RUN WITH ME

A Discovery Series Book

By Christy Major

Christy Major

Copyright 2013 Christy Major

Cover Art by Calista Taylor
www.coversbycali.com

Edited by Janet Hitchcock
www.theproofisinthereading.wordpress.com

All Rights Reserved

Author Contact:

Website: christymajor.weebly.com

Email: christymajor@yahoo.com

FB: www.facebook.com/christymajorauthor

2

Special Thanks

I want to send a special thanks to the following people for their feedback and support. Whether it was a complete read-through of the manuscript or help tweaking the back cover text, your comments made this book possible. You all ROCK!

Heather Rigney
Joseph Mazzenga
Rachel Moniz
Kathy Tancrelle
Nicole Sisco
Tara Lagner
Kristen DeAmaral
Ashleigh Gilchrist

Dedication

To you, dear reader.

Yeah, you.

You, who knows what a good run through the woods can do.

Prologue

"I don't want to go," I said. The cloud-skins' words flowed from my lips with ease. They'd taught us their words so there could be understanding between us, but today, confusion reigned.

"Doesn't matter what you want."

I'd thought I had escaped the worst of what these cloud-skins had brought to my people. The red spots that killed. The long, silver spears that sliced through everything with ease. The dark magic that even the wisest in my village could not understand.

But this? Being ripped from my family. Heading into the unknown. Tendrils of fear wormed their way into my chest.

"Chain them together and load them on the ships," the cloud-skin chief said.

Instantly, rough hands closed around my arms. I was pushed to the sand while heavy rings were fastened to my ankles. Their rough texture bit my skin. Their weight made lifting my feet like trying to haul full trees with each step.

"Let's go," another cloud-skin said.

He yanked me forward, but I tripped over the chains, nearly fell to my knees. Only the cloud-skin's grip on my arm stopped me.

"Clumsy oaf, aren't you?" He turned to his chief. "Are you certain you want this one? He's no steadier than a newborn colt."

"Look at him," the chief said. "He's strong, his teeth look good, and he's young. He'll fetch a high price. Plenty of working years in him."

They shared serpent smiles, and my flesh prickled. I had already worked for many years. In my village. With my people. Where I belonged. Why were they taking me away from my home?

I was led to a small canoe that carried me to an enormous canoe farther out in the water. Though the sky was blue, the air warm, and the water tranquil, a storm brewed inside me. I had never left my village. Never had any reason to leave. Everything I needed was in the village. My stomach twisted painfully as I glanced back at the shore.

"This way." A cloud-skin dragged me and several of my kin to a dark hole in the floor of the massive canoe. "Get down there." He pushed me to a set of stairs. I stumbled on most of them, my feet barely hitting the steps.

The others piled in behind me. Darkness swallowed us all. A smell like rotting livestock made me cover my nose, but it was too late. The stench had already reached into my throat and grabbed hold of my stomach, squeezing it, turning it inside out. My kin reacted similarly from what I could hear.

Flesh met flesh as we were packed into that stale, wooden pit. No light seeped in. No sea air blew the odors away. The floor was wet and hard and strange.

Would I survive the voyage? Would I ever see home again?

Would no one save me?

1. Jobah

Roots reach into the soil,
bringing life,
yet a slight tug
severs the ties.

I always knew I was a tree. Not literally a tree, of course, but a kindred spirit to one. When I was a little boy, I used to sit in the middle of the woods, close my eyes, and listen to the trees. Their branches creaked in the wind. Their leaves flapped and fluttered. Sap ran inside the maples just as blood coursed through my veins. Were we so different? I hadn't thought so.

Now my grandmother had confirmed it.

I, Jobah Everleaf, am not like the others of my tribe, the Kiyuchee. I have been in this village for seventeen winters, but I am something else. I have lived beside these people, have learned their ways, have worked among them, but I will never be one of them. Not with this secret Ninae, my grandmother, has told me.

She thought I was special. She wanted to hold a ceremony to announce what she believed me to be. I convinced her to wait. I'm not the person I thought I was. I needed time to get used to the idea.

Run With Me

I don't think I will ever be used to the idea.

Do I go on living my life in the village? Do I stay among these people who have raised me as their own? Do I share my secret with the tribe or pretend I don't know what I am? I've hidden this long.

Could I do it for a lifetime?

Should I?

"But there will be much excitement to know someone like you is among us," Ninae had said.

How could she be so sure? Our people didn't like different. We went to great lengths to keep our tribe separated from the rest of the world. We never let anyone into our village. It wasn't safe. Denri, our shaman and chief, told of times long ago when the Kiyuchee let explorers from faraway lands into the village. Sometimes I dreamed of that time, as if I'd lived through it myself. I always awoke covered in sweat with a foul scent in my nose.

Since then, our people have lived in the security of the woods. We'd left the world beyond our palisades to the cruel and dangerous outsiders.

On some level, I understood the need for seclusion, and we did have everything we needed inside our village. Now, as I walked through my home of seventeen winters, I surveyed the sturdy dwellings made of wood and ferns. Beyond that, I took in lush, fertile fields that produced fresh vegetables. I knew firsthand that our hunting grounds were full of meat. The lake supplied us with fresh water and fish. Some would consider our village a paradise.

Yet another world existed beyond the palisades surrounding our village. I wasn't allowed to be part of that world. I lived in the safety of our tribe.

But now? Now I was the outsider. I was different. I stopped walking and looked at some of my people, busy in their daily chores. I shared many features with them. Same dark skin, same black hair, same brown eyes. My body resembled that of the other boys my age, lean and muscled from the work we did farming or building. I followed their traditions, laughed at their stories, played their games. I'd recently built my own dwelling near my grandmother's home and had dug out a patch of land to plant.

My gaze settled on several females about my age cooking over a central fire pit. Recently, I had begun looking for a mate among them. Several had caught my eye. Two young women had brought me food while I constructed my dwelling. A nice gesture, but I knew they were surveying my work. I wasn't the only one looking for a companion. They were seeking too.

All this time, I had been making plans to live as one of them. To continue the traditions I had learned. To make these woods my home until I took my last breath.

Now I felt like running. Running until I reached the edge of Great Earth. I wasn't sure what I would do once I got there, but I no longer fit here.

Maybe I didn't fit anywhere.

2. Olivia

I stared at the ceiling in my bedroom. My throat was seriously sore from screaming at Mom and Dad, but it had done me no good. I could have set myself on fire in protest of the news they had delivered to me, but it wouldn't have changed their minds. They were rocks like that.

Damn archaeologists. Always so sure of themselves. So right all the time. Only their opinions mattered. Whatever they wanted, they got. Let's get this straight now. I do not live in a democracy.

Dictatorship all the way.

I rolled to my side, and the bed creaked beneath me. A Target bag rested on my beanbag chair in the corner of the room. The red and white bull's-eye symbols decorating the bag looked at me like disappointed eyes. Three red T-shirts, two pairs of tan pants, and a shiny new nametag announced me—Olivia Bradford, employee—to the world of Target shoppers. My whole summer waited inside that bag.

All of it was useless.

I'd have to kiss that sweet summer job good-bye. Yeah, I know it was only Target, but Kevin was working there, too, on the days he wasn't lifeguarding at Narragansett Beach. We had it all planned out. Drive into work together, take lunch breaks at the same time, and flirt in the cat food aisle at precisely 1:34 p.m. each day. After our shifts we could drive home together and make out in the car in my driveway. If Doctors Madeline and Peter Bradford, my resident Indiana Jones 'rents, weren't home, I would invite Kevin inside for an after-work snack and some general making out.

It was a good dream.

Apparently not *my* dream. Not since I'd be spending the tail end of June and all of July in frickin' Montana.

Yeah, Montana. I'll wait until you're done swallowing that one. It doesn't go down easily. I'm still choking on it.

Flathead Lake, Montana.

Yeah, you heard right.

Actually Woods Bay, about four miles south of Bigfork. The doctors had been contracted to lead a dig near the lake, and for some stupid reason, that meant I had to leave my lovely Sunderfield, Rhode Island and go with them. Usually my parents didn't take assignments during the summer when I was out of school. Not that we went on fun family outings together, but I guess some part of their overdeveloped brains figured they should be around when I was around.

When they did go on digs, it wasn't for more than two weeks at a time. My grandmother would usually come to stay with me while they were gone, but she passed away last year. I guess I should be sadder about that, but Nana was like a prison guard.

Although, right now, I'd take her over disappearing for six whole weeks with my parents.

I'd reasoned with them.

I'd pleaded.

I'd screamed.

I'd cried.

And still, I was going. Not even an attempt to pull out the responsibility card had worked.

"But, Mom, I've been hired for the Target job," I'd said. "I can't quit before I even start."

"Your father will call and straighten it out, Olivia." Mom continued writing out one of her infamous packing lists. Only a tiny fragment of her brainpower was being used to deal with me.

"I can't rely on you and Dad to get me out of these situations," I'd offered. "I made a commitment. I should keep it. Besides, I need the money."

I'd been saving for a car. Babysitting on the weekends wasn't exactly a booming business lately. Parents weren't going out as much anymore with the economy being what it was. Instead, they were doing movie nights after the kids went to sleep, making my work obsolete. This Target job meant steady pay and a few steps closer to the used car of my dreams.

Okay, maybe it just meant a few steps closer to something with four wheels and hopefully a radio that worked. I didn't really care. I just wanted the independence that came with car ownership.

"How about if she helps with the dig and we pay her a little something?" This had been from Dad who often speaks as if I'm not standing right beside him. He filters all his comments through Mom who then translates.

Mom had tapped her pen on her pad and got that let's-consider-this-from-all-angles look she sometimes gets. Eyes squinted. Lips puckered in and out. Head leaned right, then left.

Mom nodded in a way that told me a decision had been made. "A great idea, Peter. There's plenty for her to do on this trip."

Then I threw out the impossible.

"What if I stayed in Rhode Island? I'm seventeen for crying out loud. I can take care of myself."

"No," both of my parents answered in unison.

Never good when they answer in unison. It meant total agreement between them. I didn't have a prayer to convince them otherwise.

"How about if I stay with Carrie?

Carrie was my much older sister. At twenty-seven, she lived in a swanky little apartment by T.F. Green Airport with her tattoo-artist boyfriend, Jett. Though some of Jett's tattoos were… questionable… he was actually the nicest guy you'd ever want to meet. And seriously talented. The tattoos I was allowed to see were works of art.

My sister was a pilot, hence the boyfriend named Jett, I guess. Carrie flew mostly domestic flights. She and Jett had insane schedules, which would make staying with them a real bonus for me. Little supervision, lots of freedom.

A teenage paradise.

"Carrie's too busy, Olivia." Mom had actually looked up at me. That's how I knew she'd thought I'd suggested something truly ridiculous. She only used her full gaze when she was trying to figure out how brainiacs like her and my father could have been so burdened with an offspring as ordinary as me.

"She's coming with us," Dad had said before disappearing from the kitchen.

And that's how my summer vacation had been totally, irreversibly, pathetically destroyed.

3. *Jobah*

I am a Tree Penta.

A Kiyuchee woodland spirit.

I forbade my grandmother to use the word *fayishe,* or *fairy,* but that was the official word for it. Something about that word made me feel small and transparent.

I had known something wasn't right with me. Throughout winter I hadn't needed my wolfskin cloak, as if the cold north wind had no effect on my body. Staying out late into the evening hunting for my people hadn't caused the shivers it usually did.

We'd eaten well.

When spring came, I'd run through the meadow near our village with my cousin, Ashlo. I was going at full speed like always, but Ashlo's voice had tugged me back.

"Jobah! Come see this!"

I jogged to him, my eyes growing wide at the fully bloomed flowers lining the path.

"Where did those come from?"

Everything had been brown and dead when I'd run by not even a moment ago. How could there have been bright petals and thick green leaves already?

"When you ran by," Ashlo began, dropping to his knees by the flowers, "they just... bloomed. The petals burst open."

Not believing that I'd done anything to make the flowers bloom, I'd stooped beside him to inspect one of the flowers more closely.

"It can't be me, Ashlo. That doesn't make any sen—" I stopped abruptly as the closest flowers opened their petals wider, their colors growing more vivid, their fragrance more potent. Simply breathing on the petals caused them to blossom even fuller.

Ashlo agreed not to say anything to anyone about what he'd witnessed. He was true to his word too, but I couldn't hide from Ninae. She saw everything even when you thought she wasn't watching.

Summer was here now, and I waited to see what other oddities would be revealed about me. Would I grow roots, sprout leaves, let woodpeckers nest on my shoulders?

"We won't know what will happen until it happens, Jobah," Ninae had said. Not at all comforting. "The Kiyuchee are descendants of the Pentas, but none have been around for ages. You have been given a great gift."

Gift? A gift would be to find firewood already cut and stacked. To have the south field weeded. To have the bows waxed, the arrows sharpened.

Finding out I could *feel* the trees was not a gift.

I heard rustling behind me and swiveled around on the boulder where I was sitting by the brook.

"Here you are." Ninae weaved through the low-growing ferns and sat on the boulder next to me. She rested her aged hand on my knee. "Is your plan to hide?"

I shrugged. "I don't exactly have a plan."

"You always have a plan, Jobah. That's what makes you so important to us." Ninae took her hand back and turned her dark eyes to the brook cascading over rocks and cutting a watery path into the land. The rocks were smooth from years of rushing water.

"Does Great Earth on either side of this brook lament the loss of its former self? Or does it embrace each new incarnation?" Ninae tilted her head at me.

"How should I know?" I didn't normally take this tone with her. She had raised me. My parents had gone hunting one day when I was six winters old and never returned. No one knew what happened to them. Some said their curiosity—a trait I shared with them—got them killed. Others said a fierce animal attacked and devoured them. Still others said outsiders with their evil hearts lured my parents away from the village.

It didn't matter what happened. What mattered was they were gone.

"I think if you truly listen, child, you will know what to do." Ninae patted my knee then rose from the boulder. She shuffled away through the woods, sending a flurry of bees out from a rotted log.

Normally I'd head the other way when bees came around. We'd found out two summers ago that I was deathly allergic to bee stings. My uncles had ignored tribal rules and taken me into the town of Bigfork, near our great lake, because they didn't know what was happening to me. My throat closed, my skin hived, my heart raced.

I'd thought I was dying. I should have.

I'd never been out of the village before the bee sting. Truthfully, I didn't get to see much. Not being able to breathe prohibits you from observing your surroundings.

What I did see, however, was… stimulating.

A passing *truck*—a word I had never heard before that day—had stopped to pick us up once the driver realized we needed help. My uncle, Ranen, had been carrying me. At ten, I was very tall and mostly limbs. Add to that the fact I was choking on each breath. Toting me couldn't have been easy.

They slid me into the back of the driver's truck. Uncle Ranen and my other uncle, Wynde, hovered on either side of me while the vehicle bounced over ruts in the road. I had been stung on my arm, and it had swollen to double its normal size. I could barely move it.

At the *hospital*—another new word—my uncles had trouble getting someone to help us. We didn't have the cards the women behind the semi-circular barrier, or *desk* as I later learned it was called, had asked for. Neither of my uncles could write on the papers the women pushed at them. My vision had grown hazy. Spots danced before my eyes, and then I fell.

When I awoke, I was in a soft bed that smelled so unlike the woods. The scent was harsh and made my eyes water, but I could breathe again. My skin was back to its dark smoothness. My arm felt like a part of me once more.

People I didn't know bustled into the room, checked lighted metal boxes attached to me, and scurried out like squirrels. Some of the people looked like me with black hair and dark skin, but there had been many with fair hair and pale skin. Eyes the color of sky and grass. They were all nice to me. All seemed to care about my well-being.

Then they released me. I came back to the village, but paid closer attention to the things we passed on the trip back home. Dwellings, not like ours at all, dotted the fields. Wheeled things zoomed by us, churning up dirt from the road. Small children chased each other around their yards. Dogs whined, barked, and ran after balls.

One building caught my attention in particular. All stone and surrounded by huge, cleared fields, the structure hypnotized me.

"What is that?" I asked my uncle, Wynde.

The driver of the truck had generously waited to give us a ride back to where he'd picked us up, and he answered my question. "It's a school."

When my uncles and I didn't show any signs of understanding, the driver pulled over. He stared at the breechclouts around our waists, the moccasins on our feet, and said, "Where are you guys from anyway?"

We didn't reply. Our shaman chief would not approve of us revealing our village's location to this outsider.

The driver shook his head as he continued driving. "Okay," he said slowly, "a school is where we teach our young people. It's a place for learning."

At the time, I had wondered what could possibly be learned from the inside of a dwelling like that one. Everything I had been taught had to do with the outside. That night, however, I dreamed of the school. I was inside one of the rooms and great secrets were shared with me. Secrets that took me far beyond village life. Far beyond my simple existence of surviving day-to-day in the woods.

The next day, after my uncles had been cast out of the tribe for taking me to the outside, I secretly ran to a hill past the meadow where I could see the school from the village. I went there almost daily. No one knew about that spot. No one knew about my watching, my obsession with that place for learning.

I so desperately wanted to know what happened inside.

4. Olivia

"This is social suicide, Olivia." Eden Bennington sat on the end of my bed as I pulled shorts and T-shirts out of my closet and chucked them into a suitcase. Who even cared if they matched or not?

"Thanks, O Best Friend, for stating the completely obvious." I stalked over to my dresser and ripped open the top drawer. Balling up pairs of socks, I hurled them at Eden who shielded her head.

"Okay, okay," she said. "I'm sorry, but I can't believe this is happening." She gathered the sock balls and dumped them into the suitcase beside her. "This was supposed to be *our* summer. The one with the jobs and the parties and the boyfriends."

I rested my forehead on the top of the dresser and breathed a forlorn sigh into my underwear drawer. "I know. Now it's the summer where I get totally forgotten because I'm stuck at a stupid lake in the middle of stupid nowhere with my stupid parents."

I lifted my head slightly and caught sight of the purple silk underwear I'd hidden under my standard, everyday whites. I had been hoping to mention the sexy unmentionables to Kevin soon. That would have to wait until August now.

"What if you ask to stay with me for the summer?" Eden jumped up from the bed, her curly, chestnut hair bouncing around her shoulders.

"It won't work, Eden. My parents are solid about me going with them. There is no way out of this. I tried. I really did." I flopped onto the bed and threw my arms out to either side of my body. "The doctors said something about helping me find my direction with this ridiculous trip. Umm, am I lost? I'm not lost. Maybe I don't have every detail of my future mapped out, but I have time."

Don't I?

There have to be people out there who didn't come out of the womb knowing they wanted to be archaeologists.

Right?

"It's as if I'm stuck in a cheesy horror movie where the main character keeps trying every door, but they're all locked tight. No escape." I sighed again. Such a pathetic sound.

Eden pushed my suitcase over and sat beside me. "This officially sucks, Olivia."

I opened my mouth to agree, but my cell phone chirped from the nightstand. After pulling myself upright, I grabbed the phone and checked the screen.

"It's Kevin. He's on his way over."

Eden made a face as if to say, "I wouldn't want to be you right now." An appropriate face. I didn't want to be me right now either. Hell, I would have settled for being the homeless guy I'd seen sitting outside the parking garage at Providence Place Mall last Saturday.

"Should I stay or go?" Eden asked.

I stood and paced in front of her. "Go, I guess. No reason you have to subject yourself to hearing this truly wretched news all over again. So far, I only told Kevin to stop by. I didn't go into details."

"This news calls for a face-to-face conversation, even if Kevin is a—"

"Don't, Eden. Please." I held up my hands.

Eden was forever bashing Kevin over something. The two of them just never hit it off.

"Fine. Okay." She stood and picked up a sock ball that had rolled to the floor. She tossed it into the open suitcase then clamped her hands on my shoulders. "I'm going to miss your sorry ass. How am I supposed to get into trouble without you?"

Despite my current misery, I had to smile. Eden had a way of doing that for me.

"You'll get into trouble just the same." I rested my hands on Eden's arms, and she sent me a devilish grin right before pulling me into a hug.

When she released me, Eden walked to the door of my bedroom then backtracked to my open closet, her eyes scanning its contents.

"Go ahead," I said. "I'm not going to need it where I'm going. You should enjoy it for me."

"Are you sure?" Eden stood in front of the closet with her hand outstretched.

I nodded. "Take it. I'll wear it when I get back."

"You're the best, Olivia." She carefully extracted the electric blue slip dress I had bought last weekend. My great aunt in Florida had sent me a gift card to the mall for my birthday. I would have preferred cash to put in the Getting a Car Fund, but who was I to begrudge a gift card? Besides, blue was Kevin's favorite color and his eyes would have popped out of their sockets over that dress. Money well spent.

Or so I had thought.

Sigh.

Again.

I walked Eden to the front door. With one more hug and a promise to find some way to communicate with each other while I was nestled in No Cell Service Land, Eden left. As she pulled out of the driveway, Kevin pulled up in his green Jeep Wrangler. He'd taken the roof, side windows, and doors off so when he cut the engine, he merely jumped out in all his Kevin Rogers loveliness.

He wore his red lifeguard swimming trunks and a light gray T-shirt with the words "Narragansett Beach Lifeguard" printed in a neat circle around a yellow anchor on the front. It should have read "Sexiest Boy on the Planet," because that's what he was.

Honest.

Kevin's blond hair was disheveled in that sand-and-surf way. His legs were muscled and tanned, as was the rest of his six-foot frame. He spun his keys around his finger as he pulled his sunglasses off and dropped them into the Jeep. Whenever he walked toward me, it was like watching a movie star approach.

How was I supposed to go a whole month and a half without him? We'd only been dating for about three months, but we definitely had something good going on. Everybody said so at school. People didn't say Olivia without saying Kevin in the same sentence. I hoped Kevin wouldn't miss me too much while I was gone. Poor guy.

"Hey." Kevin gave me one of his smiles. The kind that made my insides do jumping jacks.

"Hey." I gazed down at him from the step I was on. I was at a perfect level for leaning forward and pressing my lips to his.

So I did.

He returned the gesture, adding a little more heat to the kiss, and those jumping jacks quickly turned into a full-out cardio blast. When his arms came around my waist and tightened, I nearly forgot all my troubles.

Nearly.

Kevin pulled away and said, "Sorry if a little sand got into that kiss."

"More salt than sand," I said, licking my lips. "Very tasty."

He grinned and I wished I had my cell phone on me. A snapshot of him with that smile would help me make it through the rest of June and all of July without him.

"You hungry?" I took Kevin's hand and led him inside. The brilliant Doctors Peter and Madeline Bradford were not home from packing equipment for this voyage, so we had the house to ourselves. "You want a sandwich or something?"

"Sure." He was always hungry. He followed me into the kitchen and sat at the island.

I scrounged around in the refrigerator for some lunchmeat and condiments, but when I turned around, Kevin was facing the living room. The living room where my parents had efficiently placed their packed suitcases.

"Are your parents going on a trip?" Kevin swung back on the stool to face me again. His eyebrows wiggled above perfect blue eyes. More kissable lips never existed.

Was there a way to fit Kevin in my suitcase?

"Yes, my parents are going on a trip," I said as I built a masterpiece of a sandwich. Toasted rye bread. Layered meats folded with precision. Lettuce, tomato, hot peppers stacked colorfully. I cut the sandwich into perfect isosceles triangles and garnished the plate with pickles. I slid it in front of Kevin and poured a glass of lemonade. I opened a bag of chips and sat beside him.

"Sweet," Kevin said around a bite of sandwich. He made a yummy noise and wiped his mouth with the napkin I handed him. "Where are they going?"

I almost didn't hear the question, because, as usual, once I got this close to Kevin, my mind could only think about getting closer. He smelled like the ocean and sunscreen, and I wanted to inhale until I had consumed the entire scent.

Shaking out of my stupor, I said, "Montana."

"That's not around the corner." Kevin took a swig from the lemonade then grabbed a handful of chips. He elbowed me. "How long are they going to be gone?"

The hormonal gears were turning in his teenage male brain. Two parents away plus one available house plus one girlfriend equaled many hours of partying and questionable activity. Too bad the "one girlfriend" part of that pretty simple equation was missing.

Gripping the countertop, I sucked in a breath and said, "We'll be gone for the rest of June and all of July."

Kevin stopped mid-chew and stared at me. His stunned silence hung in the kitchen like smog. I heard every moan of the washing machine running in the basement, every grumble of the refrigerator, every whoosh of the central air conditioning. Finally, Kevin swallowed and put the sandwich down on his plate.

"You're going with them?"

5. Jobah

*To control one's destiny
is to let it fall
upon the hands
of Fate.*

The summer sun beat down on my bare back as Ashlo and I weeded the south field. If you didn't keep on top of the weeds, an entire crop could be choked out. The soil near our great lake was rich, which was good, except for the weeds.

"Have you told anyone else?" Ashlo wiped sweat from his forehead and dumped a handful of wide-leafed weeds into the pile we'd made. He was my closest kin and friend. We'd spent nearly every day of our lives together.

"No. Only you and Ninae know." I stopped yanking, wiped my hands on my breechclout, and looked at my cousin. "I'd like to keep it that way for now."

"I won't say anything." Ashlo went back to weeding, but then said, "What's going to happen to you?"

"Happen to me?" I shielded my eyes from the sun and studied Ashlo's face. Ninae had often called us her twins though she wasn't Ashlo's grandmother. Our mothers had been sisters, and Ninae was my father's mother. It didn't matter though. Ninae considered all the people in our tribe her kin. She'd do anything for any one of them.

"I saw what you did with the flowers, Jobah. You can do things the rest of us can't. What's the purpose of it?"

"I don't know what the purpose is, Ashlo. Being able to make flowers bloom before they're ready doesn't strike me as all that important. Maybe there is no purpose."

But Ninae thought there was.

I kneeled and plunged my fingers into the dirt to continue weeding. I reached deeper than I had all morning. A strange warmth traveled up my arms and across my chest, and I ripped my hands out. I'd been feeling hotter than usual lately, but this sensation was new.

Almost frightening.

After staring at my hands for a moment, I sunk them back under the soil. The heat was there again, and my nose flooded with the scent of Great Earth and rain and sun. I tasted corn, carrots, potatoes, and everything else we grew in the field. I heard the plants growing, a soft hiss of expanding stalks, stems, leaves.

And then it was gone.

"Jobah! Jobah, are you all right?"

Ashlo had a tight grip on my forearms. He'd pulled my hands free of the dirt. My head ached, and my eyes burned. I closed them and shook my head.

"I'm okay." My voiced sounded weak and scratchy. I opened my eyes, wiggled out of Ashlo's hold, and got to my feet.

He rose beside me. "I kept calling your name, but you didn't answer me. You sounded as if you were choking."

"Choking?" That would explain the scratchy throat, but I didn't remember gasping for air. All I remembered was the fabulous feeling of Great Earth surrounding me, filling my senses with her gifts.

"I think I should walk you back to your grandmother's dwelling. You've done enough out here for today. Maybe the sun is getting to you." Ashlo took my arm as if to escort me.

"No," I said, freeing myself of his grip. "I'm fine. Let's finish. There will only be more weeds to gather tomorrow. We can't let them win." I smiled as if making a joke.

Ashlo stared at me with his mouth opened.

"What's the matter?" I crouched to begin picking weeds again.

"Your eyes." Ashlo backed up a couple steps.

"What about my eyes?" I rubbed at them. "They do burn a little. Are they bloodshot?"

"Bloodshot is not the right word." He was starting to scare me with the way he kept backing away.

"What is the right word, Ashlo?"

31

"Green."

"What are you talking about?" My eyes were dark brown, nearly black, like every other member of the Kiyuchee tribe. I'd seen them reflected in the lake. They were the same as Ashlo's.

"There's green in your eyes." Ashlo raised a hand to point at my face. "Right around the black part, like a halo of green."

We weren't near the water so I had no way of seeing my reflection at that moment. Ashlo wasn't funning with me, however, as he liked to do sometimes. His own dark eyes were opened so wide that the whites were extra bright. He stood stone still and stared at me as if he'd never seen anything so odd in his life.

I wasn't sure what to do.

So I ran.

I ran out of the field and into the woods. I ran through the ferns and past boulders. I ran until my lungs felt as if they might explode in my chest. My moccasins slapped on the ground and carried me swiftly to a destination I hadn't quite decided on. Branches scratched my arms. Fallen twigs jabbed at my heels through my moccasins. Sweat leaked into my already irritated eyes and set them on fire. I almost couldn't see where I was going.

And yet, I didn't need my eyes.

My legs kept carrying me forward until finally I dropped to the ground with exhaustion. All my muscles twitched. My heartbeat pounded in my ears, but not enough to drown out another noise. Another pulse. Another drum thudding below the ground.

I flattened my palms over Great Earth beneath me. A faint vibration tickled against my skin as if something alive was trying to slip into my veins. I scampered to my feet and resumed running.

Strangely, I ended up at my dwelling though I had not taken a path known to lead there. I ducked inside and dropped on top of my moose hides. Curling up into a ball, I squeezed my aching eyes closed and willed my stomach to calm. Everything was jumbled inside me. Nothing felt right. I was so tired, but I'd only done half a morning's work with Ashlo. I usually kept going until the sun sank below the horizon, and sometimes I didn't even quit then. There were always things that could be done by firelight. I liked to make the most of each day.

But today was different. Not good different. Not bad different. Just different.

What if tomorrow was different too?

6. Olivia

I studied my fingers, now white from my death grip on the kitchen island. Never noticed exactly how many veins crisscrossed over the backs of my hands. Gross.

"I have no choice." My voice sounded small. "I have no choice," I said with more volume but just as much disgust.

"What about the Target job? Track practice? Summer fun at the beach with me?" Kevin looked about ready to throw an all out tantrum. His voice had risen as each word left his lips.

Did I mention how kissable those lips were?

I believe I did.

"I can't take the job. I don't know what I'm going to do about track practice, and the summer fun with you will have to be *late* summer fun in August instead."

I fiddled with the ends of my hair, noticed the blond split ends, and swiveled a little to the left then to the right on my stool. My knees brushed up against Kevin's thigh, but he didn't react as he normally would with a hand on my leg, or a kiss on the cheek, or a squeeze around the shoulders.

No, he was a statue beside me instead. A chiseled, lifeguard sculpture whose summer had been ruined along with my own.

"I don't want to be without a girlfriend during the summer, Olivia," Kevin said.

Hmm. Interesting.

Not "I don't want to be without *you*, Olivia," but "I don't want to be without *a girlfriend*," as in substitute any random female into this position.

A twinge of something nasty prickled my flesh. Could Eden have been right about Kevin this whole time?

"Trust me, Kevin, I don't want to be hanging around Montana for June and July, but there's no getting out of it. I tried, but the doctors are serious about this one. They won't even let me stay with Carrie."

I got up and put the lemonade away. I needed to be doing something while Kevin got over the initial shock of me going away. He just needed a few moments.

Kevin pushed his half-eaten sandwich to the middle of the island.

Not good. That boy was always eating and that was one hell of a sandwich I had served him.

"How long have you known about this vacation?"

Why did his voice have a tone? He wasn't the one who had a half-packed suitcase waiting upstairs. He wasn't the one who would be away from all his friends, all the fun, all of civilization for six weeks. If anyone should have a tone, it was me.

"I only found out yesterday, Kevin. I needed a day to swallow it myself before telling anyone else. And I wouldn't exactly call it a *vacation*."

I picked up his dish, tossed the uneaten sandwich in the garbage disposal, and hit the switch. As the grinders minced bread, ham, turkey, and cheese into a mustard-swirled glob, I thought about how my social life had slipped into a garbage disposal as well.

Grind, grind, grind until nothing recognizable was left.

"Well, we should probably call it quits then." Kevin stood and pushed in his stool.

I turned around from the sink.

"Wait. What?"

Had I heard him right? Had the garbage disposal pulverized his words?

"We obviously can't keep up a relationship with you in Montana and me here in Rhode Island. Six weeks in the summer is a long time, Olivia. There are parties to go to, beaches to visit, other places to be that are more fun with a date. I don't want to miss out on that. And this summer is our last summer as carefree kids. Next year we graduate. That summer is going to be filled with shifting into college mode and figuring out the rest of our damn lives. This summer is all we have."

When he put it that way, I wanted to hurl myself off the deck in the backyard. But a broken neck probably wouldn't stop my parents from dragging me to Montana.

Kevin shook his head and folded his wonderfully muscled arms across his wonderfully muscled chest, but I couldn't enjoy it the way I usually did. Instead, I felt like a rock on the shore when the waves come in and pull all the sand out from underneath it. The rock gets real loose and...unsure of itself.

"Look, Kevin, I don't think we have to get all crazy here. Six weeks is going to fly by." Yeah, right. "We'll still have all of August to have our fun. Plenty of beach days and party nights to be had together."

"Olivia, I like you. A lot. We've had a good three months, but let's make this easy for both of us."

Easy? What was easy about breaking up? What was easy about one's boyfriend acting like a royal prick?

Kevin was already picking his keys up from the island and walking toward the front door. I stood a moment in the kitchen, my arms hanging loosely at my sides, as he increased the distance between us. None of this was right. He was supposed to say he'd miss me terribly. That he'd think about me every day and night we were apart. That he'd go to work at Target and lifeguard at the beach, but spend every other moment simply dying for my return.

We were supposed to be making out enough to last me six weeks.

Kevin wasn't supposed to be walking out my front door right now without even waving good-bye.

"Wait!" I jogged after him and stopped in the doorway.

Kevin turned around. What struck me first was that he didn't look upset about dumping me. He had ended a three-month relationship as if it had been the simplest thing in the world to do.

Maybe for him it was.

This was Kevin Rogers we were talking about here. Girls—except for Eden—flocked to him even when I was standing right beside him. He was a chick magnet with his looks, his Jeep, his I-know-CPR-and-can-save-your-life confidence.

I was but a rusty paper clip, inferior metal helplessly attracted to his pull, and apparently easily tossed aside.

7. *Jobah*

"Are you in there?"

I rolled to my side. Soft moose hide brushed against my cheek, and I squeezed into a tighter ball.

"Jobah? Are you in there?"

My eyes opened and the log sides of my dwelling filled my vision.

Yes, I remembered now.

The total exhaustion. The fiery burn in my eyes until the only reprieve was to close them. To put my head down and forget everything for a while.

Daylight crept into my dwelling, but a shadow blocked it for a moment. My back was to the door, and normally I would have turned to greet a visitor. At this moment, however, I didn't dare. I'd seen my eyes in the water trough where the horses were kept.

Ashlo had been right.

A clear ring of green encircled the black parts.

I wasn't normal.

Ninae had said some of the Penta abilities would bring changes. I didn't realize she'd meant ones that others could so clearly see. Perhaps the decision to stay in the village or leave would be made for me. Once people saw my eyes, they'd know I wasn't the same. They'd know something was wrong with me. They had knowledge of Pentas, but Pentas were legend now, something buried deeply in our tribal past, not something that walked among us in our woods. Actually seeing one would make them afraid.

A cold hand touched my shoulder. "Ashlo said you weren't well."

Keryun. She'd been among the female visitors as I built my dwelling. I'd caught her surveying the structure from all sides. She'd commented on how perfectly round I'd gotten it. She'd noticed mine was a little taller, a little wider than the others in the village and my roof was tightly thatched. Keryun had even suggested arranging the exterior bark in a pattern so the curved doorway was accented. She'd also helped me gather rocks for the cook fire in the center and was skilled at stacking rocks so they formed a sturdy wall. My fires were well contained.

I had enjoyed working alongside her. She was strong and beautiful. She would make a fine mate.

"Jobah, look at me." Her voice was close to my ear, her breath warm on my skin.

I burrowed my face into the moose hide below me. "Go away."

"Not until you look at me." She poked my bicep.

"Keryun, please. Ashlo was right. I'm not well. Leave me alone."

"I will not leave you alone."

Shuffling sounded around me and though my face was full of moose hide, I knew Keryun was now on the other side of me. She nudged my shoulder back so I either had to show my face or completely change my position. I lifted my head slightly and realized the light in my dwelling was dim. She probably wouldn't be able to see my eyes.

I raised my face to her, and Keryun smiled. A truly wonderful smile, full of white teeth and dimpled cheeks. Her long, black hair was loose about her bare shoulders and the hide dress she wore only covered from just above her breasts to the tops of her slender thighs. Summertime was always good for viewing the females of the tribe. The sun darkened their smooth skin. Their hair took on the scent of wildflowers.

"You look well enough." She cupped my chin in her hand and tilted my head as if studying me. Light from outside reflected off her face. Her eyes were huge dark pools, bottomless and hypnotizing.

I quickly shrugged off her grip, nervous that she would see what I didn't wish her to see. "I'm tired."

"I watched you build this dwelling. I've seen you work in the fields. I know you like to run and that you're fast. You never tire, Jobah." She sat back on her heels. "What's wrong?"

For a second, I wanted to tell her. I wanted someone besides Ninae and Ashlo—someone besides blood relations—to know. If Keryun could handle the odd news, perhaps everyone in the tribe could.

"You've slept some, yes?" she asked.

I nodded.

"Perhaps you need fresh air now. Walk with me. The sun will be going down soon. It's a little cooler outside."

Keryun stood and held out a hand to me. She wiggled her fingers, and the movement hypnotized me as if it were the most fascinating thing I'd ever witnessed. A walk. I could probably manage a walk. My eyes didn't sting as they had earlier today, and my muscles no longer throbbed. The headache that had plagued me was gone as well.

I shot a glance out the door. With the fading light, I might be able to conceal my changed eyes from Keryun. This could, in fact, be a simple walk.

I took Keryun's hand and let her pull me to my feet. She was petite, much smaller than me. I had to crouch down to exit my dwelling, but Keryun could walk right out the doorway. Her size, however, was deceiving. I'd seen her haul rocks that would have given Ashlo trouble.

Not me, but definitely Ashlo.

I steered Keryun toward the lake, leading the way through the low brush. The night bugs chirped their melodies, and small creatures squeaked and twittered around us. Normally, I loved the sounds of nighttime. Tonight, however, I heard them a little too crisply, almost as if I were making the noises myself.

We walked on without talking until the lake appeared. Moonlight rippled on the surface, and a warm night breeze tickled my skin.

"Feeling better?" Keryun craned her head back to look me in the eyes, and I silently thanked the spirits for sending the darkness.

"Yes. A walk was a good remedy." I picked up a rock and skipped it across the water. It bounced four times before sinking into the watery abyss.

"It is not only my mother who knows remedies."

Keryun's mother was our tribe's healer. She knew everything about roots, herbs, and plants in the woods that could be used to treat various maladies. She cured many illnesses. My reaction to the bee sting had been the exception.

"You have been studying your mother's ways?" I asked Keryun.

"I have. She wishes me to take her place as the tribe's healer when her time has ended." Keryun zigzagged her way to the water, dipped her feet in, and wandered back to me at the tree line.

"Do you want that calling?"

"I do. I think I will be good at it." Keryun stood in front of me and walked her fingers up my arm.

"I think you will be good at it too."

I envied her. She knew her place in our tribe. Her future was clearly defined. No questions. Not like me.

"Do you want to know what else I'm good at?" She leaned her body against mine and backed me up against the closest tree.

Before I could answer, Keryun pressed her lips against mine. At the same time our mouths connected, a tingle ran along my spine where it rubbed against the tree behind me. I was able to ignore the sensation for a few moments as she drew me deeper into the kiss. Her arms encircled my waist, and I cupped her face in my hands, let my fingers get lost in her hair.

When the tingle grew into a more powerful vibration, I was still able to push it aside. I focused on only Keryun in my arms. Her warm lips. Her soft hair. Her flower fragrance. I should have been shocked that she had made such an advance, but my brain could only register how wonderful it felt to be kissed.

We continued for a few moments more, then Keryun took a step back. She actually licked her lips, which made me want to dive back into kissing her. I'd made a plan to do just that, but she slipped into the trees behind me. As soon as I thought about the trees, that tingle flared to life again. It zipped down my back and radiated into my limbs.

I stepped away from the tree and ran my hands along my arms as if I could dust away the odd feelings, the *awareness*. I thought about something else, mostly Keryun and how her hair shimmered in the moonlight.

Heading into the woods and ignoring the dull vibration pulsing inside me, I followed Keryun.

As she walked, she broke off a thin branch from a birch tree.

My stomach clenched.

She snapped the twig in half, and I doubled over with an ache in my gut.

When she cracked the twigs again, I dropped to my knees. The pain was so sharp I half expected to find one of the twigs lodged in my stomach.

"Keryun." Her name came out like a strangled groan. Sickness rose up my throat, and I crouched on the ground.

I was like an animal.

Or maybe something much worse.

8. Olivia

I got stuck in the middle seat on the airplane. Mr. Doctor on my left. Mrs. Doctor on my right. Each of them was already entrenched in their pre-dig analysis. Laptops open, keys tapped, daughter ignored.

Another perfect Bradford family adventure.

Repositioning my earphones, I turned up the volume of my music until nothing but a sick guitar solo filled my head. Yeah, so I resembled a blond-haired, blue-eyed, cheerleader type, but my choice of music fit better with the black-clad, combat-booted, lip-pierced, tattooed metalheads that hung out under the bleachers of the football field. They'd never accept me as one of their own even though my playlists featured bands I'd seen on many of their ratty T-shirts.

Didn't matter anyway. I wasn't in search of a new set of friends. I was in search of a way to survive for six weeks in the woods while my best friend partied without me, and my boyfriend—no, scratch that—my *ex*-boyfriend enjoyed the summer of his life with some new girl.

Before we'd left for this stupid-ass trip, Eden texted me that Kevin was already spotted at the beach with Charity Matiste's cousin. A cousin from France.

France!

"Unbelievable."

A sharp jab to my arm made me pull out one of the earphones.

"What's unbelievable, Olivia?" my mother asked.

Had I said that out loud? Damn. Great time for my mother to actually listen to me.

"Nothing." I plugged my ear again and let the raging drumbeat fill my head. Perhaps if I could keep a constant flow of agitated rock music going for six weeks, I wouldn't realize how much my heart ached. Breaking up with Kevin, or more accurately, being dumped by Kevin, should not have hurt so much. I mean, we'd only dated for three months. Only gotten to somewhere between first and second base. Why did I care so much about him not wanting to wait for me?

Or the fact that he was already French kissing a French girl?

I bit my bottom lip to keep from saying something else out loud. Bad enough I was sandwiched between the doctors. I didn't need them asking me a million questions about why Kevin and I had called it quits.

I gave them both a sideways glance. Why weren't they asking at least a few questions? They'd seen me ripping up the box of Kevin's cards I'd saved. Witnessed me stomping all over Kevin's track jacket he'd let me wear. Had gotten my sneakers good and muddy to do that too. My parents had even watched me throw myself onto the couch and sob for thirty minutes.

Still, not one question.

The doctors have impressive deductive skills. I knew they inferred that Kevin and I had ended our relationship, but caring humans ask about another human's well-being.

Don't they?

Aren't parents bound by some code to check the status of their teenage daughter's fragile ego?

That settled it. My parents obviously weren't humans.

Not that I wanted to answer a bunch of questions anyway.

Closing my eyes, I let myself slip into a world of guitars, drums, keyboards, and vocals involving love gone wrong. A perfect drug for my current disease. Nothing warm and fuzzy happening in seat 23B on flight 6708 bound for No Man's Land, Montana. Only cold and jagged emanated from this section of the plane, and I was its epicenter.

I wanted to talk to Eden, but I'd left my cell phone at home. A piece of crap by nature, it wouldn't have been functional in the woods anyway. I'd tried to convince my parents that I needed a better phone to keep in the loop on the happenings in Rhode Island, but my case fell on deaf ears.

Again.

"Olivia, you can write her a letter. Besides, it won't kill you to unplug for a few weeks," my mom had said.

Like I had some sort of technology addiction. I didn't.

If I could talk to Eden, she would at least commiserate with me over the odd turn of events. She'd go over the play-by-play more than once, trying to get to the root of what went wrong. We'd analyze this breakup from all angles and blame Kevin for his male stupidity. Eden would gloat about being right about him, and we'd eat away my woe with pints of chocolate chip cookie dough ice cream. The universe would once again be in balance.

Instead, I was on this crowded plane, with two android parents. And was that a six-year old Karate Kid behind me kicking the seat every damn minute?

Perfect. Just perfect.

I reached into my carry-on bag under the seat in front of me and extracted one of the books I'd chosen for summer reading. Figured this Trip of Extreme Boredom would be a good time to get this assignment crossed off the list. That way when I returned to Rhode Island, returned to My Life, I'd be free to... to... do something with... someone.

Heaving in a breath, I opened to the first page and started reading.

Samantha Rigby thought she'd never fall in love. But she had and it was everything she'd ever dreamed.

I snapped the book shut as a lump formed in my throat. Five hours in a plane reading this stuff was not going to end well.

Christy Major

After digging around in my bag again, I pulled out my second book. With a glare over my seat at Karate Kid who nestled against his mother under the force of my laser eyes, I tried reading again.

Cold, wet blood covered my shaking hands. They hardly looked like my hands anymore. Surely they belonged to someone else. A madman perhaps. A fragile soul.

A murderer.

Now we had something that could get me from Rhode Island to Montana without twisting my heart until I wished it no longer beat. I settled into my seat, lowered the volume of my music, and continued reading.

By the time I'd gotten to the middle of the third chapter, a flight attendant came around with lunch. If you could call it that. A flimsy cardboard box with disappointing contents. A rubberized sandwich with a mystery meat I wasn't willing to touch. A small bag of animal crackers. Really? What am I, four years old? A box of raisins. Look, if my raisins aren't covered in chocolate or sugar, they're just shriveled grapes to me. And the crowning piece? A pickle. Loose. Wet. Soaking through the cardboard box.

This, of course, was what happened when your parents worked from grant to grant. All the doctors' funding was spent on equipment and hiring specialists in the field. Flights that involved edible food didn't concern my parents. Neither did the healthy nourishment of a still-growing teenager, a track athlete.

If the food was going to be this bad on the entire trip, I hoped bears ate me in my sleep while visions of clam cakes and chowder at Narragansett Beach danced in my head.

Could you actually feel a heartache? Did the organ really throb in your chest with each breath in and each breath out?

And what the hell fixed it?

9. Jobah

A wonderful, flowery scent filled my nose, a lilting melody sang in my ears, and I snuggled closer to whatever was under my head. Soft, smooth, warm. I slid my hand out from under me and flattened my palm on a... knee?

I opened my eyes and lifted my head. A thigh bore the imprint of my ear.

The singing stopped. "How do you feel?"

I snapped my head up and met Keryun's gaze. Pushing up to sitting, I scanned my surroundings. The lake. The moon. The trees. Keryun.

"What happened?" My stomach was cramped, and I was warmer than ever.

"I honestly don't know, Jobah," Keryun said. "One minute you were following me into the woods. The next you were calling my name. When I turned around, you were on the ground and in pain. Lots of it."

I got to my feet, and Keryun rose beside me. She put a steadying hand on my arm. That touch was the only thing holding me in this world. If she let go, I wasn't sure what would happen.

"Do you want to go home?" Keryun lifted her hand to touch my cheek.

I looked at her and nodded. "It must be late."

She studied the sky for a moment. "Probably. I fell asleep for a little while myself. Not sure how long we've been here." Keryun's dark eyebrows raised and if it weren't for the moonlight, I might not have seen the grin on her beautiful lips. "I know you didn't feel well, but I liked having you close, Jobah." She rested her head against my chest and squeezed me around the waist.

"Next time, I promise not to get strange on you." I knew it wasn't a promise I could keep. Not if things were going to continue the way they'd been going lately. I'd be lucky if I could make it back to my dwelling without incident.

"I like strange." Keryun took my hand and pulled me into the woods. "I could live with strange."

Was she asking to be my mate? I'd been prepared to choose her, but would she still want me once she found out what I was?

We moved swiftly and quietly as was the way of the Kiyuchee. After a short time, we stood in front of my dwelling. The village was cloaked in silence and darkness. I glanced at my grandmother's dwelling and knew she had most likely been asleep for hours. She was certain I was supposed to be a Penta, that it was my calling, as Keryun's was to be a healer. The only difference was that Keryun had her mother to learn from.

Who did I have?

No one.

"If your stomach still hurts tomorrow, come find me," Keryun said. "I'm sure my mother has something to help you in her supplies."

Could she transform tree spirits back into regular humans?

"On second thought…" Keryun lifted to her toes and pressed her lips to mine. Despite my fears over what was happening to me, I enjoyed everything about having Keryun kiss me. "Even if you feel well tomorrow, come find me. Good night, Jobah."

"Good night, Keryun." I dropped a final kiss on her forehead. After watching her walk away, I ducked into my own dwelling and eased onto my bedding. I'd spent far too much time asleep today and wasn't tired now. My body wanted the physical rest, but my mind was going, going, going in circles. Around and around. Spiraling from thought to thought until I finally had to sit up and shake my head.

I crossed my legs in front of me and inhaled deeply. Sifting the breath out slowly, I focused on my own pulse. I had to calm down. Getting agitated was not going to help my situation. I reviewed the things I knew.

First, I had a new relationship with the earth. I bloomed flowers and channeled energy in the soil and through the trees. My eyes had changed in color. Breaking branches caused me physical pain. None of these things appeared to be under my control. They were just happening.

Victim. I felt like a victim. I didn't like that.

"Think, Jobah." There had to be a way to make sense of this. Ninae had said Penta blood ran in our line, but why me? Why not a chief? I had no power in this tribe. Or was that the point? Was I meant to break away and carry out my own life elsewhere? Ninae hadn't thought so. She was convinced my abilities were meant to serve the people in some way. How would I know what to do? It was as if I'd been dropped into a foreign land with no tools, no sense of direction, no purpose.

I flopped back on the moose hides, hoping to catch some dreamless sleep, some peace. The moment I closed my eyes, however, a scratching sound outside my dwelling roused me. I crawled to the door and poked my head out.

A pair of dark eyes and a twitching nose greeted me. I stepped out of my dwelling only to find a semi-circle of dark shapes in front of me.

Creatures.

Rabbits, squirrels, foxes, possums, skunks, raccoons. All of them sitting as if waiting for me to give them orders. A raccoon approached. Biggest one I'd ever seen. It sat by my feet and angled its black and gray head up at me.

What could all this mean?

I walked away from my dwelling, and sure enough, the critters followed. Not in a disorderly, forest creature scamper either. Instead, they organized themselves into a line and marched—yes, marched— behind me. I tested the phenomenon by making an erratic path, veering to the left then turning sharply to the right. The creatures mimicked my movements as if they'd anticipated them. As if they knew what I was going to do before I did.

Added to the list of Penta changes: Bizarre connection to the woodland animals.

Huffing out a breath, I decided I'd had enough of these games. I'd have to deal with all this in the morning. Maybe I would go see Keryun's mother. Maybe Ninae was wrong about all this Tree Penta nonsense. Maybe I was sick, and Keryun's mother would give me a concoction to cure me.

Yes, I liked this plan.

I turned to go back to my dwelling, but the animals were underfoot. I clapped my hands and waved my arms until they scattered. All of them left except the raccoon.

"Do you need a place to stay or something?" I whispered.

The raccoon rubbed up against my bare ankle, slinked between my feet, then got up on its haunches. Its front paws folded across its chest in a human-like gesture. I almost laughed.

Almost.

10. Olivia

We stood in front of a huge cabin partially hidden by massive pine trees. It had two floors sitting atop a stone foundation. A porch wrapped around both floors, and windows glittered in the sun sifting through the trees. The front doors were already opened, and voices filtered out from inside. I glanced around at the cars parked in the lot. A white SUV was to the right of me, and a monster-sized pickup truck with a trailer hitched to the back was perpendicular to the cabin. A bright orange backhoe sat on the trailer.

"The rest of the team beat us here." Dad hated being last. My arguing about going with them had caused us to miss the first flight out here. I'd also dumped my suitcase out all over the living room floor in protest.

Childish?

Yes.

Desperate?

Absolutely.

"Hopefully, they have some of the equipment set up already." Mom brushed by me toting her two suitcases and her laptop case. No "C'mon, Olivia, I'll introduce you to the team," or "Let's get you settled first, Olivia." Instead, she went directly into archaeologist mode.

She'd be officially punched in until the six weeks were up, Dad right alongside her.

I kicked the tip of my sneaker against a stone in the gravel parking lot as I turned away from the house. The mere sight of my running shoes made my chest tighten. I'd planned to run while I was trapped here, but it'd be more like hiking. I preferred the smooth track at Sunderfield High School back home.

I preferred everything that was back home.

"Hey," a gruff voice said from behind me.

I turned around to see a giant of a guy coming down the front steps and pointing to the pickup truck.

"Can you grab that for me?" He angled his head toward a small gray crate still in the bed of the pickup truck. He walked to the truck himself and hauled a larger gray crate.

What else was I doing?

I put my suitcase down and walked over to the truck. As I got closer, I took in the full effect of this dude's size. He had to be almost seven feet tall. It was like standing beside a telephone pole. His hands could have palmed the yoga ball Eden had in her bedroom—the one we both sat on at the same time.

Though he was huge, he didn't appear to be much older than me. He wore a baseball cap, so I couldn't see his hair, but his face didn't look... weathered, yet.

"You must be Pete and Mad's kid, right?"

Pete? Mad? No one called my parents by those names. I liked this guy a little more already.

"Yeah, I'm Olivia Bradford." I reached into the truck and pulled the smaller crate to the tailgate.

"Well, Ollie, I'm Royce Kelsner, but you can call me Tower like everybody else does." He smiled, and I could totally picture him saying something like "Fe, fi, fo, fum."

"What do you do on the team?" My parents never talked about anybody named Royce or Tower. Then again we didn't have regular family dinners where we actually talked to one another about how our days at work or school went.

He wiggled the crate he still held. "Mostly I carry the heavy stuff, but officially I'm the team's excavator." Tower rested the crate on his hip then pointed to the bright orange backhoe. "That's my ride of choice right there."

"Sweet."

"I'll take you for a spin at some point. Promise."

"Well, we have six weeks to choose from." I hefted the smaller crate out of the truck and groaned. A mere fifth the size of the one Tower carried, the crate shouldn't have been this heavy. "What's in here?"

"Axes, picks, chisels, saws."

"Oh, I see. Every heavy tool you own." I followed Tower as he walked toward the front door of the cabin.

"Nah, the heavy ones are in here." He lifted his crate over his head and growled like a bear.

I laughed. The sound was foreign to my lips. Fortunately, I caught myself before entering the cabin. There could be no laughing on this damn trip. I would not give my parents the opportunity to say, "See, it wasn't that bad, now was it?"

It was bad.

The worst.

A friendly giant wasn't going to change that.

Tower set his crate in the foyer of the cabin. "Put that little crate right on top there." He jogged back outside and returned with my suitcase, which he deposited on a couch in the middle of what must have been the living room. A stone fireplace lined one wall. Photos of mountains, lakes, and close-up leaves sat on the mantle in wooden frames along with an assortment of candles. Three leather couches formed a U in front of the fireplace with black metal end tables at the corners. A matching metal coffee table took up the space inside the U, and books littered its surface. Lantern style lamps adorned the end tables as well as other nature-inspired knick-knacks.

"Beautiful room, isn't it?" Tower asked.

"Where's the TV?"

"You're one of those, huh?" Tower studied me.

"One of what?" I folded my arms across my chest to the great amusement of Tower.

"A digital kid. Have to be plugged in, hooked up, synched." He shook his head. "How old are you?"

"Seventeen. How old are you?" Again, he didn't look that much older than me aside from being ginormous.

"Twenty-three, but the six year difference between us is just enough to make you completely dependent on technology and me not. I have a sister your age who can't have a conversation without using terms like IDK and LOL."

"I'm not that bad," I defended. "I like running outside and canoeing." I didn't mention that what I liked about canoeing was sitting behind Kevin in the boat and watching the muscles in his shoulders and back as he paddled. "But if you don't tune in to the social media for even an hour, you're going to miss something going down online. Neglect enough of those events and you're out of the loop. If you're out of the loop, you're done."

I held back the tears stinging my eyes and sniffed. Six weeks was a long time to be missing events. I'd be so out of it when I got back that I'd need Eden to spend a week with me to get up to speed.

"Tough to be a teen these days," Tower said.

"Brutal." I scanned the living room through watery eyes. "So, seriously, where's the TV?"

"Sorry, Ollie. You're not going to like this answer. There isn't one."

"This is Hell." I flopped onto the couch and covered my head with my arms.

"No, it's Montana."

"What's the difference?"

61

11. Jobah

The raccoon wouldn't leave me alone. It had followed me into my dwelling last night, curled up by my stomach, and slept beside me. It showed no signs of being rabid aside from its obvious camaraderie with me. The raccoon was only guilty of strange behavior, but who was I to talk about strange behavior?

Perhaps I was rabid.

This morning, the raccoon ate scraps from my morning meal and hopped along beside me as I made my way to the south field. Weeds had been allowed to live another day because of my episode yesterday. Today, they wouldn't be so fortunate.

When I got to the field, Ashlo, two of my other cousins, Batae and Cinn, and four boys about our age were already in the field on their knees.

"Jobah," Ashlo said. "You are well today. I have been worried about you."

"I'm fine." I glanced down at the raccoon standing loyally by my ankle to keep my cousins from looking directly at my eyes. I'd stopped by the water trough this morning, and the ring of green remained.

Batae and Cinn came over, soil stuck to their knees in brown crumbles.

"What's wrong with that thing?" Batae pointed to the raccoon.

"It snuck into my dwelling last night and won't go away now," I said.

"You shouldn't have fed it," Cinn said.

As if it were that simple. "I didn't feed it, Cinn. I know better than that." My grouchy tone had Cinn raising his eyebrows. I was never this touchy. "Sorry. I'm all off balance." I quickly looked down again.

"So is my sister," one of the boys said from the field.

Sumahe, Keryun's older brother, maneuvered through the crops until he stood in front of me. I studied my moccasins to keep from meeting his gaze.

"Keryun was out long after the moon had climbed the sky last night. My friends back there say you didn't return to your dwelling until late as well." Sumahe's fists clenched at his sides as his three friends laughed.

Ashlo, Batae, and Cinn all took a step closer to me. Nice to know I could count on their support.

"Keryun and I were together, but—"

The rest of my explanation got cut off by Sumahe's fist knocking against my jaw. My teeth rattled against each other as pain exploded up the left side of my skull. For a moment, all I could see were flashes of light. Then the ground smashed into my cheek as I fell. Dirt flew up around me, got into my eyes, my mouth. Part of me wanted to stay right there until everyone left. Another part recognized that

Great Earth beneath me was calling. Softly at first. Just a whisper of my name maybe. I couldn't be sure. My face hurt and that pain was louder.

Then the ground grew warm. So warm. Was it moving? It felt like it was moving.

It urged me up to my feet. Ratcheted my arm back. Sent it forward until my own fist connected with Sumahe's gut.

He doubled over and fell to his knees with a choking sound as if I'd pushed all the air out of his lungs. Maybe I had. I'd never hit anyone like that. I'd never hit anyone period. Violence wasn't something my people engaged in. Unless you were Sumahe. He was known to be… trouble.

Sumahe's friends came rushing over, and I knew things were about to get worse. At least my cousins didn't run off. They formed a semi-circle behind me and prepared to deal with Sumahe's friends.

Only they didn't have to.

As soon as the boys neared, I looked up and all three of them skidded to a halt. One of them turned around and ran in the opposite direction, while the other two fumbled around to pick up Sumahe and drag him away with them.

"That was odd," Cinn said.

"What spooked them?" Batae asked.

"I'll bet I know." Ashlo came around to stand in front of me. He put his hands on my shoulders and gazed at my face.

"How bad is it?" I touched my jaw where Sumahe had punched me. My hand came away bloody. I tasted blood and dirt. I must have been a mess.

"Your lip is split," Ashlo said, "and you'll probably have colorful bruising, but I don't think that is what sent them away."

"What is it then?" I wiped my hand on my breechclout and ran my tongue over the split in my lip. It stung at the contact. Perhaps a trip to Keryun's mother would be in order today. Perhaps Keryun herself would tend to me.

"Your eyes are full green, Jobah. No brown at all anymore." Ashlo let his hands fall from my shoulders. "And they are bright, glowing almost."

Batae turned me around to face him. Cinn's mouth dropped open.

"What's happening to you, Jobah?" Batae asked. "Why are your eyes that color?"

"A *brogna*, a demon," Cinn whispered as he inched away from me.

"Don't be stupid," Ashlo said. "It's still Jobah." He looked over his shoulder in the direction Sumahe's friends had run. "A new and improved Jobah."

The smile on Ashlo's face made what was happening to me seem like a good thing.

It wasn't.

"I have to go." I turned around and took off through the trees. A crunching at my feet told me the raccoon was running beside me. Why couldn't I get rid of this critter? And why did I feel as if other critters were watching as I ran?

Shaking my head, I focused on my intended destination. With my eyes like this, only one person wouldn't turn me away. Only one person would accept me no matter what.

I ran with all I had, the raccoon trampling along at my heels. We snapped small twigs as we passed, and each break caused a pinch in my stomach. Thankfully, Ninae's dwelling came into view as soon as I entered the center of the village.

Ninae was sitting outside in the sun stitching hides together. She made most of the clothing for our tribe and trained some of the women in her ways.

Fortunately, she was alone right now.

I spilled into her work area. The ever-present smile on her face faded as her eyes met mine.

"Come inside, child." She got up and ushered me into her dwelling. She said nothing when the raccoon followed me. Placing her hands on my shoulders, she pushed me onto a stump she used as a chair. With my face where she could now reach it, Ninae tilted my head one way then the other.

"Who did this to your lip?" she asked.

"Sumahe."

She moistened a cloth and wiped at my jaw while the raccoon jumped into my lap. It tucked its tail around its legs and sat on my thigh.

I stroked its fur, surprised that it allowed me to do so. When a sharp pain sliced through my chin, I grabbed Ninae's wrist. "That hurts."

She wriggled free of my grip, so I resumed petting the raccoon's coarse fur instead.

"This is why we don't strike one another." She rinsed the cloth in a bowl of water, and my stomach rolled at the reddish brown stain left behind.

"I did not ask him to hit me, Ninae."

"And yet, he did anyway." She dabbed at my face again then dropped the soiled cloth into the bowl of water. "Does this have to do with you and Keryun returning so late last night?"

I'd thought she'd been asleep when I'd returned. I should have known better.

"Ninae, you know me. I would not dishonor a female of our tribe. We merely fell asleep by the lake."

"I believe you, Jobah, but you must think of this next time."

"Next time?" I barked.

The raccoon hopped off my lap and dove into a pile of hides Ninae had spread out in the corner of her dwelling.

"What next time? Ninae, look at my eyes." I leaned forward and stared into the water bowl then at her. "There will be no next time. Everyone will see I am changed. I must leave." I stood and paced the short distance across her dwelling.

"You can't leave, Jobah. You're meant to protect us." Ninae's voice sounded so small.

"Protect you from what?"

"I do not know."

"What *do* you know? Help me."

She'd always come to my aid before. I needed her now.

"I know that I love you, child."

"I love you too, Ninae, but that does me no good right now."

"Love always does good, Jobah. Never forget that." She patted my cheek gently and stared at my changed eyes. "If I only had it." Her face contorted as if she were holding back tears.

"Had what?"

She cleared her throat and scrubbed a hand over her face. "Nothing. Never mind. If onlys don't help."

"What will?" I truly wanted an answer to this question.

"Time."

"Time?" I gestured to my eyes. "I don't have time. I have to leave."

I stepped out of Ninae's dwelling without looking back.

Without saying good-bye.

12. Olivia

I sat in the big living room with my earphones crammed into my ears. Resisting the urge to tap out a drumbeat on the coffee table in front of the couch, I rested my head on the back cushions and stared at the knots in the wood ceiling. I'd slept fairly well in my room last night despite the uncomfortable bed. Tower had the room next door, and he snored like a backhoe, but I'd slept through louder noises. Staying with Carrie in her apartment by the airport a few times brought on roars every couple of minutes. When the body was tired—and bored—it could sleep through anything.

The entire dig team was assembled in the living room. Six eggheads total. My parents, the lead archaeologists, Doctors Flint Reese and Keli Sumathai, artifact analysis experts, Doctor Simon Vakker, historian specializing in Native American peoples, and one photographer, Will Tramond, who although not a doctor of anything, was a complete geek about his cameras. His long, boney fingers sort of caressed the cameras. Freaked me out a bit.

And let's not forget the only non-egghead, Tower, in charge of big excavation, who was leaning against the stone fireplace.

And then there was me, stuck with the biggest bunch of dorks on the planet. Part of me wanted to travel back in time and see these people in their teenage years. Something told me they weren't sitting at the popular table in the cafeteria. Well, maybe Tower. He seemed okay. He was the only one who had acknowledged my existence so far. That put him at the top of my People I Don't Hate list.

An earphone was plucked from my ear, leaving me off balance with music streaming into only my right ear.

"Hey!" I shut off the music and glared up at my mother.

"This is an official meeting, Olivia. You need to pay attention."

Like she'd paid attention to my desperate pleas to be left at home?

Hypocrite.

I was about to protest and put my earphones back on, but Tower threw himself onto the couch beside me. I nearly bounced right over the armrest.

"You want to ride with me on the backhoe, Ollie?" Tower looked at my mother. "She can help me, can't she, Mad?"

"It's Madeline. I've told you that, Royce. Several times." Mom let out a breath and chewed on her bottom lip. "I suppose Olivia could ride with you, but I'll need her to cart some of the smaller tools. She is here to work with us."

"Gotcha, Mad." Tower aimed an index finger at my mother and wiggled his thumb as if it were a trigger.

The veins in Mom's temples pulsed a little more than usual. It cracked me up that Tower was able to push her buttons so effectively. Perhaps I could learn a thing or two from him during my six-week imprisonment.

"We'll head over to the site," my father said, regaining the attention of the gathered nerds. "Tower will clear the topsoil. Flint, Madeline, and I will excavate using the smaller hand tools. Keli will bag and tag. Will is in charge of photographing anything we unearth, and Simon, you'll make sense of it all." My father's eyes settled on me then he looked at my mother. "We can have her assist Keli, perhaps?"

Just once I'd like the guy to address me directly. Was he afraid I wouldn't comprehend his massive vocabulary? I mean, I wasn't a straight A student, but I wasn't failing every class either.

"If Keli doesn't mind," my mother said.

As if I'd be this enormous burden to Dr. Sumathai.

"Not at all," Dr. Sumathai said in her slight Indian accent. "Does she have a delicate touch?"

Great. Now she wasn't going to talk to me directly either. Wonderful.

I leaned over to Tower and whispered in his ear. After laughing out loud, he said, "Ollie would like everyone to know that she does, in fact, understand English and can be spoken to directly without fear of miscommunication."

My mother arrowed a glare in my direction, but I let it ricochet right off me. Her glares had no power here. I had nothing to lose. No TV. No phone. No computer. No friends. No real job. No parties. No dates. No beach. The list of things I didn't have was endless. My parents had nothing they could take away from me here.

"I've mapped out the route to the site." My father checked his watch. "Let's be ready to move out within the hour."

The brainiacs nodded simultaneously as if their cerebral cortexes—check out that vocabulary—were linked together. They broke off to gather their equipment, but Tower and I stayed on the couch. I studied his profile from my vantage point beside him. Like the rest of him, his face was big-boned with a square jaw and pronounced cheekbones. His light brown hair was cut short, almost military style, and all the pockets of his cargo shorts appeared to be full. What would a man like him carry in those pockets?

I was about to ask when Tower turned to me and said, "Perspective."

"Huh?" I slouched to the edge of the couch.

"You need some. I know you don't want to be here for six weeks. I don't either. I like digging stuff up with my backhoe, but would rather be doing it back home where, at quitting time, I can hop on my Harley, ride to my favorite hangout, and drink all the cold beers I can handle." He nudged my knee with his. "But this job right here pays more than any dinky landscaping job back home would. The way I see it, six weeks cut off from the world—and my beer—is worth it for the cash and such. Perspective."

I considered Tower's mini-speech for a few moments, trying to see the positive spin on me being kept in isolation in Montana.

"I'm sorry, Tower," I said. "I got nothing. From every angle, this situation sucks."

"I had to try." He got up and motioned to the front door. "Get whatever you're taking with you and meet me out back."

What did one bring on a backhoe ride into the woods? A ride where one's parents would play in the dirt hoping to find trinkets they weren't even sure were buried in said woods. Why couldn't I have gotten saddled with a couple of normal parents who went to work at 9 a.m. and came home at 5 p.m.? Parents who spent weekends working in the yard, or washing cars, or bike-riding.

Nope. I had to get stuck with treasure hunters. Sure, my parents were semi-famous in their museum circles. They'd made some important finds. I knew this. I should have been proud of them, but it was hard.

If I buried myself in the dirt, would my parents maybe discover me?

13. Jobah

I packed some food, seeds, water, and my dagger. I rolled several moose hides and tied them together. A shame that I had to abandon my dwelling before I'd had a chance to make happy memories inside it. After glancing around the sturdily built structure, I ducked out the door and made my way into the woods. Where I was going, I wasn't sure.

"Jobah?"

Keryun's voice. I turned around slowly, my eyes focused on my moccasins.

"My brother did this to your jaw and lip?" She stepped closer to me.

"Yes," I said. "He misunderstood what happened last night."

"I told him we had fallen asleep. That we did nothing wrong." Keryun reached a hand out to touch me, but then let it drop when I backed away.

"He did not believe you, I guess." I walked again.

"Where are you going?" She shuffled up beside me, matching my step with a little jog.

"I'm leaving."

"The village? You can't leave."

"Watch me." I hated being mean, but it was better this way. I couldn't let her see what was happening to me.

"But I want you to choose me, Jobah. I want to be your mate. I thought you wanted it too." Her voice held so much hurt, so much disappointment.

"It's not going to work out, Keryun. Find someone else, someone better." The words tasted like spoiled meat.

"Jobah," she grabbed my forearm to make me stop walking. "What are you not telling me?"

"Nothing." I shrugged free of her grasp and hitched my pack up higher on my shoulder.

"Then look at me." She maneuvered in front of me and tried to catch my gaze.

I zigzagged away from her, but she wasn't so easily evaded. Squeezing my eyes shut, I said, "Please, Keryun, let me go."

"Do you not like me, Jobah?"

"It's not about you, Keryun." I pushed forward, but still she persisted.

"What's it about then? Tell me."

"Are you sure you want to know? I can't take it back once you know."

"Of course. I want to know why you won't look at me, why you're leaving."

She deserved an explanation, I suppose. I hadn't kissed every female in the tribe. Keryun was special to me, and it pained me to leave her, but I had no choice.

Heaving in a slow breath, I raised my gaze to meet Keryun's. The gasp that rushed from her lips hit me like a thousand fire-tipped arrows. Her delicate hands—hands that had touched me in suggestive ways an evening ago—flew to her mouth.

When her hand moved, she paused for a moment, tears fresh in her eyes as she stared at me, through me. Then she screamed. I'd never heard such a loud sound within the village palisades. We generally kept quiet so as to preserve our cover in the woods. Keryun's yell, however, brought half the village scrambling out of their shelters or away from their work.

From the looks on their shocked faces, I knew Ninae had been wrong.

The people didn't want a Penta among them. They knew too little about them.

I knew too little about them.

Shouts of "What are you?" and "What's happened to you?" filled the village center. Those that had come close enough backed away as they huddled with each other. Did they think I would hurt them? Did they not see I didn't ask for any of this?

Seeing their reaction, their pure shock, made me want to dig a hole, climb into it, and bury myself alive.

I started walking again and didn't stop until I had put a sizable distance between myself and Keryun. I conjured up a picture of her from last night. All soft and warm and close as we slept by the lake. I could carry that image with me as I set off. I had to erase the vision of her reaction to my eyes. Her revulsion was evident. Her fear was tangible. I didn't want her—or the rest of the tribe—to feel that way about me, but I guess I didn't get to decide anymore. This Penta metamorphosis was going to happen whether I wanted it to or not. My best option was to be alone until I figured this all out.

If I figured it all out.

I walked until my legs burned, until my stomach rumbled with hunger. I was a good distance away from the village, but knew the lake was still close. I didn't want to stray too far from it, from all that I'd known since I was a child.

After finding a flat boulder, I set down my pack and dug out some berries. I ate them, but was still hungry. Not wanting to deplete my food stash before I'd had a chance to hunt, I choked down a few gulps of water and continued on my way. When I found a clearing in the woods, I surveyed the area and deemed it suitable for my new dwelling. Nothing fancy. Just enough to keep me dry.

I pulled my dagger from my pack and sought out a few sturdy saplings to use as my frame. When I sawed into the first young tree, however, it was as if I'd taken the dagger to my own ribcage. I'd barely left a scar on the bark, but my insides felt as if I'd swallowed hot coals. I dropped to my knees, my palms pushing into the sun-warmed soil. The tingle crept up my arms, into my shoulders, and across my back. How could I be in pain and… stimulated at the same time?

Several attempts to cut into the trees turned up the same gut-wrenching results. I had to face the fact that I would not be making my new dwelling from fresh wood. Instead, I gathered fallen branches and small logs. Neither were good for building, because they were too dry. Many pieces broke after I had gotten them into position. Fortunately, the breaking of old wood didn't cause me pain.

I finished my makeshift home as the sun reached its pinnacle in the summer-blue sky. I overturned the soil beside the dwelling and spread the seeds I'd brought. After hollowing out a stout log, I filled the vessel with water from the lake and moistened my small garden. With any luck, something would grow.

Back at the lake, I caught two salmon then built a fire to cook them. I tried not to think about what Ninae, Ashlo, or my other kin would be doing back at the village.

Without me.

I tried not to think about how I couldn't cut fresh wood and stack it to build up a wood pile for fires.

The fish should have tasted wonderful. I'd worked hard building my dwelling and planting. I was hungry enough to eat just about anything. Yet, I could not swallow the salmon easily. Every time I bit off a piece and chewed, my throat wouldn't work properly. It didn't want to swallow. It wanted to sting and choke.

I could survive in the woods. I was certain of that. My entire upbringing had been spent learning how to live off the land. I knew how to hunt and fish, what was edible, what wasn't. I knew what creatures to stay away from, what creatures were harmless. I knew what clues Great Earth gave me before the weather changed.

I knew all this, and yet, I knew nothing.

14. Olivia

I'd never ridden in a backhoe before. and I can't say I'd love to do it again. It was bumpy, loud, and cramped. Clearly, the driving area in the vehicle had been made for a single person. With Tower taking up a good amount of the room, I'd been squished. And hot. I had jumped down from the machine as soon as it had rumbled to a stop at the dig site.

My parents and the rest of the crew had driven in a comfy, air-conditioned SUV and were unloading gear from the back of it. Dad immediately shouted orders to Tower over the roar of the backhoe's engine, so I found Mom and helped her cart a few crates to the edge of the survey area.

"What are you guys looking for anyway?" I had been wondering this since they announced we were coming to Montana. I had, however, refused to ask any questions that might show even a sliver of interest in my parents' work. Seeing as how they'd managed to kidnap me and drag me across the country anyway, making a few inquiries wouldn't do much harm now.

Mom acted as if she hadn't heard me, but then she rummaged around in one of the crates and handed me a book with neon yellow sticky notes hanging out of the top.

"Page 347," she said as she pulled a black case, stakes, and rope out of another crate.

I opened the book and the words "The Veiled Tribes" announced themselves at the top of the page. Skimming, I picked up other words and phrases like *hidden, secluded, cut off from the world.* Going back to the top, I read a bit more thoroughly and discovered the author of the book conjectured that unseen Native American tribes existed all over the globe. These tribes were thought to live completely separate from the modern world. They still lived by the old ways and kept themselves buried in remote areas.

I looked around. Yep, this definitely would be a prime location for a tribe to hide themselves. Nothing but trees in every direction.

Shrugging, I dropped the book into its crate and went back to the SUV to unload more supplies. As I helped, Tower came barreling along with his backhoe. Under Dad's and Dr. Vakker's direction, Tower removed the top layer of soil. Dr. Sumathai pulled out a tripod and some weird little scope from a black case. She set it up while Dr. Reese repeatedly trotted out to the area Tower was clearing. He held a tape measure to the ground in several locations and pulled it up until it reached his shoulders. Dr. Sumathai peered into the scope and shouted out numbers.

I had no idea what they were doing, but it looked boring as hell.

Finally, the area was to the nerds' satisfaction, and they packed up the scope and tripod as Tower wheeled the backhoe out of the way.

"Where's Olivia?" Dad asked.

"I'm right here." I stepped up beside him.

"Madeline, have Olivia put stakes in every meter so we can set up the grid."

My mother actually turned to me and started to repeat the instructions. I raised both my hands to stop her.

"Really, Mom? You see me here. Of course I heard him." I shook my head and wandered back to the crates. After picking up the stakes, Dr. Vakker's abandoned tape measure, and a hammer, I stomped onto the cleared area and pounded in the first stake. Banging a stake was fantastically soothing, as if with each slam, all that was wrong in the world—well, my world anyway—loosened its hold on me. Yes, I was still supremely pissed about being in Montana, but it was real easy to picture my parents' faces on the heads of the stakes. I may have pictured Kevin's on a few too.

Stake therapy. I planned to tell the school psychologist about this breakthrough in teenage stress relief as soon as school started again. Plenty of woods around Sunderfield High School to have troubled kids bashing stakes in thirty-minute counseling sessions. Question was, was I one of the "troubled kids?"

Possibly.

I mean, I didn't feel like a crazy kid. I wasn't going to kill myself or anything that drastic, but sometimes I felt... insignificant.

Things were okay at school. Or they had been anyway. I was popular enough with my track team friends. We were a tight unit, racing together and hanging out. With the addition of Kevin, I'd picked up a few more friends, climbed a little higher up the social ladder. I could overlook being overlooked by my parents if I was considered somebody at school.

But here, with no one my age around, no social interaction or online contacts whatsoever, it was hard to disregard that my parents and I didn't know how to interact with each other. If my dad didn't give my mom things to say to me, I don't think she'd talk to me on her own aside from the general, "Clean your room," and "Are you done in the bathroom?"

Why did they even want me on this trip with them? What was their goal? Was it purely to ruin a summer they thought might be too good for me? If so, they were going to achieve that goal. I'd only been gone for a day and a half, and I was sure I'd missed a ton of things back home already. So many online statuses had been updated. If I had access to a computer, I'd have made my status say, *Olivia Bradford thinks archaeology bites.*

Although, *Olivia Bradford thinks Kevin Rogers bites* and *Riding in backhoes kinda sucks* were close second choices.

What was Kevin doing right now anyway? Probably eating crepes with Charity's French cousin, who no doubt had a model's body. Perfect for parading on beaches and slicking on sunscreen.

Shit.

I pounded a little harder on the stake in my hand as I pictured Frenchy hanging all over Kevin on his lifeguard chair. Before I knew it, the entire stake had been lost in the earth.

"Easy there, Ollie." Tower stood over me, completely blocking out the sun. "What are you thinking about?"

"Jerks, mostly."

Tower laughed. "Something tells me you know a few."

I did my best not to glance at my parents tying rope to the stakes I'd set up.

"Aww, give them a break." Tower gestured toward my parents with his chin. His hands were stuffed into his pockets, and dust covered his enormous, black biker boots. "I don't know them well, only worked a couple gigs with them, but they seem like top-notch archaeologists."

"They are. No question about that." I stood and brushed dirt off my knees and hands. "But they don't have a clue about being top-notch parents."

15. Jobah

Curiosity is the mother
of all questions,
and answers are lullabies
for the soul.

With no tribe to concern me, my list of chores was rather short. Normally the work I did in the village was for the benefit of everyone. Any food that was grown and harvested in the fields supported all the Kiyuchee. Firewood that was cut and stacked fueled all fires. I spent most of my days working on tasks that made the whole village stronger.

Now, I had only myself to worry about. The idea was both frightening and thrilling. I hadn't spent a single day completely on my own. Not ever. The tribe constantly surrounded me, and usually, I loved it. Loved knowing my labors strengthened the tribe. Loved knowing I belonged to a larger group.

But sitting here now, in front of my pieced-together shelter, with only the sounds of the forest around me, I was alone. I could do whatever I wanted, but what did I want to do?

I stared at the ground, and immediately the school popped into my head. With the changes that had been happening to me recently, I hadn't been to the hill in the woods that allowed me a peek at that beautiful place of learning.

Checking the sky now and finding plenty of blue still left, I pushed to my feet and strode a few steps away from my shelter. A trip to the hill was the perfect way to start mapping out this new existence of mine. It also gave me something to do besides contemplating what was to become of me.

Grabbing a fallen branch, I tested it and deemed it a suitable walking stick. I stepped out of the clearing and into a denser section of the woods. A loud, sloppy rustling sounded behind me.

The raccoon was back. It stopped when I stopped and regarded me from behind its mask of black fur.

"What do you want?" I asked.

The creature turned in an excited circle, its striped tail touching its nose as it moved. A small paw brushed casually over its face as if it had all the time in the world to stand there with me. Where was the rest of its raccoon family? Had it chosen to leave its kin as I had?

"What's your story, raccoon?"

A furry head tilted up at me and as I gazed into those dark eyes—eyes like mine should have been—a single word slipped into my head.

Friend.

I'd heard tales of animals talking to humans, but those tales were of people long ago. No one I knew could communicate with creatures. Another Penta talent, I suppose.

Friend.

The word came at me again, louder inside the walls of my head.

I could use a friend even if it did have four legs and a striped tail.

"I'm heading to the hill," I said. "You can come along."

The critter probably had already decided to follow me, but extending the formal invitation created the illusion that I was still in control.

Aiming for the hill, my new friend and I waded through feather-soft ferns. Each brush against my bare calves soothed me as my grandmother's hands had when I was a boy. My connection to the ferns should have concerned me, but I couldn't rustle up any panic. Not as velvety caresses filled me, empowered me with each step.

I stopped for a moment to sit on a boulder and pick brambles from my moccasins. The raccoon hopped up beside me and scratched its front paws around on its belly. A circle of white fur adorned its underside, like a full moon on a gray night sky.

"I suppose if we're going to be friends, I need something to call you." I extended a hand. "I'm Jobah. You can be Moon."

The raccoon pushed its cheek against my waiting hand and sniffed along my wrist. With a quick lick at my flesh and a strong, motherly aura emanating off the creature, our friendship was sealed.

Moon and I reached the top of the hill as the sun slipped past its highest peak in the sky. The leaves in the trees were motionless. The air, though ripe with the smells of summer, stirred nothing. Even Moon, crouched by my feet, appeared to be a statue of herself. Whiskers didn't twitch, tail didn't swish, ears didn't swivel. We were frozen in a moment.

I scanned the horizon until I faced the school. Sun beamed off its stone exterior, picking up glittering bits of rock. In one of the fields, people gathered. Every now and again, a clink sounded, sending a white rock out as people scrambled to scoop up the rock and throw it around. The person who had hit the rock ran around in a circle all to the cheering of the assembled crowd.

I had no idea what they were playing, but they appeared to be having a lovely time. Hitting and running. Throwing and cheering. I desperately wanted a closer look, but my place wasn't among them.

I sat on the hill, pulling my knees up to rest my chin on them. Moon sat beside me as I studied the school, so close yet so far. What would my life be like if I had been born into that world? A world where children went to places of learning and played games with white rocks. A world where sickness meant machines and bright white beds, not chants and herbs. A world where great distances were traveled, not by foot or horse, but by invention.

A taste of it. That's all I wanted. A taste of that other world. To see what was so bad about it, what made my people stay hidden in fear. Maybe they had it all wrong. Maybe there was nothing to be afraid of out there. How would we ever know if someone didn't go and investigate?

Was I that someone?

The woods had been my home for seventeen winters. I knew the woods and how to live in them. I was beginning to know the woods on a whole new level as well. My connection to the trees, the soil, and the animals tied me to the woods in a much deeper way. I still wasn't sure where that would all lead or if I wanted to travel down that path in the first place. I guess I didn't get a choice in the matter either way.

What if I did go into that other world and another change happened to me? How would those people, clapping and screaming in the field by the building react? Would they have seen someone like me before? Would they know how to fix me, how to change me back to the regular boy I was only seasons ago?

That thought made me pop up to my feet. Moon let out a little squeak at my sudden movement. If those people could stop or at least explain what was happening to me, I had to talk to them. Living in the woods alone was going to get tiresome quickly. Deep down, I wanted to go back to the village. I wanted to see if Keryun and I could be mates. I wanted to care for my grandmother as she had cared for me.

I wanted to be the person I had believed myself to be for seventeen winters. I wanted the old Jobah Everleaf to return.

Leaving my walking stick behind, I ran down the hill with Moon bounding along beside me. I moved like the wind and headed toward the school and the people. Whispers slithered through the forest as I ran, but I ignored them. I ignored the trees. I had to get to the school, to the outside world. I had to do something, even if it was the wrong something.

I needed answers. That school, those people, might have them.

So I ran.

16. Olivia

My parents had finished setting up the survey grid, all the while mumbling things to each other in their own little language. I assisted Dr. Sumathai in organizing her bagging and tagging station at the edge of the dig site.

"What if they don't find anything?" I motioned over my shoulder to my parents on their hands and knees in the dirt. Dr. Reese had joined them, and they had their small shovels and brushes at the ready. My mother was explaining something to the two men, then they all nodded at the same time and began digging, brushing, sifting, blowing.

"If they don't find anything today," Dr. Sumathai said, "then we try again tomorrow, and the day after that, and the day after that."

For six whole weeks. How was I going to survive this?

"Don't worry," Dr. Sumathai said. "Doctors Peter and Madeline Bradford always find something." Her eyes widened with admiration for my parents. What was she, a groupie or something?

I tossed a black Sharpie marker up in the air, let it spin then caught it in my other hand. I did this a few times, amusing myself, until Dr. Sumathai reached over and snagged the marker before I could catch it.

"You don't want this to end up in there." She pointed to the dig area.

Had she not seen me catch the marker at least ten times prior to her swiping it? Was there really any danger of a simple marker "contaminating" the dig site? Was her long black hair pulled too tightly into its ponytail? Six weeks surrounded by these people was going to kill me. For sure.

"What do we do while we wait for them to dig up something?" I leaned on the edge of Dr. Sumathai's table, which was covered with clear plastic bags, labels, magnifying glasses, my confiscated Sharpie.

"Do? What do you mean?" Her black eyebrows crawled together like fuzzy caterpillars. "We wait. That's what we do."

I so did not have the patience for archaeology. That much was crystal clear.

A quick glance around the area confirmed that every adult was engaged in some task. Dr. Vakker had his nose in a thick book with two more resting on his lap as he sat in a folding chair near the SUV. My parents and Dr. Reese were a couple of children playing in the sandbox. Mr. Tramond, the photographer, was fondling his cameras in a way that suggested he didn't date much. Dr. Sumathai was "waiting" by her table. Even Tower was busy tinkering with what he'd told me earlier was a gas-powered jackhammer.

Run With Me

I was the only one who did not belong here. I wasn't wearing the khaki cargo shorts the rest of the dig team sported. Wouldn't be caught dead in them. Not that there was anyone to notice what I was or wasn't wearing out here.

The only thing that felt right at this particular moment was my sneakers. An older pair that should have been pounding a smooth, paved track in Rhode Island instead of shuffling through dirt and ferns in Montana. A pair that had won me several track medals. Medals that now hung on a mirror in my bedroom back home. Right next to the picture of me and Kevin at the prom. Would have to burn that photo upon my return. Or at least draw devil horns on Kevin's head. No sense in ruining my part in the picture. I looked damn good in that purple mini-dress with the braided shoulder straps and sparkly silver sandals. I'd been a sight to see dancing my butt off that night.

On that thought, I dug out my music, plugged my ears, and let the volume rip. A quick run might wipe out the antsy feeling crawling around like worms in my veins. I seriously doubted anyone would miss me around here anyway.

I edged away from the dig site, slow and quiet steps, until the trees hid me. I turned in a circle, deciding I would run on the trail the backhoe had made through the brush. Flattened ferns and turned up dirt marked the path clearly. The only thing worse than being in these woods would be to get lost in them.

Christy Major

I could imagine the headline in *The Providence Journal* already:

"Local Sunderfield Track Star Lost in Desolate Montana Woods."

Okay, so I may have been overdoing it with the "track star" part, but that was my right.

Stretching out my legs, I started at a slow jog to get the feel of running on uneven ground. I had to watch for roots and logs sticking out here and there, but I fell into a steady rhythm in a matter of minutes. Though I hated being here, I had to admit the air was fresher. Hot, but pure somehow. Each inhale charged the rest of my body, pushed me further along. Each exhale siphoned out some of the tension, some of the disgust.

As my legs started to burn, I actually laughed. Laughed at how I had ended up in this situation. Laughed at how I'd lost my Target job. At how Kevin had dumped me. At how I'd ridden in a backhoe, rubbing elbows with a man who referred to himself as Tower.

I mean, it was all so comical if I thought about it as happening to someone else. As if I'd read it in a book instead of lived it. Maybe that was a strategy for dealing with this whole predicament. Pretend it was happening to a book character. Not me. Not Olivia Bradford, but some other poor soul with unreasonable parents.

Increasing my speed, I sang along with the music until I had officially moved into The Zone. That place where only me, my sneakers, and the ground existed. A perfect connection between the three propelled me forward. My hair, caught up in a long ponytail, bounced from side to side as the wind—a wind my movement created—slid over my cheeks. I was a bullet racing through the air, a bird soaring with wings outspread, a star shooting across the sky. Nothing could stop me.

I came to the end of the bulldozed trail and spilled into the parking lot in front of the cabin. I had run all the way back to camp and wasn't tired. How was that possible?

After pausing to shuffle through playlists, I jogged across the parking lot and found the narrow road we had driven on when we'd arrived at the cabin. It was a suitable track for running as well, so I turned up the volume and continued. Figured I had plenty of time before the dweebs back at the dig site noticed I was gone.

If they noticed I was gone.

I went along for a while until a raccoon ran across the road a few feet ahead of me. It was cute with its bushy, striped tail and scurrying little legs. I slowed as it dove into the brush. As I was preparing to run again, something—something big—rammed into me. My body got flattened to the ground, my palms digging into stones and sticks.

A scream shot from my throat, and I struggled to get out from under whatever was atop me. Warm flesh pressed against my bare legs.

Wait. *Flesh?* Not fur? Not a wild animal full of claws and teeth waiting to rip into me?

I stopped squirming and rolled over. Jet-black hair fanned across the front of my T-shirt. A set of very tanned arms rested on either side of me, and a low groan sounded as I moved to slide away.

"Are you all right?" I asked as my eyes traveled over a bared back, also tanned. And muscled. Better-than-Kevin-Rogers muscled.

The arms moved at my sides, and the body pinning me to the ground slowly lifted. A pair of leaf green eyes—a color I'd never seen before on a real person—stared at me through long, black eyelashes. They glowed in a face of dark, smooth skin.

I felt I should say something, but those unusual eyes had me paralyzed and made me forget how to speak. Made me forget everything.

The setting around me dropped away as I stared at those eyes. I didn't feel the rocks and twigs beneath me, didn't hear leaves rustling above me, didn't smell sun-warmed soil.

There were only the eyes.

I should have been pushing this body off me, skittering away from this stranger in the woods, slapping this intruding face so close to mine.

I should have been *doing* something.

But I didn't want to.

17. Jobah

"You're bleeding." This was not the first thing I'd noticed about the female beneath me, but my brain registered it as the most urgent observation.

She blinked slowly, sat up, and studied her palm. Strands of light yellow hair fell about her pale face as blue eyes inspected the cuts in her skin. Blood dripped down one slender wrist, and she pressed the wound to her shirt as she looked back at me.

She was... her face was... well, I'd never seen anyone like her. I didn't have the right words to explain her to myself.

Pulling her hand away from her shirt, she groaned softly.

"I'm sorry." I kneeled back on my heels so I wasn't hovering over her. "I didn't see you." I'd been running along behind Moon, thinking only of reaching that school.

"I didn't see you either." Her voice reminded me of the wooden flute Uncle Ranen used to play around the fire in the evenings before he was made to leave the village.

Fresh blood had already pooled in her hand.
"Shit."

I didn't know what that word meant, but it appeared to express her disgust at being injured.

97

"It needs to be cleaned," I said. "There's water just beyond those trees." I stood and held out a hand to help her to her feet.

She stared at my hand for a moment then her gaze met mine. "Your eyes are so green."

I let my hand drop and closed my eyes. Even this outsider knew something was wrong with me.

"I won't hurt you." If I reached the school, would the people in the field fear me as well? Would no one want to be around me because I was a Penta?

"I didn't say you would hurt me." She reached up and slid her uninjured hand into mine. Her skin was warm and soft, but her grip was strong. "I'm Olivia Bradford." Her gaze traveled down the length of me, a puzzled expression flitted over her delicate features. "Are you in costume or something?" She gestured to my breechclout and moccasins with her free hand.

"Costume? No."

"So you just run around the woods dressed like that?" She laughed as she slid her hand from mine, and I felt as if I had just lost something... something important.

"This is what I always—" I was about to say I always wore a breechclout and moccasins, but a voice like my grandmother's filled my head with cautions.

Outsiders are evil.

They are selfish beasts.

It is not safe to be in their company.

But this Olivia didn't look evil or selfish or unsafe.

She looked like sunshine and clear, blue water. She smelled like summer fruit. Her skin had felt softer than feathers.

Olivia narrowed her eyes at me, but then widened them quickly. "Wait a minute. Are you one of the tribes? Like in the book? A Veiled Tribe?" Her mouth dropped open.

"I don't know what book or tribes you speak of." I shrugged. Were all outsiders this intelligent? It had only taken her moments to figure me out. I had to go.

Now.

I turned to start up on my run again—to get away from Olivia—even though most of me didn't want that. Instead, I wanted to tell her everything and know everything about her.

Had she cast some kind of outsider spell on me?

Her hand clamped onto my forearm, stopping me from resuming my run.

"Let go of me." My voice crackled on the word *me*.

Olivia tightened her grip. "Not until you tell me why you are dressed like that."

"You were right. I am in costume." I folded my arms across my chest to look surer of myself.

She shook her head. "Too late for the costume bit, Green Eyes. Don't let the blond hair fool you. I'm smarter than you think."

What did the color of her hair have to do with her intelligence?

"Why are you wearing what you have on?" I gestured to her garb.

"Because this is what people wear when they go running. T-shirt, shorts, sneakers. Standard running gear."

"And what are these?" I tugged on the two circular pieces dangling from a box at her waist.

Olivia picked up the pieces and swung them around on their cord, a smile easing across her lips. Light, pinkish lips. Not dark like mine or the females in my tribe.

"Now see, that question right there reveals it all. You are so from one of those tribes. Anyone else would know that these are earphones and this plays music when you are on the go." She unclipped the box from her shorts and touched it a few times. She held out one of the earphones. "Here, listen."

I hesitated.

"It's not going to hurt you."

She stepped closer and put the earphone next to my ear.

Drums. Only not like the ones from my people. These drums were many and angry and loud. Other sounds I didn't recognize mixed in while Olivia's foot tapped and her head bobbed.

"Cool, right?" She smiled again, and I didn't feel even a little cool. "So 'fess up. You're from a Veiled Tribe, aren't you?"

I nodded once. If I didn't actually *say* I was from a hidden tribe, I hadn't broken any rules. At least that's what I told myself.

Olivia smiled brilliantly and a small indent appeared on her left cheek. "What's your name?"

"Jobah Everleaf." There were no rules about stating my name. "How do you know about my tribe?"

"Well, Jobah, my parents are back that way digging in the dirt looking for artifacts about hidden tribes." She laughed and the sound flooded over me like a refreshing summer rain. "They're the PhDs, and yet, here *I* am with a living, breathing member of such a tribe." Her eyes examined me, and my face grew warm under her scrutiny. "Are there more of you?"

"There's only one me." Why would there be more than one me? Had she bumped her head on her fall? My fingers itched to check for bruises under all that golden hair.

Olivia chuckled. Why did she find me so amusing?

"No, I didn't mean are there more of you in particular." She poked my shoulder with a sharp fingertip. "I meant are there others like you around here? More of your kind?"

I hesitated. I was supposed to say no. Actually, I was supposed to say nothing. I should turn around and run in the opposite direction. This Olivia Bradford could mean trouble.

Only she didn't look like trouble.

"Oh, I get it," she said. "You can't tell me about your tribe. Sworn to secrecy, right? Nod if I'm right. Then it's not like you actually told me."

She had thought the same as I had.

I nodded in response.

"Cool. I don't suppose you could show me the village, could you?" She stepped closer. I didn't have to look too far down to see her. Not many females in my tribe were almost as tall as me.

I shook my head firmly. "I can't." I wasn't heading back to the village on my own, never mind with an outsider.

She held up her still bleeding wrist. "You owe me after knocking me down."

"I didn't mean to knock you down," I said. "It was an accident."

"Because you weren't paying attention." She wagged a finger at me. "Where were you going in such a hurry anyway? There's nothing around here but trees and more trees."

I volleyed between telling her where I was headed and keeping it a secret. As an outsider, however, Olivia might be the one to help me.

"Do you go to school?" I asked.

"Yeah, but not in the summer. Do you?" Olivia dabbed her cut wrist on her shirt again.

I pointed in the direction of the lake up ahead, and Olivia started walking beside me.

"No, my tribe doesn't have a school. I learned how to plant, care for animals, cut and split wood, hunt, make dwellings, and build fires from the others in my tribe."

"That's all you need to know to live out here?"

"It's all I need to know. There are others that know about tanning hides, healing, and communicating with spirits. None of that is my concern." It hadn't been anyway. Now that I was a Penta, who knew what my concerns were?

"Wow. Wish I could say that Calculus was none of my concern, because it isn't, yet I have to take it."

"What is Calculus? Where do you have take it? Is it heavy?"

Olivia shook her head and laughed again. "*Take it* means to study it, learn it. Calculus is extremely boring mathematics. You know, stuff with numbers." She checked her hand again. "Where are we going? This is starting to burn."

I guided her to the lake. Olivia kneeled by the water's edge and dunked her hand into the water. A sigh escaped her lips as she swished her hand back and forth. Sunlight glinted off her hair, making it shimmer gold in some spots. Muscles coursed along her bent legs as she hunched over the water.

When she pulled her hand out, little drops of blood seeped to the surface of her palm.

"It won't stop bleeding," she said. "Why won't it stop? The cuts are not that deep."

I scouted around the area until I found some yarrow. I curled my fingers around the plant, but hesitated before plucking some leaves. If I felt it when trees were sawed and live branches were snapped, wouldn't I feel the leaves of this plant being torn as well?

Olivia still kneeled by the water, looking with great concern at her palm. Gulping in a breath, I quickly ripped three yarrow leaves from the plant. Three sharp pricks arrowed into my stomach, but the pain was tolerable.

Stooping by the water, I wet the leaves and rolled them around in my palm until they got soggy and pasty.

"Give me your hand," I said.

"What are you going to do?" Olivia looked at me with untrusting eyes. The sun reflecting off the water wavered over her face. Her skin was so fair, so flawless. She didn't look like a real human crouched beside me. She looked like a spirit, or what I imagined one to look like.

"This plant will stop the bleeding and make you heal faster." I motioned with my fingers for her to hold out her hand.

Slowly, Olivia did so. I placed my hand beneath hers, cradling it in my palm. I pressed the yarrow paste into the small wounds, spreading it thinly over her skin.

"It should be wrapped to get the full effect and so it doesn't dry out too quickly," I said.

"My T-shirt." Olivia stood and angled her hips toward me. "You can rip off some material at the bottom."

I took the edge of the shirt in my hands, and my fingers brushed against her stomach. The skin there was warm and smooth like the rest of her. Something stretched awake inside me.

Focusing on the gray shirt instead of the feel of her flesh, my eyes zoomed in on the green and gold symbols across the front. "What does that mean?"

"SHS Track? Sunderfield High School Track team. I'm a runner." She smiled again. "That is, I'm a runner when boys don't plow into me and send me crashing to the ground."

Using my dagger, which Olivia eyed carefully, I finished ripping her shirt until I had a suitable strip of material to tie around her hand. "Again, I'm sorry. Moon made it by, so I figured my path was clear as well."

"Moon?" Olivia's eyebrows rose as she took her hand back.

"A raccoon." I swiveled in a tight circle, searching the area. "In fact, I don't know where she went."

"I saw a raccoon," Olivia said. "That's partly why I didn't see you. I was too busy watching that fluffy, striped tail slip into the ferns that I didn't hear you barreling through like a train."

"Train?"

"Oh, uh… a bunch of… well, there's railroad tracks… and… never mind. Not important." She puffed out a breath.

"What were you doing in the woods?" I asked.

"Running." Olivia cleared her throat. "Running away, I guess."

"You too?"

What could she possibly be running away from? She didn't look as if anything was wrong with her. In fact, she was probably the most perfect looking creature I'd ever seen.

"We all have things to run away from, Jobah. Not that running solves anything." She lowered to the ground and crossed her long legs in front of her.

I should have gone. Parted ways with her. I had a school to get to after all. I had the rest of my life to figure out. She was an outsider. I wasn't supposed to have contact with her.

But I couldn't go.

Olivia was so vulnerable sitting there, drawing circles in the dirt with a stick. Something inside me had to find out why she was running. Something inside me made me sit beside her.

Something inside me wanted to know her.

18. Olivia

Mountains rose like purple, triangular shadows across the lake while trees hugged the closer edges. I didn't want to admit it, but the scenery was phenomenal. I'd only seen landscapes like this in books or online. Sunderfield still had unpopulated spots, but nothing like this. Nothing this serene, this natural.

The sky was dusky over the lake, but I didn't move from my spot next to Jobah.

Jobah Everleaf.

What a wonderful name.

His legs were stretched out in front of him, and I'd spent the last five minutes memorizing the muscles in his thighs. That strip of…of…God, I guess it was animal hide encircling his waist didn't cover much, but that was okay. I desperately wanted to inspect his face, but with him sitting so close beside me, it was impossible to look and not look like I was looking.

"How old are you?" If I asked a question, I had to look at his face. Common courtesy, right?

"Seventeen winters." His voice reminded me of a bass guitar, low and steady, keeping the song on track.

"Me too. If you went to school, we'd be seniors together."

Why did that thought excite me? A vision of parading down the busy hallways of Sunderfield High School with Jobah beside me made my cheeks warm. Eden would absolutely die.

Maybe Kevin would be jealous. Maybe he'd want to get back together. Maybe I'd tell him to screw.

Why was I even thinking about this? Jobah wasn't a shiny new toy to be paraded around. He was a person, and I wasn't that shallow.

But shit, he was gorgeous.

"Seniors?" Jobah shifted his legs so one bent, and he rested his arm on his knee. Good thing he was facing the water. Otherwise, I would have gotten to view…umm… all of him. He didn't seem to care that he was flashing the fish in the lake.

"That's what they call you when you are in your last year of high school." I fiddled with the end of my ponytail.

"How many years of schooling have you had?"

"Six years of elementary school, three years of middle school, and three years of high school. I have one more left then it's off to college for about four or five more years. Assuming I can figure out what I want to be when I grow up."

Jobah's dark eyebrows rose over those evergreen eyes. "That is many years spent on schooling, but you still don't know what to do with your life?"

Great. He sounded like the doctors. Expected me to have everything all figured out.

"Knowing what to do with your entire life is a pretty big decision, don't you think?" Boy, did I sound bitchy or what? I shuffled away from Jobah a bit. Just my luck I'd run into a guy in the middle of the woods who was so judgmental.

"It is a big decision, and sometimes what you had planned for yourself can no longer be." Jobah stared out over the water.

"Your plans have changed?" I scooted closer to him again. Maybe he understood my situation better than I'd thought. Maybe he wasn't judging, but agreeing.

"My future is uncertain."

"You're not alone."

He turned those magnificent eyes my way. "That's good to know." He sifted out a breath and twisted on the sand to face me, his legs folding beneath him so he was resting on his knees. "What do you do besides go to school?"

I turned to face him so our knees were nearly touching, one eye on that animal hide, hoping it'd cover what it was supposed to cover.

"Lots of things. School is only during the day for about six hours. After school, I have track practice. I hang out with friends, do homework, talk on the phone, baby sit sometimes. I used to spend time with my boyfriend too, but he dumped me when he found out my parents were making me come here for part of the summer."

"You did not wish to come?"

"Not at all. I had plans to spend my summer in a much different way."

"What's being dumped mean?" Jobah's face crinkled around the eyes, showing his confusion.

"It means Kevin didn't want to be with me anymore."

"Like he didn't want to be your mate?"

"Umm…yeah, I guess that's what it's like." Being mates sounded a bit deeper than anything Kevin and I had going, but if it made sense to Jobah I could go with it.

"Kevin does not make wise decisions then," Jobah said. "You appear to be a fine mate."

When I looked at Jobah, he stared right into my eyes. *A fine mate?* That may have been the nicest thing anyone had ever said to me even if it was a bit Neanderthal.

"Thank you." I straightened out my legs to the left of Jobah and glanced toward the water, not sure where else to look.

"Is that why you were running?" Jobah asked. "Because Kevin dumped you?" He hooked some of his chin-length black hair behind his left ear. The tanned skin at his neck was the color of coffee.

Shifting my gaze to study my wrapped hand, I said, "I was running because I didn't fit in with the dorks back at the dig site." I held up my hand before Jobah could speak. "Dorks are super smart people who have almost no social skills. They are consumed by their work and don't have time to waste on daughters, on family."

My eyes stung, and I warned myself not to cry in front of Jobah. Way to seem like a total loser. I swallowed the hurt and cleared my throat. "Why were you running?"

Slowly, Jobah's legs stretched out next to mine. If he moved an inch my way, we would have touched. He leaned back on his palms, his stomach muscles tightening as he did so, showing off movie star abs.

"I wonder if you can handle the truth of why I was running." Jobah tilted his head at me, and those green eyes were so full of sorrow.

"Try me," I said. "What have you got to lose? If I can handle it, then you'll feel better having unloaded it. If I can't, then you never have to see me again, so who cares?"

Jobah nodded, considering my logic. "Your words make sense. Others must come to you for wise advice."

I thought of Eden always asking my opinion on everything from purses to science fair topics. Several of my friends sought out my thoughts on various matters, but I never considered myself a source of wise advice. Maybe I was. Could that be my life's calling?

Jobah rubbed a hand over his face. "It is probably better if I show you why I was running instead of tell you."

He stood and offered me a hand again. He pulled me to my feet and led me to a patch of plants to the right of the lake.

"Kneel with me." He pointed to the spot beside him as he got to his knees.

I did as he asked. My arm touched his as we kneeled together over waist high stems. I didn't know what kind of flowers the plants were because none of them had bloomed yet. They all had tight green buds at the tops of the stems just waiting to blossom.

Jobah curled his long fingers around the nearest stem. Pulling it so it angled toward him, he leaned down. His lips almost kissed the bud, and I thought he was going to eat it. Instead, he parted his lips and blew out a gentle breath.

I put a hand to his bare shoulder when movement on the bud caught my attention. The sides of the green bud peeled back, and bright, pink petals unfurled themselves. Within a matter of seconds, the flower was completely bloomed. It was like watching that rapid-frame photography you sometimes see in documentaries when the director is trying to show the development of something over time. This flower had gone from bud to blossom in mere moments.

How was that possible?

When I didn't say anything, Jobah blew his breath over the entire patch of stems. The buds exploded pink, and a sweet fragrance perfumed the air.

"They're beautiful." My voice was barely a whisper. "How did you do that? What are you, Jobah?"

"Not normal. That's what I am." Jobah pushed to his feet and gazed down at the bloomed flowers.

"Why so sad about it?" I said. "What you did was amazing."

Those green eyes darted to my face. A look of sheer surprise tightened Jobah's features. "Amazing? You sound like Ninae, my grandmother. She thinks this is good. That I'm important somehow."

"You don't agree?" So far Granny sounded right to me.

"I had a plan." Jobah faced the water now. "I had made my own dwelling, was choosing a mate, was happy to continue my life in the village as part of my tribe. Then little changes in me became big changes, like my eyes for example." He looked at me. "Two days ago, my eyes were brown, almost black, like the rest of the Kiyuchee. Now they are the color of—"

"Summer leaves," I finished. "They're wonderful." I hadn't meant to say that last part out loud.

"They are different from everyone else's." Jobah thrust out a hand to the flowers at our feet. "I can control the flowers, I can feel the trees, and a raccoon, wherever she's hiding, has decided to be friends with me. It is all too strange. I don't know what it means, what I'm supposed to do."

"Maybe you aren't supposed to do anything. Yet." I pulled at the strings hanging loose at the end of my torn T-shirt. "Maybe you'll just know when you're supposed to do something." I hoped that was how I'd figure out my own life's direction. That it would come to me, like a strike of lightning illuminating a path for me.

Jobah smiled, perfectly white teeth nearly glowing from his tanned face. I actually felt a little light-headed looking at that smile and the way his dark hair fell about his chin, the way those fantastic green eyes looked at me.

"You are definitely wise, Olivia Bradford."

"I just wanted to make you feel better. Life sucks sometimes. Trust me, I know, but you have to assume it all means something. Otherwise, what's the point?"

Like me being in Montana. It was wretched, but if I hadn't been here, I wouldn't have been steamrolled by Jobah on the path. I had a feeling meeting him meant something big. Something lightning strike-ish.

19. Jobah

"Officially, I'm a Tree Penta." I wasn't sure how much to tell Olivia. I didn't know her, but she was the first person to make me feel as if my future was still my own. "According to Ninae, there have not been any tree spirits in my tribe for hundreds of years."

"So why you?" Olivia said. "Why now?"

"Good questions. Ones for which I have no answers."

Olivia chewed on her bottom lip, and the action had me thinking of kissing Keryun. Keryun who only days ago touched me with gentle hands, kissed me with soft lips, wanted to be my mate. Now she was afraid of me. That thought made something in my chest ache.

I focused back on Olivia. Did she taste like Keryun? A subtle mix of pine and ginger root? Or did her fair skin and light hair give her a sweeter flavor?

"So you've left your village?" Olivia asked.

I drew my attention away from her lips. "I had no choice. My eyes were frightening people. People I've known my entire life." I closed my eyes, hoping Olivia wouldn't be afraid.

Her hand touched my chin, turned my head toward her. I kept my eyes clamped shut and held my breath.

"Jobah, look at me." Her fingers tightened on my jaw.

I opened one eye at a time and prepared for the fear certain to hit Olivia at any moment. Why did it matter? Again, I didn't know her. She didn't mean anything to me.

"Maybe I'm supposed to be scared of you," she said, "but I'm not. So relax." She dropped her hand from my chin, and her face softened, not a line, crease, or wrinkle anywhere. Just smooth perfection.

That was it? No shrinking away? No mouth agape in horror? No screaming? She was going to continue to sit this close to me? Outsiders were hard to figure out.

We sat next to each other in comfortable silence as darkness crept over the water.

"Where are you living now?" Olivia finally asked, her voice quiet.

"I've built a shelter in the woods, not far from this lake." I motioned to the water in front of us.

"You can survive out here all alone?"

"So many questions." I nudged Olivia with my elbow.

"I'm sorry. I'm trying to picture living alone in the woods without shivering in dread over it." Olivia's shoulders shook a bit, as if she were casting off a cold shadow.

"I know these woods well. I can survive."

In the darkness, I almost couldn't see Olivia's face anymore. I wanted to be able to see it.

"I don't think I could survive out here on my own," she said. "I'm not even sure I can find my way back to the cabin."

On that thought, she popped up from the ground and turned in a circle.

"What is it?" I asked as I stood.

"When did it get this dark? I should be at the cabin now. Shit, which way is it?"

Genuine fear radiated off Olivia, but it was not fear of me. I rested a hand on her shoulder and she let out a little squeak. "I can get you back to the path where we met."

"Where you flattened me, you mean."

"Where I accidentally bumped into you."

She held up her wrapped hand. "The cuts on my palm suggest more than a *bump*, mister."

I took her wrist and ran my fingers along her forearm. "Does this still hurt?"

Olivia didn't answer right away. I wished I could see her face, but there wasn't enough light.

"No. It doesn't hurt. Those leaves must have worked." Her other hand felt its way up my arm. Soft, tickling strokes. "Or maybe you're magic, Jobah Everleaf."

"Maybe."

Her body was now very close to mine. Her breath slid over my chest in little, hot bursts. She tilted her head up, and her lips were right there at my chin. All I had to do was lean down, and I could answer my questions about how she tasted.

"I'd better get back to the cabin. My parents are obsessed with their work, but they must have noticed I'm missing by now." Olivia backed up a step, but weaved her fingers between mine instead of letting go. "C'mon."

Holding her hand, I led Olivia through the brush. After a few moments, the crunch of leaves to our left made me stop.

"It sounds small," Olivia said. "Tell me it sounds small." Her grip tightened on my hand.

I squinted in the direction of the sound, and suddenly the darkness wasn't so black anymore. I rubbed my eyes, but a soft glow illuminated the area.

"Do you see that?" I asked.

"See what?" Olivia's body pressed against the back of mine. I could almost feel her heartbeat in my own chest.

"That light. It's all around us."

"I don't see anything, Jobah. It's pitch black out here."

I let out a huff. "A new ability, I guess. I can see in the dark now."

"Don't sound so down about it? I'd kill for that ability right now. What do you see? Is it big? I hope it's not big." Her nails dug into my side.

As I peeled her hand away, two eyes reflected back at me from the ground. "It's just Moon." I clicked my tongue, and the raccoon came bounding toward me, her striped tail waving like a furry flag.

Olivia jumped. "It touched me! It touched my leg!" Her arms went around my waist and squeezed. "What if it's rabid, you know, sick?"

"It's not." I thought about freeing myself from Olivia's hold, but I liked having her this close.

"These critters don't generally make friends with us humans. There has to be something wrong with it." Olivia jumped again, and Moon brushed against my calf.

"It's me," I said. "I'm what's wrong. She's drawn to me or something. Because of what I am."

Olivia's grip loosened. "Maybe you're rabid then." She poked me in the back with a boney fingertip and actually chuckled.

"You joke about what's happening to me." Hadn't I wondered the same thing though? I turned around to face her, now able to see her clearly.

"I joke to protect, Jobah. Not to hurt. If I don't laugh about my parents being more interested in their dig than in me, I'll cry. If you don't laugh about becoming one with the trees, you'll make yourself crazy. Listen to me. I'm wise, remember?"

Again, she poked me. This time between my ribs, and I did laugh. I couldn't stop myself. I caught Olivia's hand and held it as I had before. I followed Moon as she picked her way back to the path.

Once we spilled onto the flattened trail, Olivia moved so she walked beside me. She didn't let go of my hand though. Probably because she couldn't see.

When lights came into view ahead, Olivia said, "There's the cabin."

"I have never been to this part of the woods. My village does not reach to this area," I said.

"Yet, you knew where to lead me," Olivia said. "Maybe you can find your way in any woods now that you're a Penta. Maybe the trees guide you."

She made it sound so reasonable. As if being a Penta was just a part of growing older. I liked that idea.

I walked her closer to the structure ahead. A large, looming shadow surrounded by trees, the shelter emanated a soft glow from within as if a fire burned inside it. I admired its construction and wondered if I could build such a dwelling. A machine with a huge arm on the front sat next to the cabin. It was covered in dirt and smelled strange.

"What is that?" I pointed to the machine.

"A backhoe," Olivia said. "It digs up the earth in big scoops."

"It destroys?"

Olivia thought about that before answering. Her brows scrunched together. "It can, but here it's mostly moving dirt from one spot to another. My parents and the other archaeologists need to get to the deeper layers to look for their trinkets."

"Trinkets from my tribe?"

"I guess." She shrugged.

"They won't find any here. We never lived in this area. We've always lived in the village."

Olivia put a finger to my lips. "Shhh, Jobah. Let the doctors play in the dirt if they want. I assume your tribe wouldn't want to be discovered, right?"

"No, the elders have decided the tribe is not to interact with…"

"With me," Olivia finished. "But you're not part of the tribe anymore, are you?"

"No." Why did my answer not fill me with unbearable sadness?

"Meet me tomorrow afternoon," Olivia whispered. "At the end of this path." She pointed behind me. "You don't have a watch, do you?" She pushed something on her wrist and a blue glow revealed strange markings.

"I don't have one of those. Is that a watch?"

"Yes." Olivia unfastened it and handed it to me. "Take mine. When the screen says this," she crouched to the ground and drew four shapes in the dirt, "I'll be at the end of the path. Promise you'll be there too."

"I will be there." Where else did I have to be?

"Good." She smiled and that little indent in her cheek appeared again. "We'll go for a run together. I'll bet I'm faster than you." She gave my shoulder a light shove. "See ya, Jobah."

She jogged toward the cabin and leaped up the stairs. Her body moved like a deer's, graceful and quick, but I didn't think she was faster than me. A rectangle of light spilled out of the dwelling as Olivia entered. She turned and gave me a wave before disappearing.

After studying the markings she'd drawn in the dirt to be sure I would recognize them on the watch, I walked back down the path where Moon was waiting.

"What do you make of Olivia?" I stooped by the raccoon and let her nuzzle my knee. Thinking of how Olivia's hand had felt in mine, I wondered why the elders didn't want to mix with outsiders. With schools, watches, and females like Olivia Bradford, the world beyond my village seemed like a wonderful place.

20. Olivia

I closed the door carefully so it wouldn't make a noise and leaned my forehead against it. Had I really met a tree spirit, a Penta? Or had I tripped on that path and banged my head? Was Jobah Everleaf a figment of my injured brain?

Was I unconscious and still spread eagle on the ground?

I felt around my scalp and didn't feel any bumps.

I peeked under the makeshift bandage around my hand and noted that the cuts on my palm were real enough. The yellowy-green paste that had crusted over the slices was proof I had definitely met someone in the woods. Injured brain or not, I wouldn't have known to slather wet leaves over a wound to help it heal. And it was working. The cuts weren't as red and didn't hurt much at all.

Jobah was real.

That thought made something in my stomach buzz excitedly. Maybe Montana wasn't Hell after all. Surely Hell didn't have Native American boys that looked like Jobah. All that dark hair, that tanned skin, and those eyes…

"Yummy."

"What's yummy?" a voice said from the living room.

I whipped around. Tower sat on the couch facing the door. He had a magazine open on his lap and a tall glass of iced tea on the coffee table in front of him.

"Nothing's yummy." I glanced to the stairs. No way could I make it to them without having to walk by Tower, so I inched into the living room.

Mr. Tramond, the photographer, was also sitting on one of the couches. He had a slew of pictures he was sorting.

"Evening," he said without looking up.

Tower's eyes, however, immediately went to my torn T-shirt. He slid the magazine to the table. "What happened to you?"

"I went for a run and fell. Stupid. Just not paying attention." I held up my wrapped hand. "Had to use my shirt to stop the bleeding, but it's not deep. I'll be fine."

I edged toward the stairs as if the conversation was over.

"Maybe I should take a look at that." Tower made a move to get up from the couch.

"No, no. It's nothing. I'll wash it out when I get upstairs." I waved my other hand dismissively.

"You've been gone a long time." Mr. Tramond said, his eyes now focused on the jagged hem of my T-shirt. On the section of my stomach now visible.

"I know. I got a little lost. One tree looks exactly like the next." I pulled at my shirt, trying to cover my stomach. "Were my parents worried?"

"I'm sure they—" Tower started, but Mr. Tramond cut him off.

"No," he said.

"Of course not. What was I thinking?" I flopped onto the couch beside Tower. At least seated, my T-shirt wasn't as short. If I hunched down, it skimmed the top of my shorts and covered my skin.

Mr. Tramond continued to stare at me as if he were taking photographs with his mind or something equally as creepy.

I pulled a throw pillow from the couch onto my lap. Tried to look comfortable, but his gaze just stayed on me.

Maybe going unnoticed by adults was a good thing. Maybe I didn't want their attention after all. Not this kind of attention anyway.

I should have invited Jobah inside.

Tower picked up his iced tea and held it out to me. "Want a drink?"

I shook my head. What I wanted was to go upstairs to my room.

He set the glass back down. "You sure your hand is okay?"

"Yeah. It's fine." I looked to the stairs. "I should head up. I'm tired."

"More digging on tomorrow's agenda. You should get plenty of sleep." Tower gave me a wave. "Good night, Ollie."

"Night."

"Good night, Olivia," Mr. Tramond said, his attention back on his photographs, thank God.

I walked to the stairs in what I hoped didn't seem like a run and took the steps two at a time. Once inside my room, I locked the door and stood in the dark for a few moments until the goosebumps Mr. Tramond had caused faded from my arms. I made a decision to stay away from him for the rest of this damn trip.

After turning on the light on the bedside table, I sat on the end of the twin bed. The mattress barely moved, and I didn't look forward to spending another night on it. I missed my bed back home. All soft and broken in and smelling of the lavender detergent I loved. The sheets on the bed beneath me now smelled like bleach, which my mind did register as meaning clean, but the scent was too industrial to be cozy.

What was Jobah sleeping on tonight? He'd said he made a shelter, but what did he use to make it? How big was it? How comfortable was he? I pictured him alone in the dark on a pile of leaves and twigs. Wasn't in love with that vision. I'd have to ask him to show me his shelter tomorrow so I could put a new image in my head.

I unwrapped my hand and undressed. After throwing out my ripped T-shirt, I stepped into the shower in the bathroom connected to my room. The hot water washed away the grime and sweat running in the woods had painted over my body. A glance down at the shower drain revealed brownish stains in the water. God, how filthy had I been when I'd met Jobah? Better yet, how had he been so clean if he lived in the woods? No dirt had smeared his exposed body. No gunk had collected under his fingernails. His hair had not been a tangled mess. He didn't smell foul, and he should have reeked in the summer heat.

What was his secret?

Maybe Tree Pentas didn't get dirty. How should I know?

I held my hand under the spray of water. The crusty yarrow paste rinsed off, and the cuts below hardly stung. Pretty amazing that some wet leaves had that much healing power. I still thought it had something to do with Jobah as well.

The question was, how much of what Jobah told me did I believe? He definitely appeared to have some abilities. Those flowers bloomed, that raccoon followed him, and he had to have some serious night vision to find the way back to the path the way he did.

And those eyes were unusual. They didn't match the rest of Jobah's dark coloring. They were like cat eyes.

I always liked cats.

I powered down the shower, dried off, and slipped into a gray tank top and purple cotton shorts. The air conditioner had cooled off the bedroom nicely, and I was thoroughly refreshed. Deciding to keep my palm uncovered, I climbed into bed. Normally, back home, this would be the time where I'd text Eden to discuss something trivial. Or I'd be online, chatting with my track friends about practice.

Tonight, my online status would say, *Olivia Bradford discovered a Tree Penta.* That would start a flurry of comments to which I'd reply cleverly.

But I didn't have my phone or my laptop. I had my summer reading book. The one about a murderer. I dug it out and read a couple pages, then rummaged around in my bag until I found the other summer reading book. The one about Samantha Rigby falling in love.

Maybe it wouldn't be too awful reading that one first.

21. Jobah

The morning sun streamed into my shelter, and I threw my arm across my face to shield it. I would have to seal up the cracks in the roof and sides much better. One rainstorm and I'd be soaked. If only I could use fresh wood, then I'd be able to build a dwelling similar to the one I'd built in the village. Sturdy and dignified. I suppose I could use fresh wood if I didn't mind being in pain while I cut it.

I propped myself up on my elbows and grabbed Olivia's watch. Proof that I had actually met her last night. Without the watch, I would have thought I'd only dreamed of her golden hair, her sky blue eyes, her long, fit legs. I'd thought about her all night, wondering if the watch would show the markings she'd made in the sand while I was sleeping. Then I figured she wouldn't meet me in total darkness, and surely the markings would match when day appeared. But what part of the day? When the sun kissed the horizon? When it reached its peak? When it lost its brilliance and gave way to the moon? When?

I wasn't usually this impatient.

After securing the watch on my wrist as it had been on Olivia's, I rolled off my moose hides and stood. Moon was a tight gray and black circle of fur at

129

the corner of one of the hides. I petted her back, and she wriggled under my touch, a soft little sigh escaping from her. She was crazy to follow me around, but I did appreciate the company. Being alone in the woods was so different from what I was accustomed to. The silence made the whispers of the trees a little louder in my head. What were the trees trying to say to me?

If only I knew.

I stepped out of my shelter and headed to the lake. I waded into the water, bathed, and caught two small trout, which I cooked over a fire beside my shelter. After filling my stomach, I watered my seeds and asked Great Earth for a good harvest. I checked the watch every now and again, but the markings still didn't match the ones Olivia had drawn.

I made small improvements to my shelter with sticks and leaves already on the ground and set up a few traps hoping to catch something for dinner. Moon surprised me with her ability to run after sticks and bring them back to me. We played that game as the sun climbed the sky, but my lack of actual purpose bothered me. I was used to having tasks lined up for the day.

Finally, I couldn't wait anymore to see Olivia. I found the path we'd walked on last night and followed it until I was in the woods bordering her cabin. The backhoe, as Olivia had called it, had been moved from its position. I was about to step into the clearing before me to have a closer look at the digging machine, but a huge man hopped down from inside the backhoe. He whistled a tune as he wiped his black-streaked hands on a piece of cloth.

I crouched in the brush, hiding myself from this man, this outsider. He dropped to the ground and crawled underneath the backhoe. Several clangs echoed in the woods as he did something to the underside of the machine. When he reemerged, the cabin door opened.

Olivia walked out and the sunshine beamed a little brighter. Truly, it did.

Her hair was loose today, spilling gold around her shoulders. The black shirt she wore had no sleeves so her arms were bared. Short, green material hung from her waist and encircled each of her legs down to her upper thigh. I'd seen clothing like this on the people in the field by the school yesterday. Like the leggings my people wore in colder weather but much shorter and not made of animal hide. Whatever they were called, they looked wonderful on Olivia.

She skipped down the stairs of the cabin toting tools I could not identify. After loading them into a vehicle, she turned when the big man under the backhoe called to her. They had a brief exchange then another man joined them. With long, brown hair tied back at the base of his neck and something black and rectangular hanging around his neck, he was much smaller than the first man. I noticed how Olivia kept looking back at the cabin since this second man had arrived. Did he make her nervous? Why? Should I go to her? I hated not knowing what to do.

Two more people came out of the cabin. One man, one woman. Both had Olivia's fair skin and gold hair. Olivia stood in the same manner as the woman. Arms folded across chest, left leg bent at the knee, head tilted to the right. If they had been wearing the same clothing, it would have been like looking at reflections. Olivia had the man's height though. No doubt these were her kin.

Seeing the three of them had me wondering about my own mother and father. They had been lost to me for so long, I barely remembered them. Did I have my father's build? My mother's patience? What pieces of them did I carry inside me?

Did they know I would become a Penta? Could that be why they'd left me?

A loud noise from the backhoe had me leaving those thoughts for another time. The big man was inside the machine now and shouting something to Olivia's father who nodded and corralled Olivia's mother into the vehicle Olivia had loaded with tools. The brown-haired man climbed into the back seat of the vehicle.

Suddenly, Olivia grabbed her stomach and bent over. Her mother touched her on the shoulder, and I nearly bolted from the trees to go to Olivia's side. Three more people came out of the cabin, two men and a woman. The woman put a hand to Olivia's forehead and shrugged. It took all my energy to keep myself hidden. What was wrong with Olivia? Was she in pain?

Olivia waved to the vehicle her father still stood beside. She shook her head several times and urged her mother toward her father. The men and woman who had come out of the cabin followed Olivia's mother and climbed into the vehicle. Within moments, the vehicle drove around the back of the cabin with the backhoe rumbling along behind it. Only Olivia was left standing in the clearing in front of the cabin.

Olivia, who was no longer bent over. Olivia, who no longer looked unwell. In fact, she was smiling.

She ran toward my hiding spot and down the path. I looked at the watch on my wrist and realized the markings matched Olivia's drawing. The time had come.

I raced to the end of the path and found Olivia leaning against a tree, twirling a curl of hair around her finger.

"Hiya," she said.

"Hello."

She looked over my shoulder. "Why are you coming from that direction? Isn't your shelter somewhere back that way?" She pointed behind her.

"It is, but I…" Did I tell her I had spied on her? Would that make her angry? I didn't want to upset her. She was the only human I had to talk to outside my village.

"You what, Jobah?" She kicked dirt off her shoes. "You were skulking around my cabin, just waiting to see me?" Her eyes rolled up to the sky, then settled on me.

How did she know? When I didn't answer right away, she pushed off the tree and stepped closer to me.

"You were, weren't you? You were outside the cabin."

I nodded. "Are you unwell? You grabbed your stomach. Are you in pain?"

Olivia laughed and shook her head. "The only way to get the dig team to leave me behind was to be sick."

"But you're not sick."

"Nope." She came another step closer. "It's an old trick. One you have to use sparingly. Not that my parents would ever be suspicious. Do you know they didn't wonder where I was so late last night? Didn't even ask." She shrugged. "Guess that means I've got the whole day to spend with you, Jobah Everleaf."

"It will be an honor."

She smiled, and I was warmed from head to toe.

"Show me your shelter," she said. "I want to see where you're living now that you're on your own out here. And where's that raccoon?"

"Moon chose a nap over exploring," I said.

"So she likes to sleep. My kind of critter. Sleeping is a lovely thing."

That was not the only lovely thing in the woods today.

22. Olivia

Jobah's black hair was wet and hooked behind his ears. He must have gone swimming in the lake. That notion conjured up images in my mind. Images of Jobah's arms and legs moving powerfully through the water. My cheeks grew hot, and I quickly looked down to my sneakers.

Running. Think of running. Think of anything else.

Jobah led me to a hut of sorts in a clearing not far from the cabin. Branches had been stuck into the earth to form a circle. A few branches had been left off the perimeter to create an opening to get inside the shelter. The roof was made of sticks and leafy ferns woven together. The entire structure leaned to the left a little, and I feared a strong breeze would topple it.

"My dwelling back at the village was much better than this," Jobah said, "but I can no longer cut fresh saplings." His broad shoulders sagged.

"Why not?" I peeked inside. Hides covered the floor and a small gray lump took up one corner. Moon's head popped up when I ducked into the shelter. She let me pet her then stretched out her front paws before rising.

Jobah followed me into the shelter, and it was tight with both of us crammed inside.

135

"When I cut into live trees and plants, I feel it." His lips turned down as his brows lowered over those beautiful, green eyes.

"It hurts you?" I sat on the hides, and Moon wandered into my lap. Never had a raccoon in my lap before. Eden would not believe this.

"It feels as if someone is cutting into my gut." Jobah's hands went to that smooth, muscled stomach of his as he kneeled across from me. Our knees touched, and my petting of Moon became a way to keep my hands busy.

Unfortunately, Moon abandoned my lap to sniff at Jobah's knees. She slithered around the back of him and nudged his right elbow until he shifted so she could climb onto his lap. The raccoon clawed at the hide Jobah wore around his waist. Was he comfortable in that attire? I pictured the boys at Sunderfield wearing something similar. They would look ridiculous, but Jobah didn't. Not at all.

"What if someone else cuts them for you?" I said.

"I was in pain when another person snapped branches and I was standing close to her."

Her? Hmm.

"How close?" Hugging her close? Kissing her close?

"Maybe three armspans."

"Did you try increasing the distance?"

Jobah shook his head. "I was weak after the experience. I collapsed and fell asleep."

"Up for some experiments then?" I leaned forward and ran my hand across Moon's furry back. She rewarded me with a lick to my hand.

"Experiments? What do you mean?" Jobah took my hand and inspected my palm. He gestured to the light pink scratches. "These look better."

"Thanks to you, so now let me return the favor. C'mon. I'll cut some fresh stuff while you stand at different distances. We'll see what kind of range this ability—or limitation, I guess—has on it." I impressed myself with my scientific thinking on this matter. Were the doctors rubbing off on me?

Shit, I hoped not.

"You will stop if I tell you to?" Jobah followed me out of the shelter.

"Of course. I don't want to hurt you. I want to help you." I turned to look at Jobah and found that he was standing very close though there was plenty of room outside his shelter.

"I'm glad I ran into you yesterday, Olivia," he said.

I put my hand on his chest more to steady myself than anything else, but the moment I touched him, I grew even dizzier.

"Me too." I pushed against him slightly. "Now back up."

He offered me a lovely smile and gave me some space. Not sure I wanted it anymore.

Jobah reached to his hip and pulled a dagger from his belt. "Use this to cut into the saplings, but please stop if I tell you to." He placed the dagger in my hand, but didn't let go of it right away.

"I know you have no reason to trust me, but you have my word. If you say stop, I'll stop." I pried the dagger out of his grip.

He nodded and led me to a young birch tree. "This one. I'm going to stand on the other side of my shelter."

"Okay." I let him get into position. When he waved a hand at me, I rested the blade on the bark and gently slid it back and forth, barely scoring the tree. "Did you feel that?"

"Yes, but it was only uncomfortable, not painful. Keep going."

I gripped the handle tighter and made more of a sawing motion with it. Jobah instantly went to his knees, one arm up to signal me. He let out a groan and stayed on all fours. I ran over and crouched beside him.

"That bad?" I rested a hand on his back.

He nodded, his breathing coming in labored gasps. His flesh was warm, warmer than mine.

"Okay, clearly that distance was too close. Are you all right?"

Jobah leaned back on his heels. Sweat dotted his forehead as he squeezed his eyes closed.

"Another test." His voice was strained. How much pain was he trying to hide?

"Are you sure, Jobah?"

"Yes, but you'll have to come to me after you cut in case I can't yell to you."

"I don't like these experiments anymore. Not a good idea." I held out the dagger, prepared to give it back to him.

"No." He pushed my hand back toward me. "I need to know more about what is happening to me. I can't do tests like this with my kin. It will frighten them. They are already so afraid."

"It ain't exactly thrilling me, Jobah. I don't want to cause you pain."

He clamped onto my arm and motioned for me to help him to his feet. When he was steady, he walked deeper into the woods. He waved that he was ready, and I returned to the birch sapling. I cut a gouge into it.

Jobah's cry echoed in the forest. I dropped the dagger and ran. When I found him, he was on his side, legs curled up in a fetal position. He was shaking, coated in sweat, eyes fluttering.

"Jobah?" I kneeled next to him, brushed his hair back from his face. "Jobah, can you hear me?"

"Yes." The word was a whisper. Jobah's lips continued to move, but no sound came out.

"We're done with experiments for today," I said. "Results indicate no trees should be cut in your presence." I touched his forehead. "Shit, you're burning up!"

"Fever," he rasped. "Water."

"Do you have some at your shelter?"

A noise slipped from his throat that I took as a yes.

"Be right back."

I sprinted to his shelter and dove inside. Moon let out a little sound of protest at my intrusion. "Sorry, girl, but I need water."

As if understanding my words, Moon scurried to a hollowed log and stood on her hind legs next to it. I picked up the log and let out a breath when water sloshed inside. I raced back to Jobah, Moon at my heels this time. The raccoon got to him first. She nuzzled his cheek, and his eyes shot open. He rolled to his back, his arms cradling his stomach as if only his hands could hold his body together.

I slipped his head into my lap then lifted him to a sitting position. His back pressed against my front, and heat jumped from his body to mine. It was like touching the sun.

"Drink this, Jobah. Can you hear me? Drink this." I put the neck of the hollowed log to his lips, tilted his head back slightly, and poured out some of the water. A few streams slipped down his chin, but he appeared to drink a few gulps as well.

After a couple moments of Jobah leaning against me and taking deep inhales, he said, "Help me up. Need to get into the water. Too hot."

I put the now empty log down and hooked my hands under Jobah's arms. "You're going to have to help me here. You're not exactly light as a feather."

We did the best we could manage. It wasn't graceful, but I got us both to our feet. I slid under Jobah's left arm, and he leaned on me for support. Taking small, slow steps, we made it to the lake. We waded right into it until the water reached my upper thighs.

Jobah let go of me and sunk into the cool water. I was nervous that he wasn't strong enough to keep from drowning, but once the water surrounded his shoulders, he turned to me and smiled, those green eyes shining like polished emeralds.

Umm…who felt feverish now?

23. Jobah

The water was a glorious reprieve from the burn consuming my body. Never had I been this hot, as if a fire were growing inside my stomach. Why did being a Penta have to involve this? What good was I if I couldn't cut wood to use for cooking and building? How could my grandmother think I was important?

I was useless.

"Do you feel better?" Olivia swam to me. Her hair was darker now that it was wet, but the sun reflected off pale gold streaks. She pressed her hand to my forehead and lowered her brows. "You still feel hot."

My heart pounded against my ribs at her touch. Now I couldn't tell if cutting trees had elevated my temperature or if Olivia had. Perhaps it was a little of both.

"I need some time." I drifted away from Olivia so I could focus my attention on cooling down.

"I'm sorry, Jobah." She studied her hands resting on the surface of the water. "I didn't want you to get hurt."

"It's not your fault." I stood and stepped closer to her. "It's my fault. It's what I am now that causes me pain."

"You didn't choose to be a Penta." She looked up at me with eyes as blue as the sky. "It's not your fault either."

"Maybe not." I exhaled a slow breath. "I just wish I knew what it all meant. What am I supposed to do in this life as a Penta?"

"I barely know what I'm supposed to do in this life as a regular human." Olivia shrugged, and droplets of water rolled down her smooth arms. The expression on her face suggested that she'd spent many nights awake trying to figure out her future with no success.

"Right now," I said, wanting to see her smile, "we're supposed to swim."

I cupped my hands, filled them with water, and splashed Olivia. Her lips immediately turned up at the corners as she shook out her hair, spraying water onto me. She laughed and dove under the surface. Her body rubbed against my leg, and I plunged my arms into the water. I grabbed her around the waist and lifted her. She let out a shriek as water rained off her.

"Put me down, Jobah!" She wriggled like a fish in my arms, but I didn't think she was trying her hardest to be freed. Her left arm came around my shoulders, and she held on, pressing her body against my chest.

I sunk to my knees so the water was touching my shoulders. Olivia was submerged to her neck as I held her. She stopped thrashing and pulled her wet hair from her face. The water settled around us, and Olivia looked at me.

"What?" I finally asked.

"I know you preferred your brown eyes, but these green ones are amazing. I've never seen anything like them."

I looked away, but Olivia pulled an arm out of the water and touched my cheek, making me face her. "Green is my favorite color."

She hooked my hair behind my left ear, let her hand linger on my cheek a moment longer, then hopped out of my hold. She dove back into the water and swam away. She popped up to the surface occasionally, each time farther from me. Finally, she stopped and waved her hands from a good distance away.

"You said swim, so swim already." She disappeared again.

I dove in and tried to catch up to Olivia, but she was fast. Each time I thought I'd reached her, she darted away like a water snake. I hadn't played like this since I was a small boy. Since Ashlo and I used to run throughout the village chasing each other until we couldn't breathe anymore. I hadn't had the freedom to let myself go with so many tasks to do in the village. I had it now and it was wonderful.

Finally, Olivia started swimming toward the shore. After she passed me, I turned around and followed her. Watching her shed the water like a liquid coat as she walked onto the sand stirred up my insides. Her clothing stuck to her body, showing all of its muscles and curves. Her hair sent streams of water to the ground as she ran into the woods. She gathered her shirt and wrung it out while her shoes made loud, slurping sounds.

I ran after her, knowing that I wanted to be wherever she was going. When we reached my shelter, neither one of us was panting from the run. Olivia's endurance was impressive. She sat on the ground and removed her shoes.

"These are totally ruined." She dumped out a puddle of water from one of them. "I didn't think to take them off. I just wanted to get you into the water."

"Does my eternal gratitude make up for the ruined shoes?" I asked as I collected twigs to start a fire.

Olivia smirked. "No." She poured water out of the other shoe. "Maybe I should get a pair of those." She pointed to my moccasins. Though they were wet, they'd dry out soon and not be damaged.

"They are the superior footwear. Animal hide is naturally waterproof." I picked up one of her soggy shoes and turned it around in my hands. "What are these made from?"

Olivia shrugged. "How should I know?"

"You didn't make them?"

Her laugh echoed through the woods. "Of course not."

"Did your kin make them?" I set her shoe down and arranged kindling before rubbing sticks together to make a spark.

"My parents wouldn't waste their time making anything for me. It would take them away from their precious archaeology." She twisted her hair up and somehow made it stay in a knot at the base of her neck. "Where I'm from, you don't have to make your own clothes. You go to a store and buy what you need. Somebody else, or nowadays probably a machine, made those sneakers. I bought them for running track at my school."

"You do the same for food and other supplies?" I rubbed sticks together until a curl of smoke wafted up.

"Yeah." Olivia leaned forward and placed some of the kindling nearer to the smoke. She blew out a gentle, but steady breath while I rubbed the sticks, and the kindling caught fire.

I added more wood, and soon a sizable blaze rose skyward. Olivia huddled a little closer, and I realized that in those wet clothes, she was chilly. I ducked inside my shelter and emerged with one of my moose hides.

"Here." I draped the hide on her shoulders, and she eyed it for a few moments, sniffed at it, then wrapped it around herself.

"Thanks."

I nodded and sat across from her on the other side of the fire. "Tell me about your school."

"What do you want to know?"

"Everything." I thought of the school I watched from the hill. With Olivia here, I had a piece of that place—of the outside—with me.

"Sunderfield High is a good school. Lots of nice teachers, cool kids. Most of them anyway. There's always a few pricks, but they're easy to avoid."

"Pricks?" Did she mean thorns?

Olivia giggled, and the sound washed over me. Firelight danced in her eyes and shimmered off her hair. "It's a word we use for people who are mean or rude. Surely, you have some people you don't get along with at your village."

I immediately thought of Sumahe and how he had hit me in the south field.

"Yes, we have pricks."

"Unfortunately, they're everywhere. I told you about Kevin who dumped me. He's a prick."

"Sumahe, a friend's brother, hit me before I left my village." I ran my tongue over the thin slice in my lip that remained from my encounter with Sumahe. "He's a prick."

"Feels good to call them that, doesn't it? It's cleansing." Olivia wiggled her fingers in the air around her. "Not that I should be teaching you to call people names, but when you see a deer in the woods you call it a deer, right?"

"Yes."

"Then when you see a prick, you should call him a prick."

"Are only males pricks?"

"Generally speaking, yes." Olivia chewed on her bottom lip. "Females are called bitches. I know far more pricks than bitches though."

"This is not what I expected school to be about," I said. "I thought you learned there."

"You do, but the social element is just as important. Maybe more so. In my… culture, I guess you'd call it… being a teen in high school is all about finding your place in the social order. You don't want to be at the bottom. You want to be at the top."

"Are you at the top?"

"I was pretty close." Olivia's shoulders slumped under the moose hide. "This trip to Montana, however, could be undoing all the work it took to get there. Six weeks in the woods is more than enough time for someone else to slip into the top spot. I could be a social zero when I get back. Who knows?"

She closed her eyes and rubbed her hands near the fire.

"What do you study?" I asked.

Olivia's eyes opened and she gathered her legs up so she could rest her chin on her knees. I wanted to go to her side of the fire, but made myself stay where I was.

"Mathematics, Literature, Science, History. All things my culture thinks we need to know to survive in the world. Probably seems pretty foolish to you. I can recite Edgar Allen Poe's *Telltale Heart*, but didn't know that yarrow was good for closing up bleeding wounds." She held up her palm. "Makes all that studying I've done seem useless."

I didn't know who Edgar Allen Poe was, but couldn't imagine Olivia studying all those things for nothing. "I'm sure what you've learned will help you in the future."

"Assuming I figure out what I'm going to do with my future." Olivia's brows lowered as her fingers tapped on her legs.

"You still have time to decide, don't you?"

"Not much. I'll be in college after one more year of high school, so I have to start thinking about it. My best friend, Eden, knows she wants to be a teacher. She's known it since we were kids. She has three younger brothers, and she's helped them all learn to read and memorize their multiplication tables. She's a natural. Eden will make an excellent teacher."

"I got to be a builder and farmer in my tribe because I am good at both." I waved a hand toward my decrepit shelter. "Do not judge by that. It is not a good representation of my skills. My *former* skills, I guess." I shook my head and wished I could take Olivia to my village to see the dwelling I had constructed there. "What are you good at, Olivia?"

She pulled the moose hide off her shoulders. Her pinked cheeks told me she was now warm enough.

"What am I good at? I don't know. Texting, emailing, shopping, irritating my older sister, cooking...running." She peeked at me through the climbing flames. "I'm good at bumping into strangers in the woods, but I don't think I could make a living out of that."

"Not a great deal of strangers wandering about in the woods." I motioned at the growing shadows around us.

"I sometimes wonder if my parents want me to become an archaeologist like them."

"Why else would they take you along on their work trip?" Without meaning to, I shifted closer to Olivia.

"To ruin my summer." She narrowed her eyes in disgust.

"Pricks."

Olivia chuckled. "Pricks. You're catching on, Jobah."

I was definitely caught.

24. Olivia

What exactly was I doing? Sitting in the woods with a strange boy who thought he was a tree spirit wasn't on my normal list of leisure activities. Yet, the words came easily when talking with Jobah. No need to put up a front, try to be cool, or game-play with him. There was no risk in being myself here. Being Olivia Bradford. If Jobah didn't like me, so what? I never had to see him again once I left for Rhode Island.

I never had to see him again. That thought echoed in some hollow space inside me.

"Are you hungry?" Jobah asked. He had shifted closer to my side of the fire, and the thought of him holding me in the water earlier flashed into my mind. He'd picked me up as if it hadn't taken any effort at all. Would Kevin have struggled a bit? Probably. When I'd come in first at my last track meet, Kevin had twirled me around in celebration, and it hadn't gone so smoothly. We'd both ended up in a tangle on the grassy field in the middle of the track. I hadn't cared then. It'd been pretty funny actually.

Now it seemed lame.

"I'm a little hungry." I focused my gaze on the fire.

151

"Probably from all that swimming away from me you did in the lake." Jobah was close enough to press his elbow into my arm.

"You're the one who said we should swim." I wagged a finger at him, and Jobah gently knocked it away.

"I'll be more careful how I say things around you."

As if he wanted to be around me some more? I might be in favor of that. Hard to tell just yet.

Jobah stood, stretched, and poked at the fire until it burned brighter. "Want to check the traps with me?"

"Traps?" I put on my sloshy sneakers and stepped out of the moose hide Jobah had g
iven me.

"To catch meat." He walked past his shelter and into the woods more. "You are able to buy meat where you come from?"

"I certainly don't hunt it down myself." I made a face as I thought about catching my own food. "In my culture, some of us don't even eat meat."

"They deny themselves a great pleasure then."

I followed him until he crouched beside a cage-like box made of sticks. A lump of fur huddled in the back corner of the box.

"Caught one." When Jobah stood, he held a brown rabbit by the back legs in his hands. The animal wiggled in his grasp, wide eyes looking all around.

"Tell me you're not going to kill that." I almost didn't want to look at the rabbit for fear of falling in love with it. I had a soft spot for furry critters. We didn't have any pets at home because the doctors were allergic to dander. Another huge inconvenience to living with them, but Eden and Kevin both had dogs that I absolutely loved.

"How else are we going to eat it?" Jobah pulled his dagger from his waist.

"No!" I yelped. "Jobah, please, don't."

I grabbed the rabbit around its middle and took it from Jobah. The animal immediately pressed its little body against my chest as I hugged it to me. It looked up at me with big, brown eyes while its long ears flopped back. The entire rabbit shook in my arms.

"Shhhh…" I whispered. "It's all right. No one's going to hurt you."

"Then no one's going to eat either." Jobah stepped closer, and I turned away from him to shield the bunny.

"I'll get us food from the cabin. We don't need to kill anything." I stroked the soft fur on the rabbit's back until the shudders stopped, and its twitchy nose sniffed around my shirt.

"I kill to survive, not to hurt." Jobah's voice sounded offended.

I turned back around to face him. His arms were folded across his chest, but his dagger was back at his waist.

"I didn't mean to imply that you killed for the sport of it. I realize this is the way of your people, but when you're with me, there is another way to get food. Okay?"

Jobah studied my face for a few long moments. I feared he was going to tell me to leave, but instead he reached out a hand and petted the bunny. Moon appeared from under the low-growing ferns and weaved between Jobah's legs. Jobah tilted his head as if he were listening to something, then he nodded.

"You can free this rabbit. It is not her time to leave this place." He started back toward his shelter, and Moon hopped after him.

I set the bunny down. It sniffed my fingers then bounded off through the ferns becoming no more than a brown speck in moments. I'd saved that one, but how many would Jobah have to sacrifice in order to survive out here on his own? How many had he already killed in his lifetime?

When I caught up to Jobah at the fire, he was kneeling beside it. Moon was up on her hind legs with her front paws resting on Jobah's lap. They looked as if they were sharing secrets.

A twig snapped beneath my sneaker and both boy and raccoon looked at me. As I came closer, Moon rubbed cat-like against my ankle, then slinked away into Jobah's shelter.

"You want to get some food my way?" I asked.

Jobah stood and though I wasn't much shorter, I was suddenly struck by how tall he was. Much taller than Kevin. Did he just appear so tall because so much of his flesh was showing?

"I should not go with you to your cabin. I should not be seen." Jobah turned to poke at the fire again.

"No one will be at the cabin. It's early. I'm sure the team is still digging. Unless they found something."

"They will not find anything where they are digging." Jobah sounded convinced.

"You don't know how determined my parents are, Jobah. They always find something. They must have a reason for digging there." I squeezed the remaining water from my hair and redid my ponytail. "How about if I go first to the cabin and scope it out? If they aren't there, then will you come in?"

Why did I want him in the cabin with me? What was I hoping would happen?

Jobah looked at me for a silent moment. Was he mentally listing the pros and cons? "Only if you are certain no one is around."

We ran back toward the cabin, and having Jobah for company made the run better. He kept up with me, but didn't try to show off and surge ahead like some of the guys on the track team would.

I was surprised at how easy it was to find the cabin. Was I becoming familiar with these woods? Scary thought.

When the cabin came into view, Tower's backhoe and the SUV were still missing.

"I'll run in and check, but I don't think anyone's here," I said over my shoulder.

Jobah merely nodded his acknowledgement, so I bounded into the parking lot then up the front steps. Once inside, a thorough check of each room proved the dig team was still digging. I opened the front door and waved Jobah over. He hesitated at first, and I thought he wasn't going to come. When he did step into the parking lot, my eyes lost track of his movements. In an instant, he was on the porch with me.

I stumbled back, but Jobah caught me before I fell.

"How did you do that?" I asked.

"Do what?' Jobah's hands still gripped my shoulders, but his eyes scanned the living room behind the open cabin door.

"How did you move like the wind?"

Jobah looked down to his feet, then said, "Add it to the list of unwanted abilities. Who knows what I'll be able to do next?"

For some reason, I wanted to be around to see what he'd do next.

25. Jobah

Following a path
to see where it may lead
brings pleasure,
pain,
and possibility.

My grandmother would not approve of me being with Olivia at an outsider's cabin, but I suppose it didn't matter anymore. I was no longer part of my tribe. Kiyuchee ways were losing their grip on me. Ordinarily, I would never have let a catch go. Especially a nice, plump rabbit. The meat on that creature would have been tender and filling. I could have eaten well tonight.

Instead, I was following Olivia into the cabin, searching the big room she led me into, smelling scents I'd never detected before. I was a spooked squirrel, twitchy and ready to run. Yet, the notion of spending more time with Olivia kept me from fleeing.

Olivia must have sensed my unease, because she put a hand on my forearm and tugged me through the big room into a smaller one with lots of silver surfaces in it.

"We'll hear the backhoe rumbling long before any people come into the cabin. We'll have plenty of time to hide or get out." She squeezed my arm before letting it go. "Trust me, Jobah."

I had absolutely no reason to trust her. I'd only met Olivia yesterday. I didn't know her, yet I felt like I did. I had already memorized the color of her eyes, the smell of her hair, the way she moved. I let a rabbit go just because she asked me to.

Was Olivia more than human too? Did she have shaman-like abilities? Was she controlling me?

That thought made me back away from her. Had I been wrong to tell her about being a Penta? Did she seek to use my abilities somehow?

"What are you?" I asked.

Olivia turned around from a huge, silver box, her hand still resting on what appeared to be a door. "Huh?"

"Why did I let that rabbit go? I would never do that on my own. What powers do you have?" I searched the room for weaponry, and my gaze settled on a set of small daggers resting in a block of wood. They were no better than the dagger at my waist, so I curled my fingers around my own hilt.

"I don't have any powers, Jobah. I'm a boring, normal human."

She pulled open the silver door and light spilled out. Olivia ducked into the box. When she straightened and turned toward me, her arms were loaded with things, some of which I couldn't identify.

She spread them out on a high table in the middle of the room.

"You let the rabbit go, because you saw that it bothered me to kill it. You took into consideration my feelings and changed what you'd normally do to make me happy. It was very sweet, and now I'll repay you by making you a feast you won't soon forget." She surveyed the items she'd put on the table and frowned. "Well, at least it'll be an awesome sandwich. I'll have to cook for you using all my skills when we have more time."

Looking at her, I forgot to be scared about being in the cabin, forgot to be wary of her, forgot all the things that had kept me alive for the past seventeen winters.

"Sit." Olivia pointed to a seat beside me.

Again, I followed her orders and wasn't convinced she didn't have a hold over me. But I was hungry, and whatever food Olivia was preparing smelled wonderful. She busied herself with thin slices of meat she pulled from a clear container. Where was the rest of the animal? I recognized something that looked like the bread Ninae made only it came from a crinkling, see-through sack.

A thick, yellow liquid shot from a bright yellow container onto the bread, and Olivia used a dull dagger to spread the liquid around. She added lettuce and tomato, which we grew in the village as well. She cut the entire assembly in half, placed it on a plate, not a plate carved of wood though. She made a second assembly and put it on another plate. After putting all the supplies back into the silver box, Olivia poured a purplish-red liquid into a see-through container and set it in front of me with one of the plates.

I turned the plate around several times, studying the concoction from all angles. It was very…colorful.

"Don't stare at it, Jobah. Eat the sandwich." She pointed to the plate. "Drink the cranberry juice." She waved a hand over the container. "You'll like it. I promise."

Olivia dove into her own sandwich and drank the juice. I watched her chew and swallow before picking up my sandwich and biting into it. The meat tasted vaguely familiar as did the lettuce and tomato, but there was something foreign about the way the ingredients mixed together. The yellow liquid, though tart and unexpected, was tasty. I finished my entire sandwich before Olivia finished hers.

"Do you want another one?" She gestured to my empty plate.

"Are you having another one?"

Olivia looked down at the remaining quarter of her sandwich. "No, but I don't eat that much. Something tells me you require more fuel than I do." She knocked her shoulder against my upper arm.

"Yes, I'll have another. It's delicious."

Olivia nodded, took a bite of her sandwich, and went to the silver box. I stood as well, curious to peer inside. When the door opened, the light revealed all sorts of unknown objects, and a coolness chilled my skin.

"Where does all this come from?" I stepped around Olivia to examine the back of the box. It was separate from the wall behind it and didn't reach to the outdoors at all.

"We bought the food at a grocery and put it in this refrigerator to keep it cool. Some foods last longer if chilled." She shuffled over to a wooden door beside the refrigerator and opened it. No light or cold came out of this door. "Food that doesn't have to be cold goes in these cabinets."

She pointed to two more silver boxes smaller than the refrigerator. "That one is the stove for cooking and heating things like you would on a fire. The other is a dishwasher, which will clean our plates and glasses when we're done eating. And that," she indicated a silver spout over two, deep silver bowls, "is the sink." She touched the spout and water came trickling out.

"Amazing," I whispered. "No one has to go to a lake to get water?"

Olivia shook her head. "We figured out how to bring the water to us."

Why did my people not want to be a part of Olivia's world? Everything was easier here. Food and water readily available. Clothing that didn't have to be made by hand. Vehicles that moved much quicker than any human or horse or ox. Places of learning.

Females that looked like Olivia.

Sitting in that room with her made me feel as if I'd passed onto another place, another time. My old life in the village seemed like a dream now. How could I go back to it?

Did I want to?

26. Olivia

I didn't want to overwhelm Jobah, but at the same time, I wanted to show him everything. If only I had my phone, laptop, and television. Those would have blown his mind. We could have created an online account for him and made his status say, *Jobah Everleaf thinks the 21ˢᵗ century rocks.*

He'd been peeved about letting the rabbit go earlier, but sitting next to me now at the kitchen island, eating his second sandwich, he didn't seem so unhappy. He reminded me of a young child learning about the world and taking it all in with wide eyes. Wide, sexy, leaf-green eyes.

"Why is it cooler in here than outside? Is it not summer inside this cabin?" Jobah finished his juice and swiveled on the stool to face me. His knees pressed into my thigh, and I silently thanked whoever had designed this kitchen for making the island so... cozy.

I pointed up at one of the ceiling vents above us. "Air conditioning is a system for cooling the insides of places when the weather outside is hot. It lets us be comfortable regardless of the outdoor temperature."

Jobah stood and stretched his hand up toward the ceiling vent. He wiggled his fingers and nodded as if feeling the cool air blowing down gave credence to what I had said. He walked back into the living room, so I followed him. He traced the stones of the fireplace. "And this heats, like my fire?"

"It does, but we also have heat that flows around the house through radiators or vents." I indicated the radiator lining the exterior wall of the living room. "And it's not just wood that can make the heat. Oil, natural gas, electricity, and water can make heat too, but I don't know how it all works."

Jobah nodded again as he picked up some of my dad's books heaped in tidy piles on the coffee table. He flipped through the top few then turned one around to face me.

"Your parents search for this?"

I sat on the couch and took the book from Jobah as he slid into the space next to me. Focusing on the book as I pulled my hair free of its ponytail so it would dry, I examined the picture he had shown me. It was the typical Native American village that you see whenever textbooks talk about Native American villages. A few huts encircling a central fire. Animal hides hung on poles. Females bent over wooden bowls, grinding cornmeal. Males making bows and arrows. I'd seen pictures like this one thousands of times.

"I guess it's what they're looking for. They hope to discover an undiscovered tribe," I said.

"They hope to discover my people." Jobah's brows furrowed. "They should not look for my village. The Kiyuchee do not wish to be found."

"Your people could have all this if they were found." I held my hands out to indicate all the things Jobah had marveled over in the cabin.

"I find these things interesting," Jobah started, "but most of my tribe is quite content to live the way they do. It was decided long ago that our tribe was better off without such things and without mingling with outsiders."

I closed the book and put it back in the pile where my father had it. "I don't think you have to worry, Jobah. My parents are archaeologists. Yes, they want to discover things, but they don't wish to change them. They are all about preservation. They'd be much more excited to study your tribe's ways than to alter or erase them."

I was absolutely certain of this. Don't know how. Generally, I didn't pay much attention to the doctors and their work. We stayed out of each others' ways, but I did know that aside from plucking this teenage girl from her Summer of Fun in Rhode Island, they didn't tamper too much with things. Most unearthed treasures ended up in museums, but if the relics belonged to someone, the doctors usually wrote a book about it and let the owner keep his or her trinket. My parents gained the recognition they craved, added their knowledge to historical academia, then went on to the next hunt. For them, it was all about the search.

Jobah slid his leg off the couch, and I finally looked at him straight on. His skin matched many of the wood accents in the room, tan and rich. I totally wished I had my camera or my phone so I could take a picture and send it to Eden. She definitely would have considered Jobah a huge upgrade over Kevin.

Not that Jobah was mine to show off. Someone else knowing he existed would have made him more real though. I mean, I could still wake up, be miraculously home in Sunderfield, and have dreamed meeting him in the woods.

"Pinch me," I said.

"What?" Jobah picked up a pair of Tower's binoculars and shook them. He tried looking in the wrong end then flipped them around. He shot back on the couch, when the far wall no doubt appeared to be right in front of him.

"Those are binoculars. They help you see things that are far away."

He looked through them again and pawed the air in front of the binoculars. He lowered them and saw the far wall was still across the room.

"So pinch me," I said again.

"Why? Won't that hurt?" He put the binoculars down.

"Yes, but I want to make sure I'm awake."

At this, a smile slid across his lips. The motion enchanted me as little lines crinkled the skin at the corners of his amazing eyes. His hair fell loose from behind his ear, and that movement weaved a new spell over me. My gaze wandered over his smooth, broad chest down to his narrow waist and muscular legs.

Shit, this boy needed some clothes. Like right away.

"I wondered if I were dreaming as well," Jobah said. "Last night, in my shelter, I only had your watch to convince me you were real."

"Well, I need something to make me believe you're real right now. So pinch me."

"I don't want to pinch you. That will hurt." Jobah locked his gaze on me. "I have another option."

"I'm all for it."

"Good."

Jobah leaned forward slowly. I had a moment to think *OMG*, and then his hand cupped my cheek. His palm was hot, and as soon as the contact was made, his heat jumped to me. A fire zipped throughout my entire body.

When Jobah's lips touched mine, there was no doubt.

I was awake, and he was real.

27. Jobah

Olivia tasted like nothing I'd ever known. I had no words to describe her flavor besides intoxicating. Her lips were smooth and warm. The skin at her cheek was soft against my palm. I smelled the lake on her hair and sunshine on her flesh. My hand moved to the back of her neck and up into her still wet mane of hair. A small sound vibrated in her throat, and the noise made my heart pump faster.

I wasn't sure what to do beyond kissing Olivia. Keryun and I had gone no further than this. I had been content with kissing Keryun, but being this close to Olivia was a different experience. My lips were simultaneously enjoying their contact with hers and yearning for more.

Olivia's hands ran along my shoulders causing a wave of goosebumps to flood my skin. We kept kissing, but I forgot to breathe while I explored the depths of her mouth. The room around us spun in dizzying circles. Still, I continued kissing her. My heartbeat pulsed in my ears like a ceremonial drum, and I wondered how long my ribs could keep my heart caged.

Something thundered outside, and Olivia broke away. We both skittered to opposite ends of the couch. Her lips were puffy and red, and a thrilling jolt zipped through me at the knowledge that I had made them that way.

"Shit," she whispered. "They're back."

I jumped up from my seat and searched the room for an exit. My mind was foggy, as if kissing Olivia had stolen away my ability to think.

"This way." She got up and clamped a hand onto my wrist. She led me through another room that had two doors leading out to a wooden-planked area. When we reached the doors, Olivia peeked out. I looked over her shoulder and exhaled a breath when only trees sprawled out in every direction.

"I wish you could stay," Olivia said as she turned around to face me, "but I'm not ready to share you with the doctors yet. I think it's in everyone's best interest if we keep you a secret for now."

"I agree." I lost myself for a moment in the blue of Olivia's eyes. So deep. So endless. Her pupils were huge, black holes beckoning to me, pulling me in, wanting to consume me. She had said she didn't have any powers, but she was wrong. So wrong.

"You want to meet again tomorrow?" she asked.

Now that was an easy question. "Yes." I traced a finger along her jaw. Her eyes closed, and she took in a shivery breath.

Olivia fussed with her watch on my wrist for a moment, then said, "When this beeps, go to the lake. I'll be there waiting."

"Olivia?" a woman's voice called out.

"Go," Olivia said to me. "Hurry."

She opened the door and pushed me out. With a short wave, I took off into the trees. I let them swallow me. Let them create a barrier between my world and Olivia's. A temporary barrier. There would be a tomorrow with her.

I crouched in the ferns as the backhoe stopped its rumbling. The big man jumped off the machine and joined Olivia's parents and the rest of the team already out of their vehicle. Everyone had dirt stains on their knees and weary expressions on their faces. They were foolish to dig where they were. My people were vigilant about keeping to one area. As far as I knew our tribe had never moved from their current location. That's what Ninae had told me anyway. No one had ever discovered the Kiyuchee so we had no reason to find another home.

What if Olivia's parents did discover us? I thought of my grandmother. I missed her. She'd taken good care of me all these years. I didn't want outsiders to frighten her or worse.

On this thought, I wandered deeper into the woods away from Olivia's cabin. The sun was still shining. There would be enough time to go to the village. To warn the tribe to be careful. To make sure Ninae was all right.

I slipped through the forest on silent feet, stopped at my shelter where Moon decided she would join me on my trip back to the village. Again, I welcomed the company.

Within a short time, Moon and I stood on the fringe of the village. Olivia was right. I now moved at increased speeds. Looking to the sky, I noted that the sun had barely moved. What did this quickness mean?

After picking Moon up and letting her settle in my arms, I stepped beyond the vine-covered palisades surrounding the village perimeter concealing it from the eyes of outsiders. The moment I did so, Ashlo spotted me. Casting a swift look to the left then to the right, he jogged over.

"Say you are back, Jobah," he said.

"Only with a caution, Ashlo." I accepted the hug he gave me after Moon jumped down from my hold.

"Come sit with me." Ashlo gestured to the stumps he'd pulled up around his fire.

I glanced around the area. Too many of my people were around. One look at them, and I remembered why I had left. I was no longer like them. The raccoon standing loyally at my feet was proof. There were the physical changes and the Penta abilities, but more set me apart now. I'd mingled with an outsider.

I'd more than mingled.

I wanted to more than mingle again.

"I can't stay, Ashlo. I came to say that outsiders are looking for this village. Tell everyone to be extra careful."

Ashlo's face paled. "How do you know this?"

"I have seen the outsiders." That was all I planned to tell him. He didn't need to know more than that. "You must keep everyone safe and hidden."

"Of course, but isn't that your job?" Ashlo stared at me with dark brown eyes. Eyes like the ones I used to have. Eyes that had made me belong with these people.

"I am of no use to this tribe anymore."

"Then why are you here?" Ashlo stepped closer, his voice becoming a low whisper. "If you stayed, people would get used to your eyes, Jobah. They'd come to respect what you are and look to you for guidance. You could be a great leader for the Kiyuchee."

I shook my head. "I am not a leader. Promise me you'll keep everyone safe, you'll watch over Ninae."

"I will, but your absence breaks her heart. She wanted to send out a party to find you, but I was the only one to volunteer to search. Then Denri ordered me to stay inside the village. He listened to Keryun's account of your eyes turning colors, and I think he knows what you are."

"But he does not wish for me to return?" I knew Ninae had been wrong about me being important. If our shaman chief did not want anyone to search for me, he couldn't have thought I was of use to the tribe in my new state.

"I think he just wanted Keryun to stop screaming." Ashlo patted my shoulder. "Sorry."

"I must not linger here then. Someone will see me, and there'll be screaming all over again." The speed at which Keryun had changed her feelings about me stung. Stung deeply. How could I have misjudged her as a possible mate? How could I have been so wrong?

Was I wrong about trusting Olivia too?

Moon clawed at my moccasin as if to say we had to go.

"You are not so different from the boy I've known all my life. You are my kin, and you belong here with us." Ashlo shook me gently as if willing me to understand his logic. "I can't protect them all on my own."

He did have a point there. My people weren't warriors. We hadn't needed to be. Our best defense was the forest that hid us.

"Jobah?"

I looked past Ashlo.

Ninae stood there, her eyes full of unshed tears that pulled me toward her.

28. Olivia

"Are you feeling better?" my mother asked.

How sympathetic of her to wonder about my health. I turned away from the doors in the study, sure that Jobah had disappeared into the trees. My lips still buzzed from his kiss, and I hoped my mother couldn't tell that I'd been making out with a seriously hot tree spirit.

"Yes. My stomach has settled," I lied. My stomach was anything but settled. My entire body was more excited than it had ever been. Kissing Kevin was like kissing a watermelon compared to what I'd just experienced with Jobah. "Find anything out there?" Why did I hope they hadn't discovered any artifacts that might indicate the existence of Jobah's tribe? Why did I want him to be *my* secret?

My mother rubbed at a spot of dirt on her T-shirt and shook her head. "Nothing today. Maybe tomorrow." Her voice held a note of disappointment, and for a moment, I felt bad for her. "This is why we need your help, Olivia. Why we brought you. The more hands and eyes we have working with us, the more likely we are to succeed at this mission."

If she only knew that the mission was already a success. I'd found Jobah. I'd found proof.

But I couldn't share it with her. Not yet.

How was I going to get away tomorrow to meet Jobah? I had to. No question about that. I would not give up seeing him to play in the dirt with the doctors. Not after the kiss we had shared.

My mother sat on the burgundy leather couch in the study. Her gray eyes were washed out, and her hair had frizzed in the Montana heat. She looked older somehow.

"What happens if you don't succeed?" I asked.

"Your father and I will lose our grant. We won't be able to continue our research into the Veiled Tribes without producing some evidence that they do in fact exist. The university had to make funding cuts. Lots of universities are shifting gears and putting their funds toward the study of technology for the future, not artifacts of the past. It's unfortunate." She rubbed the bridge of her nose like she did whenever something was bothering her.

I sat in the chair opposite the couch and looked at my mother. So many times I had wished she were like my friends' moms. You know, normal. A mom with a job that didn't involve sifting through dirt or poring over gargantuan texts looking for links between the puzzle pieces of history. A mom with time to take me shopping for a prom dress, to teach me the proper way to apply eyeliner, to bake cookies with me on a Friday night and watch a chick flick.

Instead, I had Dr. Madeline Bradford, a mom who could dig a ditch with a spoon if need be. She had an impressive vocabulary, unlimited knowledge of all things ancient, and a determination that wouldn't quit. She was more like someone you read a biography about and did a book report on than someone you knew in person. She was definitely scientist first, mother second.

I'd often wondered why she and my father had reproduced in the first place. They were rarely home, and when they were, their eyes were glued to their laptop screens, reviewing notes, maps, photographs, making discoveries. I was just in the way most of the time, so I learned to stay out of the way.

When I asked if they had planned to have me and my sister, my father said, "The only way to truly pass on a bit of oneself is to procreate. We did so twice just to be sure."

Great.

Even my birth and Carrie's were part of a science experiment. Well, the joke was on them, because other than the physical resemblance, I wasn't anything like them. I didn't share this great passion for learning or history. I could care less what was buried under the dirt. I didn't want to read dry, boring books about things that no longer applied to my day-to-day functioning in today's world. I didn't want to follow in their footsteps.

I was Olivia Bradford. I was my own person with my own interests and plans for the future.

Sounded good anyway, didn't it? The only problem was the discovery I'd made on this trip. Jobah. Finding him had produced a rush of enthusiasm I hadn't experienced while doing anything else so far in my life. Was archaeology like this? Like unwrapping an unexpected present? Like turning over a rock and finding magic coins underneath?

No. No. I was *not* interested in archaeology.

"Why are you wet, Olivia?" My mother gestured to my hair and clothes, still moist from my afternoon swim.

"I went outside to get some fresh air." I twisted the heart-shaped earring in my left ear as I thought of a plausible story. "Then got hot so I came inside and stepped into the shower."

"With your clothes on?"

Shit. I shrugged in that teenage way that makes adults roll their eyes. As if the things I did weren't supposed to be logical.

"You should probably get to bed early," my mother said. "Try to catch up so tomorrow you'll be recharged."

"Right."

My mother stood and wiped at the layer of dust she'd left behind on the couch. Mumbling to herself, she left to no doubt shower, find my father, and plan tomorrow with the rest of the team.

I had some planning to do myself. I'd set my watch on Jobah's wrist for 1:00 p.m. I'd hoped my mother would see my complete lack of interest in their work and leave me to amuse myself. That was how it usually worked at home. It figured the rules had changed in Montana.

If I played sick again, my mother would get suspicious. She may not have been the best mother in the world, but she wasn't an idiot. She probably knew I was lying about being sick. If I tried it two days in a row, she was sure to catch on.

Why did I care if she caught on? If she finally realized I had no desire to work at the dig site, would she let me hang out at the cabin? The doctors rarely punished me. They had to be around to catch me doing something to punish me, and they couldn't force me to dig with them.

Could they?

Mulling this over, I wandered back into the living room. The book Jobah had looked at caught my attention on the top of the pile. I slid onto the couch and pulled the book onto my lap. Opening to the picture of the village, I imagined my parents unearthing some relic that proved Jobah's people inhabited this area. A part of me wanted to be there if they did find something.

Maybe I could help them get some proof without revealing Jobah to them.

Chewing on my bottom lip, I considered this notion. Did I want my parents to continue to get funding? Although it would have been nice to have them around more, I did understand that their jobs were what allowed us to live in a nice town like Sunderfield in the large, waterfront house. Their discoveries and books allowed me to live the life I lived. Generally speaking, I loved that life.

If they lost their funding, it would affect my life. Can't say I cared for that too much. If they found out about Jobah and his tribe, it would affect his life. Didn't care for that either.

Something clattered in the kitchen and I headed that way, a little relieved to have something else to think about for the moment. That relief lasted all of three seconds.

The photographer, Mr. Tramond, leaned against the kitchen island where two plates, two glasses, and the remnants of two lunches lay out in plain sight.

"Hungry?" he asked.

More like speechless.

29. Jobah

"Jobah, my child, you've returned." With Moon trouncing along at our feet, my grandmother corralled me toward her dwelling. Beyond hers, mine still stood. If only I could move that superior structure to my new spot in the woods.

That was a thought. Ashlo would probably help me. Something about removing the dwelling from the village appeared too permanent though, as if I could never return to my people. Probably the case, but still I had hope.

"I have not returned for good, Ninae." I followed her to the back of her home. Moon stopped along a row of low-lying bushes and darted between them. "I come with a warning about outsiders. They are in these woods searching for artifacts from our people."

At this, my grandmother's hand went to her mouth. "Oh, Jobah, how do you know this?"

"I have seen them." I looked away, not wanting to tell my grandmother more than was necessary. If I met her eyes, everything would come spilling out. Ninae was magical that way.

"Where?" She lowered to one of the tree stumps she used as a seat.

I sat on the one across from her and smoothed the dirt at my feet with the heel of my moccasin. Moon came back out from the bushes and nuzzled my ankles until I reached a hand down and petted her.

"West of here," I said. "There is a team. They are searching for what they call The Veiled Tribes. Hidden tribes like ours."

"This is not good, Jobah. If they find us, our way of life will be in danger. Shaman Denri has told of what happens when we open ourselves to outsiders." My grandmother wrung her wrinkled hands in her lap, one eye keeping a close watch on Moon slinking around my feet.

I thought about Olivia telling me her parents wouldn't want to change my people or harm them. Could I trust her? I wanted to. I wanted to believe that anyone who tasted as she did was sweet all the way to the core.

"That is old thinking, Ninae. These outsiders just want to study us. To learn." I stopped moving my feet, and Moon settled into a tight circle between my grandmother and me. The silence that hung over us was a great weight pressing down on my shoulders.

"You have talked to them." She said it as if she were positive it was the truth, as if she were accusing me. When I didn't look at her, she placed two fingers under my chin and gently coaxed my head up so my gaze met hers. It pained me to stare into the dark brown color of her eyes when my own had turned to the color of leaves.

"I have talked to one of them," I admitted. "A girl."

"What have you told her?" My grandmother's hands settled on mine resting on my knees.

"Not much. She knows what I am. She's witnessed what I can do." I told Ninae of the additional abilities in hopes it would trigger forgotten knowledge about Pentas for me. Some remembered tidbit that put the puzzle together.

Instead, Ninae was quiet for a long time. Finally, she stood and exhaled a long breath. "Let me feed you, child. Let me do that at least."

Inside her dwelling, she ladled out a thick stew of meat, corn, and potatoes. It tasted… familiar. Not at all like the sandwiches Olivia had made me this afternoon. Though I had always been quite content with the food we hunted, grew, and gathered in the village, I was curious about what else resided in the silver box at Olivia's cabin. What secret delights did that refrigerator hold? What was the place where she bought food like? What else would I enjoy eating? What had I been missing all these years?

"How long do you expect to live out there on your own?" Ninae gestured to the woods beyond the village palisades.

"I don't know," I said. "I need to figure out these Penta abilities. Sort out what I'm supposed to do with them."

"Maybe you won't know what to do with them until you *need* to do something with them," my grandmother offered.

"That sounds like poor planning, Ninae, and you said I always have a plan. I can't live just wondering what abilities I may have and when I'm supposed to use them. I need to know now."

"Is this outsider, this girl, helping you plan?"

"She did help me determine that I can no longer be anywhere near trees being cut down. Another reason I can't come back to the village. Every time a tree or branch is cut nearby, I feel it. To the point of getting sick."

I finished the stew before my stomach recalled the pain of the tree-cutting experiments. "I would be no use as a builder anymore if I can't cut and gather fresh materials."

"You have many other uses in this tribe, Jobah," Ninae said. "Not to mention I miss you. You are my closest kin, child. The only thing I have to remember my son, your father, by."

Her dark eyes were full of unshed tears. When the first one spilled onto her leathery cheek, I immediately went to her.

"I love you, Ninae," I whispered. "You know that. It is because I love you that I leave. You have given me so much and I wish to take nothing away from you."

"Leaving takes *you* away, Jobah. It makes me feel so empty to be without you here."

She reached out her arms, and I stepped into the embrace, throwing my own arms around my grandmother's delicate shoulders. She shook with tears for a moment then drew herself out of the hug.

"If I were a younger version of myself, I'd go with you. We could discover your Penta abilities together, but I'm an elder now. My place is here. I understand why you think you must go, but know that you will always be welcomed back. Some might be wary of you now, but they will grow to see how important you are to us all."

There she went with that "important" talk again. She almost had me believing it until I ducked out of her dwelling only to see Sumahe and Keryun. They both stopped abruptly when they saw me. Keryun shrank away behind her brother as if she'd seen a *vornahl*, a dead soul.

Sumahe's hands clenched by his sides, but he made no advance toward me. In fact, the fear in his eyes was a tangible thing. I could almost touch it, throw it around, make a hole in it with my dagger. Sumahe was brave enough, however, to spit at my feet.

Moon scampered out from wherever she'd been hiding and hissed at Sumahe. Both he and Keryun backed up several steps, and I couldn't stop the smirk from tugging at my lips.

"We shall have to talk to Denri," Sumahe said as he arrowed a glare at my grandmother. "Jobah left us. That makes him an outsider now. Anyone who still speaks to him is acting against tribe rules. Besides, he is a *brogna*, a demon who does not belong here."

I knew as well as anyone else that acting against tribe rules could get you marched out of the

184

village, but not before Denri *cleansed* you. Anyone who left for good couldn't be allowed to leave knowing where the village was hidden. As our chief and most powerful shaman, Denri had ways of plucking the memory of our location from the mind. In my time with the tribe, I'd only seen two people ordered to leave, my uncles, who went willingly and did not resist the cleansing.

I think Denri had done something to my memories too, because I didn't feel responsible for my uncles' exile. I should have. They only went to the outside to save me after the bee sting. Where were they now? What were their lives like? Why was I thinking about them? Were they the reason I was so curious about the outside world?

Pushing these thoughts aside, I considered Ninae. I certainly didn't want my grandmother to be told to leave the village, the only home she'd ever known. Stepping closer to Sumahe, I glanced at Keryun first, but she wouldn't meet my gaze.

Olivia hadn't judged me, hadn't been afraid. She just accepted.

Ignoring Sumahe and his threats to go to Denri, I turned to Ninae and placed my hands on her shoulders. "I must go."

Moon hissed at Sumahe and Keryun again until they walked away, no doubt to seek out Denri.

"Be careful what you tell the outsider, Jobah," Ninae said. "It is not safe to trust her."

I nodded, but trusting Olivia was the only thing that felt safe.

30. Olivia

"You're having an adventure after all, aren't you, Olivia?" Mr. Tramond gestured to the lunch remains while I stood dumbly in the doorway between the kitchen and living room. How could I have been so stupid? Leaving evidence like this was a rookie mistake. And I was no rookie.

When I was twelve, Eden and I wanted to get tattoos. We hadn't settled on designs yet, but we knew we were headed to Ricky's Branding Station, a small tattoo parlor at the edge of Sunderfield. We also knew that our parents would never in a million years let us get tattoos, but if we just went out and got them, the 'rents wouldn't be able to erase them.

We'd made plans to have a sleepover at my house, a common occurrence. Eden's parents were around more than mine, but they loved it when they could dump Eden and her brothers off at friends' houses and go on one of their romantic getaways. My parents were waist-deep in research at the time, and my sister, Carrie, was supposed to keep an eye on us.

Well, Carrie had broken up with boyfriend #683 and was literally a sobbing mess. I could invited twenty heavy metal bands into our living room for a jam session, and Carrie wouldn't have noticed.

Run With Me

It had been so simple slipping outside once night fell, hopping onto our bikes, and pedaling like the wind all the way to Ricky's Branding Station. We walked into the tattoo parlor ready to get inked and pretty darn impressed with ourselves.

Until Ricky asked for some ID.

Had it not been for the mere fact that Eden and I were only twelve, we'd have some killer tats right now. This was only one of the many escapades she and I were almost successful at executing.

But this? Leaving blatant evidence that I'd had a lunch guest? One I was trying to keep a secret?

Beyond stupid.

"I had two sandwiches," I said. "I like a fresh plate each time. You know, like when you go to a buffet at a restaurant and they make you take a new plate for your second round."

Mr. Tramond grinned and not in that okay-I-believe-you way I was hoping for. Instead, it was an aren't-you-cute-when-you-lie grin. It prickled my skin.

"You Goldilocks, too?" He came over to the two stools, both of which were pushed away from the island. "These both look as if they've been used."

"Maybe I'm obsessive-compulsive."

I had two friends at Sunderfield who suffered from OCD. One of them, Renee, was on the track team with me. She couldn't run at a meet unless she put her left sock and sneaker on first, then the right sock and sneaker on second. Seemed like a small

187

detail, but she was all out of sorts if that routine wasn't maintained.

My other friend, Jess, organized and reorganized everything. Her locker, her bedroom, the food on her lunch tray. You could give her a pile of just about anything and in ten minutes, she would have shuffled the pile into thirty different arrangements.

I could be that way about plates and kitchen stools, couldn't I?

"Okay, Olivia," Mr. Tramond said, that grin on his lips freaking me out. "Whatever you say. I'll keep your secret, but I've got my eye on you." He pulled the camera strap around his neck off and set the camera on the island.

Though he wasn't much taller than me, he backed me up against the refrigerator. He didn't touch me, but kept coming forward, so I kept going backward.

When the cool stainless steel of the refrigerator pressed against my shoulder blades, I said, "What do you want?"

"I haven't decided yet." Some of his hair had slipped from the low ponytail at his neck. It was sweat soaked and sticking to the side of his face. He took a step back and his gaze traveled down the length of me over my tank top and shorts still a little wet from swimming with Jobah.

"Everything all right in here."

I shifted so I could see around Mr. Tramond. My father stood at the island, his hands pressed onto the countertop. His gaze never wavered behind his glasses as he waited for a response.

Mr. Tramond turned around to face him. "Everything's fine, Doctor Bradford." He reached around me to grab the handle of the refrigerator door. "Just getting something more to drink after the lunch Olivia made us."

My father didn't move.

I shuffled away from Mr. Tramond as he opened the refrigerator. "On second thought," he said, "perhaps I'll go develop the pictures I took today." He gestured to the two plates still on the island. "You'll clean that up, Olivia?"

I nodded.

"Great. Thanks for lunch." He grabbed his camera and left the kitchen, the sound of him whistling through the cabin raising the hairs on my neck.

My father and I just stood staring at one another.

Finally, my father said, "When you finish in here, come find me in the study. I've got a job for you."

Stunned that he'd actually spoken directly to me, I nodded and made my way on shaky legs to the island where I picked up the plates. My father hesitated for a moment, staring off in the direction of where Mr. Tramond had exited then left the kitchen.

I rinsed the plates and stacked them in the dishwasher. Grabbed the glasses and did the same. Wiped the crumbs off the counter. Sat in the stool

Jobah had occupied. Wished Jobah would magically appear.

If my father hadn't come into the kitchen when he had, what would Mr. Tramond have done? I was glad I hadn't had to find out. I hoped he'd stick to playing with his cameras and leave me alone for the rest of this trip.

But he knew I was hiding something, and he'd helped me hide that something from my father. Why?

After pushing away from the island, I settled the stools back in their places and was actually relieved to report to my father in the study. I didn't know what job he had for me, but I didn't want to be alone in the cabin right now. Not with that photographer giving me the heebie-jeebies. Had to wonder if he only took pictures of dig sites or was he slimier than anyone on my parents' team knew?

I knocked on the closed study door. "Dad?"

"Come in." Again, it was odd hearing his voice directed at me and not funneled through Mom.

I eased open the door and walked inside. My father was sitting in the chair opposite the couch with his laptop on his lap and the usual spread of books and papers strewn all over the table in front of him. A faint smudge of dust still remained on the leather couch where my mother had sat earlier, and it reminded me of a fingerprint. An indication that my mother had been here and had left something of her day behind.

"You have a job for me?" I wasn't sure what else to say to my father without my mother around to translate.

"Yes." My father pulled a notebook out from the academic debris on the table. "I need you to type up these notes here. Can you read them?" He tapped at the first page of his small, scratchy handwriting before handing me the notebook.

I flipped through ten pages, fronts and backs, filled with his notes about the digging they'd done so far. All this and they hadn't even found anything yet. I couldn't imagine how many notes he'd have if they'd actually uncovered an artifact.

If they actually met Jobah.

After successfully reading the first paragraph to myself, I said, "Yeah, I can read it."

"Good. Here." My father passed me the laptop and motioned to the couch. "Work there."

I sat where he'd told me, placed the notebook on the armrest of the couch and got started, tap-tapping away on the keyboard. Technically, I could have worked anywhere in or outside the cabin with the laptop. Something kept me rooted in that study though. Something kept me from wanting to stray too far away from my father, from someone who may not know how to talk to me, but may know how to protect me.

31. Jobah

The night sky was my favorite. Different shades of blue melded like spilled paint. The moon, a silvery-white slice tonight, offered little light, but my changed eyes were able to see in the shadows. As I lay on my back beside the lake, the stars above were holes poked in the black web of the sky. I envisioned a great fire blazing on the other side, and the only evidence of that fire was what came through those star holes.

One clear memory I have of my parents was of a summer night much like this one. The air was hot and thick, immovable. I had complained of being too warm, and my mother had scooped me up. She roused my father, and the three of us came to this lake.

With a finger to her lips, my mother had led my father and me to the water. Its temperature reflected the heat of the day. We waded in to our ankles, knees, thighs, stomachs. My father went out the farthest, my mother next, then me closest to the shore.

"Face the moon," my mother had said.

My father and I did as she had asked.

"Wise Mother," she said, "let your white eye watch over us, keep us bound to you, to Great Earth, to the winds, to the spirits of the Five Trees. Should we stray, guide us back with your light, your pull, your power." She sung songs of our people in our native language, her voice rising clear and strong in the silence of the night.

When she was done, the three of us emerged from the water, and miraculously, I was cooled and comfortable. We returned to our dwelling, and I slept the sleep of someone who was worry-free, weightless.

My parents disappeared two nights later, and everything had been heavy since.

Ninae took care of me as if it were the only thing she lived for, and perhaps it was. She schooled me in the ways of our people and made sure I spent enough time around the men of our tribe. I had learned everything with ease and speed, relishing working with my hands from sunrise to sunset.

At night, however, I wondered about the outside. What was it like out there? Were the people really as Denri and the other elders said? Were they vicious, full of malice, demons? Did they wish to destroy all we held dear?

Thinking of Olivia now, I didn't believe that all outsiders were evil. She had only been kind to me, but she did tell me of the pricks among her people. Much like my tribe, some people would be loyal to you always and some people would turn on you in a heartbeat. Ninae and Ashlo were examples of the first group, Sumahe and Keryun the latter. I never thought Keryun would side against me, but clearly I'd frightened her. Didn't she see that I hadn't changed on the inside? My eyes were different and I had new abilities, but most of me was still the same Jobah Everleaf.

At least I thought so anyway.

Something bounded onto my stomach, and I crunched up my legs in defense. I raised my head and got a mouthful of raccoon tail.

"Easy, Moon." I shifted to my side and poured the animal off my chest where she had settled. She let out little critter noises of protest, then got distracted by the fringe on my breechclout. She pawed at the strands, batted them this way and that, ran around behind me, climbed over my side. She put her face right up to mine, nose to nose, her whiskers tickling my skin.

I ran a hand down her back, stroking between her ears all the way down to the tip of her bushy tail. She let me do that a couple times before standing on her haunches and sniffing the night air.

After sitting up, I did the same. Summer flowers and sun-warmed water perfumed the air. As I exhaled, movement in the shadowy brush to my right caught my keen eyes. No, the movement was in front of me.

Behind me.

Everywhere.

I hopped to my feet and turned in a circle, holding my hands up as if ready for attack. Why hadn't I brought my bow, my arrows? I had the dagger at my waist and closed my hand around the hilt now as I rotated. A dagger meant I had to let whatever was out there get close enough before I defended myself. Not a good situation. A flurry of fireflies signaled to one another as if keeping time to a rhythm I couldn't hear.

Or could I?

I stopped circling and stood absolutely still by the water. Leaves shushed though no wind blew. The air was motionless, yet the leaves moved, animated by some unseen force.

Evolve.

The word flashed into my head, and when I looked down at Moon, she stared back up at me, her forepaws neatly clasped at her belly. The position was so… human.

I squeezed my eyes shut, but that did not stop the rustling of the leaves on this windless eve. The noise rose in volume, came from all sides at once, bored into me, past flesh and muscles and bone down to my soul.

I left my body.

When I opened my eyes, I was back at my village, looking down on Ninae's dwelling through a filter of branches and leaves. I knew the perspective—an enormous pine tree beside my grandmother's shelter. I had climbed it often, because you could see the entire village from that vantage point. How had I gotten there now?

I studied the scene below. A soft, orange glow flickered at the back of Ninae's dwelling. A dark figure huddled beside the light. I wanted to go to her. To tell her I'd come back to the village. To tell her I'd take care of her as I'd always promised as a boy.

Christy Major

Her voice rose to my ears. "Protect my Jobah, spirits. If you have chosen him as one of your Pentas, it is with good reason, but give him the strength and the courage to serve you well. Help him find himself, for right now he is lost."

Hearing Ninae call me lost stabbed me in the heart. I made a motion to climb down the tree, but found I had no legs, no arms, no body.

I *was* the pine tree.

As soon as this realization solidified in my mind, I got thrown out of the tree. Not merely off it, but *out* of it. As if I had inhabited its insides and now had been cast aside.

I was back in my body, sprawled on the ground by the lake, Moon still sitting on her haunches eyeing me with a flick of her tail every now and again. I rose to all fours on shaky limbs.

"What was that?" I half-hoped the raccoon would offer an answer.

I rubbed my eyes and soared again. Now I was in a tree looking down on Olivia's cabin. Lights inside the cabin winked like giant eyes, and I had a natural urge to step back into the cover of deeper woods. Again, my body was not my own to control. I looked out the eyes of a birch tree somehow.

I only stayed at Olivia's cabin for a few minutes then I came rushing back to the lake. Weak-kneed, I fell to the ground. My palms braced my fall, but I collapsed into the sand, my breath coming in shallow gasps.

Had I traveled to different trees in these woods? Had I borrowed them? Had they borrowed me?

32. Olivia

"Do you need this printed?" I saved my father's notes.

"Hmm?" My father drew himself out of the textbook he was reading. He pulled his glasses off and rubbed his eyes.

"Do you need these notes printed out?" I asked again.

"You're done already?" My father squinted at his watch as he polished the lenses of his glasses on his T-shirt.

"I text, IM, and email like 24/7. I could type up an entire book in my sleep. This was nothing." I held up his notebook then closed it. Sliding to the edge of the couch, I set the laptop and notebook onto the table between us.

"Impressive." Dad put his glasses back on and peered at me with eyes the same exact color as mine. Mom's were more gray, but Dad's and mine were that true blue you see back in Rhode Island when you're on a boat in the middle of Narragansett Bay on a steamy July afternoon.

Which is where I could have been today had I not been in Montana.

I touched my lips. Remembering Jobah's kiss made me not miss boating all that much.

"So do you?" I pointed to the laptop.

"Do I what?"

"Need those notes printed." Maybe we did need Mom to translate for us.

Dad shook his head. "No. I'm only collecting the notes for now. I'll add to them as our work continues."

"Why did you and Mom pick the site you picked?" If Jobah was right, they weren't going to find anything where they were currently digging. Should I tell him that piece of very important information? What if they changed their location and still didn't find anything? Did I want them to find something?

Man, I was expending too much brainpower on things I shouldn't be worrying about.

Dad shuffled around in the books on the table. He extracted the one Jobah and I had looked through earlier. "The author of this book is a friend of ours. He did some digging north of here prior to writing this and postulates at the end of this work that these woods hold a Veiled Tribe. He wasn't able to continue his research due to health concerns, so your mother and I figured we'd pick up where he left off. Our current dig site is the result of Dr. Sumathai's, Dr. Reese's, and Dr. Vakker's study of the area." He shrugged. "We had to start somewhere, but it's basically a needle in a haystack situation."

My parents worked hard, too hard, and I didn't want to see them waste their time. I also wanted to protect Jobah. He was having enough trouble with his Penta stuff. He didn't need a bunch of scientists on his case too. Not before he was sure about what he was becoming.

"Do you need me to do anything else?" I wasn't ready to roam the cabin by myself. Didn't want to bump into Mr. Tramond.

"I have your mother's notes here," Dad started. "You could type those up too if you want." He pulled another notebook from a canvas pack on the floor by his chair.

"Sure." I held my hand out for the notebook.

Dad rested it in my hand but didn't let go when my fingers closed on the spiral binding. We engaged in a brief tug-of-war until my father let go.

"It isn't too terrible, is it?" he asked.

"What?"

"Being here with us."

I exhaled a long, slow breath. "My friends have probably forgotten that I exist, some other teenager has my Target job and is watching her bank account grow, and I'd die for clam cakes and chowder at the beach right now, but no, it's not too terrible being here." I grinned and started typing my mother's notes, which were considerably easier to read.

My father stood, watched my fingers fly over the laptop's keyboard, and went to the door of the study. "Want something to drink?"

"Okay."

When my father came back, he toted a tray of sodas, a plate of hotdogs already in their buns, potato chips, apples, and brownies. My eyes opened wider when my mother trailed into the study after him.

"Your father microwaves hotdogs like a world class chef. I couldn't resist," she joked.

"Olivia's already typed all my notes and has moved on to yours, Madeline." Dad set the tray down after I cleared a spot on the table.

"Excellent. One less thing we have to worry about. You're our official data entry person, Olivia." Mom sat beside me, picked up her notebook, and pulled a pen from the mass of blond hair she had gathered into a tight ponytail. She crossed out some things, added in some things, circled five words she wanted typed in bold, and placed the notebook back on the couch cushion between us.

"Let's take a break now for this elaborate dinner." Dad unfolded a paper napkin and draped it on his lap after he sat in the chair across from Mom and me.

"I'd hate to see non-elaborate," I said with none of my usual biting sarcasm and attitude.

"Non-elaborate is when you have to rip open a pouch and spoon the nearly unidentifiable contents out with your own hand." Mom opened one of the soda cans and took a long sip. "I imagine it's like eating cat food."

"Non-elaborate is when you have to crack open a beetle and eat its innards," Dad said.

"Tell me you guys haven't eaten bug guts for dinner." I looked at Mom then Dad.

"Sometimes when you're out in the field—" Dad stopped when I held up a hand.

"Please don't. I won't be able to get this hotdog down if you do, and I'm hungry. Let's save that disturbing revelation for another time."

Had Jobah eaten insects? Had I kissed someone who had let the gushy insides of beetles fill his mouth?

Shit, think of something else! A vision of Eden and I playing Dance Camp III on her Wii popped into my head. We'd dressed up as 80s punk rockers complete with mohawks and leather pants. We bopped around her living room for hours until her mother finally told us if she heard "Girls Just Want to Have Fun" one more time she was going to make sure these two girls never had fun again. It was the biggest threat Mrs. Bennington had ever made.

With the idea of eating bugs pushed to the recesses of my mind, I concentrated on the hotdog in my hands. I generally don't adore hotdogs, but something about this one my dad had nuked and I had slathered in ketchup hit the spot. Every now and again, I stole glances at my parents who never remained still long enough for me to inspect.

Both of them had showered and changed into clean cargo shorts and T-shirts after their dig. My mother's hair was still a little wet in her ponytail, but Dad's short, blond buzz cut had only needed towel drying. The outline of a watch marked my mother's otherwise tanned arm, while my father's arms both looked a little sunburned. Fortunately, I had my mother's ability to tan, though I had my father's fairer hair and lighter eyes. By the end of the summer, I was a lovely shade of golden from running track outside every day.

By the end of most summers anyway. Not this one. This one had me running around under the shade of broad-leafed trees and only going into the sunshine to swim with a mysterious boy claiming to be a tree spirit.

"How would you like to actually do some digging tomorrow, Olivia?" My father wiped ketchup from the corner of his mouth before looking up at me.

Mom stopped chewing and volleyed her gaze between my father and me. This was one of those moments where you know your answer to what appears to be a simple question is really one of the most important answers you'll ever give.

"Okay." A rather mundane response, but the smiles that beamed from both of my parents' faces told me it was the right response.

What was happening? Something unfolded inside me. Something that started in my chest. A thawing if you will. The ice that had hardened around my heart regarding matters of my parents cracked, tiny fissures giving way to ragged seams, until a strange warmth poured out and radiated throughout the rest of me. We were having one of those Hallmark Original Movie moments that in no way made up for the years of barely speaking to one another.

Still, it was something. Maybe it was a beginning.

33. Jobah

I managed to make it back to my shelter without any otherworldly experiences. Moon escorted me the entire way, chittering as if telling me secrets of great importance. I threw myself into the simple task of making a fire, an act I did instinctually at this point in my life. I worried about the time when I would need to cut fresh wood to build up my fuel pile. A man could not survive in the woods without fire. I had enough dead and dry pieces to get me through the summer and fall, but normally I'd spend a good portion of those seasons collecting fresher stock to dry out for future use. And what would I do through the winter and spring?

Not wanting to think of those concerns, I concentrated on the fire at my feet now. I wasn't hungry. Ninae's stew still filled my belly. I was concerned more with what filled my head—visions of seeing places from the trees' points of view. Being inside those trees was both frightening and comforting. Discovering one has no control over his body was enough to scare the hair right off my head, but at the same time, being able to see through the trees brought about a peace in me. I wore the bark like a second skin, the spirits' energy coursing directly through my veins, uniting me with every tree in the woods. I could be any one of them.

Control.

I snapped my head up to find Moon on the boulder beside me. Her whiskers twitched forward, twitched back as she nodded slightly.

She was right. If I had control of these Penta abilities, then I'd have control over me. Perhaps my purpose would come to me if I weren't so concerned about the effects of the new abilities.

After grabbing a long stick, I dragged it in a wide circle around the fire. "I create this sacred space, Wise Ones, so I may purify myself and hear your counsel, so I may quiet the noise inside me and receive your gifts."

Moon hopped down from the rock and wiggled into the circle with me. Instantly, the fire surged higher in the center as if the addition of Moon's natural force had strengthened the blaze, strengthened me.

I sat on the ground with my legs crossed in front of me. Placing my palms together at my chest, I cleared my mind, envisioned my soul as a misty white cloud, and opened myself to my surroundings. I dropped all shields and let Great Earth flow into me. Deep breath in, deep breath out. Deep breath in, deep breath out. Over and over again until the rhythm was memorized. Flowers nearby opened and closed their blooms as I inhaled and exhaled. I was aware of my hold on them, my power connecting me to them, them to me. Their fragrances mingled and filled my nostrils, became a part of my own scent.

I closed my eyes to block out the minute details I could see even in the dim blackness of night. Images still came. Tribe images of the village and the people I had called my own. Outside images of a world I'd only visited once, but could never forget. Olivia images, her soft lips simply waiting for me.

A gush of wind made me open my eyes. Olivia's cabin was before me, closer than when I'd visited it earlier. The front door was but a few steps away. I looked down and saw the trunk of a small pine tree. I pushed forward and my body came into view. Two legs, a torso, arms. I was not inside the tree anymore. I had used it as a doorway instead. I was actually in the dirt lot in front of the cabin.

But how?

I bent down and picked up a handful of dirt, which I let sift through my very real fingers. I was solid. I was me. Only I was here instead of at my shelter, and the switch had happened in an instant.

Footsteps crunched on gravel to my left, so I hid behind the vehicle Olivia's parents had used. Over the sound of my heartbeat pulsing in my ears, I heard a man's voice.

"They haven't found anything yet, but we knew it was going to take some time. We have to be patient. The pay-off will be worth it. I'm doing some poking around myself when they aren't watching."

I wanted to peek around the vehicle to see who it was, but didn't dare risk being seen.

"No, no. We should stick to the plan. Changing it now would be stupid, and we're not stupid. At least I'm not anyway." A gruff laugh sounded as boots scraped on wooden steps. "It was a joke. Take it easy, Xavier. I didn't mean anything by it."

Why did I only hear one voice? He sounded as if he were talking to someone, but why was no one answering him?

"All right, I have to go. Got some young, fresh eye candy on this trip, and you know how I like candy." Another laugh. "I'll keep you posted. Bye."

A soft beep echoed in the dark. Light spilled out from the cabin as the front door was opened, then all was black again as the door closed.

I hunched by the vehicle for a few silent moments, making sure I was alone before stepping out of the shadows. Silhouettes passed by windows, but I couldn't make out details through the window coverings. It felt wrong to be peeking in anyway, so I turned away from the cabin, closed my eyes, and thought of my own shelter.

Another gush of wind brushed against my face and when I opened my eyes, I was back in the woods, staring at my fire from the base of a birch tree. Moon clapped her forepaws together and whipped her tail from side to side as I stepped from the bark. She was obviously pleased with whatever it was I had accomplished. Traveling, I guess you could call it. Only I didn't need to do any walking. I thought of a place and the trees took me there.

207

I filed that away with the blossoming and keen vision abilities, all seeming as if they might be positive aspects of being a Penta. Only cutting trees appeared to be a problem, a big problem. One I couldn't solve this evening, for my travels tonight had made me tired.

After poking at the embers, I retired to my shelter. Moon scurried in and chose her spot at the corner of the moose hides. I spread out on top of the animal skins as well, and though I had figured some things out, I still had so many questions. Questions about being a Penta and my future, questions about strange, one-sided conversations and eye candy, whatever that was. Questions that needed answers.

I closed my eyes and focused on picturing the moose hides beneath me. Didn't want to accidentally travel in my sleep. What I did want was to see Olivia tomorrow. Everything about my situation seemed better with her around.

On that thought, I sat up and pictured the lake in my mind. A breeze blew and I saw the lake from a pine tree on the shore. I took a step and was ankle deep in water a moment later.

I was getting good at this.

Searching under the shallow water with my hands, I freed several stones from their sandy homes. I rinsed them and inspected them in my palm. Tossing three that were too large back into the water, I was left with two pieces of slate. I brought them both back to my shelter where I smashed them against a big boulder. I sifted through the fragments and found a piece that looked like the shape I'd seen hanging from Olivia's ears today. I didn't know what the symbol meant in her world, but she must have liked it to decorate herself with it.

I ducked inside my shelter and freed my dagger from my waist. After cutting a single, thin strip of hide from my breechclout fringe, I made a hole in the slate shape and threaded it onto the hide. My people gave gifts to those who were important to them. I had only just met Olivia, but she felt important. She'd helped me, taught me, fed me, hid me.

Kissed me.

34. Olivia

I woke early the next morning, the evening I'd spent with my parents still fresh in my mind. Sure, the food sucked and I was still trapped in Montana, but maybe I didn't hate it as much as I had pre-hotdogs.

Or pre-Jobah, more specifically.

After hopping into jean shorts and a green tank top just to show Jobah how much I truly did love the color, I went downstairs and out to the back porch where I'd left my sneakers to dry from their swim in the lake. They were pretty beaten up, but at least they weren't soaked anymore.

As I sat on one of the steps and tied my shoes, I wondered what Jobah was doing right now. Was he up and fishing maybe? Were he and Moon still snuggled in his shelter? What was Jobah like first thing in the morning?

Shaking my head at these questions—the time for Jobah would come later today—I came back into the cabin and ran smack into Mr. Tramond.

"Easy there, Olivia." He grabbed me by the biceps and held me firmly in place. "What's the rush?"

I maneuvered out of his hold. "No rush. Just hungry." I started for the kitchen, hoping he wouldn't follow.

Of course he did.

"Going to make yourself *two* breakfasts? I know how you like to double up on meals."

He wasn't going to let go of what he'd seen yesterday in the kitchen, was he?

"How about if I make you breakfast and you agree to keep your mouth shut?" I asked the last part in a low whisper, almost a growl.

"Deal."

I continued to the kitchen and let out a breath.

"Don't think this squares us though." He sat on one of the island stools. "I know you're up to something, and one breakfast isn't going to even everything out."

Shit. I didn't like this hanging over my head. No one could know about Jobah or his people. Not yet. I felt bound to protect them for some reason.

"Whatever." I pulled eggs, milk, and cheese out of the refrigerator. "Omelet?"

"Perfect." He pulled some glasses down from the cabinet and filled them with orange juice while I cooked at the stove. He kept making excuses to squeeze by me. He needed to get at the dishes. Needed a paper towel. A coffee mug. A fork. Bread for the toaster. He passed by so many times, he nearly wore a rut into the tile floor. Each time his body brushed against mine, I got a little more spooked. His proximity didn't feel like friend.

It felt like predator.

You can outrun him. This sentence looped in my mind as I folded the omelet over, sealing in the cheese.

Where would I run?

To the lake, because I think I could outswim him too.

Feeling better with this plan if needed, I plopped the omelet onto a dish and set it in front of him. He'd already buttered two pieces of toast and eaten one of them.

"Wow," he whistled as he looked at the omelet, "who taught you to cook? I'm guessing it wasn't your parents."

"Rachel Ray. I like to watch cooking shows." I shrugged and got started on an omelet for me.

"Hidden talents," he said. "Nice. What else can you do?"

I didn't turn around or respond. I busied myself with the eggs instead. If I focused on the stovetop, I didn't have to watch him watch me. I wanted the eggs to hurry and become an omelet, but like waiting for paint to dry, the eggs took their sweet damn time.

When the omelet was done, I faced a new predicament—where to eat them. I tried piling everything onto my dish and scooting out of the kitchen to eat up in my room, but Mr. Tramond grabbed my arm as I passed. Not too hard, just a loose clamp to keep me from leaving.

"You're not going to make me eat alone? That'd be ever so impolite. I might accidently mention something to your parents about your guest yesterday if you're impolite to me." He didn't look at me, which was actually more unsettling than if he had. As if he knew I would pull out the stool beside him and sit. I had to.

To protect Jobah.

Sitting on the edge of the stool, I ate my omelet and toast, drank the juice, and counted down the moments until Mr. Tramond was finished and gone. Unfortunately, he appeared to be feeling leisurely this morning, savoring every bite. I was about to stand and say I was done so I could get out of there when Dad walked into the kitchen. He skidded to a halt in his work boots, but then recovered before coming all the way to the island.

"Good morning, Olivia. Will," he said.

"Peter." Mr. Tramond raised his orange juice in salute.

Dad's eyes narrowed. He knew something was off here.

"Hey, Dad," I said in hopes of renewing our family bonding of last night.

My father focused on me and offered a tentative smile. He should definitely smile more. "You ready to get dirty?"

A snickery noise sounded from Mr. Tramond, and there was a moment where I thought Dad might reach around me and hit the guy.

I stood, using my body to break Dad's line of sight on the photographer. "I'm ready." I held up my empty plate. "Do you want me to make you some breakfast?"

Dad shook his head. "I already ate. Your mother and I have been up since five."

"Ugh," Tower grunted as he walked into the kitchen. I had to agree with him. "No one should be up at five. No one." He gave Mr. Tramond a curt nod then smiled at me. "Mornin', Ollie. How's it going?"

"Okay." Now that all these people were in the kitchen.

"Fab-u-lous." He smacked his hands together and looked at what remained of the omelet on Mr. Tramond's plate. "Where can I get one of those?"

"In this kitchen, *tomorrow* morning," Dad said. "For now just eat something quickly, because we have to get going. We've got the day planned out. We're going to move slightly east. See if we have better luck."

I had difficulty swallowing for a moment. East was closer to Jobah's shelter. How far east were my parents planning to go? Keeping a boy a secret was turning out to be harder work than I thought it would be.

"Perhaps you want to learn more about photographing relics, Olivia." Mr. Tramond took his plate to the sink then turned to face us. "You could be my assistant today."

A tremble worked its way through my body, and Dad rested his hand on my shoulder.

"She doesn't need to be bored to death by you, Will," Tower said, clapping the man on the back until he almost fell forward. "Ollie can ride with me in the backhoe again, if she wants."

Though I didn't really want to sweat it out in the backhoe, it was preferable to hanging out with Mr. Creepy and his cameras.

"What do you say, Ollie?"

"We need O-liv-ia," Dad said each syllable separately, "to ride with us today. Got a few things to debrief her on." He made it all sound so official.

"Gotcha." Tower did that pulling-the-trigger thing again with his thumb and forefinger, then grabbed a power bar from one of the kitchen cabinets. "See you all on the battlefield." He gave us a wave and disappeared into the living room.

Mr. Tramond mumbled something I couldn't make out and left too.

As soon as he was gone, my father slid his hand off my shoulder. "Has he...did he...He hasn't..." He didn't seem able to pick a question and finish it, but I knew what he was asking.

"No." I stared at Dad, hoping that what went unsaid was still understood. Mr. Tramond hadn't done anything, but I didn't feel comfortable around him anymore.

"We'll keep you busy. Stay with us. Or Royce. He's an ape of a man, but trustworthy." He went to the sink, filled a glass with water, and drained it in under two seconds. "Come on. Let's go find your mother and load up the SUV."

Nice to know Dad had the desire to defend his young, even if he wasn't entirely sure how to talk to me. He was getting better though, or maybe I was getting better at speaking his language.

After brushing my teeth and grabbing my father's laptop in the study as I had been instructed, I met my parents outside by the SUV. Tower was positioned in his backhoe, the engine rumbling like thunder.

"Morning, Olivia," my mother said. "You ready to get dirty?"

I looked at Dad, who smiled as he held the back driver side door open for me.

"What?" Mom asked as she climbed into the passenger seat.

"I asked her the same thing about twenty minutes ago." Dad closed my door then got in behind the wheel.

"Great minds." Mom grinned at Dad, and they actually looked like a regular mom and dad for a split second. For this brief moment in time, they were just a man and a woman, not brainiacs obsessed with archaeology.

Interesting. They actually had the capacity.

The moment passed as the rest of the dig team loaded themselves into the SUV. Dr. Reese and Dr. Sumathai squeezed in next to me, while Dr. Vakker and Mr. Tramond sat in the way back behind us.

Good. The farther away the photographer was, the better.

The drive along the bumpiest path in creation to the new dig site was quiet, and I figured they were all reviewing their strategies for the day, so I kept my mouth shut. Not that I was sure what to say to them anyway. I was just only learning how to converse with my own parents, never mind an entire team of nerds and one possible pervert.

One step at a time.

When we arrived at the site, my dad instructed me to set up the grid as I had done at the first location. This time, however, he kneeled in the dirt beside me, handing me stakes and showing me how to tie more secure knots in the lines comprising the grid. My mother had me develop a sketch on her tablet of the grid and watched over my shoulder as she told me codes to type in the squares.

They were both letting me into their world. Maybe they would have let me in a lot sooner had I shown any interest. Had it been me keeping them out all this time? Had they merely been waiting for the day I'd stop thinking about myself for two minutes and open my eyes to what they were doing with *their* lives?

I'd stepped across an imaginary bridge. One Olivia—the popular, everything revolves around me, Rhode Island version—stood on one side, and a second Olivia—the digging in the Montana dirt and liking it version—stood on the other side. Perhaps the world as I knew it wouldn't crumble at my feet if the Rhode Island version took a hike for a while.

35. Olivia

*Small discoveries
reveal what we keep secret
from the world,
from each other,
from ourselves.*

I used a small hand shovel to loosen the dirt in the square my parents had assigned me. Wasn't exactly sure what I was looking for, but both Mom and Dad said I'd know an artifact when I found one. Again, I was divided. I didn't want to find anything that might put Jobah and his people at risk, but I also was a little fascinated by the prospect of unearthing some treasure.

I dug for hours, streams of sun filtering through the trees and beating down on my back. My parents were in the squares on either side of me. Doctors Sumathai, Vakker, and Reese were in their own squares toiling away as well while Mr. Tramond took photographs of us and the nearby woods. We were all in our own worlds, focused on our work, but at the same time, we operated like a well-oiled machine, methodically overturning dirt in almost perfect synchronicity.

"I've got something!" My mother's voice.

Instantly, my father hopped over to her square. "Easy now. Steady." He shined a flashlight into her square, which had been dug to at least three feet deep.

I crawled over to my father's side, unable to straighten out after being hunched over my own square for so long. Squinting, I peered into my mother's square.

What did she have? Should I be concerned for Jobah?

Holding my breath, I watched as my mother freed the dirt around whatever it was she had found. She wiggled and tugged until something came loose.

"Hand it up here, Madeline," Dad said, "where we can see it better."

She did so then took the hand my father extended down to her. He pulled her up where she landed across his lap, a girlish laugh slipping from her in the process. My parents may have been geeks, but they were geeks still in love after all the years they'd been married.

I focused on the rectangular object my father held in his hand. A book. Animal hide cover, aged pages, scribbly writing and symbols inside. A circle with a leaf in the center had been burned into the hide on the cover.

"Simon," my mother called. "Come take a look at this."

Dr. Vakker, having left the square he'd been poking around in, kneeled next to my mother. "What have you got there?" He took the book from my father and flipped through it carefully. His long, thin fingers ran over the markings on the pages. "I'll need to check these with the reference books I've brought along, maybe send some pictures back to the university, but I'd say you've made our first official find here, Madeline. Nice going."

My father helped my mother to her feet and gave her the biggest hug I'd ever seen one human give another. He lifted her right off her feet and did a half spin with her. When he set her down, they both righted their rumpled T-shirts, gave each other a raised eyebrow, and fetched their notebooks from the ground by their respective squares.

Dr. Vakker and Dr. Sumathai hovered over the book at the bag and tag table. I stared at them until movement behind them caught my attention. Just a subtle shift of ferns and leaves. My eyes darted to the ground where a raccoon emerged from the brush.

"Moon?" I said.

"What?" My father looked up from his notebook.

"Noon? Is it noon?" I said. God, what time was it? I'd been fooling around in the dirt for so long, I'd lost track of the day.

"Way past noon, Olivia," my mother said. "It's three o'clock."

Three o'clock! Shit. I'd missed my meeting time with Jobah. Had he sent Moon to fetch me? That thought made me smile as I looked down at the raccoon waiting patiently at the fringe of the dig site, her head angled toward the trees behind her. I studied those trees and found him.

Jobah stared at me from behind a tall pine tree deeper in the woods. His body was hidden, but those eyes practically glowed green at me. They were much brighter than yesterday. The moment I realized he was this close, I wanted to be with him. Like magnetic attraction, I almost couldn't stop myself from running into the woods.

But I had to.

"What's the matter, Olivia?" My father rested his hand on my shoulder and I jumped out of my skin. "Sorry. I didn't mean to scare you."

"No problem," I managed.

"It's exciting to make a discovery, isn't it?" He gestured to Dr. Vakker leafing through the ancient book.

"Yes." Exciting and potentially dangerous for the hot tree spirit still watching me. "How much longer are you and Mom going to dig?" I added a touch of my former whiny self to the question.

Dad threw a look up to the sky as if checking the position of the sun, then glanced at his watch. "With a find like that book, we'll probably go into the night. We have lights we can set up. Best to continue digging in case it rains tonight or an animal tampers with the site."

"Into the night, huh?" I rubbed my forehead then brushed at the dirt I figured I had streaked across my face.

Dad pulled an old-fashioned handkerchief from his back pocket and handed it to me. I wiped my forehead, looked at the brown smear soiling the handkerchief, and hoped the stain would come out in the wash.

"Why don't you head back to the cabin, take a break." Dad slid his gaze to Tower tinkering with the backhoe. "I can get Royce to drop you off, and you'll have some time to yourself."

"I think I'll go for a run instead. The cabin isn't far. I've run longer distances."

Dad nodded. "I'll keep Will busy photographing your mother's find."

A moment of awkward silence passed between us until Moon scampered over to me, tagged me on the ankle, then ran off into the brush.

Dad stumbled back a bit. "That was odd behavior for a raccoon."

"I think she wants to start a game of chase," I said. "Apparently, I'm *It*."

Dad considered this before he realized it was a joke, and he let out a short chuckle. "Well, don't let her win."

"Got to," I said already starting to jog in place. "Raccoons are sore losers. Everyone knows that."

That got a full laugh from Dad as he turned to join my mother in her square. I had a few hours before they'd be back at the cabin.

A few hours to tell Jobah his tribe might be in trouble.

36. *Jobah*

She ran straight toward me, but I waited until she passed and disappeared into the woods behind me before I turned and followed her. Moon led us to the lake where I collapsed onto the sand beside a heavy-breathing Olivia.

"Nothing... like... a... run... to... get... the... blood... pumping." Olivia put a hand to her chest and drummed her slender fingers along her collarbone.

I rolled to my back next to her, my arm touching hers from shoulder to elbow. Her skin was warm and having her so close made me happy I'd gone to find her. When her watch on my wrist beeped, I had raced to the lake only to find she wasn't there. I'd waited and waited, but she never came. Finally, I couldn't take it anymore. I feared she wasn't coming and that left me empty.

Moon was the one who egged me on, ran back and forth between me at the shore and the tree line. Following her at least gave me something to focus on besides obsessing over where Olivia was. The raccoon led me directly to the dig site as if she'd known where it was all along. I'd thought Olivia had said it was further west, but I must have been wrong.

"Why didn't you come?" I asked.

Olivia shifted to her side, strands of her golden hair spilling over her neck. "I'm sorry, Jobah. I lost track of the time. I was… having fun?" Her eyebrows crinkled together. "I'm not sure how that could be, but digging with my parents was interesting." She looked down to her hands, not meeting my gaze.

I lifted her chin with a finger. "Isn't finding your parents' work interesting a good thing?"

"It is," Olivia said, "but my mother found something today."

I'd let my hand trail down Olivia's neck and along her shoulder, but now I froze just above her elbow. "What did she find?"

"Well, the dig crew moved the site east, because they weren't having any luck in the original location. We set up a new grid and after hours of digging, my mother uncovered a book."

I pulled my hand off Olivia completely so I could think. "What did it look like?"

She described the book then picked up a stick. Drawing in the sand between us, she said, "There was a symbol like this on the cover of the book." She'd drawn a circle with a leaf inside.

"This is the symbol of the Kiyuchee, the Clan of the Five Trees, my people," I said. "It marks our homes, hunting grounds, and decorates our clothing." I lifted one of my feet to Olivia so she could see the symbol on the sole of my moccasin.

"Clan of the Five Trees?" Olivia asked.

I sat up and took the stick Olivia had used to draw the symbol. I sketched five simple trees in the dirt. "The Kiyuchee tribe started from five trees planted by the spirits who created the five elements." I wrote *Earth, Air, Water,* and *Fire* under four of the trees. "Trees represent those four elements. They grow in the earth. They give air. They take water. They burn with fire so the people can survive. The fifth element is Spirit itself." I labeled the last tree. "Earth, Air, Water, and Fire all had places to exist, but the spirits needed a place to put the fifth element. They put Spirit in humans."

Olivia appeared to be filing this information away somewhere in her mind.

"What else can you tell me about the book that was found today?" I asked.

"That's all I know. As soon as my mother dug it out, she gave it to one of the crew members to analyze."

What if that book told of Pentas? What if it could tell me about my abilities, my changes, my purpose?

I had to have that book.

"Is there any way I can look at that book?" I asked.

"Not for a few days at least," Olivia said. "The doctors are going to be examining that thing from all angles. I won't be able to sneak it away."

Every day that passed was another day I was lost, another day for a new ability or change to surprise me. I wasn't fond of surprises. Not all of them were good.

"Mr. Tramond," Olivia started, "the photographer, the guy who takes pictures of my parents' work?"

I nodded.

"He knows something's going on," she said. "He found our lunch plates yesterday. I tried to cover, but he's not letting it go. He's hanging it over my head. He thinks I owe him something for keeping the secret that I had a guest."

"What kind of something does he think you owe him?" I did not like the sound of this.

"That's the million dollar question." A shiver rippled through Olivia. "I don't think I'm going to like the answer."

"He won't do anything to harm you, will he?" All the muscles in my body tensed at this thought.

Olivia shrugged. I could tell she was wary of the man. That made me want to protect her as she was protecting me.

"What if we told your parents about me?" I heard myself say. What was I doing?

Olivia's blue eyes widened. "They'll want to know everything, Jobah."

"Not if we control what they know." I pushed to my feet and paced in front of her.

"What do you mean?" She rested her elbows on her knees and squinted up at me.

Good question. What did I mean? My gaze fell upon the tiny "SHS" written in bold green lettering on the bottom of Olivia's sneaker.

Sunderfield High School. School.

"Come with me." I yanked Olivia to her feet and pulled her along behind me into the woods again. I let go of her hand when I started to run, but she kept up with little effort, bounding over fallen logs and rocks like a lithe deer. Moon rustled over the terrain and passed us. She always knew where I wanted to go.

I stopped at the top of the hill where I'd gone on so many occasions to peek at the outsiders' school. This afternoon, people littered the field to the right of the stone building, some dressed in bright yellow, others wearing blue. A black and white, round something was being kicked around by the people, and voices carried on the warm, summer breeze.

"Soccer," Olivia whispered in my ear. She leaned into me from behind, her hand on my left shoulder.

"What?"

"Soccer. They're playing a sport called soccer." Olivia pointed to the field. "See those two nets on either end? The point is to get the ball into the nets, but you can't use your hands."

"Have you played this sport?" I had an urge to try it. It looked like a lot of running, which I always enjoyed.

"Yeah," Olivia said. "When I was a little kid, I was on a team. I decided, however, that I liked the running around part more than the kicking the ball part, so when I got a little older I joined the track team instead."

"Soccer and track," I said. "Are they the only games you play in your world?"

Olivia let out a short chuckle. "Soccer and track are only two of the many games we play. There's baseball, basketball, football, hockey, lacrosse, tennis… God, I could list sports all day and still not get them all." She squeezed my shoulder. "On the outside, we love our games. You'd have fun out there."

I turned around to face Olivia and loved having her right there with me. "Could you get me some clothes? You know, like the males you know wear?"

She looked down to my breechclout and moccasins. "Why? Tired of showing off your body?" Her fingers played along my stomach causing me to tighten the muscles there. The black parts of her eyes swelled until the blue was almost gone completely.

I grabbed her wrist to stop her from tickling me then weaved my fingers between hers. "If I dressed like one of you, couldn't I be one of you?"

Olivia chewed on her lower lip and the gesture had me wanting to taste those lips again. "Like I could have met you over there?" She pointed to the field. "I could have been on my run, saw the school, wandered over to check it out, and met you."

"It's more reasonable than you bumped into a tree spirit, isn't it?"

228

"Then you could come back to the cabin with me, be introduced to my parents, the team, ask all the questions you wanted about the Veiled Tribes and the book my mother found." Olivia's smile widened with each word she uttered as did mine.

"I'd just be a curious high school student. You could help me say the right things."

Olivia shook off my hand to clap her own together. "This is a brilliant plan, Jobah. I wouldn't have to hide you anymore, and Mr. Tramond wouldn't have a secret to blackmail me with." She pressed her hands to my chest. "You know, for a guy who's lived his whole life in the seclusion of the woods, you're a genius."

I wasn't sure what a genius was, but by the look on Olivia's face, it was much better than being a prick.

"Let's get back to the cabin," she said. "No one is there right now. It'll be easier to raid my parents' room and find you clothes that fit when we have the place to ourselves."

I followed Olivia as she led me down the hill, her hand in mine. Tugging her in the right direction to get to the cabin, I broke into a run beside her. I was reminded of the story my grandmother used to tell me every time she saw two animals together. She would say the spirits paired the animals so there would be balance in the world, so no one would have to travel through this life alone.

I'd thought the story only applied to animals. With Olivia running beside me, I knew it applied to so much more.

37. Olivia

I went into the cabin first while Jobah crouched behind a boulder in the woods. After poking my head into each room, I confirmed that the team was still knee-deep in dirt at the dig site. I opened the front door and waved Jobah over.

Watching him run across the parking lot reminded me of the time Eden and I pay-per-viewed an X-rated movie while having a sleepover at my house. Again, Carrie was in charge and otherwise engrossed in one of her teenage problems. I so loved when my parents left her in command.

We were in the living room, a gargantuan bowl of popcorn sitting between us, oozing butter like lava flowing from a volcano. We'd spread out my Barbie sleeping bag in all its pinkness and were sprawled out on our bellies, feet up and flopping around.

"What do you want to watch?" I'd asked.

"Something we've never watched before," Eden had replied. This was a surprise response from Eden who always wanted to watch **Sixteen Candles** because she was totally in love with the kid who played Jake Ryan, whatever the actor's name was. Every year, to this day, she eats her first piece of birthday cake sitting on her dining room table, hoping

231

some hot guy will show up to eat it with her. Hasn't happened yet, but who am I to ruin her birthday wish?

I'd scrolled through the cable menu and somehow stumbled to the pay-per-view channels. We'd found a movie called *The Secret*. Now, who doesn't enjoy a good secret, right? Well, let me tell you, there was nothing secret about that movie. No way. Everything... and I mean *everything*... was right out there for everyone to see. I don't think Eden or I blinked for the entire two hours the movie played. It was the first time either of us had seen a completely naked male body, and we were right at that age when boys didn't seem as gross as they did when we were younger. I remember going to school the following Monday and wondering if the boys in my class were hiding six-pack abs under their grape juice stained T-shirts.

I didn't have to wonder about Jobah. His abs were right there for me to see as were the muscles in his thighs as he ran toward me. Wished I could hit a slow-motion button so I could check him out in detail, but he was quick and crossing the threshold before I could drool any further.

"Come upstairs," I said. "I think some of my dad's stuff should fit you."

Jobah followed me up the stairs. "What's eye candy, Olivia?"

I stopped climbing the steps, and Jobah bumped into me. I had to put my hand on the next step to keep from slamming into it.

"Sorry." Jobah snaked his arm around my waist and maneuvered me to standing. "Are you all right?"

"Yes, but why do you ask about eye candy?"

"I overheard it somewhere. Just thought you might know what it means."

I had the sense he wasn't telling me the whole story—where would he overhear that?—but I was in a position to teach him, and it would only help him play the part of one of us.

"Eye candy is what you say to describe someone you think is attractive." My cheeks instantly got hot. I purposely looked over Jobah's shoulder to the living room below so I wouldn't be reminded of how attractive he was. "It's not really a compliment though," I added, "because usually it means that the person only has good looks and not much else. You could be insulting someone's intelligence by saying they were eye candy, so I would be careful with that one."

Jobah seemed to be digesting this bit of information, and I thought he was going to ask me more about it. Instead he climbed one more step so he was a few inches below me. He reached up a hand and coiled some strands of my hair around his fingers. Dark skin became striped with light hair.

"What do you say if you want to tell someone they are both beautiful and wise?" The green of his eyes pierced through me, electrocuted me with a leafy zap, showered me with emerald sparks. I would have been quite content to stay on that step for an eternity.

"I don't think there's one word to do both," I said once I'd regained use of my brain.

"My people have a word for it," Jobah whispered, his fingers gently winding and unwinding my hair.

How had I ever thought Kevin was something to get excited about? He'd never gotten my insides to dance like Jobah had right now just by standing so close to me.

"*Nahderhi*." The word rolled off Jobah's tongue slowly, his voice low and seeping into me. I would never forget the word or him saying it. Not ever.

"Have you used this word often? You know, back in your village?" I was sure any girl he'd said it to would have melted at his feet.

"I've never called any female this," he said. "I've had no occasion to in the past."

The left corner of his lips turned up slightly as his eyes darkened to a rich, hunter green. He let my hair twist free of his fingers and brushed his knuckles along my cheek. I rubbed back, cat-like, and closed my eyes.

"I want to kiss you again, *Nahderhi*." Jobah's hands cupped either side of my face.

I didn't have to open my eyes to know his lips were mere centimeters away from mine. Leaning forward, I pressed my mouth to his and tasted forest. Not any forest, but summertime forest when all the leaves are green and the earth is sun-warmed and alive. When things are growing and changing. When the days are long and the nights are filled with cricket lullabies.

When Rhode Island is a distant memory and Montana is all I want to know.

Jobah and I kissed on the stairs until the sun streaming in from the huge windows in the living room lasered across us. With a final taste, we broke apart, and I led us to my parents' room. My eyes kept darting to the bed in there, while bits and pieces of *The Secret* came flooding back to memory, only I was the female lead and Jobah the male.

I dove into my father's section of the closet he and my mother shared. He had about a half dozen pairs of tan cargo shorts. I'd have to make it seem as if he always had a few in the laundry basket. Maybe I'd take up doing the laundry. Then he'd notice even less.

Rummaging around, I found a plain, green T-shirt. The thought of Jobah's eyes and that shirt had me nearly cheering aloud.

"Here," I said, holding the shorts and T-shirt out to Jobah. "These ought to fit."

He took them and set them on the bed. "Thanks."

"No problem. This is a good plan, Jobah." I was about to say I'd get him some underwear when, with his back to me, he let the animal hide around his waist drop to the floor.

"Jobah!" His butt was right there, perfectly sculpted, the left cheek dimpled as if his maker had left her mark on him.

He started to turn around.

"No, don't!" I quickly put my hands on his shoulders to stop him. Being this close to him while he wore no more than his moccasins literally made my head spin.

"What's wrong?" He looked over his shoulder, putting those dream lips right there in range again.

"Where I come from you don't strip down in front of another person like this." Although with a butt like his, I wasn't against changing the rules completely.

"Why not?"

"It's embarrassing." My grip on his shoulders was loosening by the moment. I knew if I let go of him, he'd turn around and I'd see it all. Parts of me wanted that.

"I'm not embarrassed," he said.

"Clearly." I looked to the ceiling and asked every deity I could think of for the strength to keep him from turning around. Time was short, and we'd already wasted some making out on the stairs. My parents and the rest of the team could be back at any minute. I did not need to be found with a naked boy in my parents' bedroom. I did not want to have to explain that.

"Okay, look," I began, "I understand that perhaps in your village, nudity is no big deal, but on this side, it is. Huge. So could you stand just like this while I make an exit? Then you can get dressed and meet me downstairs. How's that sound?"

"It sounds like you're afraid of me." Hurt laced his words.

I leaned forward and pressed my lips to his bare shoulder. "I'm not afraid of you, Jobah. I'm afraid of me, of how much I want you to turn around."

After letting my hands run down his arms until bumps rose on his tanned flesh and maybe taking one more look at that phenomenal butt, I jetted out of the room and ducked into mine. Closing the door and leaning against it, I tried not to think about Jobah on the other side of the wall, nothing but wood and plaster separating us.

38. Jobah

The clothing Olivia had given me was comfortable, but I wondered how hot I would be outside with so much of me covered. More clothing didn't make sense, but apparently outsiders didn't like to expose themselves. I'd been around nakedness my entire life. In the summertime, most men wore only the breechclout and the women wore only short hide dresses. Their chests were often bared, nothing but their long, black hair to cover their breasts.

Olivia appeared to always be covered. The sleeveless shirts she wore were the closest I'd seen her to revealing herself. They hugged her body and hinted at what was hiding underneath. I'd only just met her, but I wanted to know all of her.

I fished the necklace I had made for Olivia out of the small pouch sewn inside my breechclout. After sliding my dagger into one of the many pouches in the short leggings Olivia had given me, I folded my breechclout and left the room with it. I descended the stairs to find Olivia sitting in the room with the huge stone hearth. When I approached her, she smiled and I wanted to see that smile again and again.

"You look…" Olivia started, a hand going to her chest. She shook her head and the smile returned. "Did you see yourself?"

"No." I didn't remember seeing a pool of water anywhere in that room to see my reflection.

Olivia held her hand out and wiggled her fingers. I took her hand, and she tugged me into a smaller room. She flicked something on the wall beside the door, flooding the room with light, and two people were already in the room looking at us. I skittered to the back of the room, my shoulders slamming into the wall. The boy in front of me did the same.

Wait a minute. The girl was Olivia.

"Why are there two of you?" I asked as I brushed my hair out of my eyes. The boy did the same.

"That's a mirror, Jobah." Both Olivia's pointed at each other. My Olivia hooked her arm around mine and the other Olivia did the same to the boy in the mirror. "Those are our reflections." She dragged me closer. "That's you."

I had only seen myself reflected in water where the details always wavered and the color was never as bright as the real thing. This image in the mirror, however, was crystal clear and still. Was my hair really that black? My skin that tan?

My eyes that green?

"Is this the first time you've actually seen how hot you are?" Olivia asked.

"I don't feel hot." I turned to look at Olivia beside me, but couldn't tear my eyes from the Jobah in the mirror, so dark compared to the Olivia next to that Jobah.

Olivia laughed. "Not hot like warm, hot like incredibly handsome, nice to look at, pleasing." She slid in front of me and reached up on her tiptoes. Her fingers raked through my hair. She played with letting it hang loose, bunching it all up similar to how I'd seen her wear her own hair, and finally settled with hooking some of it behind my left ear.

"Lucky for you, long hair on guys is in style. You'd fit in with the skateboarding crowd." She fussed with it a bit more, and I loved the feel of her fingers against my scalp, along my cheek. "I'd kill for hair this thick and shiny."

I gathered her hair and let it spill down her right shoulder. "You need not be envious of my hair. This is like spilled sunshine."

Olivia's cheeks reddened and she lowered her gaze. "Thanks." She wiggled out from in front of me so I could see myself again in the mirror.

I leaned on the table-like structure below the mirror and stared at my face. Two pure brown dots sat above my left eyebrow. I rubbed at them thinking they were specks of dirt.

"I think those are permanent, Jobah," Olivia said, pressing her fingertip to each of them. "Freckles. Like mine." She indicated similar brown spots on her right shoulder. One on her left elbow that stood out much more than mine against her light skin. Another one on the side of her neck that wasn't quite circular. She stopped there, but I imagined where other freckles might be hiding.

Looking back at myself, I inspected my lips, which were full and dark, my teeth, which were straight and white, my tongue, which was long and pink. I was a child just discovering myself. And Olivia let me. She leaned against the doorway watching me, a pretty half-grin on her lips.

"My eyes are so green. I feel as if they belong to someone else." I widened my eyes, and the black part shrank away revealing more green. "Can you make it dark in here?"

Olivia hit that place on the wall again, and the light blinked out of the room.

"You want it back on so you can continue to admire yourself?" Olivia asked.

"I can see in the dark," I said.

"Oh, right. See, you already had me fooled that you're a regular guy."

"I hope it's that easy."

I followed Olivia out of the room. She took my breechclout and said, "I'll put this in a bag and bring it to you tomorrow. We don't want the team to see it." She scurried up the stairs with it.

When she came back down, she stopped at the glass doors at the rear of the room. Opening one of them, she stepped aside as Moon scooted in. The raccoon jumped to the back of a seat in the large room so that her head was about level with my chest.

Caution. She stared at me with coal black eyes.

I didn't need her to tell me I was risking a great deal with this plan, being here with Olivia, being in contact with outsiders. I knew it was dangerous, but what did I have to lose? This was a way to keep the tribe safe and not have to be alone at the same time. Perhaps I could steer the dig team away from more discoveries while I got to enjoy Olivia's company. While I figured out what I was supposed to do with my life as a Penta.

"She looks like she's mad at you," Olivia said, standing slightly behind me.

"She wants me to be careful. My people don't trust outsiders for good reasons."

"Do you trust me?" Olivia tugged me around to face her. Moon hopped down and went off to investigate the rest of the cabin.

I pulled out the necklace and took Olivia's hand. Turning it palm up, I placed the necklace in her hand. "I made this for you, and yes, I trust you."

Olivia picked the necklace up by the cording and inspected the slate I'd threaded onto it. She had the same shaped earrings on again, and her hand went to them.

"Do you know what this symbol means?" She dangled the necklace between us.

"No, but you like it, right?"

"It's one of my favorite symbols." After fingering the slate and taking a long moment just to look at it, she put the necklace around her neck and motioned for me to tie it.

I scooped her hair out of the way, loved the way the silky strands slipped between my fingers, and secured the necklace. Olivia turned around and the slate symbol fell right in the hollow at the base of her throat. I liked how it nestled there, safe and warm against her body.

"Are you going to tell me what the symbol is, what it means?" I asked.

"Not yet. We'll let it work its magic first." She winked a blue eye at me and dropped a kiss on my lips. Merely a quick brush, but my insides rushed around at the contact.

Was it magic? It was definitely something.

39. Olivia

I couldn't stop looking at him. Jobah sat beside me on the couch sharing a bag of potato chips—something he had never eaten before—and every time our hands touched reaching into the bag, fireworks went off inside me.

"So we'll keep the story simple," I said, trying to focus on the important business of inventing Jobah Everleaf, normal high school male. "You're seventeen, right?"

Jobah nodded. "Like you."

"Yeah, so that would make you a senior like me as well. That means you've completed three years of high school. Do you know the name of that school we saw from the woods today?"

"No." Jobah crunched noisily on chips, and I pictured him in the cafeteria at Sunderfield High. Eden would drop her Jake Ryan fantasy quicker than it would take her to blow out a birthday candle.

I got up and went to the kitchen. After rummaging around, I located a phone book and brought it back to the living room.

"How many high schools can be in Bigfork?" I said half to myself.

Jobah scooted closer and leaned over to see the pages in the phone book. "What's this?"

"This is a list of all the people and businesses in the area. Their names, addresses, and phone numbers are in here."

"So many people in the world." Jobah's voice was a whisper as he fingered a page.

I held up the book. "This is just the list for Bigfork, Jobah. Most towns have a book about this size or bigger."

His eyes widened. He appeared to be equally amazed and afraid.

"Didn't realize there were so many of us outsiders, huh?" I said.

"I didn't. No." He brushed chip crumbs off his hand and sat back on the couch. "What is where you live called?"

"Rhode Island. It's the smallest state in the United States. Montana's one of the bigger ones." And maybe it didn't suck as much as I thought it would.

"What is it like there? Is it like here? Are there woods?" Jobah came back to the edge of the couch and shifted a tad closer.

Struggling to keep myself from climbing into his lap and making out with him again, I said, "There are woods, but there are also cities. Do you know what a city is?"

"Yes, I've been to the one near here. A bee stung me when I was younger and I got sick. I couldn't breathe and our healers didn't know what to do, so my uncles took me to the outside to get help. I found it all very interesting. Once I could breathe again, that is. I haven't been outside since, but I am so curious."

He looked at me as if he wanted me to tell him the entire history of the world outside his own. I didn't know where to begin.

"Go back to telling me about Rhode Island," he said.

I let out a breath. That I could manage. "It's called the Ocean State because so much of it is coast along the Atlantic Ocean. One of the best things about Rhode Island is the beaches. Normally, in the summer, I'd be at the beach every day with my best friend, Eden, and probably a pack of other people."

"What would you do at the beach?"

"Swim, stretch out on towels and sunbathe, have lunch, play games, judge bathing suits." I laughed, but Jobah stared at me, soaking up every word. I cleared my throat. "We might build something out of the sand too, like a castle or a sea creature."

"Why would you build out of sand?" The skin at the corners of Jobah's eyes crinkled. "It won't last very long."

"That's the point. You build it just for fun, and when the tide comes in, or the sand dries out, it's like the slate is cleaned for the next person to create something."

Jobah's lips puckered in and out as he considered my explanation. "Maybe we could build something by the lake. There is enough sand there."

"I'd like that." I also liked that Jobah was making plans for us to do something together. Had Kevin ever made plans, or had I always been the one to suggest stuff?

"What's wrong?" Jobah asked.

"Huh?"

"Your eyebrows are down here." He tapped his finger to the tip of my nose.

"I was thinking about home." I shrugged.

"Do you miss being there?" Jobah traced circles on my forearm, his touch like feathers on my skin.

"Not as much as I thought I would," I said, "but I think you have something to do with that."

"Me?" He stopped moving his fingers, a slight grin turning his lips up at the corner.

"When my parents said we were coming to Montana for six weeks during my precious summer vacation, they neglected to mention the possibility of meeting a Tree Penta in the woods." I nudged Jobah's hand so he resumed running his fingers along my arm.

"And I thought you said your parents were intelligent."

"Guess they don't know it all."

Jobah pushed the phone book off my lap so it slid to the cushion beside me. He let his fingers trail to my bare thighs, pressed his palm flat to my flesh, and ran his hand back up so he carved a path over my shorts up to my waist. Hooking his hand there, he pulled me closer until I sat on his lap, my legs falling to either side of him. Both of Jobah's arms came around my back, and his hands snaked upward toward my hair.

A little sound slipped from my throat as I circled my arms around Jobah's shoulders. My fingers coursed over the muscles in his back under my father's borrowed T-shirt.

Why had I overdressed him?

Jobah's lips pressed to my neck, slow and warm like drizzling fudge over vanilla ice cream. He forged a trail down to my collarbone and then up to my jaw, finally arriving at my lips. His movements were precise and careful, as if he didn't want to get anything wrong.

I didn't see how he could be anything but absolutely perfect.

40. Jobah

This was not like me at all. With Keryun, kissing had been enough. I had only kissed her because I thought she wanted me to, because it was what a man did when he chose a woman to be his mate.

With Olivia, it was different. So different. I thought she wanted me to kiss her, but what surprised me was how much *I* wanted it as well. Sitting next to her generated a heat between our bodies that I could not ignore. My entire being wanted to respond to that heat, to be encompassed by it, devoured by it. When Olivia accepted my kiss, my touch, and kissed and touched me in return, that heat erupted into a fiery liquid that flowed throughout my body.

Olivia's skin tasted like berries, summer ripe and sweet. Her pulse drummed against my lips as I kissed her neck, and she pressed her body against mine. She fit in my arms as if she had been made to be there. Nothing else mattered while she was this close. Not the fact that I'd become a Penta. Not the fact that I'd had to leave the village. Not the fact that I'd made contact with an outsider and traded my breechclout for an outsider's clothes.

Not the fact that I was pretending to be something I wasn't.

Olivia shifted and pulled me down on top of her. I slid the strap of her shirt off her shoulder and nibbled on the soft skin there while she slid her hands under my shirt. Her delicate fingers ran along my stomach, and my muscles tightened at the sensation. Olivia laughed and did it again.

"I like how that happens," she whispered as she hooked my hair behind my ear so it didn't hang in her face.

"It tickles." I moved to catch her lips with a quick taste.

"I know." Olivia's lips turned up under my own as I kissed her again.

She made a move to pull my shirt off completely, but a sound outside froze her for a moment. A loud crunching thundered at the front of the house.

"Shit." Olivia let go of my shirt and pushed me up to sitting. "They're back again. Sit over there." She pointed to a chair across from us.

The thought of being that far away from her made a chill ripple through my body.

"I don't like it either," she said, "but we have to play it cool. I'm going to give us away completely if you're too close." She dropped a light kiss on my cheek. "Now get over there, and let me do the talking."

I did as she said, but it was hard quieting everything she had stirred to life inside me. Watching her straighten her shirt and finger comb her ruffled hair made me want to rush back to her side. Instead, I dug my fingers into the sides of the chair I sat in and braced for meeting more outsiders.

"Olivia?" a voice called as the front door opened.

The woman who looked like Olivia stepped inside the cabin. When her eyes met Olivia's, she called over her shoulder, "She's here, Peter." When she caught sight of me, she darted her gaze back to Olivia.

Olivia's father came in next followed by three men and a woman.

"Hey, Mom, Dad," Olivia said. She cleared her throat as her parents and the team approached. "This is Jobah Everleaf. He lives nearby."

No lies. I was Jobah Everleaf. I did live nearby.

"Dr. Madeline Bradford." Olivia's mother extended a hand to me, and Olivia brought her two hands together, shaking them slightly up and down behind her mother.

I stood and took Dr. Bradford's hand, shaking as Olivia had indicated. Was I supposed to say something? I was afraid to say the wrong something.

Olivia's mother let go of my hand and her father stuck his in my grip.

"Dr. Peter Bradford. Olivia's father." He made the introduction as if it were a warning, and I had a little trouble swallowing. My throat was sandy dry.

The rest of the doctors and the big guy who ran the backhoe introduced themselves to me, saying,

"Nice to meet you," and "How are you doing?" So far, I was doing all right as indicated by Olivia's subtle head nods and smiles.

The photographer, or Mr. Will Tramond, as Olivia's mother introduced him, was last to look me over. I was taller than this man. He had to look up to see my face, and I liked it that way.

His own face was weathered. I wasn't sure how old he was, but his dull, brown eyes took in the details of me. He alternated his gaze between me and Olivia. I was no longer a secret he could use to force Olivia into doing something for him, and he didn't like it.

His jaw was tight when he said, "Nice moccasins."

Instantly, everyone's gaze shot down to my feet at the moccasins Ninae had made for me last season. A quick survey of their feet showed they all wore brown boots that laced up the front except for Olivia who still wore her sneakers. Clearly, my footwear was not of their world.

"It's the style around here," Olivia said with a slight shrug.

"They look comfortable," Olivia's mother said.

"Wouldn't mind a pair right about now," her father added. "My feet are killing me after today."

"Let's clean up," one of the other doctors said. I already forgot which one he was. "And I believe it's Keli's turn to whip up dinner." He poked the arm of the female standing next to him.

"If by 'whip up dinner,' you mean crack open a can of something, then yes, it's my turn." The woman tapped the man back on the shoulder and the team laughed.

"You'll join us, Jobah?" Olivia's mother asked.

"Yes, thank you." It was the first time I'd spoken, but my voice came out steady.

"Great. It'll be nice to have a local around." She offered Olivia a little smile then the team dispersed to clean up.

Everyone except the photographer.

He stayed standing in front of me, still looking at my moccasins. "Your lunch partner, Olivia?" He swept his gaze to her. His voice was familiar. I thought back to when I'd discovered I could travel in the trees. This was the man talking outside the cabin.

Eye candy. Watching the way he looked at Olivia, I understood who he had been talking about, but not who he had been talking to. I also understood what kind of favors he wanted from Olivia.

He wasn't going to get what he wanted. I'd make sure of it.

"We met when I was running in the woods. He was doing the same." She made it sound like nothing to get excited about, and still she hadn't told any untruths. I was impressed with her skill. She was a *Nahderhi* for certain. Beautiful and wise.

Mr. Tramond let out a growl and pushed his way past me. He disappeared out the glass doors at the back of the cabin leaving Olivia and I staring at one another. Leaving me with a desire to keep Olivia away from him.

"That went better than expected," Olivia said. For the first time, I noticed the shake of her hand as she brushed her hair out of her face.

I gestured to the photographer outside with my chin. "He's not happy."

"We ruined his fun."

"I don't like the fun he had in mind." I stepped closer to Olivia.

She smiled and it was easy to forget about the photographer for a moment. Easy to imagine Olivia and I had long summer days to spend together.

Easy to be one of the outsiders.

41. Olivia

I sat between my parents at the dining room table, Jobah across from me, while plates of pasta rotated around the table. Dr. Sumathai had cracked open a jar of tomato sauce instead of a can of something, and now a semi-fine Italian feast was ready for consuming. I wished I could take Jobah to Mama Rosa's in Sunderfield. That place had an eggplant parm to die for and a violinist who played Italian songs. It was like stepping into Rome for a little while. Was it coincidence that Roman and romantic shared so many letters?

"So how did you come across our Olivia?" my father asked once everyone—except for Tower—was seated. He was probably tinkering with one of his excavation tools.

I nodded slightly at Jobah indicating that he should answer my father.

"I ran into her," Jobah said.

The entire table waited for him to say more while I stifled a laugh. When he didn't, I said, "Literally, Dad. Jobah ran into me." I slapped my hands together and let them fall away from each other until they flopped onto the table. "We were both running in the woods, off in our own little worlds, and then boom."

"We knocked each other down," Jobah added.

"More like he plowed over me," I said, a teasing edge to my voice.

"I apologized," Jobah defended, a slight grin on his lips.

"Do you belong to your school's track team like Olivia?" Mom asked.

"Jobah doesn't run for competition," I said quickly. It was almost a game now to see how far I could go without telling an outright lie. "He runs to get in touch with the earth."

"Nature can be a religion," Dr. Sumathai said reverently.

Yes, help my cause, Dr. Sumathai. Excellent.

"What can you tell us about Bigfork?" Dr. Vakker asked around a mouthful of pasta, sauce dribbling from his fork onto his T-shirt. He swore and rubbed at the spot until a bright orange circle marked him.

Jobah didn't look at me first, which was good. Made him seem more relaxed. "I spend most of my time in the woods, so I'm afraid I'm out of touch with city news."

"I'll bet you know some great spots for taking pictures," Mr. Tramond said. "Maybe you could take me out?"

"Sure," Jobah said.

Why did I get the feeling Jobah wouldn't bring Mr. Tramond back if he took him out?

"What's the story with the book you found, Mom?" I casually reached for bread and offered Jobah a piece. He took one and dragged it through the sauce still in his plate when he saw me do the same. He caught on quickly.

"We won't know until we examine it more and decode the symbols," Dr. Vakker said. "I've got some texts I can consult, but I don't immediately recognize the picture language."

I looked at Jobah, who read my mind.

"Maybe I could help," he said. "I've studied some ancient languages."

"Do you have an interest in archaeology?" My father leaned forward slightly, his fork hovering above his pasta.

Take it home, Jobah.

"Yes, Dr. Bradford. Early people fascinate me."

My mother smiled at my father. Deal sealed. They'd be ready to adopt Jobah now.

I sat back in my chair and corralled Jobah's ankles between my feet under the table. His green eyes flicked up to mine, his hair falling free from behind his ear to dangle around his chin.

"You can have a look at the book after we finish here," my father said. "Unfortunately, it's the only thing we've discovered so far. Maybe tomorrow will turn up other artifacts."

Maybe an artifact was sitting right in front of you, Dad.

Jobah was about to reply when a chainsaw sputtered to life outside.

"What is Royce doing?" Dr. Reese slid back his chair so he could look out the window behind him.

Before he could report on Tower's doings, the chainsaw revved louder as it no doubt met the side of a tree. Instantly, Jobah dropped his fork and grabbed his stomach, a low howl erupting from his throat. He pushed away from the table and stood, but as the blade chewed through bark, Jobah bent over until he was on his knees.

I popped up from my seat and rushed over to his side of the table while everyone else did the same.

"Keli's cooking sucks," Dr. Reese said, "but it's never made anyone sick."

"Shut up, Flint," Dr. Sumathai said. "I think the boy's really in pain."

I pushed through the circle of people and dropped to my knees beside Jobah. I rested my hand on his shoulder. His T-shirt was moist with his sweat.

"Make him stop," Jobah whispered to me.

I scrambled to my feet and bolted outside. I called Tower's name, but he had on a helmet with earphones to block out the roar of the chainsaw. Running at full speed, I got into Tower's line of view and waved my hands. He continued cutting until a thick branch crashed to the ground, then he powered down the chainsaw.

Lifting one of the earphones, he said, "What's up, Ollie?"

"Stop cutting." I started running back to the cabin to see if Jobah was all right.

"I need to clear this area so I can get the backhoe through tomorrow," he yelled back.

He yanked the cord that started the chainsaw and mowed through the saplings in front of him. They fell like spilled toothpicks.

I could only imagine what this was doing to Jobah. I ran back and clamped a hand on Tower's forearm. He shut off the chainsaw and took off his helmet.

"You're hurting Jobah," I said.

"What? How?"

I didn't stick around to explain. When I got back into the kitchen, Jobah was a limp heap on the floor. My mother had a towel pressed to the back of his neck.

"He's passed out," she said when I reached them. "I can grab the medic kit I brought along and examine him, but we need to cool him down first. He's developed an instant fever."

When I pressed my hand to Jobah's forehead, it was burning. I wished we were near the lake. It had worked so well last time, but we'd have to settle for the bathtub now.

"Fill the downstairs tub with cool water," I said to Dr. Sumathai.

Thankfully, she dashed off to do what I'd asked without any questions. My father and Dr. Vakker lifted Jobah and carried him toward the bathroom. They placed him in the tub, clothes and all, while it filled. I kneeled beside the tub and dunked the towel in the cool water.

I was vaguely aware of Mr. Tramond watching everything, but not doing much to help.

Movement on Jobah's tanned skin stopped me before I could press the towel to his forehead. Twisting green vines drew themselves on Jobah's neck. Leaves unfurled off the vines, tattooing his flesh as if he were a blank sheet of paper.

Or a Tree Penta.

A single flash blinded me for a moment as Mr. Tramond took a picture.

42. Jobah

I knew I was in a dream. The edges of the vision were misty and blurred, all the details of the scene fuzzy and faded, yet I recognized the two figures floating toward me. My mother wore a long, white robe that flowed around her narrow frame like a snow-covered stream. Her black hair was buried under the robe's white hood, only a few strands blowing about her delicate face. My father glided beside her wearing leggings made of white hide. A gray and white wolf's fur wrapped around his torso, and a silver dagger glinted at his waist. His hair was twisted into a long, black braid that snaked over his shoulder like rope.

When they reached me, they both stretched out an arm. I took their offered hands, and they pulled me into an embrace—one that felt familiar and right. The wolf's fur was soft against my cheek as my father hugged me. My mother smelled of glacier lilies, and her voice whispered in my head.

Jobah, you have become what you were meant to become, my son.

I stepped out of their grasp and looked from my mother to my father. "What do you mean?"

You are Penta. A gift. You are important. My father braced my shoulders with his hands. He had to reach up to do so, and I was struck by the fact that I had grown taller than him.

"You sound like Ninae."

She is wise. My mother cupped my cheek.

"But what am I meant to do?"

You will see, my father said. *When the time is right, you will know what to do. You must listen. Listen to the trees.*

I hated answers like that. Ones that didn't tell you anything at all. Ones that raised more questions.

"Why are you here?" If they wouldn't tell me my purpose, at least they could tell me theirs.

To push you back to your world, Jobah, my mother said. *It is not your time to be here with us in this one.*

Was she saying I was dead?

I smoothed a hand over my stomach, down my arms. I felt alive.

"What world are you in? What happened to you?" They owed me answers. Real answers.

We fell upon outsiders when we were hunting on that summer day, eleven winters hence. My mother's dark eyes filled with tears. *We didn't want to leave you, Jobah, but it was the only way to protect you and the village. The outsiders tied us, packed us into their machines, and took us far away. They made us work in cold, damp dwellings made of stone. We had little food, little water, little sunshine. Our fingers bled, our stomachs grumbled, our souls ached. We missed you so much.*

My father put his arm around my mother's shaking shoulders and brought her closer to him. She buried her face in his wolf cloak.

We both got sick, so sick, until our bodies let our souls go, my father said. *We thought of you every moment, Jobah.*

My throat stung as I listened to this horrible story. My parents had not deserved a death as cruel as that. I wasn't sure if not knowing how they had died was worse than knowing this. I had always imagined their death to be noble somehow, but the demise they'd described was degrading. Perhaps the elders had been right to force the tribe into seclusion.

Still, not all outsiders were like this. I had seen the proof. I had met Olivia.

The tribe will need you, my father said, *but we will be here waiting for you.*

Always waiting for you, my mother added.

Before I could ask another question, my parents floated away from me. They ascended up into the treetops of the vision and vanished among the leaves. I didn't get to tell them I missed them, loved them.

The next thing I became aware of was the sound of Olivia's voice calling me.

"Jobah, can you hear me? Jobah?"

I slowly opened my eyes, and her face came into sharper focus each time I blinked. I reached up a hand to touch her cheek, but then realized we were not alone.

And I was wet.

"Hey," Olivia said. "You had us scared there for a few minutes." She helped me to sitting.

"How do you feel?" Olivia's mother asked as she shined a bright light into my eyes.

"Cold."

"Let's get him out of the tub," Olivia's father said. "Can you stand, Jobah?" He switched places with Olivia and let me lean on him as I got to my feet.

Water dribbled down my body, but Olivia was ready with a large piece of fuzzy material which she wrapped around my shoulders. She patted my arms dry, concern written all over her lovely features.

"I'm sorry if I frightened everyone," I said, but I only looked at Olivia.

"We're just glad you came to," Olivia's mother said. "Peter, get him some of your clothes to borrow."

Olivia's father let go of my arm, and Olivia took up supporting me. All my limbs were weak and shaky, and I couldn't tell if it was from being cold and wet or from the vision of my parents or from passing out.

"You can change up," Olivia's mother said. "Then come out to the living room so we can have a look at those."

"A look at what?" I shivered as droplets of water loosed themselves from my hair and rolled down my cheeks.

Olivia tugged on the fabric covering me until my left side was exposed. I stumbled back a bit, but Olivia held on to me as I inspected the green, leafy vines that snaked along the skin of my left arm from the back of my hand, up my wrist, and under the sleeve of the shirt. I let the fabric drop to the floor and pulled the shirt off completely. The vines spread across my shoulder and covered my ribs and stomach also on the left side. Olivia nudged me toward the mirror we had looked in earlier today. The strange vines continued up the left side of my neck, around my left ear and disappeared into my hair.

I rubbed at the vines, but they were somehow branded into my skin. Taking a step closer to the mirror, I inspected my right side, but found no odd vines there.

Olivia touched my left forearm, tracing a fingertip along the vines. "They're like tattoos, only they just… appeared."

"They're intriguing," Olivia's mother said. "I've never seen anything like this before."

Olivia's father came back into the room and handed me a pair of short leggings like the ones we'd already borrowed from him. "I've got a T-shirt for you in the living room, but let's examine those first." He pointed to the vines.

Olivia's parents stood there in the small room, their eyes eagerly sweeping over me as if they couldn't take the spectacle in all at once. Thankfully, the other members of the team were not crammed into the room with us.

"Can we have a minute?" Olivia said, snapping them out of their trance.

"Of course," her father said.

"We'll be waiting out there." Olivia's mother followed Olivia's father out of the room, and Olivia closed the door behind them.

"Sorry. They shouldn't be treating you like a science fair project. I knew they were going to do that." She shook her head and came to stand close to me. She went back to tracing the vines. "These are beautiful, Jobah."

"Beautiful? Where did they come from? Why did they appear? What do they mean?" With each question my voice rose higher and louder. I sat on the edge of the tub and cradled my head in my hands. Where were my parents now? Why couldn't they tell me what was happening to me?

Listen to the trees.

What did that mean?

"I don't have the answers to any of those questions," Olivia said. "I only know Tower revved up the chainsaw and started cutting. You keeled over and passed out. We dunked you in cool water to keep you from burning up, then these tattoos appeared." She ran a hand over the vines covering my shoulder. "It was as if an invisible hand drew them while you were unconscious."

Had my parents done this to me? That thought sparked a flash of anger. Did they think I needed one more thing to mark me as inhuman? I'd already made myself an outcast in my village. I'd resorted to pretending amongst outsiders, which I could no longer do with these vines just showing up like this.

Did it have to get more complicated?

"Jobah." Olivia's voice pulled me out of my panic. "I know you're confused, maybe a little scared, but I'll help you. My parents will help you. We'll figure this out."

She pulled me to my feet and wrapped her arms around my waist even though I was still wet. Her head rested against my shoulder and her soft lips pressed against the vines on my neck as she said, "You're not alone."

Without Olivia, I would be.

43. Olivia

The tattoos were a blatant reminder that Jobah was not like me. He was something different. Something more. Something truly magical.

I'd slipped out of the bathroom to let Jobah get out of my father's wet shorts and change into the dry ones. He hadn't wanted me to leave, but I'd assured him I'd be just outside. That's where I was now, leaning against the wall opposite the bathroom, studying the seam of light at the bottom of the door.

Jobah was freaked, and I couldn't blame him, but watching the vines sketch onto his skin while he was unconscious had been unbelievable. Reminded me of the time I'd drawn on Carrie with a Crayola marker after she'd fallen asleep on the couch when she lived at home. Purple had been the color of the week in kindergarten, and I was enamored with the hue. Carrie's arms were blank canvases that, in my mind, had needed some purpleness. When Carrie woke up, she hadn't been too happy to be covered in hearts, both small and large, over both her arms and down her right leg. She'd had to scrub herself red to get my designs off.

The green vines covering Jobah's dark skin, however, were not going to come off with a little soap, water, and elbow grease. I'd rubbed at them as

268

he had, and they appeared to be infused into his skin. The thing was that the more I'd touched the vines, the more I'd wanted to be touching them. They made me feel as if I were running through the woods after a light rain had fallen. Dewy leaves and damp earth scented the air. I was connected to everything when I made contact with those curious vines.

The bathroom door opened, and Jobah filled the threshold. "I was thinking..." His voice trailed off as he absently scratched the vines on his left wrist. He shook his head and clamped his hands on the sides of the doorway. "I was thinking we should tell your parents what I am. The truth."

"Are you sure that's a good idea?" My parents were curious about Jobah now, but we could still keep them in the dark about the details.

"We need their help, Olivia." Jobah rubbed his emerald eyes and tapped a moccasined foot.

I nodded and guided Jobah to the living room. As soon as we entered, my father stood.

"Do you feel better?" my mother asked.

"Yes, Dr. Bradford. Thank you." Jobah studied his feet for a moment. "I'm truly sorry I've disrupted your evening."

"Not at all, Jobah," my mother said. "The other members of the team have retired for the evening on our recommendation so we can have some privacy." She patted the space beside her on the couch. "Come sit here."

I nudged Jobah toward her.

"You mentioned wanting to take a look at this." My father held out the book my mother had unearthed today.

Jobah sat next to my mother and held his hands out for the book. My father, however, held up a finger, then paged carefully through the aged volume. When he found whatever he was searching for, he flipped the book so Jobah could see the page.

"I'd thought the designs on your skin looked familiar," my father said.

I scooted around to the back of the couch and leaned between my mother and Jobah. My eyes instantly darted to the vine tattoos on Jobah's neck, and I had to clasp my hands tightly in front of me to keep from touching him. They called to me, but I forced myself to focus on the book.

The same leafy vines crawled along the edges of the page my father had opened to. Jobah raised his arm and rested it against the page so we could see both the book and the skin designs at the same time. When Jobah's skin touched the paper design, the black ink on the page turned green.

"What the…" My father's eyes were so wide I thought his eyeballs were going to roll right out of his head. "Madeline, did you see that?"

"I saw it." My mother looked up at me then shifted her gaze to Jobah. "Why don't you tell us who you really are, young man?"

"He's Jobah Everleaf," I quickly jumped in.

"That may be his name," my father said, "but it says nothing about what he *is.*"

Jobah had grown quiet on the couch with the book still open on his lap. He'd flipped through a few pages, his fingers smoothing over the symbols drawn on each.

"I'm this." He tapped a fingertip on a symbol that looked like a tree with eyes carved into its bark.

"What does that symbol mean?" my mother asked.

"It means I'm a Tree Penta," Jobah said.

"What is that?" My father lowered to sit on the end of the coffee table in front of Jobah.

I rested my hand on Jobah's right shoulder, careful not to touch the tattoos. They had a power over me, and I needed a clear head to control the situation unfolding before us. Jobah was still rattled. The tight knots that had formed in his shoulders were proof of that.

Jobah sucked in a breath and told my parents about his abilities. He left out the fact that he was part of a hidden tribe still living in the woods nearby, but he told them why he'd passed out when Tower cut into bark. He told them he could make flowers bloom with his breath, see in the dark, move faster than normal, and travel through the trees. That last one was a new revelation to me, and I wondered how he'd figured out he was able to do such a thing. Was it fun traveling that way or was it frightening?

When Jobah was done telling his story—or the parts he wished my parents to know anyway—the doctors looked at him for long, silent moments.

"Say something," I finally said, the quiet getting too loud for me to handle.

"What do you want us to say?" my mother said. "If I hadn't seen those vines appear out of nowhere myself, I'd say this boy was delusional. That the fever he suffered earlier had damaged his brain somehow. That we ought to take him to the closest hospital right away."

Jobah burrowed his head in his hands again, and I shot my mother a look of death. "But you did see the vines appear," I said through semi-clenched teeth, "so what would you say instead?"

"I'd say the boy is what he says he is," Dad said. "He's got no reason to make all this up, we did see the vines appear, and I'm sure if we needed him to, he could demonstrate some of the other abilities he claims to have."

I could hear the gears turning inside my father's head. "No. We are not putting Jobah through a series of tests meant to validate his claims. I've seen most of them in action myself. Today is not the first day Jobah and I spent together."

At this piece of news, both my parents lasered their gazes into me. For a couple of dorks, they did the scary parental look pretty freaking well.

44. Jobah

Olivia's parents were angry when they found out Olivia had pretended to be sick to come see me the other day.

"We took you here in hopes you'd find something that interested you, Olivia," her mother said.

"I found *someone* that interests me." Olivia thrust out an arm in my direction from her position across the room, and I instantly wanted her closer to me.

"I know we're not around much, but we do care about what becomes of you," her father added. "You're only interested in your friends, running track, getting a car—"

"Correct me if I'm wrong," Olivia interrupted, "but I think a quick poll would show that most teenagers my age behave in a similar fashion."

"You're not most teenagers," Olivia's father said. "You are *our* teenager, and we have high expectations for you."

"Since when?" Olivia shot back.

I volleyed my gaze between Olivia and her parents. It made my head swim. I was still a little weak from passing out, and their voices cut through my brain like daggers.

"Since always," Olivia's mother said.

A puff of air left Olivia's lips as her gaze rolled up to the ceiling. "Well, you both fooled me. Neither one of you has been Parent of the Year. It's like you raised Carrie, then said, 'That's it. We're all done. This one's on her own.' You don't know anything about me." She stuck out a finger to point to her father. "And you only started talking directly to me like yesterday."

Olivia's mother looked as if she had been slapped. Her mouth hung open, no words coming out. Her father blinked several times in rapid succession as if he'd gotten the shock of his life.

Wedging the book under my arm, I got up and trudged over to Olivia using furniture in the room to support me along the way. After sinking into one of the chairs near her, I gently grasped her wrist and turned her to face me. Her entire body was tense, rigid.

"Olivia."

She looked at me, the sound of her name softening the muscles in her hand and arm. She shook her head. "I'm sorry, Jobah. This isn't the time for this discussion. We should be helping you."

"No," I said. "These things should not go unsaid between you and your parents. They are what hold you apart." The vision of my parents crept back into my memory. "Parents and children should not be separate. You carry pieces of each other, ties to one another. You are family."

My throat had gotten so tight. I couldn't help but think that if my own parents were around right now, I might not be so confused. If they were alive, surely they could tell me the answers to my Penta questions instead of leaving me with riddles. They could guide me, comfort me.

"He's right," my mother said. "And so are you, Olivia. I know your father and I haven't given you the attention you deserve. It's not enough to provide a roof over your head and food." She pushed her hair out of her face in a move I had seen Olivia do when her hair was down and around her shoulders. "We brought you to Montana to forge a path between our lives. It may seem like we kidnapped you, pulled you away from your friends and your life in Rhode Island, but we only want you to experience the world. To see as much as you can see, then decide what your part in it is."

"Right now," Olivia said, "my part is to help Jobah." She sat beside me and placed her hand in mine atop the book her father had given me. "We'd like your help, but if you don't want to give it, then we'll figure this out ourselves."

Holding her hand calmed the storm of uncertainty swirling inside me. Her touch was miraculous. It had the ability to both soothe and stimulate, to know exactly what I needed. I should probably have left Olivia and her parents to their discussion. Let them work out their differences, heal their relationship. I knew if I had the chance to speak to my parents, I wouldn't let it slip through my fingers. Those chances were not unlimited.

Tonight, however, I needed Olivia. No longer being part of the tribe cut me off from the human connection I had to have in order to not lose myself. With the appearance of these vines on my skin, I was becoming something I didn't recognize anymore. Something that frightened me. As long as Olivia was around, I wouldn't go to pieces. I wouldn't break down and give in to the fear, the insecurity. I wouldn't show weakness. That would make me unworthy of...

Of what?

Of Olivia?

She squeezed my hand, and the questions dissipated like summer fog hanging over the lake.

"We want to help you," Olivia's mother said, "but it's getting late tonight. Did you drive here, Jobah?"

"He doesn't drive," Olivia said. "Do you?"

I shook my head.

"Peter can give you a ride ho—" Olivia's mother stopped abruptly. "Do you have a home, a family?"

This question stabbed my chest, plunged into my heart. "I had both," I said cautiously. I did not want to reveal anything about the tribe. "I have neither now."

"Where are you living then?" Olivia's father asked.

"He lives in the woods," Olivia said. "He's had a difficult night. Can't he stay here? We have plenty of room, and then we can get an early start in the morning helping him."

She let go of my hand, and suddenly I was cold. I reached for the T-shirt Olivia's father had brought out for me to borrow. Covering the tattoos seemed like a good idea while her parents decided whether it was safe to allow me to stay in the cabin with all of them.

"Madeline," Olivia's father said. "A word in the kitchen with you, please."

Olivia's mother nodded. To us she said, "We'll be right back."

As they disappeared into the kitchen next door, Olivia slid her hand under mine, and our fingers wove together. Dark skin, light skin, dark skin, light skin. The different colors didn't stop our hands from fitting perfectly.

"If they say you can't stay," Olivia whispered, angling her head toward the kitchen, "you're staying anyway."

"Olivia, I don't want to get you in trouble." I didn't want to leave her either.

"It'd be worth any trouble." She offered me a grin and brushed her lips against my right cheek. She held my right hand. Stayed on my right side.

Away from the vines.

"Why won't you touch them?" I asked.

Olivia closed her eyes and rested her head on my right shoulder. "It's not like I don't want to. In

277

fact, every single piece of me wants to touch those vines, Jobah. They have power. Until we understand that power, we should be careful."

"You're not afraid of me, are you?" I searched her face for some indication that she wanted me to leave and never come back. I braced for the worst.

Olivia cupped my cheek and dropped a kiss on my lips. "I'm going to say this once more and I want you to truly hear me." She stared directly into my eyes. "I'm not even a little bit afraid of you, Jobah."

She knew just what to say to me.

45. Olivia

The mind slowly realizes
what the heart already knows.
Allow yourself to see,
to believe,
to live.

"He can stay on the couch in the study," my father announced when he and Mom came back into the living room after their little conversation in the kitchen.

"I'll get some extra blankets and a pillow," Mom said. "Olivia, come help me."

I gave Jobah a look, silently asking if he'd be all right by himself downstairs. He squeezed my hand and released it. As I walked away from him, I realized he wasn't going to be alone. My father escorted Jobah into the study. The door closed while my mother and I climbed the stairs.

What was my father saying to Jobah? Would he trick Jobah into revealing his true roots? Would Jobah's tribe be endangered? God, I didn't have the energy to be this tense. Why did I have to run into a Penta in the woods? Would have been much easier to smack into a regular boy. Sure, Mom and Dad probably wouldn't have been too keen on the idea of me hanging out with a normal kid while they were trying to get me interested in archaeology, but socializing with a guy who was covered with vine tattoos that magically appeared didn't win me any points either.

And those tattoos were making me nervous. Not touching them wasn't enough, because merely looking at them created this overwhelming longing inside me. I'd been attracted to Jobah from the start. I could admit that. What wasn't to enjoy? Jobah was tall, muscular, had eyes the color of summer leaves, hair the color of night, and a smile that bordered on dangerous. His lips knew their way around my mouth as if they'd been kissing me for ages, not mere days. The vines covering his left side were artistic, mesmerizing, powerful. That connection to the earth had filled me like nothing else ever had. It was as if a missing piece of me had been returned.

"Take these." My mother's voice dragged me out of my daydreaming. I cradled the two blankets in my arms as Mom pulled one pillow from my bed. "You don't need two pillows, do you?"

I shook my head, and the next thing I knew, a pillow had been added to the two blankets in my hands.

"Do you think he needs more clothes?" Mom asked.

"The shorts and T-shirt he has now are fresh enough. He'll be fine." I started back toward the stairs, eager to be in Jobah's presence again.

"Olivia?" Mom stopped me with a hand on my shoulder.

I turned around to face her, shifting the blankets and pillow to under my right arm. "What?"

"I can see that you... like Jobah." She studied her fingernails, most of which still had dirt under them from the morning's dig.

"He's unique," I said. And kind, attractive, smart, entertaining, amazing. Jobah was so many things and I didn't even know him that well, but I wanted to. I wanted to know everything.

"He's very unique," Mom said. "I just want to caution you. He says he's a Penta, but we don't even know if that's something real."

"Making flowers bloom with his breath was real, Mom. Trust me. I saw it."

"Could be an exceptional illusion, Olivia. You don't know for sure. Scientists need data, hard facts. We don't have any indisputable proof that Jobah is a... a tree spirit. We only have his word." Mom leaned back on the railing of the stairs, almost blocking me from leaving the second floor of the cabin.

"His word is good enough for me," I said. "He has no reason to lie to me, to us."

"Just be careful." Mom patted my hand and led the way down the stairs.

I followed her to the study, and when Mom and I entered, Dad suddenly stopped talking. He and Jobah looked at me, but I couldn't decipher what had been going on. Dad stepped over to me and took the blankets and pillow. He handed them both to Jobah who was standing by the leather couch.

"Here you go. We'll see you in the morning." Dad corralled me toward the door.

"I want to talk to Jobah," I said.

"You can talk to him in the morning." Gently, Mom nudged me out of the room.

I caught a quick glance of Jobah's face before she shut the door. Unease fell like a veil over his features. I needed to be with him, but Mom and Dad were like a wall between me and the study door.

"Get some sleep, Olivia," Mom said. "We'll get to the bottom of all this tomorrow."

Realizing it was futile to argue with them, I nodded and trudged up the stairs. After a shower, I hopped into a light blue tank top and navy cotton shorts and climbed into bed. I wasn't the least bit sleepy. All I could think about was Jobah alone in the study right below my room. Jobah worried about what was happening to him. Jobah thinking I was afraid of him and the tattoos.

I had to settle his mind.

Crawling out of bed, I listened at my door. Everything sounded quiet on the other side. I poked my head out into the hallway, making no more noise than a mosquito. No archaeologists in sight. On silent, bare feet, I skulked down the hall to the stairs. When I reached the study door and lifted my hand to knock, the door opened before a single knuckle met wood.

Jobah's crazy raccoon that I'd forgotten had entered the cabin earlier in the day wiggled between my feet into the study.

Jobah didn't even glance her way. "Hi." His smile told me coming downstairs had so been the right move.

"How did you know I was out here?" I pushed Jobah back so I could enter the room and close the door behind me.

He shrugged his left shoulder, and I watched the tattoos that climbed up under the hem of the T-shirt sleeve. That magnetic pull tugged at me again, causing me to take a few steps closer to Jobah.

"I wanted to make sure you were okay." My voice was strained as I swallowed the desire building up in me.

"I am now." Jobah slid his left hand onto my shoulder, let it slither its way up to my neck, into my hair.

I grabbed the edge of my father's borrowed shirt and peeled it up until Jobah raised his arms. The shirt came off completely and landed on the ground. Pressing my palms to Jobah's chest, my right hand covered the vines while my left hand enjoyed pristine, dark skin.

"I'm staying in here with you." I whispered.

Jobah leaned down and just before he kissed me, he said, "Yes, you are."

His lips were like a glass of water after days of walking in the desert, refreshing, but only an abundance would quench the thirst. I drank him in.

drowned in his summer forest scent until my head was completely clouded with all things Jobah, all things wild and natural.

I wanted him. More than I'd ever wanted anything. My entire life back in Rhode Island belonged to someone else when I was standing here with Jobah, his arms wrapped around me, pressing me to him.

He lowered me to the couch and stretched out beside me. After tugging the blanket over us, Jobah nuzzled my neck with his nose and settled his body against mine. I'd never cuddled this closely with anyone. Kevin hadn't been a cuddler. Then again, I'd never attempted to sleep beside Kevin for an entire night. The thought hadn't occurred to me.

But here with Jobah, it was all I could think about. I wanted to get closer somehow. Wanted to feel his heartbeat against my own skin. Wanted to hold him and be held until the sun streamed in through the windows.

My parents would flip when morning came if they found me with Jobah, snuggled so close, but I was willing to risk it.

What else was I willing to do for Jobah?

46. *Jobah*

I fell asleep next to Olivia. Her pale skin was softer than any hide I'd ever slept upon, and she smelled wonderful. When I'd asked her what the scent was, she'd mentioned a word I didn't know.

Cinnamon.

She'd said it was used for cooking mostly. Promised to make me toasted bread outsiders ate in the mornings that used generous amounts of cinnamon. I knew no food would be as mouth-watering as Olivia.

Her father had warned me about hurting Olivia when he'd taken me into this room with him. I'd told him I would never hurt Olivia. She'd done so much for me in the short time we'd known each other. I'd never met anyone like her. Dr. Bradford said that was because Olivia was special.

He didn't have to tell me that. I already knew it. I knew it the moment I'd run into her on that path in the woods.

Olivia slept tucked under my arm on the couch, all her curves fitting against me beneath the blankets. Huddling like this seemed odd in the middle of summer, but the air in this cabin was cool like autumn. It would be easy to forget that a hot, humid night stretched on outside in the darkness.

Moon was curled up at our feet and making little critter noises in her sleep. Looking at her now, I recalled her warning to be careful. She'd made me angry, but she was right. I had to keep my head about me. Though I was more comfortable than I'd ever been, I had secrets that needed keeping. The village had to stay hidden or my people—or those that had been my people—would suffer. Their way of life depended on seclusion, though I almost couldn't understand it anymore. A few short days interacting with Olivia, seeing things from the outside world, and I didn't want to go back to my old ways. I missed Ninae and Ashlo as well as some other kin and friends, but Olivia's world had many intriguing things to explore.

And of course, Olivia's world had Olivia.

I pressed my lips to her forehead and smoothed her hair away from her cheek. She wiggled her body closer to mine so no empty spaces existed between us. I could have stayed in this position forever.

Closing my eyes, I tried to get back to sleep, but my mind wouldn't shut off and my body was far too aware of Olivia's proximity. I decided to test my traveling abilities to pass the time until morning. I slowed my breathing until my chest barely rose and fell. With eyes still closed, I pictured the tree beside Ninae's dwelling. A rush of air blew my hair around my face and when I opened my eyes, I was that tree. Hopefully, my traveling hadn't disturbed Olivia's slumber.

Run With Me

After stepping out from the pine tree's trunk, I walked over the needle-laden earth until I was near enough to Ninae's dwelling. I expected to find the area dark, but a fire still burned at the back of the structure.

Then I heard voices.

"She won't eat anything," one voice said.

"I've never seen her this sick," another voice chimed in.

"She's weak," the first voice said. "She can barely hold her head up to drink."

"This has progressed rapidly. It doesn't usually happen like this. She must have been putting up a brave front for some time."

"For her grandson probably."

"The one who left?"

"Haven't you heard the stories about him?"

"Only bits and pieces."

"Keryun and Sumahe say his eyes were changed from brown to green," the first voice said. "He's not human anymore."

Lowering my shoulders at their conversation, I crept closer to Ninae's dwelling and peeked in through the open entrance. In the hot weather, my people often left entrances uncovered to let in whatever breeze might dance by. Keryun's mother, our healer, and another woman whose dwelling was nearby kneeled next to my grandmother's pile of hides. With my keen night vision, I could see Ninae's small feet flopping away from each other at the end of her bedding.

287

A faint cough sounded and Keryun's mother leaned forward.

"Drink this, Morina. It'll soothe your throat and chest."

The other woman lifted Ninae to a sitting position and when I saw my grandmother's face, my breath got caught in my throat. Gone was the normal glow. Her brown eyes were clouded, her lips purpled. The skin on her cheeks resembled dried earth, dusty and cracked. When she coughed, her gray brows lowered over closed eyes. Her shaky hand grasped at her chest as if she were trying to keep something from choking her. She hadn't looked ill when I'd seen her last. What had happened?

"Easy, Morina." Keryun's mother wiped Ninae's forehead with a moist cloth, and I was reminded of Olivia caring for me after trees had been cut. The difference was I felt better after Olivia's attention. Ninae appeared no better off.

I couldn't bear listening to the wheezy breathing, the strangled gasps. I stepped into Ninae's dwelling, and Keryun's mother whipped her head around at the sound of my footsteps. I froze in place. Until this moment, I hadn't been sure I was really in the place I'd traveled to. I'd thought it was perhaps all in my mind, a mental trip.

Apparently, I was here in the flesh.

Did that mean Olivia was alone on the couch at the cabin right now? Was she hugging nothing but air in my absence?

"Jobah?" Keryun's mother whispered my name. "You should not be here."

"Shouldn't I?" I lowered to Ninae's side. "She is my family."

Ninae's gaze swam to my face, but she didn't truly see me.

"What is wrong with her?" I asked. At the sound of my voice, Ninae reached out a hand, groping in the air.

"My child. You have come to see me off," she rasped. Those few words sapped her strength, and the other woman kneeling beside her lowered Ninae back to the hides.

"You are not going anywhere, Ninae." I took her hand in mine and could feel all the bones in her fingers. If I squeezed too tightly, I feared those bones would snap.

"My time here is done, Jobah. I go to see my son, your father, and your mother, and all those who have gone on to the next place. They call to me and I join them." She coughed again as she held her stomach.

"No, Ninae," I said. "You're wrong. You have much to do here. Your time is not now."

"The body knows when it is being called," the other woman said. She didn't know what she was talking about.

"What is wrong with her?" I asked again.

Keryun's mother touched my forearm so I would look at her. "Your grandmother is dying, Jobah."

289

47. Olivia

Something walked on me. My eyes shot open, and I was nose-to-nose with Moon. I jumped to sitting, spilling the raccoon off me. She dug her claws into the couch cushion beneath me and hung as if she were doing chin-ups. I gave her a minute, figuring animals had their own ways of righting themselves, but Moon's left paw was stuck by a claw. She went wild trying to free herself.

"Shhh, Moon." I petted the raccoon's head and her body stilled. Gently, I unhitched her claw, and she dropped the short distance to the floor landing on all fours. She ran to the sliding doors and pressed her face to the glass.

"You want out?" I turned to ask Jobah, wondering why he wasn't stirring after Moon's commotion. When I found the section of couch beside me empty, I stood.

Where had Jobah gone? Was he thirsty? Had he needed to use the bathroom? I was certain I would have been awakened if he'd gotten up. Our bodies had been so intertwined he couldn't have extracted himself without rousing me in the process.

Moon scratched at the door and made a cat-like sound at me. I opened the sliding door, and she streaked out, becoming invisible within seconds. I squinted into the darkness. Was Jobah out there? Why would he be?

Was he okay?

I stepped out onto the porch. Humid night air stole my breath away and caused an instant sweat to break out on my skin. I wanted to yell Jobah's name, wanted to hear him reply, wanted him to not be gone.

Staying outside was useless. The darkness was too complete for me to actually go searching for Jobah if he was in fact out there. I went back into the cabin and looked around the study. Jobah's borrowed T-shirt was still on the ground where I had dropped it earlier, so he hadn't taken the time to dress before leaving. Perhaps he was in the bathroom or getting a drink. Maybe the panic and dread building in my chest was for no reason.

I cracked open the study door and peeked into the living room. No lights reflected back at me, but Jobah didn't need lights to see. I shuffled to the bathroom, but it was empty as was the kitchen. Back in the living room, the book my mother had found today was still on the coffee table where my father had left it. Jobah wanted to see that book. He wouldn't leave without getting the chance to look at it more closely.

Would he?

Maybe I'd been snoring in my sleep, and Jobah couldn't take another minute of it. Maybe he'd gone into one of the empty guest rooms upstairs. There were still two unoccupied ones.

I climbed the stairs, poked my head into my room and the guest rooms, but still no Jobah. The upstairs bathroom was not his hiding place either. I searched every room that was not being used by the team and Jobah was nowhere.

Back downstairs in the study, I sat on the couch where I was sure Jobah and I had been cuddling a short time ago. He had the ability to make me feel absolutely peaceful and completely stimulated all at once. Kissing him was like running up to a cliff and not thinking twice about diving off into the air, for you knew the soft, moss-covered earth would cushion your fall.

Had it not been the same for him? And why didn't he take Moon with him? It was as if he'd vanished from my arms while I was sleeping. As if he were a dream that faded upon waking.

I flopped back on the couch and buried my face in the blankets. They smelled of Jobah, all sun-soaked leaves, so I hadn't imagined we'd done some serious making out on this couch. He'd kissed me senseless, and I'd traveled along those tattooed vines on his skin as if they were a road map. Best trip I'd ever taken.

But where was Jobah now?

I stretched out and pulled the blankets over me. I could do nothing about finding him right now. In the morning, I'd go to his shelter in the woods. Maybe he'd gotten freaked about staying the night in an outsider's cabin. Maybe it was all too much for him. Maybe he preferred sleeping on the hides in his shelter to being crammed on a couch with a girl right against him, giving him no space at all.

Maybe he preferred being alone.

I shook my head against the pillow. He didn't want to be alone. He wanted answers. That book my mother found could have answers, and Jobah knew that. He would come back to see the book if not to see me.

Closing my eyes, I tried to go back to sleep. Back to that place of extreme comfort where nothing mattered but the sound of Jobah's breathing beside me, the feel of his body wrapped around mine, the taste of his skin under my lips. Without Jobah here, that place was gone. I was back to being lost in the night. Back to wondering what I was missing in Rhode Island. Back to wanting to talk to Eden so she could tell me I wasn't crazy for believing in tree spirits.

What if Mom was right? What if Jobah was a regular boy who had fooled me somehow? Could those flowers he bloomed have been a trick? Did cutting trees really have no effect on his body? Was he a member of a Veiled Tribe? Or was it all an act to make fun of a city girl stuck in Montana for the summer?

My teeth clenched as I mentally stomped down this path of thinking. It wouldn't be the first time a boy had duped me into believing he was more impressive than he really was. Kevin had gotten me with his lifeguard persona. He'd made himself out to be this CPR-giving, expert swimmer, gee I care about you type, when actually he only cared about Kevin and Kevin's Summer of Fun in the Sun. He could have tried to rescue me from this Montana trip. Could have brainstormed ways for me to get out of it.

Instead, he'd cut me loose without any fight whatsoever.

Jobah probably wasn't any different. Maybe he was worse. Kevin hadn't gone through the trouble of donning animal hide and building a piece-of-shit shelter in the middle of the woods. He hadn't concocted an entire story about being a Penta and having to leave his tribe.

He hadn't kissed me as if I'd meant something special to him.

48. Jobah

I refused to believe what Keryun's mother had told me. Ninae could not die. She was the formidable woman who had raised me when my parents left this life. She had fed me, clothed me, and housed me. Ninae had taught me the ways of our tribe. She'd showed me what I needed to know to survive in the woods. She'd encouraged me when I wanted to be a tribe builder and farmer. She had insisted I was something special even when my Penta abilities divided me from the tribe and from her.

Ninae loved me.

Was I being punished for thinking of only myself? Should I have stayed in the village? Could I have prevented this sickness from finding Ninae if I had been here with her?

These questions spiraled around my head as Keryun's mother mixed herbs with water beside my grandmother's bedding. The other woman had gone to her own dwelling once I'd showed up. I was thankful for the dimmed lighting in Ninae's home. It allowed me to hide my eyes from Keryun's mother. I feared she would not stay to help Ninae if she saw how changed I was.

"Sit her up," Keryun's mother directed.

I did as she asked, but had to scoot behind Ninae to keep her in a sitting position. Her body was so frail in my grip, as if a mere feather were leaning against me.

Keryun's mother put a wooden bowl to Ninae's lips. "Drink, Morina."

Ninae tried her best to swallow the offered herbs, but much of it dripped down her chin and into her lap. I wiped the spills with a cloth and eased her down to a reclining position on her hides.

"I'm sorry, Jobah." Ninae's voice was thin and scratchy.

I leaned down to hear her better. "There's nothing to be sorry about."

She shook her head before I could say more. "No. I should have made you stay. This is your home, your people. True, you are a Penta, but you are first one of us." She slowly raised an arm, her fingers curling over my shoulder as she tugged me down closer. "I am proud to call you my grandson, Jobah. I know that whatever you do will be for the good of everyone. Remember what I told you."

"What did you tell me, Ninae?"

"Love always does good, Jobah."

She let out a weak cough.

She never took in another breath.

"No." Hot tears stung the corners of my eyes. "No, Ninae. Don't." Suddenly, my hands were on her shoulders shaking her gently. "Wake up."

"Jobah." Keryun's mother put her hand atop one of mine. "Life has left her. She's on to the next place. We must let her go."

I stood and turned in a circle. The dwelling was too tight. Air didn't move. I had to get out. I bolted for the entrance and ran smack into Ashlo outside.

"Jobah, what's wrong?" He guided me to my knees when he realized I wasn't supporting myself.

"My grandmother is gone." My voice didn't sound like my own. Surely, it was someone else's grandmother who had died. Not mine. Not the one I'd known my entire life and had depended on.

"Oh, Jobah." Ashlo wrapped his arms around my shoulders and let me cry. He stayed with me on the ground until I had no more tears left to shed.

Keryun's mother came out of my grandmother's dwelling as Ashlo was helping me to my feet.

"I will get Denri and organize the journey ritual." She hesitated with her hand half reached out to me. Her eyes narrowed as her gaze swept over my left side and her arm dropped. She'd caught a glimpse of the vines. She wouldn't touch me.

I walked back into Ninae's dwelling on unsteady legs and kneeled before her. She looked so peaceful on her hides, her hands clasped at her stomach, her face relaxed. Our people believed that it took time for the spirit to leave the body and find its way to the next life, but Ninae had already found contentment. It was quicker for those who were ready for death. Her lips were turned up at the corners just slightly. Enough that she looked as if she had learned some great secret, one that held all the answers to all the questions.

"She will watch over you always," Ashlo said.

I nodded, the tight knot in my throat keeping me from speaking.

"What can I do, Jobah?" Ashlo reached across and rested a hand on my shoulder.

I wanted him to get Olivia. I wanted to hold on to her while my world slipped away beneath my feet, but I couldn't have that now. "There is nothing you can do."

Ashlo let his hand slip from my shoulder. "You will stay with us now, won't you?"

"I shouldn't be here now, Ashlo." I lowered my voice. "I have been in the company of outsiders. I have learned some of their ways. I feel a connection to one of them."

"A connection?" Ashlo frowned. "What do you mean? There can be no connections with outsiders."

"See? Even you don't understand, and your mind is more open than most here. I can't explain it, but I know all outsiders are not evil. We have been lied to, Ashlo."

"You have not been lied to."

Ashlo and I snapped our heads to the entrance where Denri, our shaman chief filled the doorway.

"You have been protected. There is a difference."

Run With Me

He passed into Ninae's dwelling making no more noise than a leaf growing. I braced myself to be told to leave the village, but instead, Denri kneeled before my grandmother and held his hands over her. He chanted in the old language of our people. It had the reverence of a prayer, a blessing.

"Your grandmother was a valued member of this tribe. Her handiwork with hides has kept us clothed for many seasons, and she has passed that skill on to many women. She will be missed among us, but we wish her well on her journey to the next place."

Denri stood and motioned for Ashlo and me to follow him outside. "Ashlo, rouse our people to pay their respects to Morina Everleaf."

Ashlo hesitated for a moment, looking to me.

"Your kin will be fine. Do as I say. Go." Denri swept his arm out to the village behind him, and Ashlo jogged to the nearest dwelling.

"Sumahe has spoken to me about you, Jobah." Denri folded his arms across his bare chest. For an elder, he was still in impressive shape. Though his skin was weathered, the muscles beneath hadn't aged. I'd once seen him carry an entire deer from where he'd killed it back to the village. He'd just hoisted the animal onto his shoulders and walked.

"Sumahe isn't fond of me," I said.

"To be sure, but the question is has he told me the truth about you?" Denri narrowed his dark eyes at me. "It is too dark out here to see if your eyes are changed from brown to green as Sumahe has said they have."

"They are green." No point in lying to him. Daylight was playing on the horizon. Denri would be able to see my eyes soon enough.

"And have you had contact with the outside? Have you spoken to people there?"

"Yes."

"What have you told the outsiders about us?" Denri took a step closer to me and my heart hammered in my chest.

"I have not told them where this village is."

"My question was what *have* you told them, not what haven't you."

Denri was close enough now that I could smell the paint he used to mark himself as shaman chief. In the dark, I could see the black and white lines running down his nose and looping over his cheekbones.

"I have only told them about me. That I'm a Penta. They know about my abilities. They were going to help me test them, figure them out, figure *me* out."

I held my breath. Denri was going to cleanse my mind and make me leave. Now that Ninae was gone, I guess the leaving part didn't bother me as much. She was the only reason to come back.

But the cleansing. That was the part to fear. If Denri erased my memories of this village, what else would be erased? Would I forget Ninae and where I'd come from? Would I forget what little I remembered of my parents?

Would I forget Olivia?

49. Olivia

I couldn't fall asleep after realizing Jobah had left. Questions circled around the walls of my mind, each one making me trust my feelings for him less and less. Why did I have feelings for him anyway? We were nothing alike. Our worlds were so completely different. I'd only known him for a couple days. Calling my reaction to him *feelings* wasn't right. We didn't know each other well enough for feelings.

And yet, I couldn't stop thinking about him.

A bond existed between us. I certainly felt it, but did he? Was this thing just one-sided?

I ran a fingertip over my lips where Jobah's mouth had skillfully explored the terrain. No, it was definitely *not* one-sided. He had to have felt something close to what I felt. His kiss and his touch went far beyond the casual and the curious. Not going all the way had been a challenge.

Frustrated, I finally threw off the blankets and went back up to my room. No sense in being found in the study if Jobah wasn't in there. It was worth the trouble I'd get in to be with him. Staying down here now was stupid.

In my room, I slipped into bed and gazed out the window on the far wall. The sky above the treetops grew bluer as the sun slid up from its resting place below the horizon. It would be morning soon, and though I knew it probably wasn't going to turn up any results, I still wanted to go to Jobah's shelter in the woods to see if he was there. I could put all this worrying and doubt aside if he'd merely gone to his shelter due to discomfort at being in an outsider's cabin.

After about an hour, I got out of bed and dressed in black shorts, a purple tank top, and my running sneakers. I gathered my hair into a ponytail, went downstairs, and stepped out onto the deck at the back of the cabin. The forest was growing ever lighter as the sun peeked through the trees. Enough light to find Jobah's shelter and hopefully find Jobah.

Meandering over ferns and around boulders, I soon broke into a run when the path was clearer. It felt great to run. My feet kicked up dewy earth that smelled of overnight rain and blooming flowers. Air swirled past my face as I sprinted through the brush. Sweat trickled down my forehead creating salted rivers on my skin. Muscles burned with use. I was so utterly human. So totally average.

So not anything like Jobah.

When I reached his shelter, I knew right away that he was not inside. The embers in his fire pit did not glow. He hadn't built a fire here recently. I poked my head into the shelter and was encouraged to find his stuff still inside. He hadn't stopped here and packed everything up so he couldn't have gone too far.

His village. That had to be where he was, but I had no clue where the village was hidden. Jobah had been careful not to talk about its location, and I wasn't equipped to wander around the woods looking for concealed tribes.

But my parents were.

I ran back to the cabin, and when I burst into the kitchen, sweat-soaked and panting, my father looked up from his coffee mug.

"Olivia, are you all right?" He stood and crossed the kitchen in three big steps.

"Jobah's gone," I managed between breaths.

Dad stepped back and looked across the living room to the closed study door. He scratched his head. "You mean he's not in there?"

"No. Look, there's more to tell you about Jobah." I lowered onto a chair at the kitchen table.

My father sat next to me. "I'm listening."

I inhaled and sifted the breath out slowly. I was betraying Jobah's trust by telling my father anything, but I couldn't let Jobah disappear on me. He was too important. If there was a chance I could find him, talk to him, then I was going to take it. Maybe that was selfish, but I'd been accused of worse. I had to at least make sure he was okay. With new Penta abilities cropping up on him, he could be sick or hurt or in some kind of trouble wherever he was.

I told my father everything. How Jobah was from a Veiled Tribe, but they'd been afraid of the changes in him so he'd left. How he wasn't supposed to have any contact with outsiders. How he'd been living in the woods in a ramshackle shelter, because he couldn't cut new trees without writhing in pain. I even told him how I'd snuck down to the study to be with Jobah.

When I was done, Dad sat there blinking. Finally, he shook his head and focused on me. "He's what we've been looking for out here."

"There has to be a way to find his village, find him, but not destroy his tribe's way of life, Dad."

"We don't want to destroy anyone's way of life," my father said. "That's not what archaeology is about. We merely want to learn. I mean, it's fascinating to think that in the technologically advanced world we live in, some humans decide to disregard it all and live primitively. And yet..." He paused, tapping the side of his glasses.

"And yet what?" I didn't have time for him to get lost in his musings.

"Jobah passed for a regular kid your age. The potential to hop into the current century is there."

"I think Jobah is different from the rest of his people," I said. "Maybe being a Penta makes him more able to blend in with us. I don't know." I shrugged then rested my hand atop Dad's on the kitchen table. "Will you help me find him?"

"Let's wake your mother and the rest of the team." Dad stood and patted my hand. "We'll find Jobah. An entire tribe of people can't hide forever."

But they'd hidden this long.

We had miles of woods surrounding the cabin in all directions. Jobah's village could be anywhere. Worse still, he may not have retreated to his village. Maybe he'd gone to the outside. Maybe he'd gone to that school he'd shown me.

The school. Jobah had said he went to that hill to spy on the school when he was living in his village. That had to mean his village was within walking—or running—distance from the hill.

"I think I know a place where we can start looking," I said.

My father smiled. "I think we've turned you into an archaeologist."

He left the kitchen to assemble the team, and I stopped in the living room to pick up the book my mother had found yesterday. I opened it and fingered the leafy vines bordering the pages.

I wasn't sure about being an archaeologist, but I was sure about my need to find Jobah. Making certain he was all right was the only thing that mattered.

50. Jobah

"A Penta only shows up in a tribe when it is needed." Denri said.

We sat around a small fire inside his dwelling in the center of the village. Keryun's mother and some of the other women in the tribe were preparing Ninae for the journey ritual.

I was numb. Part of me knew my grandmother was gone. That I'd never see her smile again, hear her laugh, learn from her advice. Another part of me, however, thought perhaps this was all a dream. Maybe it was a Penta test meant to see how strong I was, how capable I was at dealing with tragedy. If the ache in my chest was any indication, I was failing miserably.

Focusing on Denri's dark eyes, I said, "What could I be needed for? I'm not even sure what being a Penta means? I have these odd abilities, but what use are they?"

"No Pentas have emerged in centuries, Jobah, so I don't know everything about tree spirits either. No one in the tribe does."

Instantly, I thought of the book Olivia's mother had uncovered at the dig site. It could have the answers, but getting outsiders involved was risky.

307

"These markings," I pointed to the vines on my arm. Denri had inspected them before we'd entered his dwelling. He hadn't commented on them so I had no idea what the shaman was thinking. "I have seen them in a book."

"What book?" Denri's skin crinkled around his eyes as firelight flickered off his features.

"A book one of the outsiders found."

Denri's eyes widened. "So it exists." He stroked his long, silver braid of hair.

"What exists?"

"*The Penta Chronicle*," Denri said.

I waited for him to explain, but instead he asked, "How many outsiders are there? How close are they?" He stood and paced around the confines of his dwelling.

"There are eight of them total. Olivia and her parents. One man in charge of a machine that moves quantities of earth, three scientists, and a photographer. They are staying in a cabin west of here. Not far. Running distance."

Denri rubbed his forehead and shook his head. "This is why you have been chosen to be a Penta. You will keep us safe from the outsiders."

"Me? I can barely take care of myself. I've let my grandmother die while I've been engaging in nonsense with an outsider."

It hadn't felt like nonsense with Olivia though. It felt like something deep and significant. "Besides, I don't think these outsiders wish us harm, Denri."

His worried face softened for a moment, his eyelids drooping slightly as if he were remembering a sadness. He stopped pacing and after staring at me for a stretch of silence, he dug around his cache of herbs.

"Olivia is not like any of the outsiders we have learned about, Denri." I thought of leaving her on the couch in the cabin. Being close to her and kissing her had pushed the Penta matters out of mind. With Olivia, I could be the boy I had been before. She didn't judge, didn't fear.

Where did she think I had disappeared to? Was she looking for me? Was she upset?

I had a sudden urge to travel back to the cabin and let Olivia know where I was. She deserved that courtesy. I couldn't stand the thought of hurting her, especially after she had been so wonderful to me.

Getting to my feet, I started to tell Denri I had to leave, but he spoke before I had the chance.

"*The Penta Chronicle* was written by past Pentas," he said.

That had me frozen in place.

"It is said that the last Penta of our tribe buried the book for safe keeping," he continued.

"Why didn't someone keep the book in the village?" Anger shot through me. Many of my questions could have been answered by reading a record from a true Penta. I would never have had to leave the village. I would have been able to explain myself to those that feared me in the tribe. They would have understood. Someone should have kept the specifics of Pentas alive among the people.

"The last Penta wasn't able to make it back to the village. The tales say she sacrificed herself to save this tribe as she was meant to do."

She? The last Penta had been a female? She'd died trying to protect the village? Was that my fate as well?

"She was an Everleaf, Jobah. You are from her line."

My mouth opened, but no words came out.

"You will stay here and honor your grandmother with the rest of the village." Denri rested his hands on my shoulders and looked up to my face. "You will have no more contact with the outsiders, Jobah Everleaf. Forget this Olivia person. Your duty is to this tribe. You will protect us if the outsiders come."

Again, I opened my mouth to protest, but Denri opened his palm and blew a collection of herbs in my face. I took in a breath and sneezed, coughed, sputtered. My throat burned.

"What was that?" I rasped, my eyes watering as I regulated my breathing. Wiping my eyes, I tried to focus on Denri's face, but the inside of his dwelling spun around me. I put my hand to my stomach to settle it. Lowering to my knees, I squeezed my eyes shut to block out the dizziness, but it was still there, inside my skull.

"Forgive me, Jobah. Contact with outsiders is a grave offense. You know that. I will not banish you from the village. We need you, so you must stay, but as a Penta you may be more powerful than me. I just don't know. I am a mere shaman chief. I have not been chosen by the spirits. You have their strength behind you. It is already evident in your developing abilities. I can't take the chance that you will let your time on the outside change your loyalties." Denri helped me to my feet and guided me out of his dwelling.

I clung to his arm, not able to see through the spiraling haze of my vision.

"Please, Denri," I said. "I will do whatever needs to be done for the tribe, but don't make me forget the outside."

"You gave me no choice, child."

The next thing I felt was water on my face, splashing then dribbling down my cheeks. Slowly, my vision cleared, my throat stopped burning, my stomach eased. I was sitting on a log bench in front of Ninae's dwelling, the sound of Keryun's mother's voice singing pre-ritual songs wafting out on the warm, summer air. I gulped in several deep breaths and rested my head in my hands.

Looking up, I watched Denri as he walked back to his dwelling, then I focused on the vines on my hand. For a few agonizing moments, I had that feeling I was supposed to remember something, but couldn't. A sense that important information was just out of my grasp.

Squeezing my eyes shut and taking in a breath, I traced the vines on my forearm and a warmth traveled through me. Then Olivia's face came into view in my mind. The mental image shifted to her slender fingers gliding along the vines as I held her close. I thanked the spirits for letting me remember.

I would protect the tribe if that was my destiny as a Penta. I would figure out my abilities and what use they were to me. I would even withstand the stares and whispers of the rest of my people as I stayed among them.

What I would not do, however, was forget Olivia.

51. Olivia

"Well, what are we waiting for?" Mr. Tramond said. Out of the whole group, he seemed more excited about finding Jobah's tribe than the rest of the team. He wasn't even an archaeologist.

Telling my parents the truth about Jobah made me feel like scum. As if I had taken a knife and jabbed it right into Jobah's beautiful, vine-tattooed back and twisted it multiple times. He'd left me no choice though. I had to make sure he wasn't in trouble. Finding his village was about finding him. If my parents found what they were looking for in the process, so be it.

"Olivia, myself, and Madeline will take the lead," my father said. He had a bag slung over his shoulder full of maps, flashlights, food provisions, cameras, his laptop, a few books, a first aid kit, water bottles. There may have even been an inflatable raft inside that pack.

"Keli, Simon, and Flint will stay in the middle, keeping an eye out for signs of a village. Will, you'll need to be ready with the cameras, and Royce, you take the rear."

"I always have to be the ass of the operation." Tower roared at his own joke, but no one else was in the mood for humor. The rest of the team was in mission mode.

We filed out of the cabin, and the day was already heating up. Waves of warmth squiggled up from the gravel in the parking lot as we crossed it and burrowed into the denser woods. I led the team with my parents a couple steps behind me walking side-by-side. No one talked, and it felt like a covert operation in which we were looking for an elusive figure buried in the woods.

When we reached the hill Jobah had taken me to, we climbed it and Mr. Tramond let out a whistle.

"Great view up here." He turned in a careful circle as if he were surveying the land.

"Jobah was interested in *that* view." I pointed to the school basking in the rising sun. Several teens were doing jumping jacks on the soccer field, their bright yellow and black uniforms making them look like bees. I thought of my track coach back home. Luckily the notion of practicing this early on a summer morning had not occurred to her.

"He wants to learn our ways," Mom said, her voice sympathetic.

I nodded. "He's a Penta now, but I don't think he was happy living in his tribe before he changed. He's too curious to be cooped up in a secluded place."

The word *prisoner* flashed in my mind. Followed by *captive* and *caged*. Maybe I'd been spoiled living in my world with all its freedoms, but something about taking away a person's right to choose how and where they wanted to live struck a wrong note with me. Jobah deserved to experience everything the world had to offer. I wanted to help him with that.

"If we could get higher," Dr. Sumathai began, "maybe we could see the village. They must have cleared an area to build it."

"Should have brought my cherry picker," Tower said.

"What does picking cherries have to do with anything?" I asked.

"A cherry picker is a truck with a mechanical arm and bucket that can reach up high," my father said.

"Gives quite the ride," Tower said.

I craned my head back and looked at the nearest pine tree. "If Dad and Tower can hoist me up, I think I can climb this tree." I patted its trunk, studied its pattern of branches.

My father and Tower dropped their packs and took positions on either side of me. Making stirrups of their hands, they stood with their legs shoulder-width apart. I held onto their shoulders as I set my feet in their waiting hands. Feeling very much like the cheerleader I never wanted to be, I slowly stood in their grip. Once I got my balance, I grabbed hold of the first branch I could reach. Dad and mostly Tower pushed from below while I pulled from above.

When the men let go of me, I shimmied up the tree like some small woodland creature. I thought of Moon and wondered if she had found Jobah.

As I climbed, I was uber-careful not to break any branches. If Jobah was close by, I didn't want to cause him any pain. When I reached as far as I could go, I swiveled my head in all directions. The view was ridiculous. The lake Jobah and I swam in was off to my left, rimmed with mountains. I finally understood the lyric, "For purple mountain majesties," in the song "America, the Beautiful."

The high school was in front of me and much larger than Sunderfield High. It resembled a college campus more than a high school now that I could see the extent of it. Buildings dotted the grounds, yet many green spaces were woven into the overall design. The familiar black track making a giant oval around one of the fields called out to my feet.

Behind me, sunlight reflected off glass, and I knew that to be our cabin. That left only one direction to inspect—to my right. I stayed focused in the cabin's direction, almost not wanting to look where Jobah's tribe no doubt nestled, untouched by the outside for who knows how long.

Did I want to be the one who ruined it for them? Was my reason for doing so justified? Did concern for Jobah outweigh the privacy of the tribe?

Sucking in a breath and ignoring the questions both in my head and coming from the team below, I slowly turned to my right. The sun blinded me at first, and I squeezed my eyes shut against the piercing brightness. I let the warmth flood my face, adjusted my grip on the pine tree's trunk, and opened my eyes.

I only saw one thing.

52. *Jobah*

Keryun, being our tribe's finest singer, sang the songs of the journey ritual as my grandmother's body was carried in a wide circle around the central ceremonial fire. Ninae wore a robe of white fur like all the dead wore on their send-off to the next place. Her hair had been twisted into a long, silver and white braid. Her face was slack, her skin stretched tight over high cheekbones. Her lips had lost their pinkish hue, the cold purple of death painted across them instead.

She didn't look like Ninae anymore.

Ashlo stood beside me, his hand resting on my shoulder, and to be honest, that support was the only thing keeping me from slumping to the dirt at my feet. My legs felt as if they belonged to someone else. My head throbbed. My eyes stung. For someone who wasn't quite human anymore, I was experiencing grief as a human would. There were apparently no benefits to being a tree spirit.

I forced a breath into my lungs, let it sit there for a few painful moments, then gushed it all out in one long stream. The noise I made caught the attention of several people near me.

Near me.

Technically, they weren't near me. Everyone had left a wide arc of space around me. I'd heard the whispers about my eyes, about the vines on my flesh, about my contact with the outsiders. I felt the distance between the tribe and myself as if it were a kick in the shins.

Sumahe stood on the other side of the ceremonial fire. I'd felt his gaze on me earlier. He was part of the reason the tribe still feared me, and to be honest, I wanted to give him—just him—cause to fear me. That wasn't like me. I didn't usually hold grudges.

Maybe being on the outside was changing me.

Lifting my chin slightly, I focused on Ninae now being placed over the fire. Animal hides—the ones she'd used as bedding—were draped over her body. I looked at her face one last time as Keryun's voice rose over the sound of the drums. The beat started out fast, strong, and robust, but faded to a slow, soft whisper of a beat until it stopped altogether, mimicking Ninae's heartbeat in life coming to a stop as death conquered her. The hides were unrolled over her face, but that didn't change the fact that it was still Ninae under there.

I'd been to send-off ceremonies before, but nothing prepares a person for losing a loved one. Especially when that loved one had been the center of your world, the axis around which you had revolved since you were a boy.

A boy.

I wasn't a boy any longer. I wasn't a man either. I was a Penta, charged with protecting this tribe from outsiders. A foolish duty when the outsiders I'd encountered didn't wish to hurt us.

I studied my feet, hoping the ground would open up and swallow me. I didn't want to think about anything. Not about being a Penta. Not about losing Ninae. Not about Denri trying—and failing—to make me forget the outside. Not about Olivia. I just wanted to be left alone with Ninae so I could converse with her and she'd tell me exactly what to do. I knew that wasn't going to happen, but it didn't keep me from wanting it.

"Jobah?" Ashlo gave my shoulder a slight squeeze. "It is time for you to speak."

I'd forgotten about this part. The last thing I wanted to do was stand between Denri and Keryun with everyone's eyes boring into me.

"Your grandmother deserves your words, Jobah," Ashlo whispered in my ear as he nudged me forward.

Slowly, I walked over to Denri and Keryun. Our shaman nodded encouragingly. Keryun, my almost mate, took several steps back to distance herself from me. To think I once considered spending my existence with her.

I looked over the assembled tribe surrounding the fire where Ninae's body burned, her ashes fluttering into the embers only to be collected tomorrow and scattered wherever I deemed appropriate. Dozens of brown eyes studied me, and I cleared my throat. That small sound sent some of the closest people stumbling back. What did they think I would do to them?

"Morina Everleaf," I began, figuring my best plan was to get this speech over with as soon as possible, "my grandmother, your time here has touched us all, and we return you to the dust the spirits used to create you. Your soul is free now. May your journey to the next place be swift. May you watch over us until we meet again."

Keryun's voice lifted in song again, and the tribe joined in. I couldn't get my throat to work. The words, the melody, just got stuck. I could barely swallow the sadness.

When the tune ended, Denri addressed the tribe. "My people."

I slithered back to Ashlo, but Denri stopped me with a hand on my arm.

"My people," he repeated, "I see your fear of this boy. I feel it in the air."

I needed to leave. Right now. I closed my eyes and pictured the parking lot in front of Olivia's cabin, but no gush of wind puffed across my face. When I opened my eyes, I was still before the tribe, firmly in Denri's grip.

Firmly in Denri's grip.

Could I not travel because our shaman was holding me? What magic was he using to bind me here?

"Jobah has been charged with protecting us," Denri continued.

"From what?" Sumahe called out.

"Anything that may bring us harm," Denri replied. "He is a Penta. You should not fear him."

"You should honor him." Ashlo maneuvered through the people to reach me. "He is changed. That is true, but it is not cause to reject him. Jobah is still one of us."

"He has been outside." This from a faceless voice in the crowd.

"And on the outside," Denri said, "he has learned of threats to our village. This knowledge is valuable to us, and I have taken care of Jobah's memories of outside."

I feigned a confused expression and hoped no one caught the lie in my eyes. Denri's magic had not worked on me. I remembered every detail of the outside. Every detail of Olivia's face.

Those memories were more real to me than my seventeen winters living in the village. The tribe would always be a part of me. Ninae would always be a part of me, but Olivia and her world woke me from my slumber. Uncovered the blinders.

If being a Penta meant having to protect the tribe, I needed to know all I could about tree spirits *and* the outside world. I needed to do the job I'd been chosen to do and get on with my life whatever that entailed.

I needed *The Penta Chronicle*.

53. *Olivia*

I carefully climbed down the pine tree, ever conscious of not breaking branches. When I reached the last branch before the ground, my father held out his hands as if he were preparing to catch a football.

"Jump. I'll catch you," he said.

I met his gaze. Why did I believe that he would catch me? This was a man who hadn't been around much for the seventeen years of my existence, and yet, I was ready to do as he asked.

These Montana woods were a strange place.

I launched myself off the last branch and plowed into my father. He caught me in his arms, but stumbled back a few steps. I was certain the two of us were heading for the ground, but Tower quickly braced my father. My feet were on the ground before that stumble turned into a tumble.

My father shook his arms by his sides then righted his askew glasses. "Are you all right, Olivia?"

"Yeah. Are you?"

Dad nodded. "I think I just realized that you're not five years old anymore." He offered me a sad smile and rubbed a hand over his buzz cut.

"Haven't been for twelve years, Dad."

"In theory, I knew that, but you can't blame a guy for wanting to rewind and try again." He shrugged then looked up to the treetop. "So what did you see up there?"

Mr. Tramond plowed through the circle of team members around me. "Which way should we head?" He was rearing to go. Why so enthusiastic all of a sudden?

"I have no idea. All I saw was trees and more trees," I said. "I didn't see any breaks suggesting that an entire village was close by. It can't be far, but I don't see how we'll ever find it."

"You're lying!" Mr. Tramond put a chokehold on a pine sapling nearby and shook it. Needles and pinecones came down from the trees like earthen confetti, and I wondered if that would hurt Jobah too.

I actually held my breath for a moment so I could hear if Jobah cried out in pain somewhere in the woods. When he didn't, I released the breath and leveled my gaze on Mr. Tramond.

"I am not lying. There's no evidence up there that the village is in any direction." I pointed east, north, west, south, my movements exaggerated, my tone acidy. "These people are very good at hiding. They've done it for centuries."

Mr. Tramond got right up in my face, but Tower pulled him back while my father stepped in front of me.

Mr. Tramond tried to shrug out of Tower's grip but gave up when he saw it wasn't going to happen. "We're wasting our time with this area and that vine-tattooed kid," he spat. "He could be a punk pulling Olivia's leg. He tells her this tale to seem more exciting, reels her in, takes advantage of her."

"Jobah didn't take advantage of me," I argued.

"Is he blind then? Look at you in your tight tank tops and short shorts. Your damn legs go on for miles. What male wouldn't want to take advantage of that?" He thrust his hands toward me, then turned his head as if addressing the rest of the dig team, looking for their agreement.

The team's jaws dropped simultaneously, and a moment of shocked silence paralyzed them. Then they all talked at once. I only got bits and pieces, my own ears still ringing from his words.

"Inappropriate…"

"…owe Olivia an apology."

"…uncalled for."

"Not professional…"

My father's voice, however, roared above all of them. "Will, you need to leave."

Everyone fell silent. I looked at my father and he appeared to be taller, bigger, meaner. As mean as a glasses-wearing, skinny-legged archaeologist could be anyway. My mother had sidled up next to him, a hand on his shoulder as if to hold him back from hitting Mr. Tramond. Tower still held the photographer, but his knuckles were white now as if he'd increased his grip power.

"You can't tell me to leave," Mr. Tramond fired back.

"As lead archaeologist on this expedition, I most certainly can tell you to leave. I have all these witnesses to confirm you've acted unprofessionally. No one back east would question my decision." My father stepped closer to the photographer then angled his head in the direction of the cabin. "Get your things and get out of here. Your services are no longer needed."

"I'll be happy to escort him to the airport myself," Tower said.

"Thank you, Royce." My mother grabbed my hand.

Tower dragged Mr. Tramond away. I cringed over the ferns and low-growing plants that were ripped from the ground or trampled as they left. God, as much as I wanted to see him, I hoped Jobah wasn't close by.

"I'm sorry, Olivia," my father said.

I pulled my eyes away from Mr. Tramond and Tower and hugged my arms across my chest, suddenly cold in the middle of a Montana summer day. "Not your fault Mr. Tramond's a jerk." I shook my head and focused on the task at hand instead. "How are we going to find this village?" The sooner we found it, the sooner I could make sure Jobah was okay.

"Why don't we drive into Bigfork to research, interview locals, check out town records, the library?" Dr. Sumathai suggested.

"That's a better plan than wandering aimlessly through these woods," Dr. Reese said.

"I could talk to some contacts online if we can find a WiFi station in town," Dr. Vakker added. "We could scan some pages from the book Madeline found and see if anyone back home knows what the symbols mean."

If given the chance, Jobah could tell us what the symbols meant.

"Sounds like a good plan. Peter? We'll go to Bigfork, yes?" My mother squeezed my father's shoulder.

Dad finally looked at her after staring at Tower stampeding away with Mr. Tramond. "Bigfork. Yes. Let's." His voice was a little strained after yelling. My father was not used to getting all fired up like that. "C'mon, Olivia." He held out his arm and corralled me into the space beside him.

My mother walked on my father's other side, and like a three-bodied mutant creature, we followed Tower and Mr. Tramond's flattened path back to the cabin. The rest of the team trekked silently behind us.

When we reached the cabin, we watched Tower's truck churn up dirt as he left with Mr. Tramond sitting in the passenger seat. There was a general dumping of equipment, a small lunch, and a quick freshening up. As we were about to pile into the SUV, my father pushed the keys into my mother's hands.

"I think I'm going to work some angles from here," he said.

My mother raised her eyebrows, shifted her discovered book that she carried from one hand to the other. "Are you all right, Peter?"

Dad nodded, but his face was haggard. "Just a little tired."

Mom reached up and dropped a kiss on Dad's cheek, some unsaid understanding passing between the two of them.

I climbed out of the back passenger side of the SUV and stood beside Dad. "I'm staying too."

Dad slid his arm around my shoulders. Mom hesitated for a moment before giving us both a smile and easing into the driver's seat. She passed the book to Dr. Sumathai in the passenger seat. After starting the engine, she gave us a wave and disappeared out of the parking lot.

"I'm going to start with a nap," Dad said. He frequently took power naps. Mom said it helped him "get his genius back."

"Is there anything I can do while you're napping?" I asked.

Dad reached into one of the many pockets on his cargo shorts. He passed me his high-tech cell phone. The same model he and Mom refused to buy me when they'd announced this Montana trip.

"Call your friend. What's her name?" he said.

"Eden." I volleyed glances between my father's face and the coveted cell phone in my hand.

"Call her. Get in touch with normal." He saluted me and pivoted on his heel. He was back in the cabin before I could say anything.

I sat on the front steps, the tree-filtered sun fanning across my legs. I started dialing Eden's number three times and hung up three times. What did I say to her?

Hey, Eden. I've met a tree spirit, but I lost him.

Hey, Eden. My dad came to my rescue against a real jackass.

Hey, Eden. I think I may be going crazy.

I put Dad's cell phone on the step beside me and gazed out over the woods surrounding the cabin. The green of the leaves reminded me of Jobah's eyes, and the vines snaking up some of the nearby trees reminded me of Jobah's tattoos.

I dropped my head to my knees, but the feel of the sunshine on the back of my neck reminded me of Jobah too. Hell, I could even smell him.

"Olivia."

I snapped my head up, and there he was.

"Jobah?" I had a million questions to ask him, but my body had its own agenda.

I popped off the step and threw my arms around his neck. His hands slid to my hips, then around my back. We stood like that, our bodies pressed against one another, and I didn't have a single urge   to   move.

54. *Jobah*

Having my arms around Olivia again felt right. Her body was warm and soft and exactly what I needed. This contentment should have come from being in my village surrounded by my people, but it hadn't. I'd felt so out of place there. Standing here with Olivia, however, settled me.

How could that be?

I burrowed my face in Olivia's golden hair, drank in her fruity smell, ran my lips along the curve of her neck. She pulled her head back and caught my lips in a kiss that said so much considering we hadn't known each other that long. Just days. Maybe just days is all it took when you found the right person.

We explored each other's mouths for several hungry moments, hands sliding along all the skin we could reach. Every time Olivia's fingers brushed over the vine markings, my entire body buzzed.

When Olivia finally ended the kiss—I was quite willing for it to stretch on forever—she looked up and cupped my face in her hands. "Where did you go, Jobah? I was worried."

I rested my hands on her wrists. "I'm sorry, Olivia."

"Don't be sorry. Explain." She tugged me over to sit on the front steps beside her. "One minute

329

we're doing some Olympic-style cuddling, which I totally enjoyed, by the way, and the next… poof, you're gone. What happened?"

I rubbed her thigh, not able to keep my hands off her. "I couldn't sleep, so I practiced traveling. Figured these abilities are supposed to mean something so I'd better get good at using them. I ended up back at my village."

At this, Olivia's head shot up, her blue gaze more intense than I'd ever seen it. She didn't say anything, but it was as if all her attention was suddenly ultra-tuned.

"When I got there, my grandmother…" I had difficulty saying the words. I cleared my throat and tried again. "Ninae was ill. She died last night. She's gone."

"Oh, Jobah." Olivia's arms were around me again. "I'm sorry. How awful." She squeezed me so tightly. I knew that if anything could keep me from crumbling into pieces, it was Olivia. And yet, I had to tell her that my obligation was to the tribe. The tribe who feared me, distrusted me, shunned me.

"Our shaman chief, Denri, has ordered me to stay in the village." I braced for Olivia's reaction.

She let out a short laugh and gestured to me sitting beside her. "Yeah, and see how well that's going." She leaned over to kiss me again, but I stopped her with a hand on her shoulder.

"I have to go back, Olivia. Denri says I've become a Penta to protect the tribe from outsiders, from your dig team." I scratched at the vines on my forearm, wishing they would vanish. I still wore her father's short leggings, finding them much more comfortable than my breechclout. I'd kept my moccasins and now slid them over the dirt at the base of the steps where we sat.

"Take me with you." There was absolutely no doubt in Olivia's voice, and for a moment I wanted to take her with me.

"I can't," I said instead. "Denri would never let you in. He's upset that I've had contact with you in the first place."

"Exactly," Olivia said. "Take me with you, and we can show him that outsiders don't mean the tribe any harm. We'll make him see. Together."

"Denri is our shaman chief, our most respected elder. He's in charge." I thought of him trying to make me forget the outside with his magic. He hadn't been successful, so who was really in charge?

I shook this thought from my head.

I was not in charge.

"Jobah, I want to see your village. I want to know everything about you and where you came from. I want to show you everything in my world too. There's no reason you can't be a part of both ways of life." Olivia took my hands in hers, but I wriggled them free. I couldn't say what needed to be said with her touching me.

"Look, we don't live in the same world, Olivia." I stood and paced away from her, squared my shoulders. "I came back to get the book. The one your mother found."

Olivia's head went back as if I'd punched her in the jaw. I had to look down to my feet not to see the hurt I'd caused her.

"The book," she said slowly. "That's all you came back for?"

I focused on the trees rimming the parking lot and nodded.

Olivia bolted off the steps, and her fingers dug into my chin as she wrenched my head to look at her. "No, you don't get to nod. I want to hear you say you only came back for the book. Say it."

She let her hand drop from my chin, but the blue fire in her eyes burned me up completely. I'd never be rid of the scars.

"I only came back for the book, Olivia." It felt as if someone had a chokehold on my throat, on my heart. "I need it to understand my role as Penta so I can protect my tribe."

"The tribe that kicked you out? That tribe?" Olivia's voice grew louder, fiercer with each word.

"They act in fear. They don't understand." I shoved my hands in the pockets of the short leggings.

"Then make them, Jobah. You can."

I shook my head. "No. My duty is to protect them. My duty is to keep you and the team out of the village. My duty is to keep the village a secret as it has been for centuries."

My duty was to deny myself what I wanted, to deny myself Olivia and a life outside the village.

Run With Me

Olivia stood in front of me, and it took all my control not to gather her in my arms, tell her to forget what I'd said. I wanted to erase the pain—both hers and mine—and run away with her. It's not like Denri would come looking for me. He wouldn't leave the village. None of the tribe would.

But I couldn't turn my back on them, on Ashlo who'd remained on my side. Especially if they were in danger. Was this my own sense of responsibility or another Penta development meant to force me into compliance? Either way, I did not have the choice to refuse my duty.

I could only let Olivia go.

55. Olivia

Giving your heart away
is never an easy task.
Fragile as glass,
it breaks into pieces,
too many to count.

"I don't have the book." I basically spat the words out at Jobah. He wasn't any different than Kevin. He was only thinking of himself too. What was it about having a Y-chromosome that made males act like such asses?

Man, was I having a shitty day, or what? First I wake up and Jobah's gone. Then I have zero luck in finding Jobah's village. Then Mr. Tramond's Creep Factor skyrockets. Then Jobah returns, but only wants a damn book.

He doesn't want me.

The anger bubbling inside me was second only to the incredible sorrow. I'd been so worried about where Jobah was, about whether or not he was all right, that I hadn't expected to find him and have him cut out my heart.

I was glad the book wasn't here. Served him right.

"Where is the book?" Jobah asked.

He wouldn't meet my gaze directly, which was probably best. I had a feeling lasers would shoot out from my eyes and burn two holes right through his skull.

"My mother has it." I sat back on the steps. My mind told me to march into the cabin and leave Jobah out in the parking lot. My heart, however, feared that if I did, this would be the last time I saw Jobah.

Ever.

"Is she inside?" Jobah gestured to the cabin with his chin, his eyes still looking anywhere but at me.

"She went into Bigfork with the team."

Jobah looked around the parking lot as if he'd just noticed the SUV was missing.

"I know I'm hurting you, Olivia," he said, "but it's hurting me too."

"Then stop being so stupid," I said. "I can help you, but not if you won't let me."

"It doesn't help me if I bring you to the village. It causes more problems." Jobah folded his arms across his chest, covering the vines on his torso, but not the ones on his arm. How I wished he'd taken my father's T-shirt when he'd traveled. More of him covered might help me focus. Those beautiful vines called to me. It was getting hard to ignore their pull even though I was so mad at him.

"Maybe it causes problems at first, but think about it, Jobah." I stood and dared to get a little closer. "It didn't take you long to figure out that I wasn't a Big Bad Outsider. There have to be others in your tribe who are as open-minded as you. Even if you're not open-minded right now."

"Most of the tribe is older, set in the ancient ways. There are only a few my age and younger, and with the exception of my cousin, Ashlo, they are all afraid of *me*. Someone who has been in their presence their entire lives. They don't accept my changes. They won't accept you."

He was truly torn, and that stirred some waves in the little well of pity I had building inside me. Jobah didn't ask to be changed into a Penta. He didn't ask to be charged with the duty of protecting his people. He didn't ask to bump into me running in the woods only days ago.

"What happens if I get the book for you?" I retreated back to the steps and lowered to sit.

Jobah actually looked at me. "Why would you get it for me? I'm being a real… a real prick right now."

"Ten points for using a new vocabulary word." I made a little checkmark in the air with my finger and Jobah smiled slightly. That miniscule upturn in his lips was enough to have me craving his kiss even though he *was* a prick at the moment. "I said I wanted to help you. I meant it. If the book will help, I'll get it, but I want to know what happens after I do."

Jobah surprised me by kneeling in the dirt at my feet. He rested his palms on my knees and finally looked at my face. I got lost in the leafy canopy of his eyes, the fullness of his lips, the smooth coffee of his skin. Tracing the vines on his left hand stole my breath away as that earthy connection to him, to everything growing around us, surged to full power.

Shivering a little as if he felt the power too, he said, "I will use the book to learn about being a Penta so I can protect my people." Jobah's fingers slid to my cheek, tucked hair behind my ear.

"Once they are protected, then what?" I closed my eyes as Jobah's hand slid across my shoulder and down to my elbow.

"You will return to your Island of Rhode, your home, and I will live in the village." Jobah leaned forward and pressed his lips to my thigh.

"I don't think it's going to be that simple, Jobah."

I lowered my head until my right cheek rested on Jobah's back. He coiled his arms around my legs as I combed my fingers through his thick, black hair.

"It has to be that simple. We have no other choice." His voice was a scratchy whisper, and I kissed the vines snaking along his left shoulder blade. Jobah's body trembled in my lap. I squeezed him a little tighter before I realized tears were slipping from my eyes, leaving wet streaks across Jobah's back.

"I want to be with you, Jobah." I brushed at the tears, but couldn't collect them fast enough.

Jobah raised his head from my lap and wiped my tear-stained face with the pad of his thumb. "Please don't cry, Olivia. Our running paths are just not the same."

"What if I can get the dig team to leave?"

"Another team could come searching after yours leaves," Jobah said. "As long as outsiders are interested in finding us, my people are in danger."

"And as long as they are in danger, you will protect them."

Jobah nodded. "If I have the book, I can protect them better."

"I'll get it. Come back tonight, and I'll give it to you."

Jobah opened his mouth to reply, but the doorknob jiggled behind me. "Olivia?"

As soon as Dad opened the cabin's front door, Jobah disappeared and I was suddenly so cold without his body pressed against mine.

"Did you have fun talking to Eden?" Dad pointed to his cell phone still on the step beside me.

I picked it up and held it out to him. "Yeah. Doesn't sound as if I'm missing much back home." I stood and squeezed Dad's arm. "Thanks."

I walked past Dad into the cabin, but he gently tugged me back outside. "What's wrong?"

Jobah vanished, and my heart went along with him. "Nothing." I managed a smile. "I think I'll try to catch one of those power naps."

Dad followed me inside. "Fifteen minutes and you'll feel like a new person."

"Promise?"

56. *Olivia*

My alarm clock's neon green numbers announced the time. 11:59 p.m. So much for a fifteen-minute power nap. I stared up at the bedroom ceiling contemplating a bathroom run, but my body was against the notion. Having your heart broken was exhausting.

I rolled to my side and sucked in a breath, hoping to fall back to sleep. The humidity was low, the temperature not stifling, so I'd opened my bedroom window when I'd come inside. The air slipping in now smelled of summer rain. I closed my eyes and took another breath.

Wet dirt and pine.

Another breath.

Ripe berries.

All scents that reminded me of Jobah.

Trying to sleep was useless. I flicked on the light beside the bed and picked up my summer reading book. I read a chapter, but couldn't take how stupidly in love Samantha Rigby was with Stone Anderson. I mean, *Stone*. Really? Who the hell fell in love with someone named after a rock? Only a stupid teenager who foolishly threw her heart at a guy who, by the time I got to the end of the book, probably didn't even want her heart.

I set the book down on the nightstand and leaned my head back on the headboard. Staring at the ceiling, by the way, does nothing to make you feel better when you've been submerged in an ocean of despair.

Okay, overly dramatic. I know. But this level of depression made me poetic.

I closed my eyes, but sleep was still not in the cards. I'd gotten several hours during the day, and now my entire schedule was off.

When I opened my eyes again, movement outside my window caught my eye. A shadow in the tree outside my room. Though the night was a black curtain, I knew that shadow. Knew those square shoulders, those long legs and strong arms, that silky hood of ebony hair. Those haunting green eyes that didn't look *at* me, but into me. All were burned into my memory making this summer like none before it.

I threw off the sheets and rushed to the window. We stood looking at each other from opposite sides of the open window. Me with my bare feet firmly planted on the wood floor of my room. Jobah, with his feet balancing on a thick tree branch. I waited for him to say something. Anything. At the same time, I wished for him to say nothing. Not if the words he chose would dice my heart into ragged little chunks.

Again.

Our running paths are just not the same.

I never wanted to hear such things from his lips. Not from the lips that had made my insides dance, my skin tingle, my soul soar.

"Jobah," I said now. His name was a poem. A single word that meant everything to me. I started to say something more, but Jobah vanished. He did that a lot lately. I thought I heard his feet shush through the brush below the window, so I raced down the stairs to the back door of the cabin and tore it open. If I could get one more look at him, one more touch, one more kiss, one more... one more.

But Jobah had made it clear. We would never walk the same path. What we had started could never be finished. He had his life, I had mine, and the two were beyond mixing in Jobah's mind. He was wrong though. We had to be able to figure something out.

I skidded to a stop at the end of the porch and ran back into the cabin. Groping around in the silent dark of the living room, I found the book Mom had discovered. It was the only reason Jobah had come back tonight. Sighing, I tucked it under my arm and bounded down the porch steps into the parking lot where the trees stood like armed guards—a pine-needled barrier between my world and Jobah's.

As I walked toward the trees, intent on finding Jobah and giving him the book, something on the ground got caught between my feet, and I stooped to pick it up.

A single moccasin. Jobah's moccasin. A shoe that moments ago was pressed up against his skin, a part of him. Something that knew where his village was.

I held onto the moccasin as if it were a golden thread in an unraveling tapestry. How foolish to be jealous of a shoe, but I was. Jealous more of the one still on Jobah's foot, still traveling on a midsummer night's run through the misty woods with nothing but the moon and fireflies to light the way.

I felt a strange kinship to the moccasin. We had both been left behind. Discarded. Exiled from Eden. A paradise. A dream. We'd forever be a single in what was meant to be a perfect pair. It would have been better if we hadn't known what it was like being a pair. But we did know, and we couldn't undo that. I couldn't erase the memory of Jobah's leaf-green eyes igniting a fire deep inside me.

I gave the shadowed lot a careful scan, but Jobah was gone. I guess he didn't want the book after all. I turned the moccasin over in my hands, and something fell out. After feeling around in the grass at my feet, I picked up a piece of flat pine bark.

With a final glance into the night, I took the moccasin, the bark, and the book into the cabin. Under the dim glow of the light above the kitchen sink, I examined the scrap. A map was carved onto one side. When I flipped it over, my heart cartwheeled in my chest. Words had been burned into the soft wood. Jobah's words.

"Run with me, Olivia. Run with me."

57. Jobah

I landed with a thud next to the temporary shelter I had built in the woods. Running with a heavy heart wasn't easy. After ducking inside, I gathered up my few belongings and crammed them into a deer hide sack. I focused on breaking down the shelter, but my mind was fixated on Olivia. Would she follow my map to the village? Would she come to me? Or had I hurt her too deeply?

When I'd traveled away from Olivia as her father opened the cabin door, the emptiness that hit me square in the chest was overwhelming. I knew in that instant that I couldn't be without her. She'd become so important to me, as necessary as air. Being away from her was not an option I could entertain anymore.

And so, I'd made the map. A risky, potentially foolish move, but the only one I had. If Olivia simply showed up at the village, we'd have a better chance at getting her inside. Denri would not see it as me bringing her in, but more as her discovering us. I'd have a small window of time to convince Denri and the others that Olivia was not to be feared.

Assuming the tribe would listen to me, of course. Time to show the extent of my Penta powers. Maybe I could reverse the people's fear. Maybe they could be in awe of me instead as I fulfilled my duty as their protector. Maybe they too would see what I saw in Olivia and know she would never hurt anyone. All I knew was that I couldn't stand hurting Olivia. If she wanted to come to the village, I had to find a way to get her there. Leaving her the map was the best way I had.

I hurried in cleaning up the shelter area and thought of my dwelling back in the village. The gush of wind ruffled my hair, and I was back in the pine tree beside Ninae's dwelling. I stepped out of the tree and into the field between my grandmother's dwelling and my own. I stared at Ninae's home for several quiet moments until something furry slithered between my feet, one still moccasined, one no longer.

"Moon." I crouched in front of the raccoon, and she rested her head on my knee. "Where have you been?"

Moon chattered with her little animal squeaks and licked her paw.

"Thanks for abandoning me, you overgrown rat." I wagged a finger at the raccoon, but she just continued grooming herself, oblivious to the fact she'd left me to fend for myself against Denri and the village. Then the raccoon tilted her head, black nose in the air as if I'd offended her. She had it backwards.

"Yes, you left me. You're a lousy totem animal if that's what you are, Moon."

And I had officially lost my mind.

Talking to animals in the middle of the woods wasn't uncommon among my people. We believed all things shared an energy, a connected spirit, but actually expecting the animals to talk back? Well, that was a new one.

Protect. Moon narrowed her dark eyes. That single word flashed inside my head, and I knew she'd sent it. She had a habit of giving me one-word orders. Very irritating.

"I'm back in the village to protect it, aren't I?" I threw my hands out to either side of me. "What more can I do?"

"Who are you talking to?" Ashlo approached carrying a torch.

I shot a look down to Moon whose eyes reflected in the fiery light. She flicked her striped tail and slithered into my dwelling.

"No one. I'm not talking to anyone." Hopefully, I'd be talking to Olivia soon. "What are you doing up, Ashlo? It's late."

"I don't like what's going on here," Ashlo said. "The tribe isn't treating you as you deserve to be treated. They should be honoring you for doing your duty. For giving up whatever it is you've found on the outside to protect this village."

My heart twisted in my chest. Ashlo was making me out to be a hero, and I wasn't. A hero would be able to put aside his own needs and desires. I couldn't do that. I couldn't leave Olivia behind.

"I'm not as noble as you think." I ducked into my dwelling, and Ashlo followed.

"You're here, aren't you?" He lit another torch inside my dwelling, bathing the single room in orange light. I thought of the switches Olivia touched in her cabin to make light appear. Such inventions were a wonder I wanted to know more about. Not that I needed light to see anymore, but still.

"I'm here, but promise me something, will you?"

Ashlo took a step closer to me. "Anything, Jobah. You and I have been like brothers since we born. I'm with you no matter what. You'd do the same for me."

"I would. I came back to protect this village because of you and because of memories. Memories of my grandmother, my mother, my father. This tribe is part of me even if many of its members are frightened by me right now. I still owe them a debt for the seventeen winters they've supported me. I can only hope that protecting them will redeem myself in their eyes." I paused. "That being said, what I'm going to tell you now you mustn't tell anyone. Not yet."

Ashlo nodded. "I won't say a word."

"I do not plan to stay here, Ashlo."

"What?" He gripped me by the biceps. "This is your home. Things will change. Everyone will see you are the same Jobah only better."

"Perhaps, but this village is not enough for me anymore. I've gotten a taste of the outside, Ashlo, and it's delicious." I thought of Olivia's lips, how they softened against mine, parted slowly, brought pleasure. If nothing else existed on the outside besides Olivia, I still wanted to go. The fact that both she *and* other amazing things were beyond the palisades of this village only sweetened the desire to be out there.

My village was known. Familiar. Unchanging. Outside was a mystery, a discovery, an opportunity. One I didn't plan to miss.

58. Olivia

I raced back into the cabin, Jobah's moccasin clutched to my chest, the piece of bark tight in my fist. Pausing in the dim living room, I listened to the sound of crickets outside, my heart pounding behind my ribs, Tower snoring upstairs. Now was the perfect time to leave.

After scrounging around in the team's gear, I found a flashlight. I took one of the multi-tools, not that I knew what all the gizmos on it did, but going into the woods at night totally unarmed seemed foolish. If I stopped to think about any of this, all of it would seem foolish.

Online status? *Olivia Bradford is following a map burned onto bark to find a village that doesn't want to be found.* No one at home would get that status. I wasn't sure *I* got it, but one look at Jobah's moccasin and following that primitive map was the most logical thing in the world.

I had to go.

I crept back upstairs, trying not to make a sound as I slipped into my bedroom. I changed into a black tank top that had lace along the neck and waist and a pair of jean shorts. I gathered my hair into a ponytail and put on the necklace Jobah had made for me. I loved the way it looked around my neck, as if Jobah had marked me as his.

I wanted to be his.

I wanted him to be mine.

After carrying my sneakers downstairs to minimize the noise, I sat on the last step and put them on. Pocketing the multi-tool, I grabbed the flashlight and tucked the book my mother had found under my arm along with Jobah's moccasin. I studied the bark map as I made my way to the glass doors at the back of the cabin. Before going outside, I stopped. I didn't know when I'd be back. It wasn't fair to make my parents worry.

I opened a pad on the coffee table and scrawled the words, *I'm with Jobah.* Sure, they deserved a more detailed message than that, but I didn't want to give them too much information. I rationalized that I'd explain it all to them when I came back. I also rationalized that my parents wouldn't flip that I'd snuck out in the middle of the night to go to a hidden village in the depth of the woods. A village they wanted to see so badly.

Not letting the notion that I was being a brat to my parents take root in my mind, I finally left the cabin. I flicked on the flashlight and took another careful look at the bark map. Jobah had drawn it starting from the edge of the parking lot. The map was surprisingly easy to follow, like *An Idiot's Guide to Finding Veiled Tribes.*

I stopped a few times when a rustling rose around me. A crackle of leaves, a snap of a branch, a disturbance in the cricket sound. Had to be a nocturnal animal of some kind. Probably hunting. Hopefully, I didn't look tasty. I didn't care if I did. When I got to the end of this map in my hand, I'd be with Jobah. That's all I could think about.

I walked through the woods, fireflies flickering in the darkness where my flashlight didn't reach. The air was fresh, not as humid as it had been since I'd arrived in Montana. God, I'd only been here a few days, and I had almost no desire to go back to Rhode Island. Of course I missed Eden, but she would think I'd completely lost my mind if she could see me at this very moment, wandering through the dark woods, searching for a place that didn't have televisions, cell phones, or even running water.

That thought slowed my progress a bit. I was used to a certain level of civilization. How basic would Jobah's village be? I'd seen videos in school about Native Americans. Would I be able to handle such a simple way of life?

Why was I worrying about this? It wasn't as if I was going to live in Jobah's village forever. I just wanted to see it. I was more interested in convincing Jobah to come with me. Pulling him into my world made way more sense than dropping me into his. He'd already proven—minus the vulnerability to tree-cutting and mysteriously appearing vine tattoos—that he could fit into the modern world without too much difficulty. In fact, those vine tattoos would be considered artwork in some circles. Carrie's boyfriend, Jett, the tattoo artist, would love them.

Maybe Jobah would start a whole new pop fad of getting vines tattooed over one's left side. Jett could probably mimic the look for interested customers and become famous.

I let my mind focus on the reality show that would result from everyone wanting vine tattoos like Jobah's as I followed the map. Soon I reached a small lake, much smaller than where Jobah and I had done our swimming together. According to what Jobah had drawn on the bark, his village was just ahead. I scanned the darkness, let my flashlight beam slice into the shadows in front of me. There was no evidence to suggest anybody was living out here, never mind an entire village. No wonder Jobah's tribe had stayed hidden for so long.

I continued walking until it felt as if I'd walk right off the edge of the planet. Everything was still, silent in the summer blackness. I squeezed Jobah's moccasin tighter between my elbow and ribs, checked that the book was still wedged there as well, and took a final glance at the bark map.

And then... when I looked up, I saw it. A leafy wall in front of me. Covered in vines and wide leaves, the wall was well-camouflaged. If I hadn't been looking for it, hadn't had a map marking the spot, I'd have totally missed it.

I stepped closer to the wall, ran my hand along the exterior of it until I found a break in the fortification. The wall overlapped, one part of it curving inward to create a disguised entrance. I stepped inside and a village sprawled out in front of me.

Dotted with torches still aflame, a dim golden glow danced over shelters. Ones constructed much better than the one Jobah had in the other part of the woods. I wondered if he'd helped build any of the ones I saw now. If so, his talent was evident. Judging by the one closest to me, the shelters appeared sturdy and were attractive. Roundish in shape, they had slanted, thatched roofs, and were about nine feet tall. Bark had been used like shingles on the exterior, and curved doorways had been cut out. Either there weren't any doors or all of them were open to let in the night air.

Which one was Jobah's?

I stood semi-paralyzed by the entrance, not sure if I should wait until dawn when it would be easier to scope out the village and find Jobah. That was probably the most logical, but I didn't want to wait that long to see him. I was also tired from my trek into the woods. Snuggling up for the night in Jobah's shelter with him was all I wanted to do.

I took a few more steps into the village. Aside from the torches flickering their flames as a night breeze filtered through, nothing moved. The line, "Not a creature was stirring, not even a mouse," from *Twas the Night Before Christmas* popped into my head. As a kid, it had been hard for me to imaging nothing stirring. Sunderfield wasn't a big city and I didn't have an enormous family, but something was always stirring, or ringing, beeping, clicking, ticking, buzzing. I almost never heard my own pulse in my ears, my own breathing, my own thoughts.

But this place was different. Once I'd walked all the way inside, it was as if the outside world had melted away, ceased to exist, disappeared. I had an urge to turn and run back out beyond the leafy wall to make sure my world was still out there. As I backed up a step, however, something warm pressed against me from behind.

"You came." Jobah's breath tickled my neck. He slid his arms around me, rested his palms against my stomach.

I leaned my head back onto his shoulder and fought to keep a grip on the things I carried.

"I came."

Jobah kissed a line down my neck, and I turned around in his hold. I held his moccasin between us. "You dropped this, Cinderella."

"Who?"

"Never mind. Just kiss me."

Jobah lowered his head, found my lips, and I knew coming here had been right.

So right.

59. *Jobah*

All the tension that had built up in my body since watching the life leave Ninae sifted into the dirt under my feet. Holding Olivia, kissing her, having her here with me undid everything that was wrong in my world. Only the two of us existed.

I'd bid Ashlo farewell moments before I felt Olivia enter the village. Yes, I *felt* her, like the way you feel a change in the wind. Immediately, I had known where she was and that she was searching for me. She was a vision in her black sleeveless shirt, her long, sleek arms so available. As I kissed my way from her fingers, up her arms, along her jaw and into the curve of her neck, she shivered and I wrapped my arms around her tighter.

"Let's get you inside." I led her through the dark village, thankful that no one else was awake and that my vision was so keen in the blackness.

"Am I going to get you in trouble for being here?" Olivia asked as she ducked inside my dwelling. Seeing the way the torchlight glinted off her hair and skin, I didn't care what trouble came my way.

"I don't want to worry about that now." I took my moccasin from Olivia and set it beside the other one under a log bench in my dwelling.

"I have the book." Olivia held it out to me and wiggled it.

"Thank you." I took it and set it on the bench. "But I don't want to worry about that now either."

Olivia grinned. "You're concerned about the map?" She dug in the pocket of her short leggings and put the bark on top of the book. "You can have it back. Is that what you're worried about?" She raised an eyebrow over a midnight blue eye and took a step back toward my bedding of hides in the corner of the room.

I shook my head. "I'm only worried about one thing, Olivia."

She kneeled on the hides and called me to her with a curl of her finger. "I guess I only came for one reason as well. You."

I crawled onto the hides and slid into the spot beside Olivia. Moon got up from where she'd been coiled on the bedding. The raccoon paused a moment to regard Olivia. Olivia held out a hand, which Moon rubbed. With a swish of her striped tail, the creature headed for the door.

Bond.

Again, a single word from Moon, but this one gave me her blessing. Had the raccoon finally realized that Olivia was no ordinary outsider?

Olivia ran her hand over my chest, traced the vines, pressed her lips to the leaves on my skin. My heart jumped around behind my ribs, and I felt floaty, as if we were on a cloud.

"I'm happy you're here." I freed Olivia's hair from its knot, letting it spill over her bare shoulders in a golden shower. She smelled of lavender and lemons. The scent filled my dwelling, and I didn't think I could live without it.

"I'm happy you invited me, Jobah." She looked down to her lap for a moment and hooked some of her hair behind her ear. "I know you risk a great deal by letting me be here."

"The risk is easier to endure than the loss of not having you here. I realized the moment I left you that I couldn't leave you." I cupped her cheek in my hand and brushed her lips with mine. Just a soft, quick touch of mouths, but it ignited so much inside me.

"I felt a little empty without you too," Olivia said. "I don't know why I've fallen so quickly for you, Jobah. It doesn't make sense. It's only been days. I hardly know you."

"What's to know?" I said. "I'm Jobah Everleaf, Tree Penta, charged with protecting this tribe and adoring you. That's all there is to know."

"That simple, huh?"

"It's true. I love you, Olivia, my *Nahderhi*."

Olivia blinked slowly as if she were savoring my words. "I love you, Jobah. Way too much for having just met you."

With a smile, she eased me onto my back, soft animal hides below me, silky skin and curves above me. Olivia's body was paradise. Warm and fit and smooth. We kissed and teased until we were both standing on the edge of becoming one.

"I want this, Jobah. God, do I want this." Olivia's voice was a whisper above the pounding of my heart.

"So do I." I stared up at her as she sat on my thighs, her legs on either side of me, her palms lightly pressed to my stomach. The torchlight glowing behind her gave her a spirit-like quality, but I knew she was no spirit. I felt her heat, her desire, her need. I mirrored it in my own body, in my soul.

"I'm assuming you don't have any sort of... you know... protection, right?"

"What do you mean? No one will harm us in here." Why was she worried about being attacked?

"No, not that kind of protection." Olivia's cheeks pinked. She brushed her hair out of her face and toyed with the ends. "I meant protection from getting pregnant. I'm on the pill. Mom made me get on it after she read some online article about the number of teenage pregnancies increasing. I told her I wasn't having sex with anyone, but she insisted." Olivia shrugged, caught herself fussing with her hair, and dropped her hands to her thighs.

I wanted those hands on me.

"You do not wish to have children with me?" Having a family was the main point of mating. At least I'd thought so anyway. That's how it was in the village, but I knew now that the village wasn't always right.

Olivia's eyes shot open extra wide. I'd never seen that much white in a person's eyes before. "Not at age seventeen, Jobah. No, I don't want to have children with you now. Maybe someday. Like ten years from now, maybe. But not now. We're not ready for that. I need to go to college first. Get a job. A house. Lots of things need to happen before kids. Many opportunities need exploring."

I thought of the things I had seen on the outside and could understand what Olivia was saying. Her world had so much to offer.

"I like the idea of exploring opportunities." I curled some dangling strands of Olivia's hair around one of my fingers.

"You're not mad that I don't want to… ummm… have kids with you right now?" One of Olivia's hands slid along my stomach, and I was anything but mad at her.

"I'm not mad. Besides, you said maybe someday you'd want to have children with me. I can wait for maybe someday, especially if I get to wait with you." I rested my hand on top of hers.

"We'll figure out a way for you to wait with me." She brought my hand to her lips and kissed my fingers, my palm. "In the meantime, there are ways to enjoy each other safely."

Olivia slowly pulled off her tank top revealing herself to me. I'd been around half-naked female bodies my entire life, but seeing Olivia stole my breath away. Her breasts were creamy white with rosy centers and simply running my fingers over them caused Olivia's eyes to close, her head to slide back, her legs to tighten around my thighs.

Watching her reaction to my touch stoked that fire already burning inside me.

I reached up a hand and fingered the necklace I'd made for her. "Do I get to know what this symbol means now?"

Olivia traced the edge of the slate. A smile punctuated her beautiful face. "I'll show you what it means."

She lowered to me and shifted her legs so her body met mine in one long line. The feel of her skin against my own took the last of my control.

Our bodies tangled, caressed, explored. Olivia touched me in ways that made all my body parts rejoice. It was going to be hard to wait to be with her fully, but when we finally joined ourselves, I had a feeling my appetite for Olivia would be insatiable. One taste of all of her would never be enough.

After leaving no area unattended on each other, Olivia snuggled up next to me, and I gathered her in my arms, hoping that she'd want to occupy that space for an eternity. I kissed her forehead, and she sighed.

"I have never felt this alive." Olivia snaked her arm around my waist and somehow managed to get closer.

I brought her right hand to my lips and kissed the back of it. I stopped when I caught sight of her skin.

"Oh, no."

"What?" Olivia sat up when I did.

I dragged her over to the lit torch so she could see what I saw.

Her eyes widened as she examined her hand. "Vines. Like yours." She traced the leaves coursing along the back of her hand and around her wrist.

I turned her around so I could inspect the rest of her naked body, but the vines were only in that one place.

"Olivia, I'm sorry." I rubbed at the vines, wishing they would come off, but knowing they were as permanent as my own.

60. Olivia

"I'm not sorry. It means we're close. Jobah. I love everything about being close to you." I'd told Jobah after we'd discovered the tattoos on my hand. He needed much convincing that this was a good thing before he would go to sleep beside me last night.

I raised my right hand into the rays of morning sunlight now washing into Jobah's dwelling from the open doorway. Though I was going to have a hard time explaining the appearance of the vines on my skin, I did love the sight of them. It was as if Jobah himself had been tattooed onto me so I could take a part of him with me wherever I went.

The leaves were delicate, branching off the main vine that swirled around my wrist and over the back of my hand, stretching to my knuckles. The tattoos reached a little farther up my pinky finger than the other fingers, and one tendril from the main vine snaked down to a freckle on my forearm. The green of them was much darker on my fair skin compared to Jobah's darker skin.

I turned my attention to Jobah reclining beside me. He was naked and perfect on the bedding, his vines artistically showcased on his arm, shoulder blade, and down his ribs. One long leg was stretched out straight to the end of the bedding while the other was bent at the knee. He was on his stomach so all his goods were not visible, which was important. It had been difficult last night not to... well, you know.

I sat up and finger-combed my hair. I wondered how bad my I-just-woke-up look was this morning, but there were no mirrors in Jobah's shelter. I'd have to hope for the best.

I looked at the vines on my hand again and put them against Jobah's. A sigh escaped my lips as a soft, whispering hum vibrated through my body.

Jobah moved beside me and slowly lifted his head. When his emerald eyes met mine, I got all melty inside.

"You're here." He put his palm on my thigh and squeezed.

I nodded. "I'm here."

Jobah pushed himself up, and I couldn't look away from the muscles in his arms and shoulders as he did so. Such beauty.

He brushed his lips against mine, and I slid my fingers up into Jobah's hair, brought him close for another kiss.

"I've always enjoyed the morning," Jobah said, his leafy eyes focusing on my lips, "but this is the best morning. Having you here is... is..." He shrugged and pressed his lips to mine again as if he couldn't find the right words.

Normally, I hated mornings. No, that wasn't true. I despised mornings. Loathed, detested, abhorred. I always waited until the last possible second to get up for school. I'd pared down my getting ready routine so that I could basically wake up, eat breakfast, and go.

But this morning… oh, this morning was the exception. I'd never awakened in the warm arms of a Tree Penta. I wanted every morning to be just like this one.

Jobah slid off the hides, and I was actually speechless as I gazed up at him. Sure, we'd *seen* each other last night, but something about the sunlight trickling over Jobah's smooth, tanned skin made me feel as if I were at an art gallery looking at a masterpiece.

"I invite you here and don't feed you. Very impolite," Jobah said.

"Huh?"

"You must be hungry," he said. "You look hungry."

Hungry. Yeah. For sure.

"You were a fine host in other ways." I stood and trailed my fingers along Jobah's shoulder.

He grinned. "I do have some manners even if I've been removed from the outside world for so many years."

"Trust me, guys on the outside don't know the first thing about manners." I reached for my clothes and started to get dressed, but Jobah tugged my shorts and tank top out of my hands.

"Not yet," he said. "Please." He kissed a path from my earlobe to my shoulder. His lips were hot against my skin, and places deep inside me tightened. "You're so beautiful."

I kissed him back, and the vines on my own hand tingled when Jobah touched them.

"Do you feel that too?" I asked.

"Like energy running between us?"

"Yeah."

"I feel it." Jobah pressed his tattoos to mine, and the tingling grew stronger. "I like it."

"What is it?" My voice was breathy as I gave into the sensations. Having a naked Jobah up against me with that energy was a slice of heaven.

"A connection. A bond between soul mates, perhaps?" Jobah gave me one final kiss and grabbed the book I'd brought. He sat on a stump in his dwelling with the book in his lap. "Maybe this can tell us what it is."

He opened the ancient book and ran his fingers along the symbols that meant nothing to me. "This part is about the Five Trees for the five elements." Jobah tapped the page and the leaves shifted from black to green, black to green as he made contact. His beautiful eyes scanned the following pages.

"What else does it say?" I leaned over from behind him, resting my chin on his shoulder.

"That the spirits made some humans guardians so the Kiyuchee and the five elements would be forever protected."

"Those guardians are Pentas?"

Jobah nodded then handed my clothes to me as he closed the book. "I will read more of this after we've eaten."

I shrugged into my clothes as Jobah slid into my father's borrowed shorts. I loved how so much of his skin was still exposed and how I could imagine the shorts disintegrating now that I'd seen all of him. He looked at me for a second longer as if he were envisioning the same thing.

"I'll get us some food." He pushed to his feet and put on his moccasins. "Stay here for now."

"What do I do if someone finds me in here?" The thought of Jobah leaving me alone caused a mini anxiety attack.

Jobah considered my question. He held up a finger signaling me to wait a moment. He disappeared out of his shelter, and when he returned he was not alone. A boy about his age wearing fringed animal hide around his waist and moccasins stood beside Jobah.

"This is my kin, Ashlo," Jobah said. "Ashlo, this is Olivia."

We both stared at each other with wide eyes until Jobah nudged Ashlo.

"Oh, uh..." Ashlo put his fist across his shoulder and bowed slightly. Must have been like a handshake, I guessed.

"Nice to meet you, Ashlo." I nodded at him, but stayed where I was kneeling on the bedding.

"Ashlo will stand guard while I get food."

Jobah turned to leave, but both Ashlo and I said, "Wait!"

"What?" Jobah had his dagger in his hand, ready to go catch us something to eat. I tried not to picture a defenseless little bunny running for its life. How strange was this? I was so used to guys taking me to a restaurant for a meal, not trekking out into the woods to kill something.

"Why don't I go get food, and you stay here with her?" Ashlo said.

Jobah laughed and rested his hands on Ashlo's shoulders. "Are you afraid of Olivia?"

Afraid of me? Who would be afraid of me?

Ashlo puffed out his bare chest. "No, Jobah, but I am afraid of Denri. Although you have my full support, I don't want to go against our shaman if I don't have to."

"Maybe I should leave," I said though it pained me to hear the words out loud. I didn't want to go. Not at all. In fact, I was curious to see more of the village now that it wasn't cloaked by the night.

"No," Jobah said. "I want Denri to know he's been wrong to keep us all secluded. I want him to meet you. I want him to see that all outsiders are not horrible monsters."

I contorted my lips and held out my hands like claws in front of me. "Are you sure I'm the one for that job?" I let my tongue flop over my lips as if I'd lost control of it.

Ashlo chuckled and Jobah winked at me.

"You'll have to do, *Nahderhi*." Jobah gave me a wave and disappeared out of the shelter.

Ashlo didn't walk any deeper inside. He leaned against the doorway and looked at me.

"I won't bite," I said. "I promise."

"I know." Ashlo motioned to my hand. "You have the vines too?"

"I do now." I turned my hand around, loving the way the tattoos curled around my wrist.

"You are meant for Jobah then. The spirits have approved it." Ashlo glanced up to the sky as if acknowledging said spirits.

"Does that help me win favor with your shaman chief?" I straightened the animal hides as if I were making a bed.

Nervous? Umm, yeah.

Ashlo shrugged in response.

Not exactly the assurance I was hoping to get.

61. Jobah

After a breakfast of fresh fish, which Olivia spread around her bowl more than she ate it, I decided it was time to see Denri. Sounds of my people echoed from the village and hiding Olivia wouldn't be possible for much longer.

"Are you sure about this?" Olivia tugged on my hand, not letting me lead us out of my dwelling.

"Yes. Saying all outsiders are evil is like saying all Kiyuchee are wild animals. It's simply not true. Lack of knowledge keeps this tribe in the dark. I want Denri to understand why I have chosen you though you are an outsider." I cupped Olivia's face and pressed a kiss to the tip of her nose.

"Chosen me?" The skin between Olivia's brows crinkled as she studied my face.

"Yes, for a mate. Don't you want to be with me?" Why had her mouth dropped open at the word mate? Did she not feel what I felt for her? Had spending the night together, our arms wrapped around each other, not had the same effect on her as it had on me?

Nausea curled around the food in my stomach. The thought of Olivia not feeling the same as I did made me hurt all over.

"I very much want to be with you, Jobah. You shouldn't question that." Olivia reached up and rested her hands on my shoulders. Again, where she touched the vines, a warm tingling radiated right down to my core, dispelling my doubts.

Olivia was my perfect match.

"What is it then? Why do you hesitate to be my mate?" I said.

"Where I come from, people our age don't become *mates* so quickly. They date for a few years, at least into their twenties, then maybe live together. Maybe get married after that. Less people are getting married nowadays though. My sister, Carrie, is twenty-seven, and she just lives with her boyfriend, Jett."

"They love each other?" I pictured Olivia's sister looking like Olivia only older.

"Yeah, I guess so."

"Then why wouldn't they want to be mates?"

Olivia rubbed her forehead as if she didn't know how to make me understand.

"I'm not saying they don't want to be mates. I'm not saying I don't want to be your mate. You just caught me by surprise with that comment. That's all. And the fact of the matter is that at the end of my six weeks in Montana, I have to go back to Rhode Island with my parents. What will we do then?"

"We will figure that out when the time comes." I didn't like this conversation. It tasted good-byes and pain. Putting it off for as long as possible was the only defense I had. "Come. Let's see Denri."

Olivia followed me out of my dwelling where we found Moon lazing on a log bench in front of my grandmother's dwelling. The raccoon barely regarded us. I took Olivia's hand once we were both outside, and immediately the movement in the village stopped. Everyone became nothing more than a drawing, still and quiet. I spotted Ashlo on the other side of the central fire, where yesterday my grandmother had been sent off. He too had grown motionless, but was the first to recover. He touched people as he made his way toward us, and they shook off their paralysis. Eyes still followed Olivia and me as we met Ashlo halfway.

"This isn't a good sign," Olivia whispered. She pressed herself a little closer to me as if she were trying to be invisible.

"Denri is in his dwelling," Ashlo confirmed. "You'd better go directly there before someone tells him about Olivia."

I nodded and coaxed Olivia along.

"I've never been so nervous," she admitted. "God, I have to pee."

I diverted us to a spot where she could relieve herself. She didn't get all fussy about not having a bathroom like the ones in her cabin. It could have been that she was so anxious about meeting Denri that she didn't care about the comforts she was used to. Or it could be that some small part of her was comfortable in the woods.

In *my* woods.

Turning Olivia to face me before going to Denri's dwelling, I gazed into her sky blue eyes, getting lost for a moment. "No matter what happens with Denri," I said, "I will not go back to the way I've been living. You woke me up, Olivia, and I won't be asleep again."

Olivia cast a quick glance around then kissed my cheek. She squeezed my hand and took a step closer to Denri's dwelling. I slipped in front of her and inhaled a calming breath. Too bad it didn't calm me.

"Denri?" I said.

"Come in," the shaman called from inside.

I led Olivia inside and when Denri turned around, his dark eyes narrowed. "What have you done, Jobah?" His voice was a low growl, and his disapproval came off him in waves. He moved quickly, and I only had a moment to step between Olivia and Denri.

My throat was so dry, but I managed to say, "Please, Denri, you have entrusted me with protecting this tribe. I would not bring danger to it."

"I have not entrusted you with anything. The spirits have. If I had a choice of who became a Penta, it would be someone far wiser than you." He scowled over my shoulder at Olivia.

"Hey," Olivia started, but I crunched her fingers in my grip and she stopped.

"I wish for you to speak with Olivia, to see that she and those that are with her do not mean our

371

tribe any harm. They wish only to learn about us, not change us."

"Really?" Denri took a few steps back and looked me over. "Where is your breechclout? You have only just met this outsider and yet you dress as one of them. You have disobeyed me and let her come here. What other bad habits have you picked up from them?" Denri angled his chin at Olivia with disgust. "She can't stay."

"Then I must go." I squared my shoulders, stood straighter, which made Denri look smaller.

Denri shot me a fierce glare. "You are bound to protect this village, Jobah Everleaf."

"And I will, but not by being trapped in it. I will come and go so I can keep a better watch on everything."

"Do you think I can just let you walk in and out of this village? You'll compromise us all." Denri shook his head. "She must go. You must stay."

"Denri," Olivia said. She patted my arm and stepped from behind me toward Denri. "We are not asking you to let a stream of outsiders into this village. I respect your way of life, even if I don't entirely understand it, but Jobah is not ordinary anymore. Surely, you can see that. The rules that have been set in place for this tribe can no longer apply to him. He can better protect you, in fact, if you allow him to live in both worlds. He can anticipate what dangers might come and keep them from reaching this tribe."

"I don't know about that," a voice said from the doorway of Denri's dwelling.

I spun around as did Olivia. The photographer, Mr. Tramond, stood at the entrance.

"What are you doing here?" Olivia asked. Then her eyes darted to me. "I did not bring him here."

"Not on purpose," Mr. Tramond said. "But she was easy enough to follow."

62. Olivia

Stupid. I should have been more careful, but I was too wrapped up in what I wanted. Too focused on being with Jobah.

Too damn selfish.

"Mr. Tramond, you can't be here." I pushed past Jobah and headed for the photographer. I'd escort him out and leave with him so I didn't get Jobah into any more trouble.

Jobah grabbed my arm and sidestepped in front of me. "She's right. You can't be here."

"I believe me standing here says I *can* be here, now doesn't it?" Mr. Tramond folded his arms across his chest.

"Why are you still around?" I asked. "My father fired you from the team. I saw you ride away with Tower."

"As I already explained, I don't take my orders from your father." He stepped into Denri's shelter. "And Tower was easy enough to take care of. He may be bigger than me, but he's not smarter."

What had he done to Tower?

"My father's the lead archaeologist, so he *is* in charge." Why couldn't my father be here now?

"I don't care if he's God," Mr. Tramond scoffed as he came closer to Jobah and me. "My mission was to find this hidden tribe, map its location, report to my employer, and get handsomely compensated for my troubles. I've done the job for which I was really contracted."

The pieces were coming together in my mind. How could I have been so dense? "You were never interested in helping my parents or the dig team."

"I don't give a rat's ass about archaeology, preserving history, studying cultures. Me? I'm much simpler than all that. Dollars and cents, sweetheart. It's all about dollars and cents. And taking pictures of beautiful things."

He reached out a hand to touch me, but Jobah knocked it out of the way with a movement my eyes barely registered.

"Oh, Leaf Boy is quick." Mr. Tramond raised his eyebrows. "But is he quick enough?"

Suddenly, the barrel of a small handgun was pressed to Jobah's chest.

"No!" I tried to step around Jobah, but he held me back with his arm. I don't think Jobah realized what a gun was capable of doing to him.

"Let her come," Mr. Tramond said. "She really shouldn't be hanging around with an uncivilized boy."

"Olivia is not eye candy," Jobah said.

Eye candy? Why that phrase again?

"If she's not eye candy, nobody is." Mr. Tramond winked at me, the gun still touching Jobah.

My mind fast-forwarded to all the ways I would try to stop the bleeding if he shot Jobah.

Would yarrow paste work on a wound that size? I glanced behind me looking for Denri, but he was gone. Real nice of the shaman chief to bail on us. No wonder the tribe needed a Penta to protect them.

I pressed my palm to Jobah's shoulder. His vines were right under my fingers, and they shot his energy right into me.

Run. Jobah's voice filled my head. He didn't turn to look at me. His lips hadn't moved. He hadn't spoken aloud.

And yet, I'd heard him.

Run! The word came at me again. This time with a little push from Jobah's hip against mine and a hiss from outside that sounded like Moon.

No, I would not run. I wasn't going to leave Jobah here with Mr. Tramond. With a gun. It was my fault the photographer had found the village, and I would do whatever I could to keep it safe, keep Jobah safe.

"How do you get your money, Mr. Tramond?" I asked.

"Simple. I've made a call." He dug out a cell phone from his pocket. It looked exactly like my father's. "My employer is staying in Bigfork. He'll be here shortly."

"And until then?" Jobah said. "Do you plan to hold this weapon to my chest until he comes?"

"No. I wouldn't waste my time with that." His finger started to press the trigger.

"Don't!" I pushed Jobah out of the way with a strength I shouldn't have had. Jobah nearly crashed to the ground, but the wall of Denri's shelter stopped him.

Mr. Tramond relaxed his hand on the gun, but didn't stop aiming at Jobah. Online status: *Olivia Bradford wonders how lunatics always manage to get weapons.*

"If you've already given up our location, what's your purpose here now?" I asked.

"I needed this." He reached into his back pocket and produced the book my mother had found at the site. That meant he had been in Jobah's shelter, but when? We'd only just left it to come to Denri's, and we'd occupied it all night. How had he slipped in and out?

"That's my mother's find." I held out a hand for the book.

"Didn't stop you from swiping it for Green Eyes over here." He wiggled the book toward Jobah. "According to my employer, this book is a real find. Full of tribal secrets. Should make a fantastic museum exhibit once I get a worthy offer for it."

"I planned to give that back to my mother. She should be credited with discovering the book."

"Your mother should learn to lock up important artifacts. Look how easy it was for both of us to swipe it." Mr. Tramond clicked his tongue and shook his head. "She's just in it for the science, the history. Completely misses the financial side of things. Not like me. I've always got my eyes open for a lucrative opportunity." He stashed the book back into his pocket where he was no doubt crinkling the priceless pages.

"Outsiders!" a voice called from beyond Denri's shelter. "Outsiders, show yourselves."

"Well, this isn't very hospitable, now is it?" Mr. Tramond frowned, turned halfway so he could keep an eye on us but glance out the doorway at the same time.

Denri and the men of the tribe stood outside the shelter. Arrows were ready in their bows, and Denri was chanting something I couldn't understand.

"Primitive." Mr. Tramond squeezed the trigger on his gun, and a bullet sank into Denri's gut before a single arrow could be released from its bow. The shaman chief slumped to the ground, crimson blood slithering through his fingers as he covered the wound with his hand.

The men around Denri stood motionless in shocked silence. They had no doubt never witnessed the power of a gun. Too stunned over the boom of gunshot and the blood pooling around Denri's body, not one of the men fired off an arrow at the photographer.

I touched Jobah's shoulder, not sure what to do, but knowing something had to be done. Fast.

That's when I heard it.

A low whispering sound like leaves rustling in a steady breeze. Only there shouldn't have been any breeze. The summer air had been cooler than past days, but there hadn't been any wind. Not enough to make the noise now filling Denri's shelter.

You are the trees. A ghostly voice carried on the gusts. Denri's shelter creaked and moaned under the force of the wind.

"Jobah, what's happening?" I shouted as I clamped my hands more securely around Jobah's waist.

He didn't answer me. Instead, he cocked his head to one side as if he were listening to something. His body became almost too hot for me to touch. I let my hands slip away, but he grabbed my wrists.

"No, I need you," Jobah said. "Don't let go."

"What—" I started, but the wind outside grew to such a level that my words completely drowned in the roar.

Roots burst from the ground by Mr. Tramond's boots. Thick tendrils of green gushed through the dirt floor in Denri's shelter. In a matter of seconds, chunky vines snaked up Mr. Tramond's ankles, wrapped around his legs, and headed for his upper body.

"What the..." He glanced down for a nanosecond, but that was all Jobah needed to grab the nose of the gun and rip it from his grip. He passed it to me, and I nearly stopped breathing as I felt the weight of it in my own hands.

I watched in awe as the vines lassoed Mr. Tramond's arms and wound themselves around his torso, binding him like a mummy. He wiggled and wobbled as he tried to both struggle free and keep his balance. His cell phone dropped to the ground and on instinct, I snatched it up.

He started to argue, but a few leaves unfurled from the vines and filled his mouth. His words came out as a muffled gurgle, completely unintelligible.

"I need to get Ashlo and a few men to carry him out," Jobah said.

"Will those vines hold?" I cast a wary glance at Mr. Tramond, whose face was beet red and dotted with sweat. His eyes burned with rage.

"I don't know. I've never done this before. I'm only doing what the trees are telling me." Jobah squeezed by Mr. Tramond and kneeled beside Denri. "Get the healer," he said to the nearest tribe member.

Doing what the trees are telling him? Did I hear him correctly? Had I heard the trees too?

"Should I call the police?" I turned the gun toward Mr. Tramond, but knew I didn't honestly have the courage to actually shoot him. I'd seen millions of shoot-outs on TV shows and movies, but when the blood was right there, when you saw what a gun could do to a person, you locked up.

Jobah pressed a piece of cloth someone had passed him to Denri's wound. The old man winced and sucked in a staccato breath. Some females of the tribe wailed in horror over the sight of their shaman chief soaked in blood.

"Yes, call the police," Jobah said. "Mr. Tramond has greatly injured our shaman chief. He is an outsider and should be dealt with by outsiders, though I have my own ideas of justice."

I'd never seen Jobah look so fierce, so sure of himself. His eyes glowed green, and I swore the vines on his skin changed as he moved.

The area outside Denri's shelter became crowded with men as they hoisted Mr. Tramond up and out into the center of the village.

"Take him outside." Jobah sounded like a leader, an aura of confidence surrounding him.

A beautiful woman with long black hair and a girl about my age who looked just like the woman came over to Denri. They kneeled beside Jobah and spoke in words I couldn't decipher. Jobah answered them in what I assumed was their native language. Like the word *Nahderhi*, the language was smooth and sensual as it rolled off their tongues.

"Will he live?" Jobah asked the woman.

"Only the spirits can decide that, Jobah," she replied. "I will try to stop the bleeding and make Denri comfortable."

Jobah stood and nodded. His hands were fisted by his sides as he walked away from Denri's shelter. "Olivia, come with me. Bring the gun."

I didn't want to hold the gun anymore, but I did as Jobah asked. Ashlo and some of the tribe's men hauled Mr. Tramond's bound body to just outside the village, and we followed. Moon scampered between everyone's feet as if she were trying to be everywhere at the same time.

"Put him down there and get back inside. No matter what you hear, stay behind the village walls," Jobah said.

The men followed Jobah's orders, not because they looked as if they wanted to, but more as if he'd compelled them to listen.

Jobah turned to the walls and raised his arms. Trees sprouted from sapling to full-grown all around the village, and vines connected forming a protective netting. Ferns and other low-growing brush multiplied on the ground making the area between where we stood and where the village began impassable.

"It's like the village disappeared," I whispered. "Why didn't you have this around it before?" No one would ever see past the trees and vines.

"I couldn't do this until just now. I simply thought about covering the village, and it happened." Jobah had a stunned expression on his face that he quickly shook off. "Call your police now that we are outside the village, but don't mention Denri."

"But he needs an ambulance. He needs help."

"He needs to either heal and continue to lead the tribe, or die and be replaced," Jobah said. "It is our way."

"Didn't your uncles take you to a hospital when you were stung?"

"Yes, and they had their memories taken and left the village. I was deemed too young to remember much about the outside then, so my memories were left alone except for the guilt over getting my uncles exiled. Denri took the guilt away, and I never spoke of what I saw on the outside."

"But you never forgot."

Jobah shook his head. "Maybe the spirits had caused my uncles to act against their natures and take me to the outside. Maybe the spirits insisted that I survive by any means possible to become a Penta."

I dialed 911 and explained that we had been held at gunpoint. I left out everything about Denri. The 911 operator said she could trace the cell phone to get my location and would send out officers right away.

While Jobah kept watch on Mr. Tramond, I made another call. The phone rang twice.

"Hello?" my father said.

"Dad."

"Olivia, where are you? Your mother and I are worried. I thought we were becoming closer, then you dash off in the middle of the night and don't come back. The woods are full of dangers. You could have been killed."

Guilt twisted at my heart. "I know, Dad, but I had to find Jobah."

"Did you find him? Did you find the village?"

"Yes, but Mr. Tramond followed me. He's had his own plan all along."

My father literally growled on the other end of the line. "Where is he now?"

"He's right here with me, but Jobah's got him tied up. We're waiting for the police to come."

Dad paused, nothing but silence from his end.

"Dad?"

"I hear sirens now. Your mother and I are going to follow them." He hung up, and I shoved the phone into my back pocket.

I heard the sirens now too. They sounded so far away still. I looked at the gun in my hand and a full body tremble rippled through me.

"Set that weapon down and come here," Jobah said.

I cleared a spot on the ground with my sneaker and put the gun down. I kneeled beside Jobah who was on all fours and covered in sweat.

"Are you okay?" I touched his shoulder, but quickly pulled my hand away. His skin was as hot as a stovetop. My palm actually felt burned.

"It's not easy keeping these vines around him." Jobah motioned to Mr. Tramond writhing on the ground like a mutant inchworm. "If I stop focusing on them, they'll unravel." He exhaled, his shoulders sagging, and the vines at Mr. Tramond's ankles loosened.

Jobah sucked in a breath, his body going rigid again. The vines tightened, and the photographer let out a stifled cry.

"I don't know how much longer I can keep this up," Jobah said. "I'm not good at this yet."

I did the only thing I could do. I wrapped my arms around Jobah's shoulders, pressed my vine tattoos to his, and hoped it would be enough.

63. *Jobah*

Olivia's energy shot through my body, giving me a burst of power. Her simple touch filled me, and I could stand again.

"What was that?" Olivia pulled her hands off me and stared at her palms in awe. The moment her skin stopped touching mine, my strength weakened.

"More," I said as my legs grew shaky again.

"What?"

"I need more of your energy. Touch me." I took Olivia's hands and pressed them to my chest. Tiny bumps erupted along her flesh as I fed from her. The more she touched me, the stronger I became.

"Is it draining you?" I had to be careful. I didn't know how all this worked. I didn't want to hurt Olivia by accident.

"No." The word came out as a whisper. "I feel... wonderful."

Her face had a dreamy look on it. She closed her eyes and turned her head up as if she were basking in the sun. A slight smile tugged her lips up, and just looking at her caused me to become stronger.

My legs steadied, and reluctantly, I pulled Olivia's hands from my chest. I walked over to Mr. Tramond, still bound and twitching on the ground. With one hand, I yanked him to his feet. I pressed his body against the nearest tree, and when his head met bark, his voice filled my mind.

This hurts. How can a bunch of vines hurt so much? I can't feel my legs and arms. I can't breathe. Is he going to kill me? Can he? He's just a boy. Why is this kid looking at me like this? His green eyes remind me of my ex-wife's cat. That thing hated me. Is that a raccoon? Why is it just standing there? Where's the gun? Did I kill one of the natives? When is Xavier going to get here? How much money will I make off this? I have to piss. Are those sirens?

Is he going to kill me?

"No," I answered out loud.

Mr. Tramond's eyes widened when he realized I had answered his unspoken question. He murmured something I couldn't understand with the leaves stuffed into his mouth. He tried to back away from me, but there was nowhere for him to go. I clamped a hand around his jaw and forced him to look at me. His eyes locked on mine, and I spoke to him without uttering a single word aloud.

You will forget this place, what you have seen, how to get here. You will confess to threatening Olivia and me. You will tell the police who your employer is and what your plans were. You will say nothing about shooting my chief or finding the village.

Just as I finished, the sound of dogs barking and feet crunching through brush grew closer. Twinges of pain needled my stomach as fern stems broke and leaves ripped. Olivia's warm palm on my back, however, dispelled the ache.

She was my shield.

I released my hold on Mr. Tramond, and he slumped to the ground as dogs and officers in blue uniforms spilled onto the scene. Seconds later, Olivia's parents pushed through the police and encircled Olivia. Her father wrapped his arms around her while her mother hugged both of them together. They were a tight trio, a family, and I missed Ninae more than ever at the sight of them. When my eyes met Olivia's though, I knew I was not alone.

"Who's going to tell us exactly what happened?" one of the uniformed men asked.

I pointed to Mr. Tramond. "I think you will find him very cooperative, sir." I let up on the vines so that the photographer's mouth was no longer gagged with leaves. Once the police had surrounded him, I made the rest of the vines drop away. The officers looked at me as if they weren't sure if I controlled the vines or not. Fortunately, the photographer started talking before they could question me.

"I held them at gunpoint," Mr. Tramond said, his eyes glassy.

Immediately, one of the policemen pulled Mr. Tramond's arms behind his back and fastened silver cuffs to his wrists. He didn't fight them at all.

"Where is the gun now?" a policewoman asked. She eyed the discarded vines with a mix of confusion and curiosity on her face.

"It's here." Olivia freed herself from her parents' hold. She picked up the gun from the ground and carefully handed it to the nearest policeman.

"I stole from them," Mr. Tramond confessed as he looked at Olivia's mother. "In my back pocket." He angled that pocket toward the policeman that held him by the arm.

The policeman tugged the book free and held it up. "Who does this belong to?"

Olivia's mother held out her hand, but then shook her head. "Actually, it belongs to him." She pointed to me, and the policeman dropped the book into my hands.

I fingered the cover. "Actually, it belongs to both of us."

Olivia's mother smiled, a true mother's smile, and I knew, without a shadow of a doubt, that all outsiders were not evil. Some of them were caring and generous and loving. I looked at Olivia.

Some of them were perfect.

"Xavier's waiting." Mr. Tramond's voice was automatic, as if he were dumping out everything he had done wrong. Just as I'd told him to.

"Who's Xavier?" the policewoman asked. She pulled a small rectangular item from the pocket of her shirt and pressed it with her thumbs as Mr. Tramond talked.

"Xavier Alston is a black market antiques dealer." He didn't blink as he spoke. He was in a trance. A trance I'd created somehow. "He paid me to find—or steal—rare items from this expedition as well as give up the location of a Veiled Tribe if one was found."

"What's a Veiled Tribe?" another policeman asked.

I held my breath, hoping my village would be safe.

"A tribe that is hidden and lives in seclusion from the rest of the world," Olivia's father answered. He turned to Olivia, glanced at her hand covered in vines like mine, then focused on me. "Where is the village?"

"There's no village here, Dad." Olivia touched her father's shoulder and held his gaze for a moment. He narrowed his eyes, but didn't press the issue. Good man. I wasn't sure I'd be able to put everyone in a trance to make them forget. I didn't want to.

"The kid's right," the policewoman said. "There's no one living in these woods over here. We'd know about them if there were." She nodded, confident that she knew the lands she protected.

Olivia's father scanned the area. He knew he was close to my village, but didn't say anything.

"We're going to need you kids to come to the station and fill out a report." The policewoman pointed to Olivia and me.

"We'll take them, Officer," Olivia's mother replied.

"All right. Let's move." The policewoman motioned for the other policemen to escort Mr. Tramond out of the woods. "We'll see you back at the station." She glanced again at the vines on the ground. Her gaze ran over my vine tattoos. She opened her mouth to speak, but ended up shaking her head instead.

Two policemen led the way followed by Mr. Tramond and the rest of the officers.

"Wait!" Olivia called, jogging toward them.

The policewoman turned around.

"A member of the dig team is missing." Olivia looked at her parents. "You haven't seen Tower since he took Mr. Tramond to the airport, have you?"

Her parents shook their heads, and I stepped toward the photographer.

"Where is Tower?" I asked.

Still in his trance, he said, "He's in his truck just north of here. I drugged him and left him to follow her." He pointed to Olivia.

"Show us," the policewoman said, gesturing that Mr. Tramond should take the lead. She eyed two officers who immediately sidled up to either side of the photographer.

As soon as they were no longer visible, Olivia's father stepped over to me in one long stride.

"Where is it?" he said.

"Dad, forget it. Just let it go." Olivia wrapped her arms around herself as if she had to physically hold herself together.

"I'll show you, Dr. Bradford." I turned to Olivia's mother. "I'll show both of you."

"Jobah." Olivia slid between her father and me. "You don't have to do this."

"I want to," I said. "I want your parents to trust me."

Olivia's eyes softened. She took my hand and turned to face her father. "Mr. Tramond shot their chief, but if we tell the police they'll march medics in here, maybe want to take Denri out. That will upset the entire tribe."

"Your mother has medic training," Olivia's father said. "Maybe she can help your chief."

Olivia's mother nodded. "I will do whatever I can, Jobah." She rested her hand on my forearm right where the vines were. I did not feel her energy like I did Olivia's, but just the human contact comforted me.

I faced the trees that hid my village. Closing my eyes, I willed the trees to reveal a path inside. Just a small one. Little by little, the ferns separated. The trees regrouped out of the way.

"Follow me," I said.

Olivia slid her hand inside mine, and her energy was right there, strong and steady, filling me. Her parents fell into step behind us, and I led them inside. They would either help Denri and be heroes among my people, or be witnesses to the death of our shaman chief by the hands of an outsider.

I prayed for heroes.

64. Olivia

Every eye in the village was fixed on us as we headed to Denri's shelter. You would think Jobah was leading a pack of neon blue space aliens by the way the tribe froze in place and gawked. I had a ridiculous urge to stick my thumbs in my ears and wiggle my fingers to give the people something interesting to see.

Fear shimmered in the dark brown eyes of Jobah's tribe. I wanted to say they were being foolish. That there was nothing to fear about outsiders, but how could I after what Mr. Tramond had done to their leader? His one act of vile recklessness was a more powerful message than any good my parents or I could do.

We entered Denri's shelter where the healer was bent over the shaman chief's body. The girl who looked like the healer was bathing Denri's forehead.

"How is he, Keryun?" Jobah asked.

The girl motioned to the healer. "My mother has cleaned the wound and will bind it. She found this."

Keryun held something up for Jobah to see.

"What is it?"

"A bullet," my father answered. "It came from the gun."

"It's what made this hole in our shaman chief?" Keryun's mother asked.

"Yes. It is good you were able to find it." My father adjusted his glasses as he studied the bullet in Keryun's hand.

"That means it's not still inside him." My mother kneeled beside Keryun's mother. "May I take a look?"

Keryun's mother looked to Jobah as if to get permission, as if he were in charge. Jobah nodded and the healer shifted to give my mother more room.

After a few moments of examination, my mother said, "It's a straight shot. In the front, out the back. Though it looks like he's lost a great deal of blood, he hasn't really, which indicates that nothing vital was hit. Do you have something to close it up with?"

"This bone needle and sinew." Keryun's mother held up the two items then pointed to the ground beside Denri. I recognized the yellowy goo in a wooden bowl. "We'll cover it with a yarrow paste to help it heal faster."

My mother assisted where she could while my father silently took in the surroundings. He surveyed the wooden jars and pouches Denri had along one wall of his shelter. He touched several drums and rattles, careful not to make any noise. He studied a row of masks hung at eye level so it was like looking at faces.

I knew my father was taking photographs with his mind. He was cataloging everything, dying to ask questions. I nudged Jobah who looked up and saw my father lean in toward one of the masks.

"He wants to know everything," I whispered.

"If he agrees to keep it all secret," Jobah said, "I'll tell him everything."

My mother got to her feet. "We've dreamed about seeing a village like this. Dreamed about sharing it with the world." She glanced back to Denri, who was out cold. "I see how that's not possible. Though there would be those who would love to just know of this place's existence, there are also those who would seek to exploit you as Will Tramond was planning."

"Not every outsider has pure intentions," Jobah said. "Some do wish to harm us, use us for their own gain. The best protection for this tribe is to keep them hidden."

"Them?" my mother said. "You don't include yourself in wanting to stay hidden?"

I held my breath. The way Jobah answered this one question would either fill my heart or completely empty it.

"I don't wish to stay hidden," Jobah said.

Big exhale here. Online status? *Olivia Bradford is mega-relieved.*

"What *do* you wish?" my mother asked.

Part of me wanted her to leave him alone, but another part wanted Jobah to answer.

Exactly what did he wish?

Jobah looked at me, and his green gaze seeped right through my clothes, my skin, and went to my deepest places. I tingled all over, and he hadn't even touched me. Had two people ever been more connected than us? I couldn't imagine it.

"What I wish, Dr. Bradford, is to spend loads of time with Olivia exploring the world outside this village."

Notice how he didn't say, "Exploring the world outside this village with Olivia." The "with Olivia" part had come first. God, Jobah put all other guys his age to shame.

"Maybe we can arrange something," my father said as he came back over to us.

"Arrange something?" My heart did a little excited flutter in my chest.

"Your mother and I want to know about life in here." My father gestured around the shelter and outside to the village. "Jobah wants to know about life out there." He stepped out of the shelter and motioned to the palisades, which we could clearly see from the inside, but were disguised by the trees and brush outside. "What if Jobah gives us a detailed field trip around this place, and we take him to Rhode Island with us for a little while. Assuming that is okay with this tribe."

Jobah's hand had found mine while my father spoke. He squeezed my fingers together now, almost painfully so, but I was too stunned to complain about it.

Had my father just offered to take Jobah home with us?

"The university we work for is always trying to set up exchange programs," my mother added. "We could enroll Jobah, set him up on campus. You could become an official student."

"What do you think, Jobah?" I freed my hand from his. "Rhode Island is a long way from here, but you could always travel back using Penta skills if the tribe needed you, right?"

"You have trees in Rhode Island, so I assume the ability would work long-range," Jobah said.

"Only one way to truly find out," my father said. The man's eagerness for learning about the village overflowed. Got to love when his archaeological hunger also benefited me.

My mother tapped the book Jobah still held. "If you come to Rhode Island," she said, "you can decipher this. There may be tidbits from it that we can share with the archaeological community that won't endanger your tribe. There may also be things in it that clarify your role as a Penta. Judging how you handled Will though, you're probably finding your own way." She rested her hand on Jobah's shoulder then flitted a quick glance to me. "I see ways we can all get what we want."

"Do we have a deal?" My father extended his hand.

Jobah looked at my father's waiting hand for a few silent moments. What was there to think about? This was the sweetest deal imaginable. For me.

Did it not seem as sweet to Jobah?

65. Jobah

From the bud of what we were
blooms the flower
of what we are
and spreads the seeds
of what we will be.

"Go, child." Denri's voice was weak, but clear.

I kneeled beside Keryun, noticed she didn't shy away from me, and leaned over Denri so he could see me. His eyes were only opened halfway, but he focused on my face.

"You want me to go?" I asked.

"You fulfilled your duty to this tribe. You have protected it." Denri shifted and his face contorted with pain.

"Not without you getting hurt." I had failed in part of my duty.

"There are always sacrifices, Jobah. You have to look at the grander picture. One person getting hurt out of an entire tribe is nothing. Things could have been a great deal worse. That man could have lead outsiders like him into this village. You stopped that from happening. Besides, I will live, yes?" He looked at Keryun's mother.

"As far as I can see, Denri." She patted his shoulder while Keryun finished covering the wound her mother had sewn closed.

"There doesn't appear to be any damage to your vital organs," Olivia's mother said.

"Then I repeat, you have fulfilled your duty to this tribe, Jobah Everleaf. Your grandmother and parents are proud of you as they watch over us all from the next place." Denri let out a small cough and cleared his throat. "Where is the girl?" He turned his head, searching for Olivia.

"I'm right here." Olivia stood beside me.

I tugged her hand until she kneeled on my left. Keryun studied Olivia as I filled the space between them. Keryun didn't say anything, but her staring suggested a conversation going on inside her head. If her dark, narrowed eyes and the firm set of her lips were any indication, her thoughts weren't full of pleasantries.

Denri reached out for Olivia's hand and inspected her vines. "You have the mark of the Penta; you have been kissed by the spirits. They join you with Jobah, and what they deem a match, I cannot un-match. They know far better than any mortal what Fate holds for each of us. Your destiny and Jobah's are intertwined. You shall protect Jobah as he protects us."

He looked back at me now. "You wish to see the outside world. Go. See it, but remember your duty to this village, to these people." Denri found Olivia's father. "You may see this village, but do not bring others of your kind here. We have worked to keep ourselves hidden and wish to remain so. There are far too many outsiders wishing to destroy us like the one who came here today. I will not put my people in danger."

Denri had sapped what little energy he'd had. Keryun's mother motioned for us to leave him to rest.

Outside the shelter, Olivia's father repeated his question. "So do we have a deal? A trip around this village in exchange for a trip to Rhode Island?"

I shook his hand. "Yes, Dr. Bradford. We have a deal."

Olivia clapped her hands together then got a hold of herself. Her excitement bounced to me though, and I wanted to pick her up, twirl her around, and kiss her forever.

"If they'd like to start by learning about our healing practices, I can help with that, Jobah," Keryun's mother said. She bowed her head slightly, a sign that she considered me a leader.

"Thank you," I said.

Keryun's mother looked up at me and knew my gratitude was for more than volunteering to show outsiders her methods. If she could accept me, couldn't others?

"My dwelling is over there if you'd like to follow me," she said to Olivia's parents.

Olivia's father pulled a notebook from his shorts pocket and edged her mother toward Keryun's mother. "We'll spend a little while in the village," he said. "Then we'll take you two to the police station to fill out the reports."

Olivia stopped her parents and gave them each a hug before allowing them to follow Keryun's mother. Keryun's mother gave my arm a quick squeeze on her way past me.

"This is turning out better than I expected." Olivia gripped my arms and threw herself at me.

Letting my arms come around her waist, I said, "I have to agree. I like when wishes come true." I dropped a kiss on the tip of Olivia's nose, and she scrunched up her face as if it had tickled.

"Jobah?" Keryun came out of Denri's dwelling.

"Yes." My eyes immediately went to the spot of blood on her simple hide dress. Denri's blood.

"Could I speak with you for a moment?" She wrung her hands, which also had blood on them.

I looked at Olivia, asking permission I suppose.

"Why don't I catch up with my parents?" Olivia let her hand slide down my arm. She touched all the vines and leaves on my skin there, and it was as if she had stroked me from the inside somehow. She raised an eyebrow letting me know she'd felt it too.

I watched Olivia walk toward the healer's dwelling, then turned back to Keryun.

"I know I was cruel to you," Keryun started. "There was no need for me to behave the way I did. I got caught up in things my brother said, but I should have known better. You're the hero I always knew you were, Jobah."

I hadn't expected Keryun to say anything like this. She sounded sincere. "It's all right, Keryun. I can see how you'd be afraid of me. I changed."

Keryun took several steps closer. She was so much smaller than Olivia. I was a giant beside her. Had it always been that way?

"But you were the same person. That's what I failed to see. Can you forgive me?" She reached out a hand and fingered the vines on my chest.

I grabbed her wrist to stop her, and her eyes flicked up to mine. "I do forgive you, but... that's all."

"You were going to choose me for your mate, Jobah Everleaf. All those feelings are gone now? I made one mistake and that's it?"

She tried to touch me again, but I stepped away. "You and I weren't meant to be together, Keryun." I didn't want to hurt her, but she had to understand that Olivia was my perfect match. That Olivia hadn't ever been afraid of me. She had accepted me just as I was.

She ran *with* me, not away from me.

"You choose her?" Keryun angled her head toward her dwelling where Olivia was inside.

I nodded.

"What's so wonderful about that outsider?" Keryun folded her arms across her chest.

"Everything."

66. Olivia

I forced myself to go inside Keryun's shelter behind my parents. What I wanted to do was watch Keryun with Jobah. I saw the way she looked at him. She was an exotic beauty with that long, black hair, those dark eyes, that tanned skin. I was so very white next to her. So pale and boring.

My jealousy won, and I peeked out the shelter doorway while Keryun's mother showed my parents herbs she used for healing. Keryun stood with her arms folded across her chest while Jobah spoke to her. The expression on her face was not a jovial one. She took a step closer to Jobah, but he edged back, keeping the same distance between them. Moon sat on her haunches by Jobah's feet. Every once in a while, her ears would go back and a hint of teeth would show in a snarl. I'd probably be making the same face if I were standing where Moon was.

Keryun tossed a look to this shelter, and I shrank away from the doorway. No need for her to see me spying on them. Not that I was really spying. I was merely watching for when Jobah was headed this way.

Yeah, sure.

I crept back to the doorway. Keryun said something to Jobah, and he shook his head. She reached out a hand to touch him, but he stepped out of range. A boy joined them, and Jobah's shoulders squared, his legs widened as if he were bracing himself.

The vines on my hand crackled with energy as Jobah and the boy spoke. I didn't know what they were saying, but Jobah's power was right there on the surface. Building. Waiting. I took a step outside the shelter, the pull to Jobah almost magnetic. If he needed help, he was going to get it.

The boy pointed to Keryun, then to Jobah and let out a stream of words. Again, Jobah shook his head, then walked toward me.

The boy shouted something in Kiyuchee, and Keryun followed Jobah for a few feet. She stopped when she saw me waiting. Her gaze lingered on mine then she nodded once as if to surrender.

I guess I won this round.

"Hi," I said when he reached the shelter.

"Hi." Jobah buried his face in my hair. Seconds later, his lips skimmed over my neck.

"Who's the boy?" I asked.

"Sumahe, Keryun's brother."

"The one that hit you before you left the village?" I ran a finger over Jobah's bottom lip, and he closed his eyes.

"Yes. Suddenly he wants his sister to be my mate. He did not feel that way when he was telling everyone I was a *brogna*, a demon. He made the tribe fear me more than they already did."

"But now he sees your power and so you're good enough for his sister?" I glanced over Jobah's shoulder and didn't care for the snarl on Sumahe's face as he escorted Keryun toward another dwelling. "You know what? She's not good enough for you."

Jobah grinned then rested his forehead against mine. "You, however, are too good for me." He kissed me, and I knew whatever he had felt for Keryun, he no longer felt. He and I belonged to each other.

Jobah pulled away and stood by a small sapling. "Come here. I want to try something."

I went to him as he took his dagger out from a pocket on the cargo shorts. He placed the blade against a branch.

"What are you doing?" I gripped his wrist and our vines connected, sending Jobah's power coursing through my body. I bit back the sigh wanting to slip from my mouth and noticed the euphoric expression on Jobah's face as well.

"I think I can cut this if you're touching me."

"I think I can do anything if you're touching me," I said, "but are you sure you want to try this?"

"If I have a way to tolerate wood cutting, a weakness is eliminated."

"As long as I'm always around you."

"Do you plan to be elsewhere?" The arch of one dark brow over a very green, very beautiful eye made it impossible for me to imagine being anywhere but with Jobah.

I gave him a slight shove. "Don't get cocky."

"Cocky?" His grin grew wider.

"Yeah, all sure of your hotness. Thinking that I'll follow you around like a puppy all in love with you. I'm not that pathetic." I angled my head up, scraping around for some dignity.

"I'll follow you around then," Jobah said.

Online status: *Olivia Bradford has found the perfect guy.*

"Ready?" Jobah turned back toward the tree.

I pressed my hands to Jobah's vines. "Ready."

Jobah sawed into the bark. His muscles tensed under my hands, but he didn't keel over. He didn't burn up with fever as the branch came free of the sapling.

"How do you feel?" I asked, afraid to move my hands too soon.

"A little tired, but that's all. No pain." He turned to me. "I said you had magic, Olivia Bradford. I was right."

"*We* have magic," I said. "Together."

My parents emerged from Keryun's shelter, and Jobah put some space between us. Dad was furiously scribbling notes while Keryun's mother finished whatever it was she had been explaining to him.

"Fascinating," my father said as he capped his pen.

"And what's your mortality rate?" my mother asked. "Generally, how long do your members live?"

"Eighty to ninety winters," Keryun's mother replied.

"Amazing," my mother said.

"We would love to talk with you more," my father said, an annoyed furrow in his brow, "but we have to take the kids to the police station and see about our missing team member, Royce. May we come back?"

"Of course," Keryun's mother said. "You have been granted access by our shaman chief and our... our Penta." She smiled at Jobah, and I hoped her reaction to him would be shared by many others in the tribe.

"I can tell learning is important to you both," she continued. "Perhaps you can share knowledge of outside medicine with me, so that I may better care for my people."

"An exchange," my mother said. "That is what true science is about."

"We shall return then." My father looked to us. "Ready?"

"Not really," I said. "I'd rather stay here."

"We all would." My mother glanced around the village where Jobah's tribe had gone back to its daily routines, a few wary glances being thrown our way. "There is so much to see here, but we have a duty to the outside as well."

"I hate when she's right." I slid my hand into Jobah's. "We need to get Jobah a shirt." Not that I wanted him all wrapped up. I totally dug the shorts and moccasins look he had going.

"We'll stop at the cabin first," my father said. "Then hit the police station and back here."

My parents followed Jobah and me as we made our way to the palisades. They were like children at the zoo, stopping every few moments to admire something, to scrawl something in my father's notebook, to soak it all in.

Jobah's tribe gave us a wide berth, many of them skittering away as we walked by. They would not forget what Mr. Tramond had done any time soon. Some of them bowed their heads at Jobah as I had seen Keryun's mother do. They understood his power, his ability to protect them, but they didn't like him hanging around with outsiders. Guess I couldn't blame them.

"You've made my parents very happy by letting them in," I said to Jobah.

He squeezed my hand. "I didn't do it for them. I did it for us."

I dropped a quick kiss on Jobah's cheek and pulled him through the hidden opening in the palisades.

Once we were on the other side, my parents took the lead. The SUV appeared on a flattened path in the woods and several other sets of tire tracks crisscrossed the area. Jobah's jaw tightened as he followed the tracks with his eyes. He didn't like that so many outsiders had been so close to his village.

"Don't worry," I said as we climbed into the back seats of the SUV. "You protected them, and you'll continue to do so." I sat in the middle so I could be closer to Jobah. He slid his arm around my

407

shoulders, and I wanted to always be next to him like this.

"Will you help me protect them?" he asked.

"Me? What can I do? You're the one with the fancy Penta powers."

"Yes, but I'm more powerful with you around. Everything's better with you around."

That melty feeling filled me again.

"Then yes, I'll help you. I'll be whatever you need." I snuggled closer.

Jobah's green eyes deepened several shades, and I fell into them. Completely. Willingly. When he smiled, I officially decided to be his forever whether he wanted me or not.

After stopping at the cabin to freshen up, we all hopped back into the SUV. Jobah was now wearing another one of my father's T-shirts. This one was tan with the words "Archaeology Geek" on the front. I'd always thought the shirt was true to its label. One of his colleagues had given it to my father a few Christmases ago, and they both thought it was the funniest thing. Seeing it now on Jobah, however, made it anything but dorky. The boy had a way of filling a T-shirt.

When we arrived at the police station, Tower was there.

"Are you okay?" I ran over to the giant and caught him in a hug.

"I'm fine, Ollie. Just a little sleepy still." He gave me a squeeze.

"We had a doctor check him out," the same policewoman from the woods said. "And Mr. William Tramond has officially been booked and put in jail." She led us to a larger room next to her office. "Once we got him here, he rambled on and on as if he were in a confessional or something. He unloaded every petty crime he's committed. Gave us names and addresses of people he's worked with and for. And the gun he'd had on him? We traced that back to his current employer, Xavier Alston, who apparently bought those guns—wait, let me correct myself—who apparently bought those *stolen* guns from a real bad dude we've been after for years now.

"With all the info Tramond has given us, I have enough to put Alston away too." The policewoman slid her hands behind her head and took in a deep, satisfied inhale. "I love days that end like this." Her smile stretched across the room.

She gave Jobah and me some paperwork to fill out, but we basically worked together on the one that had my name on it. Jobah didn't have any official documentation of his existence. No birth date, no driver's license, no social security number. Technically, he didn't exist.

Not yet anyway.

"We'll take care of it," my father said in the SUV on the way back to the cabin after the police station. "We'll get you all legal, Jobah. Don't worry."

And just like that, I didn't worry. I had no idea what my parents were going to do to make Jobah legal, but man, it was wonderful to be working *with* the parents, not against them as it had been in the past.

As we walked into the cabin behind my parents, Jobah hesitated.

"What's the matter?" I asked.

"Nothing," Jobah said. "I just want to pay attention to the details."

"There'll be time for that. Right now, I'm starving. C'mon." I tugged him into the kitchen.

My mother pulled open the refrigerator as my father went into the living room and fielded questions from the dig team.

"What do you kids want to eat?" my mother asked.

I nudged her away from the refrigerator. "Allow me."

"Of course." With a pat on my shoulder and Jobah's, Mom left the kitchen.

Jobah came to stand behind me at the refrigerator as I combed the shelves.

"Are you in the mood for anything in particular?" I asked.

"Yes." Jobah nibbled on my neck.

I swatted him away, but giggled. It was a carefree sound that warmed my insides. "No, seriously, what do you want?"

Jobah huffed out a breath that tickled my skin and made me forget that I was hungry for food. "I will eat whatever you make, Olivia."

He deserved a meal to remember. Something that would properly initiate him into "The Outside."

"I have just the thing." I started pulling things out of the refrigerator, moved onto the cabinets, grabbed pots and pans.

"Can I help?" Jobah said.

I looked at him leaning against the kitchen island, his visible vine tattoos calling to me, and my mind picturing the ones I couldn't see. Those green eyes studied my face, and I truly wondered what Jobah saw in me that he liked. Guess I'd have some time with him both in these Montana woods and back home in Rhode Island to figure it out.

"Are you good at chopping?" I held out an onion.

"Yes." Jobah took the onion and one of the knives from the counter. "I wonder if I'll get more abilities as a Penta."

"There's got to be something in the book my mother found about that."

"*The Penta Chronicle*," Jobah said. "That's what the book is called."

"It'll have the answers." I squeezed Jobah's arm.

He nodded and started dicing the onion. I turned back to the stove and, with Jobah's help, created a culinary masterpiece. Tossed salad with carrot curls and tomatoes cut into rose-shaped blossoms. Chicken marsala over a bed of fettuccine. The yummy noises that emanated from around the dining room table filled me with… ambition? Cooking definitely interested me, but could it be my life?

Maybe.

"I wish I had time to make a dessert," I said as we finished eating.

"I do too," Dr. Reese said.

"I don't have any room for dessert," Dr. Sumathai said. "That meal was fantastic, Olivia."

"You have a gift," my mother said.

I looked up at her and saw something on her face I had never seen before.

Pride. In me.

"I had no idea food on the outside was going to be this good," Jobah elbowed me from his seat to my right.

I had no idea this summer was going to be this good.

67. *Jobah*

Olivia stood by my side as I held the wooden pot filled with Ninae's ashes. So hard to believe this was all that was left of my grandmother. A part of me wanted to keep the ashes, to bring them to the outside with me, so Ninae would always be close. Another part knew she belonged in the village where she'd spent her entire life, where she'd raised me, where she'd always believed I was something important.

By the lake now, I tugged Olivia forward until the water lapped at our ankles. I crouched and gently shook the ashes out. They coated the surface of the water, huddled together for a few moments, then got carried away from us on small waves.

We both watched until the ashes became a part of the lake. Ninae may have been gone in body, but I felt her spirit surround me. Her voice whispered inside my head.

Love always does good, Jobah.

I looked at Olivia and understood those words now. Her love had given me power.

After sitting on the warm sand by the lake for a little while, we got Olivia's parents and returned to my village.

"There isn't much here that I need to take with me, is there?" I scanned my dwelling.

Ashlo had agreed to take Olivia's parents to the south field and show them our farming methods. He had also expressed an interest in seeing the outside. It would be nice to have him around. Then we could get acclimated to Olivia's world together.

"Most of the items here wouldn't have much use on the outside," Olivia said, picking up a fur cloak. It was black with sections of charcoal gray and white. "If you wore this in the winter on the outside, some animal activist would threaten to skin you."

I walked over to her and ran my fingers over the fur. "That was my father's."

"Oh." Olivia cast her gaze down to the fur in her hands. "I'm sorry. Take it if you want." She pushed the fur at me.

"No, it should stay here. You're right. If I wear it outside in your world, I'll be raising questions that don't need to be raised. The idea is to blend in."

Olivia cupped my cheek. "I think blending in is going to be a challenge anyway, Jobah."

"Why?" I hung the wolf fur back on its wall peg. Did she think I couldn't be a part of her world after all?

"Because there's no one even remotely like you in Sunderfield, Rhode Island. You're very unique." Olivia pressed her lips to mine. "And that's what I love about you."

She had a way of making being different sound like a good thing. I'd have to wait and see if it truly would be.

Olivia looked down at the vines covering her hand. She let her fingers skim over identical vines on my forearm and the green of the leaves darkened a shade on both of us. We shivered with the tingle of power touching the tattoos caused.

"Jett, my sister's boyfriend, is going to love these." Olivia smiled up at me. "He's going to want to replicate them."

"I guess they are artistic." Something about Olivia having the vines too made me like them more on me.

I turned in a circle and looked around my dwelling. "Maybe I should leave everything here, because I'll be traveling back from time to time to check things out." No sense in leaving this place inhospitable if I'd still be using it.

"That's a good idea," Olivia said. "We'll buy you some clothes and other necessities. Things every twenty-first century male teenager needs."

"Can I keep the moccasins?" I gestured down to my feet and wiggled my toes inside the shoes. I'd hate to give them up. Ninae had made them for me.

"Absolutely. I think you'll start a new fashion trend with them." Olivia paused as if she were imagining the males she knew from her home wearing moccasins.

"Moccasins are good for running," I said.

"I'll have to give them a try. Do you know how to make them?"

"My grandmother showed me. I'm not as skilled at it as she was, but I think I could make you a decent pair if you'd like."

I swooped Olivia up into my arms, and she let out a laugh that filled my dwelling. Such a joyous melody. I set Olivia down on my bedding and took one of her feet into my lap. Moon bristled at the end of the hides, annoyed at the disturbance to her sleep. Would that raccoon follow me to the outside? I hoped so. I'd gotten used to having her around.

I flattened my palm against the bottom of Olivia's foot. "I'll have to measure these beauties first." It was about one and a half hands. "Hmm. Big."

Olivia pulled her foot out of my lap and shoved me so my back hit the bedding. Before I could right myself, she was sitting on top of me. Moon, having given up on sleep, nuzzled my ear with her wet nose, and I couldn't help laughing.

"Big? My feet are big?" Olivia waved a fist in front of my face, but the smile on her lips said she wasn't really angry. "You'd better take that back."

"I will not." I raised my nose indignantly. "You have big feet. I like big feet."

"You'd better like big feet." Olivia swatted playfully at my chest, then sat up a little straighter. "I should go on more digs with my parents. Look at the treasures I find."

She lowered herself so her forearms rested on my chest. She pressed a kiss to my collarbone then rested her head on my shoulder. Immediately, the vines there crackled with energy. I'd always been connected to the trees even as a small boy, but here now with Olivia's body in line with mine, I felt the strongest bond ever.

"I feel like running." I rose to my elbows, and Olivia slid to my side. I kissed her lips and traced the curve of her jaw. "Will you run with me?"

Olivia pulled me up to sitting and wrapped her arms around me.

"Always, Jobah. I'll always run with you."

More adventures with Jobah and Olivia in Rhode Island coming soon in *DANCE WITH ME*.
****
Until then, enjoy an excerpt from the from the next Discovery Series Book...

SAIL WITH ME
A Historical Discovery Book

*The sea kisses the sky
and stretches
to the ends of the earth
like a waiting embrace.
I stand on one shore
wondering what secrets
the horizon holds.
She whispers my name,
pulls me from my daydreams,
and promises adventure.*

Dreams

"One of these times, we're going to get caught out here, Charlotte." Benjamin huddled in the darkness beside me.

"We're not going to get caught." I scanned the docks. Empty of people, but full of beautiful boats. "And so what if we do."

"Easy for you to say," Benjamin said. "By the time your father gets back, too much time will have gone by for him to punish you. Me? I have to go home where my father will enjoy giving me a good whipping."

"You've been afraid of a good whipping since you were seven," I said. "You're sixteen now. Have you gotten whipped yet?"

"Well… no." He fiddled with the buckle on his boot. "But it's coming. I can feel it."

"Don't be silly. You're taller and healthier than your father. He can't whip you. Besides, Lady Elizabeth *would* punish me if we did get caught. Which we won't."

I motioned for Benjamin to step up onto the dock behind me. He did so because he always did what I wanted. That's why he was my best friend.

"Lady Elizabeth won't whip you," he said.

"No, she'll sit me down and remind me how a proper young lady is supposed to behave." I scurried to the end of the dock, and Benjamin followed behind me like a silent shadow.

"How many times has she done that now?" He poked my shoulder.

I had to smile at the playful smirk on his face.

"Too many times. I can't seem to get the hang of proper young lady etiquette." I shrugged. "She probably wouldn't let me see you anymore either, if we got caught."

"How come?" His mouth turned down at the corners.

"Well, I'd undoubtedly blame you for dragging me out here."

Benjamin's mouth dropped open. "Me dragging you? I don't think so, missy." He nudged my shoulder then grew serious. "You don't think she'd stop us from being friends, do you?"

"She couldn't stop us, Benjamin. Don't worry." He was always worried about something. "C'mon. This is the one."

I led him to the smallest sloop tethered to the end of the dock. The vessels around us bobbed up and down against their lines like prisoners eager to break free of their bonds. Wanderers longing to drift wherever the sea might carry them.

Cloaked by the night, we climbed up the rickety ladder at the stern and boarded the boat. We crept to the bow, a faint sea breeze awakening my senses.

When we reached the front of the ship, I clasped the railing, its splintered wood rough but welcome against my palms. I was aware of Benjamin standing beside me. He was a good sport about all this sneaking around.

"There it is." I traced the moonlit horizon that kissed the ocean's silvery surface. The scent of sea salt and sun-baked wood danced around me. The gentle sway of the ship soothed my restlessness.

"I don't know why you like coming out here so much, Charlotte. It's just water. A great deal of it." He turned around, his back to the sea, and leaned against the railing on his elbows. He didn't hear the call. Didn't feel the pull. Didn't wonder what was at that distant and mysterious line between sky and sea.

Not like I did.

"It's getting to the other side of the water, Benjamin, and seeing what's there that's important."

"What do you think is on the other side that you don't have here?"

"Something… everything."

I closed my eyes and breathed in the sea's fragrance until Calypso, goddess of the sea, whispered inside me.

"You don't know how to be happy with what you've got," Benjamin said. The moonlight illuminated his face as he looked at me.

"What have I got, Benjamin? Tell me. My father and brothers are off sailing while I'm left here slaving for Lady Elizabeth. What have I got?"

He was about to answer, but my voice had been a hint too loud. Other voices stirred below deck, footsteps knocked on the ladder amidships. A faint lantern glow built in intensity as the footsteps grew louder.

"Don't move," Benjamin mouthed. He slipped in front of me, shielding me from whatever was headed up the ladder. I pushed him out of the way, but he stood more solidly than usual. "Charlotte, please. You can get mad at me for trying to protect you later."

In all our times coming out to the docks at night—and there had been many—we had never gotten caught. I had stolen a couple of precious moments, dreaming on the bows of various ships, imagining the day I'd actually set sail aboard one of these marvelous, canvas-winged seabirds. Benjamin had accompanied me most of the time, allowing me to chase my dreams.

Now we were steps away from being found by the rousing crew of this particular vessel. The lantern light swept across us, and I caught a flicker in the eyes of our discoverers.

"You there." The gruff voice was enough to tell me we didn't want to tangle with its owner.

"A pretty treasure, Arthur, eh?" another voice rasped as the lantern light grew closer. "We'll have to do something with the boy."

"Come on." I grabbed Benjamin's wrist and hopped up onto the bow rail. He climbed up behind me.

"What are we doing?" His grip tightened on my hand.

"Hold your breath!"

"No!" the voices bellowed together behind us.

"Charlotte… I can't—"

"Jump!"

I leaped off the rail, pulling Benjamin with me. We swooped down to the water, the men cursing from the deck above me and Benjamin howling beside me. When I hit the water and slipped below its surface, all sound was replaced with the rippling melody of the ocean.

With powerful strokes, I towed Benjamin to the shoreline and pulled him up onto the sand. He coughed and sputtered for some time before raking his shaky fingers through his tangled, brown hair. He rose to his feet, wrung out his soaked tunic, and glared at me with fiery green eyes.

"Charlotte Denham, if you ever do that again, we're through. You know I can't swim." Water ran down his face in rivulets. He spun on his heel and stomped away.

"But I saved us," I called to his retreating back.

"Saved us? You could have killed us!" Benjamin marched over the sand. His hands flapped out to either side of him as he ranted to himself.

I sat and drew wavy lines in the sand with my finger. As far as I was concerned that jump into the water had rescued us from an inevitably unpleasant situation. Who knows what those men would have done to us if they'd caught us?

The night breeze coming off the water raised goosebumps on my wet skin, and my heart was still pounding from the moment of fear, the glorious swim, the excitement of being this close to the ocean. This close to my dreams.

Get your copy of *SAIL WITH ME* to continue the voyage.

Check www.christymajor.weebly.com for release information and buy links.

About the Author

Christy Major tried not being a writer. She attempted to ignore the voices in her head, but they would not stop. Pesky voices. The only way she could achieve peace and quiet was to write the stories the voices demanded. Today, she spins tales about characters that have that little something "extra."

Christy lives in Rhode Island and occasionally Vermont with her husband, two cats, a big, black German shepherd, and a lizard. This is her first book for young adults, but she's been writing for adults for years.

Find her online at christymajor.weebly.com or on Facebook at facebook.com/christymajorauthor.

Coming Soon

SAIL WITH ME (A Discovery Series Book)

CAST WITH ME (A Discovery Series Book)

DANCE WITH ME (A Discovery Series Book)

WISH WITH ME (A Discovery Series Book)

CPSIA information can be obtained at www.ICGtesting.com
Printed in the USA
LVOW08s1614281214

420643LV00032B/1129/P